A GRIMM SACRIFICE

JEFFERY H. HASKELL

aethonbooks.com

A GRIMM SACRIFICE
©2022 JEFFERY H. HASKELL

This book is protected under the copyright laws of the United States of America. No part of this publication may be reproduced, stored in a retrieval system, or transmitted, in any form or by any means, without the prior permission in writing of the publisher, nor be otherwise circulated in any form of binding or cover other than that in which it is published and without a similar condition including this condition being imposed on the subsequent purchaser. Any reproduction or unauthorized use of the material or artwork contained herein is prohibited without the express written permission of the authors.

Aethon Books supports the right to free expression and the value of copyright. The purpose of copyright is to encourage writers and artists to produce the creative works that enrich our culture.

The scanning, uploading, and distribution of this book without permission is a theft of the author's intellectual property. If you would like to use material from the book (other than for review purposes), please contact editor@aethonbooks.com. Thank you for your support of the author's rights.

Aethon Books
www.aethonbooks.com

Print and eBook formatting by Josh Hayes. Artwork provided by Vivid Covers.

Published by Aethon Books LLC.

Aethon Books is not responsible for websites (or their content) that are not owned by the publisher.

This book is a work of fiction. Names, characters, places, and incidents are the product of the author's imagination or are used fictitiously. Any resemblance to actual events, locales, or persons, living or dead is coincidental.

All rights reserved.

ALSO IN SERIES

AGAINST ALL ODDS
WITH GRIMM RESOLVE
ONE DECISIVE VICTORY
A GRIMM SACRIFICE
KNOW THY ENEMY

CHAPTER ONE

CONSORTIUM SPACE. PRAETOR SYSTEM. 2APR2935 0805HRS

Consortium Navy Rear Admiral Endo stood above the holographic table, glaring daggers at the map of the six systems the emperor had charged him to protect, willing the Caliphate to attack the one he was in. Instead, reports of heavily armed raiders arrived from the systems south, toward the rim, away from the wormhole.

The wormhole.

He glanced at the panoramic display showing the binary star coupling of Praetor. He didn't pretend to know all the science, but something about the pulsar, white dwarf, and gamma radiation made the wormhole possible. When it was first discovered, excitement spread throughout the galaxy like wildfire.

Everyone who could field a ship and a space time detector went looking for the next great discovery.

No one had struck gold yet. Two years seemed like a long time to come up empty, but then again, the man who discovered the first one spent his entire life looking. After all, it was a big galaxy. Maybe there were only a few?

While Professor Bellaits was a hero to the people of the Consortium and Alliance, he hadn't taken any compensation. He did, however, find himself enough funding to put state-of-the-art outposts on both sides of the wormhole for scientific study. Part of the reason Endo was there in the first place was to oversee security while the one on his side was built. Not to mention the rampant buildup of infrastructure to support the new traffic coming through the system.

Endo didn't know if the wormhole was a blessing or a curse. There was nothing to be done about it but defend the system and the cargo ships passing through. Cargo his people desperately needed to keep their economy growing so they could afford to fight the impending war.

To keep the goods flowing and protect his people, he had three squadrons of the most advanced heavy cruisers his people could build. Nine ships in total, each in its own right capable of inflicting brutal amounts of punishment to an enemy ship foolish enough to close with them. With six systems to defend, he'd chosen to remain in Praetor where the wormhole opened to the Alliance. Which was proving to be a mistake.

He couldn't leave the wormhole undefended. He knew, without a doubt, the Caliphate would attack the moment he did.

Three of his ships, including his own, *Star Phoenix,* had to remain on station to deter such a move. That left him six ships to defend five systems.

He scrolled through the reports from the planets under his

protection that were enduring raids and assaults. Nothing constant, just infrequent and random enough that he couldn't justify leaving the wormhole undefended.

Everything had its cost, though. With the Consortium able to call for help, and the Caliphate that much closer to attacking the Alliance, the regime of slavery stepped up their raids, enslaving his people and bombing their planets. The Consortium government wasn't in a position to declare war on Hamid, not when the Caliphate had three times the manpower and a twice as many ships.

With the new influx of revenue and the ability to call on the Alliance, the Consortium Emperor and parliament had upped military spending and were busy charging forward with the most ambitious building program Rear Admiral Endo had seen in his life. In another six months, they would half the Caliphate's advantage.

Any move against the Consortium *had* to start with the Bella Wormhole. If the Caliphate attacked and didn't secure this side of the passageway, then the Alliance would come to the Consortium's aid. Which was why the Caliphate navy's behavior vexed him so.

In three months of heightened *tension* between Consortium and Caliphate forces, not a single enemy ship had entered the three systems surrounding the wormhole where he placed his squadrons. Report after report, though, told a much different story for Uryu, Ayama, and Tein. He mourned the losses at the first two, but the third one was untenable.

Tein's taxes represented a tenth of the Consortium's total revenue. Since the wormhole opened, the luxurious vacation planet had steadily increased in value. For the first time since they settled the Perseus arm, people could come and learn about his culture and experience it for themselves. Before the wormhole, no tourist in their right mind would brave the Corridor. Bella had turned a dangerous, monthslong journey into about an hour, bringing more goods, people, and opportunities to the Consortium. Almost overnight, his nation had doubled their GDP.

Endo hated himself for thinking of money over lives, especially after what his grandniece had endured. If it weren't for the *Alliance Marines* rescuing her, he would never have known what had happened. As much as he wished to split his forces and defend all three, he simply couldn't. Tein had to be his priority.

His perfectly pressed blue uniform felt suddenly tight around his chest. Since his arrival, he'd fought to keep his forces together, to avoid scattering them. Concentrated, it would take more than a few ships to dislodge him from Praetor. Even if the Caliphate sent a full-strength battlegroup, their losses would be severe.

Were they planning a surprise, then? Focusing on systems almost five days away to make sure he left the wormhole lightly defended? Or were they upping their raids because they knew he wouldn't leave the wormhole, thus allowing them to reap his people as profit. It sickened him to his core that the Caliphate considered Consortium women to be the "best" in the galaxy. If it were up to him, they would have already gone to war. Better to die in defense of his people than live knowing they were captured and sold as slaves.

At times like these, Admiral Endo regretted his navy's focus on heavily armed and armored ships, and wished they had more light units for patrol.

Light units might just be the key.

The Alliance was mustering a force to come help, but perhaps, with their policy of light, fast elements, maybe there was someone they could send ahead of the main force? A ship, or ships, that were fast enough to get in and out of trouble, and able to give him some much-needed reconnaissance? Surely they could spare a handful of those?

He pressed the comm stud in his ear.

"Yes, Admiral?" his executive officer replied.

"Hiro, I want you to dispatch CruRon 17 and 18 to Tien. ConCru 11 will remain here. We need to stop the raids with a heavy fist."

"Aye aye, sir. I will proceed with those orders immediately. Anything else?"

Endo decided to try. The worst they could do was say no.

"Yes, I want you to prepare a dispatch to the Alliance Ambassador on Zuckabar."

"Ready to record."

"Ambassador Earle, request light units ahead of schedule. Send whatever you can spare to Praetor with all haste. Message ends."

"I'll send it with the next transit, sir." Hiro paused for a moment. "Uh, sir, are things really that bad that we need the Alliance?"

It was the question of the hour. What Endo needed was intelligence on where the enemy was. They had more forces massed than the ones attacking, so where were they?

"I hope not, Hiro. I hope not."

CHAPTER TWO

THE NEW PALISADES, ALEXANDRIA. ALLIANCE.
10APR2935 1100HRS

Fleet Admiral Noele Villanueva glared at her NavPad as if she could make the information change by a sheer act of will. If that were the case, though, she would be on the flag bridge of USS *Alexander*, leading the Navy to victory over the Caliphate.

She had three active battle groups available to her, with the fourth battleship perpetually awaiting refit. Sighing, she changed the screen, moving away from the depressing report from Congress letting her know there wasn't enough room in the budget to complete *Enterprise*'s repairs. It was bad enough the penny pinchers were desperate to decommission their oldest battleship without replacing her first, but they wouldn't even let Noele finish her refit.

"Admiral?" Chief of Staff Leilani Kahale waved to get her attention. "The president is running late. I'm very sorry for the inconvenience, but it will just be a few more minutes," she said.

Noele gave the dark-skinned woman a tight-lipped smile

and a nod. There wasn't much President Axwell would likely do, regardless. Noele was simply out of options. The Consortium request for light units had arrived that very morning. If she hustled, she could peel three or four destroyers out of the available pool and send them to Admiral Endo's aid on the other side of the wormhole. But the Consortium had requested an entire battlegroup, and Noele almost laughed aloud at the thought of sending one. The SECNAV and CNO would never go for it. Not ever.

She needed the president's permission to override them. Which was why, on a sunny morning with the birds singing, she was at the residence of her CIC.

What she would really like to do was send *Alexander,* but without a declaration of war from Congress that was never going to happen. With the Consortium and Caliphate at near war levels of conflict, she could use their treaties to hammer Congress into doing more, but only just.

A bird flew by the window, casting a momentary shadow over her. At least with all that was happening, the land around The New Palisades rehabilitated rapidly. Green grass spread out for hundreds of meters in every direction, ending up against tall trees to block the wind. If she closed her eyes, the memories of what Anchorage Bay used to look like could almost replace the nightmare it had turned into after the Caliphate nuked it from orbit.

Had they not been so eager to decapitate the seat of power, the stealth ship could have spread nuclear fire over a dozen cities and murdered ten times as many people. Instead, they spent their entire payload on Anchorage Bay. It was pure luck that the president, herself, and several key members of Congress were out of the system at the time. Otherwise, they might have achieved their goals.

If not for a certain destroyer commander, they might even

have attacked again. A commander she was desperate to promote and put in charge of something more significant, with more responsibility. In the meantime, though, the best she could do was to get his crew out into the Navy as a whole and spread their experience, and by extension, his ethics, around. If she could find a way to put Grimm in a squadron, then she could use any success he achieved as a way to move him off *Interceptor* into a cruiser. They needed him. What she wouldn't give to have him on the bridge of a bat—

"Admiral? The president will see you now," Leilani said from the partially open door, interrupting the admiral's thoughts.

Noele stood, straightening her uniform and making sure she looked every bit the fierce fleet admiral. It was hard enough getting what she wanted out of politicians; the last thing she needed was to appear weak in front of them.

Leilani held the heavy oaken door for her as she walked through. Noele didn't miss a beat as she scanned the room, marched right to the president's desk, and saluted. It wasn't strictly necessary, and she wouldn't have done it if not for the presence of the Secretary of the Navy, and Speaker of the House Bradford from Seabring.

If there was anyone in all the Alliance that was dead set on dismantling her Navy, it was those two men. If only Bradford had stayed on Alexandria. She chided herself for the thought. It was unworthy of her. While he opposed her politically, he was a member of the duly elected civilian leadership. For her ideals about society to work, the military must be under civilian control. She just disliked this civilian in particular.

"At ease, Noele," President Axwell said.

She turned, nodded to the other two men, and only then noticed Senator Talmage St. John in the far corner. The New Austin native gave her his trademark tip of his non-existent hat.

Inwardly, she sighed in relief, knowing she had at least one ally in the room. With St. John's help, she and Wit DeBeck had managed to trick the senate into annexing Zuckabar. For a brief time after the wormhole was discovered, they were politically untouchable. Things in politics, though, moved quickly, and that major win had faded since the attack on Alexandria.

SECNAV Russo smiled tightly at her as she passed him to sit down. The soft leather couches were comfortable, but they always bothered her because she had to sit forward at attention or feel like she would sink into them. Meanwhile, the SECNAV and the Speaker lounged back as if they were home watching a movie.

That was fine with her. She'd spent her life preparing for combat, and today was no different.

"So tell me, Noele, what can I do for you?" President Axwell asked.

Noele placed her NavPad on the small side table and activated the holographic function. A 3D map of Praetor and the surrounding systems sprang to life. Three green dots and one blue dot blinked softly in the system. For several systems beyond the wormhole, angry red dots sprang to life.

"As we know, sir, the Caliphate has increased its conflict with the Consortium to near-wartime levels. Consortium forces are spread thin over a thirty-system border, and while the wormhole is important, they also have to protect their population centers. With their naval doctrine emphasizing large, powerful units, they are hurting for screening and reconnaissance units. Units we have to spare and can provide. I suggest we—"

"Now hold on," Russo interrupted. "We're not at war with the Caliphate. We can't go provoking them into a conflict over a border dispute that has nothing to do with us."

Noele clenched her jaw hard enough her teeth hurt.

Grimm's mission to Medial had proven both a blessing and a curse. The Caliphate would leave them alone, for the time being. With Hamid's son in their custody and a potential alliance with the Iron Empire over the rescue of the princess, they were safe for the moment. Russo was aware of the situation and was attempting to hide behind it. He was still solidly in the "appease" camp of the government who were desperate to avoid another war, no matter how illogical their stance.

As if Noele hungered for conflict. Did they think she was some sort of warmonger? It would be she who sent men and women to die thousands of light-years from home. It would be she who lived with the cost. As the only officer of flag rank who had fought in the last war, she knew the horror of those actions and didn't wish them on anyone.

What she wished and what was necessary were rarely the same.

"Sir, we're not provoking anyone. Our *ally of record* is requesting aid. Under the terms of our current treaty, we are legally obligated to send help." She didn't mention they were bound by duty to aid them because she didn't think the SECNAV would relate to that. Despite the Navy motto "Duty, Honor, Courage," she found few actually lived it.

"Sending in a battlegroup would most certainly provoke them, *Admiral*," he emphasized her rank to remind her she was beneath him.

Bradford showed a smug, superior expression. As if he were letting the SECNAV do the talking, but it was his words that were spoken.

"Sir, with respect. A full Alliance battlegroup in Praetor could prevent the very war you're afraid of..." Noele could bite her tongue for such a slip. The SECNAV's face went tight and his eyes wide.

"How dare you accuse me of cowardice? I will have you know that—"

"Secretary Russo, Admiral Villanueva, please keep it civil," President Axwell interrupted.

Noele resisted the urge to glance at the president. "My Apologies, Mister Secretary, I didn't mean to imply cowardice. I understand your concern, and believe me, the last thing I want is a war with a logistically superior foe. I was simply pointing out that if we had a large force defending the wormhole, the Caliphate would be less likely to attack. We have different opinions on how to achieve that goal. I'm just going with what I know will work to prevent another war."

Bradford's lack of concern and his continued arrogant demeanor worried her. She had hoped coming into this meeting she could ply loose a heavy cruiser squadron and associated elements to send, but the meeting was already on the wrong foot.

"The Caliphate aren't going to attack us though, are they?" Bradford spoke up.

He knew. She didn't know how he knew, since it was well above his civilian's clearance, but he knew they held the Caliph's son, Imran, and that as long as they had him, there would be no attack. Did he know about the other development that came out of Medial with him? The quantum FTL communications the ONI agent had downloaded might one day prove to be the single most important piece of technology ever invented. Though only if they could figure out how to use it.

"I'm not sure what you mean, Mr. Speaker?" she asked. If he wanted to admit to knowing it, fine, but she wasn't going to confirm it for him.

"Don't play coy with me, Admiral. You've got Hamid's boy locked up somewhere. They won't dare strike at us while we have that kind of leverage. So why should we risk a war you admit we can't win, when we have an insurance policy?" Bradford leaned back, daring her to disagree with him.

Noele glanced at the President for confirmation. He gave a slight nod of the head.

"I see," she said. "Well, Mr. Speaker, I wasn't *playing coy,* as you so eloquently put it, I was protecting national security, as is *our* duty. Which is exactly why we need to send aid to our ally. We have a duty to uphold our treaties. I can scrounge the ships we need from other posts, but I can't pay for it. If you are unwilling to allow me to do so, then I will have no choice but to order *Alexander* to the wormhole for temporary duty, which I can do under my authority."

Bradford about lost his bearing, leaning forward with a sharp jerk. "Now hold on. You can't send *Alexander* away. That's our only protection against further Caliphate attacks. Don't be ridiculous."

President Axwell let out a very unprofessional pshaw. "I've known Noele a long time, Mr. Speaker, she's anything but ridiculous." Axwell, to his credit, took a moment to ponder her suggestion. "I'm sorry, Admiral, we can't give you a full battle group at this time. You technically have the authority, but I would have to override you. All three battle groups will stay where they are needed. Any other suggestions?" he asked.

"You're giving in to her threats?" Bradford said, all pretenses lost as his face heated. In any other situation, Noele would have laughed. Giving into her threats? He just told her no. But it wasn't the slap down the Speaker wanted.

"No, Mr. Speaker, I'm listening to the Fleet Admiral of our Navy. Someone who knows more about warfare and strategy than anyone else in the room, or quite frankly, on this *planet.*"

"Sir, with respect," Noele said to Bradford, "you can't insist we won't be attacked on the one hand, then balk at me sending away the fleet for fear we'll be attacked on the other. As you pointed out, *Alexander* deters attacks on our system. As it would in the Praetor."

"Don't play word games with me. You know very well leaving our home planet defenseless would be disastrous to morale. You're so eager to run headlong into another war, you don't care who gets hurt along the way. If you had done your job better, then this wouldn't be necessary."

Noele stiffened, and if she were twenty years younger, she would have slapped the man across the face for suggesting she failed in her duty to protect Alexandria. She had, but she didn't need him to tell her.

"Mr. Speaker," President Axwell interrupted sharply. "You are here as a courtesy. You're welcome to leave."

Bradford did just that, looking at Noele with spite in his eyes as he marched out, followed by Secretary Russo. At least the SECNAV had the decency to look embarrassed as he departed the president's office, his proverbial tail between his legs.

For the first time since Noele entered, St. John spoke up. "I guess we know where his priorities lay. Now that we can speak more freely, what did you have in mind, Noele?" he asked. Compared to her accent, Senator St. John always seemed out of place in society with his antiquated drawl.

"It's an open secret he's gunning for my job," President Axwell said. "If he could find a way to take credit for not starting a war while making it look like I wanted to, he could win."

"Sir," Noele said, "you said you couldn't authorize any of the *three* battlegroups, but we have four. Let me take *Enterprise* out there. I can scrape together escort ships to go with her."

"No," Axwell said. "Not you, Noele. As much as you want to, not you. Admiral Spencer is next in line for a battlegroup, and he's a good man. I think you served with him? I need you here and in command of the Fleet. You can't go out on a ship. I simply can't risk losing you. I'm sorry."

"Aye sir. I understand. Spencer is a decent paper pusher, sir, but he has no combat experience besides piracy patrols. He can run the battlegroup, but he can't fight with it."

"You just told me that having it in Praetor will mean we don't have to fight," Axwell said.

St. John grinned. "He's got you there, Admiral. Spencer will work. Besides, he may not have the experience, but one thing our fleet nails is training. He's good at that."

"Agreed," Noele said, relenting to the two men.

"What about light units?" Talmage added, deftly deflecting the awkward silence. "We're stretched pretty thin as it is."

Noele nodded, letting the reality sink in. Her days aboard ship were likely done. As much as she hated the idea, she was just too important to go gallivanting around looking for trouble.

"I have four destroyers in-system waiting for assignment. Three light cruisers and a single heavy. I can throw together a temporary task force with them all and send them on their way. They could be in Praetor inside of a month," she said as she looked out the window, her mind far afield as the reality of what had just happened seeped in.

"We can do that, Noele. Also, pull a couple of heavies from *Alexander*'s group. But," Axwell added, "send the destroyers ahead to screen. I'm sure Admiral Endo would appreciate the rapid response, not to mention I don't want to risk losing a BB to a surprise attack. *Enterprise* might be old, but we need her." He leaned down to his NavPad, thumbed the screen, and proceeded to issue her official orders. "As of this moment, you have Task Force Sixteen. Send it to Praetor and assist with the defense and reconnaissance of the area."

"As you command, sir." A thought occurred to her. "I could

send five destroyers, sir. There's one just about to come out of drydock from her last engagement. I would need special authorization to assign her to the Task Force."

Talmage grinned like a fool and the president chuckled.

"You've got my blessing, Noele. Send five."

CHAPTER THREE

Commander Jacob T. Grimm leaned his forehead against the cold transparent steel to gaze out on Utopia shipyard. Within a few seconds, the train leaped out into the moon's exterior. Free from any atmospheric restraints, it rapidly accelerated across the barren landscape.

Utopia's surface held a scattering of mining and refining platforms digging deep into the mineral rich celestial body. They were visible from a distance, but the real spectacle for Jacob was the ships. The train's transparent bulkhead and overhead allowed him to look up at the vast number of military and civilian ships docked, orbiting, and transiting at any given moment.

Motion caught his eye as an all-white S&R Corsair flashed by the train, heading for Alexandria's orbit. He followed it for as long as the twin-tailed dropship stayed visible to the naked eye. He'd served as a back seater on a tour of a bird just like that one... what felt like forever ago but, in reality, was only eight years.

Green lights flashed as the train slowed in preparation for docking in Utopia City. When the city was first constructed in a massive impact crater, only the very top of the dome rose above the surface, but after centuries of advancements and expansion, the crater had all but vanished, turned into a wide valley with the central point being the twelve-hundred-square-kilometer dome that reached almost a klick above.

His view of the city ended as the train entered the long tunnel entrance, wrapping around the exterior of the city as it came to the final leg of the journey. In preparation for exiting, Jacob examined himself in the window, making sure his SDB uniform hadn't suffered anywhere. His eyes lingered on the red-white-red service ribbon with its gold ship's silhouette—his Navy Cross.

All the men and women who had died under his command owned real estate in his head, and it was right that they did. Who better to remember their gallant sacrifice than the man who ordered them to their fate? Each letter he wrote, each family he visited, was a brutal reminder that his actions had consequences, and for him to never *ever* take them lightly.

"First stop, restaurants, shopping, hotels. Next stop, transportation. You have thirty seconds to disembark," the train's pleasant, pre-recorded female voice notified him.

Jacob stuffed his NavPad into his trouser cargo pocket and headed for the door. As he exited the train, he lifted his stark white combination cover until the bottom edge paralleled the deck and the visor came down just above his eyes. His normal, red-colored cover was reserved for when he commanded a starship. Something he currently didn't do. The only red on his uniform was the twin stripes down his right leg, denoting his multiple combat operations.

He was proud of his command. The USS *Interceptor* was the finest ship he'd ever served on, with the finest crew. Which made his meeting today all the more bittersweet. He'd known this time would come from the moment he took command.

Junior officers rarely served on a ship for more than a year, and that had passed months ago. It was time.

Leaving the train, he paused for a moment to collect his bearings. He'd never actually visited Frosty's Bar, but it was a popular place for Navy and Marines to hang out, even if they did let in the occasional civilian. Most didn't stay upon seeing the sea of uniforms.

A few minutes later, he found what he looked for: a large sign bore the Alliance Navy motto in ancient Latin—*Officium, Decus, Virtus*—curving around the top of a representation of Alexandria, while the Marine Corps traditional motto, *Semper Fidelis*, around the bottom. In the middle, it simply said, *Frosty's*.

Jacob took another deep breath, held it for a few seconds before letting it out slowly. Knowing what he was about to do didn't make it easier. He loved his people. They were his brothers and sisters and part of him, a selfish part, wanted to hold on to them.

"Okay, Commander, do your job," he said aloud. Decision made, he strode through the archaic wooden doors into Frosty's. The jovial atmosphere lightened the burden gripping his heart the moment he entered. Too-loud laughter from every corner hit him, and suddenly, he was with family. At least a hundred service personnel occupied the multilevel bar, and the only time Jacob had felt more at home was on his ship, or in his actual home.

He removed his cover while scanning the crowd, looking for his crew.

"Skipper," a deep baritone cut through the noise of the bar like a knife. First Lieutenant Bond's voice brought an instant grin to Jacob's face.

As if by magic, the crowd parted and he spotted them all the way in the back, occupying a large circular table in the corner. He waved as he made his way across the crowded room. It wasn't luck that almost all his officers were there together. They formed a tight team and tended to hang out off duty at the same time.

Kimiko Yuki, Mark West, Carter Fawkes, Roy Hössbacher, and Vivienne Boudreaux crowded around the table. Only Lieutenant Gonzales and Lieutenant Krisper were missing. They had been transferred off *Interceptor* almost the moment they returned from their mission to Medial. The only noncom at the table was Jennings, and she was probably there to see Lt. Bonds, the former Marine OIC on *Interceptor*.

With the exception of Lieutenant Bonds, whom he hadn't expected to see, they were dressed in civvies. Bonds wore the gray and white combat uniform. As he sat, he noticed Bonds' hand resting easily on Chief Boudreaux's thigh, and it all clicked. Jacob raised an eyebrow at her and she blushed.

"He made an honest woman of me. What can I say?" Viv replied to his unasked question.

"I'm happy for you. I am." But he wasn't happy. Knowing what he was about to tell them was going to put a damper on their blooming relationship. That was life in the Navy. He'd had his own goodbye that morning and Nadia's scent lingered in his mind. Who knew when he would see her again?

"Skip, why so glum?" Kim asked.

"I shouldn't be, but I am." The table lit up, requesting his order, and Jacob punched up a pineapple juice.

"Always on duty, eh sir?" Bonds said.

"You know me, Paul, always. Plus, I don't drink. Master Chief Melinda Grimm taught her son to always be the best, and I'll never outdrink a Marine, so why bother?"

Bonds laughed and even Jennings snorted.

"That's very wise of you, sir. Know your place," Bonds said.

Once his drink arrived, he used it as an excuse to delay the inevitable, but nothing could last forever.

"Okay, sir, spill it. I've served with you for two years now," Kim said. "I know when you're stalling." A worried look flashed across her face.

"It's okay, really. I'm just... enjoying the moment," he said to ease her concern. "But, as an ancient philosopher once said, tempus fugit. Time is fleeting." Jacob placed his NavPad on the table and pressed the center button with the flat of his thumb. The computer read his clearance and activated pre-programmed orders. Kim, Mark, Carter, and Roy all jumped as their NavPads alerted them to new orders.

After studying hers for a moment, Kim looked up, and he could see both the excitement and sorrow.

"Congratulations, Kim," Jacob said. He slid a velvet wrapped black box across the table to her. "Admiral Villanueva gave me these, and I'd like you to have them."

"I don't know what to say, Skipper?" she replied. Kim opened the box, revealing a lieutenant commander's insignia.

He slid more across the table, one to each of his officers, all of whom received a promotion.

"All of you have worked hard and endured much. You deserve this," he said.

"Sir," Roy started while he gazed at the junior grade lieutenant's bars in the box, "there aren't that many lieutenant's billets on a destroyer."

"I know. This is why I stalled. You're all being reassigned to new ships. Mark and Owusu are heading for *Alexander*. Roy, they are sending you to Fleet Electronic Warfare school. Kim and Carter are off to command school on Blackrock."

Carter's eyes went wide with realization. He was a fine officer and Jacob had pushed hard to get him in early. He would make a great captain one day.

"Sir... I..." Carter fumbled for words and eventually settled on a clipped nod.

"I wish there was more time to say our goodbyes, but if y'all don't get going, you're going to miss your connections. These orders come with *all-haste* attached," Jacob said.

In order for them to leave, he had to stand. Jacob shook each hand in turn as the re-assigned officers said their goodbyes. Finally, it was down to Kim.

"I knew this day would come, but I'd hoped I would have more time," she said.

"I know what you mean. You're going to do great things, Kim. Especially once you learn how to shove all the paperwork off on your XO," he said with a smile.

Despite being in uniform, Kim leaned in and hugged him. "Thank you, Jacob. Before you, I..."

"You did the hard work, Kimiko," he whispered. "I just opened the door."

She stepped back, snapped to attention, and performed the most precise salute he'd ever seen. Which he returned with just as much passion.

"Good luck with your next XO, sir," she said.

Just like that, they were gone. Jacob sat back down. Only Viv, Paul, and Jennings remained.

"What about the rest of us, sir?" Jennings asked.

"I think *Interceptor* isn't the black sheep she once was, Gunny. Normal duty rotations should resume. Which means new and old crew," he glanced at Bonds.

"You know something I don't, sir?" Bonds asked.

"I do. Obviously, I can't go into it here, but I can say that you two," he nodded to Viv and Paul, "are about to be in the same chain of command again, albeit on different ships."

Paul frowned, lifting his hand. Viv grabbed it and forced it back down on her thigh.

"We're not in the same chain yet. Let's go have some fun

while we still can," she said. "Thank you for letting us know, Skipper."

The happy couple exited, leaving just Jacob and Allison.

"Anything you want to know, Gunny?" he asked.

"Negative, sir. I know I'm still on *Interceptor*."

"And how do you know that?" he asked.

"Someone has to keep you alive when you're off the ship, Skipper."

CHAPTER FOUR

Newly promoted Captain (JG) Ganesh Hatwal fidgeted with his uniform in his cabin on the O-Deck of USS *Firewatch*. He needed his first impression to be his best one. His heart raced, and he forced himself to take a deep breath and let it settle. After all, he was a captain with over fifteen years in service to the Navy. There was no reason for him to doubt his ability.

No reason except for one.

Jacob T. Grimm, Commander. Of all the rotten luck. Ganesh had his first squadron command and the most reviled officer in the navy was assigned to him.

Ganesh closed his eyes for a moment, letting the anger and frustration flow out of him. He was an officer. This was his job. It wasn't like he'd never served with someone he didn't like before.

This assignment was too important to screw up. Admiral Villanueva had stressed the significance of the mission. Head to Praetor, support Admiral Endo of the Consortium however he could. The *Enterprise* battle group would be a week behind the squadron and DesRon Nine only had to operate independently for that long. All in all, an easy first squadron command.

One last glance in the tall mirror assured Ganesh his white uniform was spotless. Reaching across his chest, he adjusted his good conduct ribbon. The men and women he was about to assume command of were only a few years younger than him, and he didn't want to risk losing their respect with a bad first impression.

"Command them, Ganesh, command them," he said to his reflection.

The hatch parted and he crossed the passageway to the briefing room. It slid open with a whoosh as it sensed his approach. He was still getting used to all the automatics the ship had, and part of him missed the manual controls. At least the Griffin class, despite their much larger footprint, were laid out as tradition demanded, with the main briefing room opposite the CO's quarters and only meters from the bridge.

Inside the spacious briefing room were his squadron commanders and their XOs. Griffins were purpose-built as command-and-control vessels, and the designers took that into account when laying out the briefing room. Of the three aboard, the O-Deck Brief was the largest, with more than enough room for double the people currently occupying it.

Commander Grimm saw him immediately and jumped to his feet like a first-year cadet. "Captain on deck," he said.

Ganesh didn't like the way he announced it. Like he was trying to gain favor.

"At ease," Ganesh was forced to say before he was ready, and ended up stumbling over the words. His neck heated, and he resisted the urge to pull at his white collar. Why, of all days, had he picked that day to wear his service dress whites? They were hot and uncomfortable and no one liked wearing them. But they also looked the most respectable. Three of his new commanders had also worn their SDWs, but Grimm wore his day uniform with the white turtleneck shirt and space-black sweater with only his name, rank, and service labeled on it. Of course, the red stripes down his leg contrasted with it, which led Ganesh to think the man was showing off. No one else in the room had the red stripes of combat, let alone two. Did he really consider shooting a bunch of ships full of children combat? How preposterous.

They remained standing while Ganesh made his way around the large table and found his seat. He realized that they were on the other side, and too far away for him to make the kind of personal connection he would like. But he'd already told them to be at ease, so he couldn't exactly make them move without looking the fool.

Once he was seated, they took their seats as well. Ganesh took a moment to activate his NavPad and used it as an excuse to examine the officers in front of him. Destroyers were generally a lieutenant commander's or commander's billet. Including his ship, the squadron had five in total. USS *Firewatch*, which acted as the squadron flag, USS *Kraken*, USS *Tizón*, USS *Saber*, and of course, *Interceptor*. He frowned as the last ship's file appeared. That couldn't be right. The file showed the near forty-five-year-old destroyer with a recent Navy Unit Commendation awarded to her. What could that outdated rust heap have possibly done to win such an award? Ganesh, his guests forgotten, followed the link on his NavPad to find out the reason for the award, only to hit a wall where his clearance wasn't high enough. That infuriated him even more.

"Fine," he muttered. He looked up, remembering why he was there, and choked down another surge of embarrassment. He'd let his anger and curiosity get the best of him, and now his captains had been waiting for more than a minute while he satiated his desire to know why the *Butcher of Pascal* had won that decoration.

He cleared his throat. "Welcome to DesRon Nine, I'm *Captain* Ganesh Hatwal, your CO. Shall we begin?"

Jacob squirmed ever so slightly in the too-comfortable chair of *Firewatch*'s briefing room. Whoever designed it was thinking of civilian offices with their easy environment. He felt like he was going to sink to the bottom of the chair and not be able to stand when it was time to leave. At the very least, the chairs could allow him to stay low, but it didn't even do that.

He felt out of place, he realized. Like he didn't belong. The feeling gnawed at him and wouldn't let go. He'd chosen to wear his day uniform because he didn't want to upstage his new CO or draw unnecessary attention to himself by displaying not only a Navy Cross and a Silver Star, but also a handful of other medals. Including the Order of the Rising Sun given to him by the Consortium for rescuing her citizens and the Badge of Honor of the Bundeswehr from the Iron Empire. He wasn't exactly clear why he had received that one, though he suspected it had to do with the ground part of the mission. The security classification around his operation to Medial was actually higher than he had clearance for. Other than the things he directly witnessed, he had no idea what had happened. They weren't even allowed to talk about it with each other, let alone with people who weren't there.

Unfortunately, that left him wearing black while all the officers of the new DesRon Nine wore white. They all looked every inch the naval officer. Lieutenant Commander Novak of *Kraken* had the regal appearance common on Weber's World, the only planet in the Alliance that had a monarchy. Though they were required by the Alliance constitution to elect leaders, they maintained a hereditary parliament. Since a full third of the Alliance's ships were built on Weber, they were given leeway on how their planet's government operated when the Alliance was formed. Her XO, Lawrence Kantor, had a slim figure and a lazy, bored expression. Something about him rubbed Jacob the wrong way, but he was determined not to let it interfere with his duty.

Lieutenant Commander Carl Gustav of the *Tizón* was perhaps the most surprising. Though he was obviously older than Jacob, he was lower rank. Which meant he had either been at his current rank a long time or made it late. The man had a bulldog expression and the shoulders of a giant. His XO tapped the NavPad nervously while drumming his other hand against his chair. Jacob didn't catch his name—the angle was wrong.

Last but not least, was Lieutenant Commander Roberto Carlos of the *Sabre*. His XO, Lieutenant (JG) Jean Louise, was a full head shorter. They seemed to communicate with looks and gestures. The kind of relationship most COs never had with their XOs.

Then it hit him. He could slink out of the room in that moment and never come back. He still hadn't retaken command of Interceptor from the yard. His officer watch was gutted. He *had no XO*. His first meeting with his new squadron commander and he showed up flying solo.

The tight grin that played across Jacob's face wasn't of mirth.

"Commander Grimm, something you would like to add for the rest of us?" Captain Hatwal said.

Jacob glanced up, realizing he must have let his emotions show on his face for a moment. He scrambled to remember the last few seconds of the captain's briefing. Something about ammo stores? He rushed to add a comment, fumbling over his thoughts as he did so.

"Sir, if we wanted to save time, instead of waiting for Fleet Space-Lift Command to top us off, we could always stop at Fort Kirk and get what we need there?" he asked. It was a risk because he wasn't one hundred percent sure that's what the captain had even been talking about.

"Interesting suggestion, Commander. However, Fort Kirk's ammo reserve is for training. We will follow the *regs* on this and wait for our squadron's supply officer... if that's okay with you?" Captain Hatwal said.

Jacob plastered a pleasant smile on his face and inwardly reminded himself that Captain Hatwal was likely just as nervous. The first briefing wasn't the best place to formulate a read on his character. It took time for COs and their subordinates to really gel.

"Aye sir," Jacob said. The words felt weird in his throat. After two years of essentially serving as his own master, he'd almost forgotten how to address a superior.

"Now, with the questions of supplies resolved, there are a few logistics problems we need to address. Commander Novak will operate as the squadron XO. *Kraken* has an excellent and up-to-date comms suite and should be the right fit for the role."

Jacob flinched but said nothing. As the second highest ranking officer, he should be the squadron XO, but it was in the purview of the squadron commander, and if Captain Hatwal wanted Novak as his XO, there wasn't much he could do. It was either a calculated insult, or captain's prerogative. Jacob would hold on hope it was the latter.

Sideways glances from the other officers told him that they knew it wasn't right. Hatwal went on and Jacob did his best to put it behind him. He reminded himself that an assignment to a squadron and a battlegroup was a huge step forward.

"I'd like to schedule some training. We have two weeks before we depart, just ahead of the battlegroup. While we won't have time to get into the field, we will link our computers and do some simulated exercises. Since we'll likely only face one or two ships at any given time, USS *Interceptor* will play the OPFOR, if that is okay with you, Commander Grimm?" Hatwal asked.

"Of course, sir, we would be honored to," Jacob said without hesitation.

That didn't seem to make Captain Hatwal happy. Jacob thought his willingness to serve would smooth the waters. But the man seemed even more perturbed than the moment before.

"Excellent. You all have two days to get your crew situated. On the third day, I wish to start at 1200 hours. I want link up by 1400 and…"

The rest of the meeting was more about learning what the captain expected and how he wanted his squadron to perform. It was all fairly standard, and Jacob, while paying attention, was also thinking about how he would have his ship combat ready in two days when he wasn't even in possession of it. However, he was from the school of, "you don't tell your CO 'no,' you find a way." He would do just that.

"Dismissed," Hatwal said. The commanders and their XOs departed one by one.

Commander Carlos surreptitiously bumped him in the shoulder with his fist, giving him a smile. Did Jacob know the man? He searched his memory but couldn't come up with a time or place they had met.

"Commander Grimm, a moment?" Hatwal requested.

Jacob dropped into parade rest and faced his CO.

"Yes sir?"

Hatwal waited for the hatch to close behind the last of the officers.

"You may not be aware, but it's customary for officers to attend staff meetings with their XOs and wearing their service dress whites. At least for the first meeting. Obviously, it isn't practical for every meeting."

Jacob swallowed hard, pushing down the confusion welling up inside him. He hadn't thought about his missing XO since he didn't have one, but since he'd never attended a staff meeting as a ship's commander before, he wasn't aware of the uniform customs. It was doubtful there were actual regs, or if there were, they read something like, "Commander's discretion."

"Sir, I haven't officially resumed command of *Interceptor*. The yard dogs have her until 0730 tomorrow and NavPer hasn't issued me any personnel files as of yet. Until then I won't know who my XO is." He hated how it sounded like an excuse. It wasn't, but it sounded like one even to his ears.

Hatwal frowned. "And I suppose you're going to tell me you don't have any SDWs?"

Jacob opened his mouth to explain why he'd chosen his dress the way he had, then decided better of it.

"No excuses, sir. It won't happen again." He remained still, not betraying emotion on his face despite the war inside him.

"One more thing, Grimm. There's much of your file that's blacked out. Obviously, I know about the business in Pascal." Jacob flinched. While the events that led to his disgrace no longer plagued his heart or mind, they still influenced his career. "While I see the authorization for two blood stripes, along with other unspecified medals, I don't see the corresponding actions in your jacket. Care to explain why?"

Hatwal peered at Jacob like a hawk. No, like a teacher speaking to a lying kid. The idea that Jacob, as an officer, would wear medals he wasn't authorized for, stunned him. How could Captain Hatwal think that would ever be a thing any officer would do? He'd never seen a noncom do that and only heard about ratings who had gone home with unauthorized badges. Perhaps, he mused, the captain was trying to break the ice? That had to be it. He let the tension out of his shoulders.

Jacob grinned roguishly. "I'm afraid it's classified, sir. I could tell you, but then I... I would..." He stopped as he realized his captain was not amused. All the tension instantly returned.

"Fine. Know this, *Commander,* I will not tolerate any insubordination or cowboy actions while under my command. You will do what I say when I say, and you will not question why. Understood?"

"Crystal, sir."

"I expect an aye, or aye aye, as appropriate, Commander Grimm."

"Aye sir."

"Dismissed."

Jacob snapped to attention, executed a left face, and marched out into the passageway. That couldn't have gone worse for him if he had planned it. What had he been thinking, trying to be funny? The hatch slid shut behind him and Jacob paused to lean against the wall. He had his own ship to get to and there was very little time to ponder his mistakes.

CHAPTER FIVE

Rear Admiral Wit DeBeck, head of the Office of Naval Intelligence, felt anything but intelligent.

More like the Office of Naval Stupidity.

Talmage St. John, the distinguished senator from New Austin, sat comfortably across from him, occasionally adjusting his eyepatch as they spoke.

"Does it still bother you?" Wit asked with a gesture to the eyepatch.

"It would bother me less if my DNA would allow a vat grown replacement or a cybernetic one, I suppose."

When Admiral Villanueva had first suggested bringing the senator into their schemes, Wit had researched everything he could about the man. Given his detailed personal files and his official clearance, he knew more about Talmage St. John than the senator knew about himself.

Like how he had lost his eye in a Corsair crash a few weeks out of Army Officer Candidate School here on Alexandria. And how he was cashiered when it became clear that his biology wouldn't allow for a replacement. Which was too bad for the Army. Wit had a very high opinion of the senator.

Wit turned to the panoramic view of Melinda Grimm Naval Base. It formed a massive complex of buildings spreading out before him. The fifteen story Naval HQ was the tallest, but not the most important or largest. The small dome—a kilometer in the distance—was by far and away the single most important building on the planet. Maybe even the Alliance.

The Office of Naval Research housed the faster-than-light quantum communications prototype they stole from the Caliphate. It might take years for Alliance scientists to put together a working device, but when they did, it would give them a tremendous advantage.

"Is that all, then?" Wit asked. "They know about Imran Hamid, but do they know about anything else?" The real question Wit wanted to ask was how they knew? How? His operation with *Interceptor* was completely off the books. Very few people even knew it happened. However, not even a year later and the information was in the hands of civilians.

"As far as I know, Admiral. That's all. They weren't exactly talkative in the meeting. If I had to guess, SECNAV told him. It was all Noele could do to pry odds and ends out of their hands to form an ad hoc task force. A small one at that," Talmage said.

"I wish I couldn't believe the SECNAV would betray his oath that easily, but... here we are. At least Noele got her task force," Wit said.

He looked down at his monitors, each one showing him different intel reports on Caliph movements and spies. While he celebrated President Axwell's decisive action in ejecting the Caliph's ambassadors, it had crippled his intelligence network, forcing him to rely on *alternate* means of gathering information.

"From what I gather," Talmage said, his archaic accent seeming out of place, "Speaker Bradford is still solidly in the *appease-and-ignore* camp. Which, if I may be so bold, is totally asinine."

Wit couldn't agree more. The current congressional attitude was wholly unsupported throughout history. No nation ever stopped an aggressor through appeasement.

Maybe if they had tried forty years before, when Hamid's father ran the Caliphate and they were more reasonable, but Hamid ended all that when he murdered his father and kicked off the largest war the galaxy had ever seen.

If it were up to Wit, they would have sent every ship they had the moment the wormhole was discovered and forced a battle on the Caliphate's doorstep.

It wasn't up to Wit, though.

"Thank you, Talmage. I appreciate the help."

"Whatever I can do for you, Admiral. You have but to ask."

Wit watched Talmage's air car ascend into the atmosphere a few minutes later. The far wall silently parted and Nadia stepped into his office.

"Do you believe him?" she asked.

"Who are you talking to? I don't believe anyone." Wit stepped around the desk and leaned against the edge.

"What's the plan?" she asked as she sat in the unoccupied chair.

"We need to infiltrate Congress," he said.

Nadia chuckled. "You never do anything in half measures, do you, sir?"

Wit shook his head. "No. I don't think this one's for you, Nadia. You're too well known. Too easily identified here on the homeworld. We're stepping outside the line on this and we can't risk anyone recognizing you."

She grimaced, knowing it was the truth. "Who did you have in mind?"

Wit turned, looking out the large window again. He hated to ask her to do this, but once again, he would sacrifice anything or anyone to save the Alliance from the death and destruction coming her way. Including sacrificing his best operative's life if need be.

"I don't need you on the ground, but I will need you here, running the op from behind the scenes."

She stiffened. "Who?" she asked again.

"You're not going to like it."

CHAPTER SIX

Jacob never tired of looking at *Interceptor*. Her sleek form evoked beauty and lethality in his mind. From the freshly painted shark on her nose down to the closed aperture of her gravcoil, all the way back to the boat bay. There wasn't an ounce of unnecessary metal on her.

"Looking good as always, Skipper," Chief Boudreaux said from beside him. They stood on the platform connecting to his ship, waiting for the shore patrol to process the remaining yard dogs off before he was allowed on to inspect. Still no refit, to his chagrin, but a decent number of repairs.

Utopia's CO, Commodore Tut, had authorized repairs on his DD with great reluctance, and found every reason she could to delay or dismiss any work she found unreasonable. Which, to her, was everything. She'd made it very clear that *Interceptor* was a waste of resources. Thankfully, Fleet Admiral Villanueva disagreed.

Why a commodore went out of her way to interfere with his ship boggled his mind. The admiral had warned him, though, that he'd made a lot of enemies.

The two SPs checked the last tech out the gangplank and then formally saluted Jacob, which he returned.

"Thank you, gentlemen."

"Yes sir," they both said before departing.

Once they were gone, he stood for a long moment at the gangplank absorbing the moment.

Empty as the day she was built, but his.

"No returning officers, sir?" Boudreaux asked as she walked up beside him.

"No. We're going to have to make do with an all-new command crew. I haven't received any jackets yet. The good news is we have about eighty percent of our enlisted and noncoms returning, which means we'll have experienced hands."

Jacob was about to step onto the gangplank when an unbreakable vise-grip clamped down on his elbow and forcefully pulled him back.

"If you don't mind, sir, my Marines and I will check it out first," Jennings said. She brushed past him, not waiting for his okay, followed by Lance Corporal Naki, PFC Owens, and a female private with dark hair and reddish skin he didn't recognize. They carried their gear slung on their backs, leaving their hands free.

Jacob was about to say something when he realized the last time he'd protested Jennings' caution, he'd wound up in a nutrient tank induced coma for a week.

"Very good, Gunny. Let me know what you find," he called out after her.

He turned and gestured to Boudreaux to take a seat on the nearest bench, where friends and family would await the ship's disembarkation.

As they sat, his NavPad beeped, informing him of two messages. The first, from Nadia, letting him know she was going to be out of contact for some time. Her life in ONI wasn't one she could talk about, and he understood. He was just happy to see her when he could. He'd hope to see her one more time before departure, but that wasn't looking likely. The truth of the matter was that his new deployment could last years, and a lot could happen in that time. They just enjoyed the time they had.

"Looks like we got our crew list," he told her. Using the holographic feature, he pulled up the officers and immediately noticed a problem. "This can't be right."

Boudreaux glanced over and frowned. "That's unfortunate, Skipper. But I don't think NavPer would accidentally assign us a group like that. It has to be intentional. Have you spoken with your admiral?" Boudreaux asked. She leaned over and massaged her vat-grown leg while he scanned through the personnel jackets.

Jacob gave her a sideways glance. "She's not *my admiral*, Chief. She's the Fleet Admiral of the Alliance."

She gave him a look that told him she didn't believe him. With a shrug, she changed the subject. "How is our new CO?"

"We have about two hours to get the crew loaded, and another two after that to join in a simulated squadron action."

"You're kidding, right, sir?" Boudreaux asked.

"I wish I was. And now," he pointed at the NavPad, "all I have are midships and ensigns. No first officer..." He glanced over at Boudreaux, a thought occurring to him as his smile spread. Chief Warrant Officer Three Boudreaux had plenty of time in service, and she was already an accomplished leader in her division. The boat bay sparkled under her command.

He'd briefly considered recommending her for OCS last year, but then the secret mission to Medial had changed all that. With a frocking and a good recommend under her belt, she'd be a shoo-in for the challenging course. Since her injury leaving Wonderland, she had been less of the cocky, carefree aviator he had first met on Zuck. She'd matured, he thought, taken her duties more seriously, and overall had become a better officer.

She could do it, he decided. Her experience, mental fortitude, and attention to detail would serve her well. Would she take it, though? Most warrants loved the special privileges their rank afforded. Both a part of and *apart from* the chain of command. Officers had no such privilege. Once she put on the bars, she would have to answer for her actions to a higher-up instead of living in her own specialized bubble.

Jacob needed her, though. Her experience and presence would be invaluable. She might just want to be a pilot, but there was so much more to her.

"This is good news, Skipper," Boudreaux pointed at his holo.

"MKIV decoy torpedoes. State of the art? We've never had decoy torpedoes onboard before," Jacob said. "Would have come in handy a few times."

"I'll just be happy if we get a Corsair," she said.

"Skipper," Jennings voice crackled over the small speaker on his NavPad, "all clear."

"Roger that," he replied. He tapped Boudreaux on the shoulder. "Let's go in."

She followed him across the gangplank. The airlock led them into the mess deck, and Jacob stopped for a moment to examine the parts of the hull the yard had repaired while he considered his next step.

Yard dogs had his ship for the last three months, which meant he'd spent three months filling out forms and shuffling virtual paperwork on his NavPad. Once aboard his ship, he couldn't help but feel like home. Some of the battle damage from their top-secret engagement with the Caliphate heavy cruiser was still evident in the mess. The outer bulkhead looked too new and had thin weld marks over the attachment points.

"I miss the old mess," Boudreaux said, pointing at the wall.

"How's this different?" Jacob asked.

"You see an ice cream machine anywhere?"

Now that she mentioned it, he didn't. There were a few things spacers needed to survive the rigorous duty of outer space. Coffee, soft-serve ice cream, and plenty of leave when at port. Miss any of those and even the best ships would risk mutiny.

Jacob looked around for a moment. "Change is inevitable, Chief. We can embrace it or rage against it, but most of the time it happens without caring if we like it or not."

"Oui, Skipper, I want ice cream though," she said with a grin.

"Get your gear stowed, Chief. Then I want to see you on the bridge."

"Aye aye, sir," she said. Boudreaux gave him a sideways look at the unusual request, but slung her bag all the same and headed out.

Jacob's bags were still in his portside quarters. With any luck, they would arrive via the pursers service before they had to launch. They had a week, after all. Plenty of time.

Midship Travis Rugger approached his new ship's birth with a mix of dread and building anticipation. Assignment aboard ship was the final test of a cadet's worth. A passing grade meant joining the Navy as an ensign. An exceptional report could mean advancement to the coveted rank of lieutenant junior grade. For Travis Rugger, it was everything he ever wanted.

The intellectual responsibilities of a cadet were hardly a

challenge for the sharp-minded young man, but the physical ones were a different matter entirely. If only he could be someone who loved those things and excelled at them. He enjoyed studying, reading, and the pursuits of the mind, but when it came to running, lifting, and fighting, Travis' small stature put him at an inherent disadvantage. The Academy presented him with a problem he'd never had before: it wasn't enough to be smart.

He only carried the one duffel since his orders were for a four-week deployment, and he managed to make his way to the ship via maglev all the way to the outer shipyard area. His new ship occupied a pier among a row of empty births.

A long line of ratings and NCOs wound around ahead of him. Unfortunately, the enclosed passageway didn't allow for him to step aside and see how far ahead the line went. Technically, he was an officer, but it wasn't like he could just order people around.

"Rugger, right?" a young woman said from behind.

Travis turned, his duffel on his shoulder swinging wide. The young woman jerked back in surprise to avoid being hit in the face.

"Oh gosh, I'm so sorry," he yelped.

"It's okay, happens all the time," she said with a smile.

He glanced down to see her name tag and remembered who she was. "Mariposa Marino, right? Second class biology?"

At the Naval Academy, the years were divided into classes. He wasn't entirely sure why first year cadets were in fourth class, but now he and Mariposa were both *Firsties,* their last year in. They spent half their time in the classroom, and half experiencing the jobs they were training for.

"Yeah, that's right. I'm heading to Fleet medical after I graduate. You?" she asked.

"I'm not sure yet. Haven't gotten my orders."

"You'll get a cushy assignment, I'm sure, considering you have the highest electronic warfare scores in our class," she said with a playful smile.

Travis wanted to respond with something witty, but there was a problem. Mariposa was beautiful, and the second she complimented him, his brain stopped working.

"Thank... thank you," he stuttered.

"Line's moving," she said, bumping him with her duffel.

Move it did. Whatever had held it up seemed to have vanished as they walked, almost nonstop, to the gangplank. As they turned the corner to the final stretch, massive translucent bay windows displayed the parked ship. It wasn't exactly the shining example of Alliance power he thought it was going to be.

Destroyers were ideal training grounds for midships and the only reason he received the assignment was his high scores, but the *Interceptor*...

"What a wreck," someone said from behind him and Mariposa.

Travis didn't turn his head to look. He couldn't take his eyes off the ship. Wreck was one way to describe her, and accurate too. The forward keel hull plating looked brand new, while the rest of the bow had pits and scratches marring the armor. The nose of the ship, with its open-mouthed shark painting, wasn't any better. The gangplank obscured his view of the forward turrets, but he could see the con and rear turrets just fine, and their *used* condition didn't fill him with confidence. In fact, he felt more than a little fear welling up inside him.

"Wait, I thought all the ships in the fleet had tri- or quad-barrels?" he said to no one in particular.

The man in front of him turned, and Travis, who was short to begin with, looked up into his Asian features and gold rank bars.

"Ensign Kai," the man said with an amiable smile. "It's a Hellcat, if that means anything to you. She's, like, forty years old." His unabashed awe seemed out of place to Travis.

"Thank you, sir," both Travis and Mariposa said as one.

"I didn't know there were any still in the fleet until I got my orders yesterday," Kai went on. "I'm excited, though. If she's still in service, then she's fast, probably the fastest ship in the fleet. I can't wait to see her insides."

Travis got the distinct impression Ensign Kai was no longer talking to him, per se, but anyone who heard his words.

"Next," the chief petty officer manning the hatchway said.

"Ensign Akio Kai, reporting, CPO Sandivol."

"Good to meet you, sir," Sandivol said. "And you can just call me Bosun if you like." The bosun tapped up a button on his NavPad and Kai's beeped. "That will guide you to your quarters. There's a map of the boat as well. Report to CPO Redfern in Fusion One once you're ready.

"Report to who?" Kai asked.

"I know, it's not normal, but Fleet, in its infinite wisdom, is sending us off shorthanded. We're all making do," the Bosun said.

"Roger that, Bosun," Kai said as he stepped past.

"Next."

As Travis started to move, a large man shoved by him and took his place.

"Wait your turn, *middie*," he said before turning to the Bosun. "Ensign Mateo Lopez."

Bosun Sandivol looked the officer up and down for a moment. "Ensign Lopez, the end of the line is back there. If you're having trouble seeing, I suggest you report to sickbay for an eye exam once we're under way. Next."

Lopez's jaw flared and he squared his shoulders. "When you address me, Chief, you will say *sir* or I will have you up on charges of disrespecting a superior officer," Ensign Lopez said.

Travis was floored. Bosun Sandivol had multiple hashes on his sleeve, with more time in service than Travis had years alive. Why would Ensign Lopez treat him like some spacer on his first deployment?

"My apologies, *sir*." Sandivol's tone didn't sound like an apology to Travis. "The end of the line is back that way, *sir*. The Ensign will need to be processed in the order of arrival, *sir*. Please return to the end of the line, *sir*."

Sandivol's repeated use of *sir* seemed to make Lopez even more angry, but there wasn't anything he could do unless he wanted to force his way onto the ship. Until the Bosun checked you in, you weren't officially reported for duty.

After a long staring contest that left Travis wanting to go to the end of the line, Lopez turned and marched past him, knocking into Rugger and pushing him aside as he went.

"Next," the bosun said.

Mariposa pushed Travis gently when he didn't move. He stumbled forward, gulping to find his voice.

"It's okay, son. Name?" Bosun Sandivol asked.

"Uh, Midship Travis Rugger, sir... I mean Bosun."

Sandivol gave him a fatherly smile and hit a button. Travis' NavPad beeped, updating him on where in the ship he would be birthed. "Look's like you're assigned to Comms, Mister Rugger. Welcome aboard *Interceptor*."

Travis stepped onto the ship, taking it all in. As he walked through the mess, he was amazed at how tight the ship felt. He was glad there was no claustrophobia in his family.

CHAPTER SEVEN

Jacob, still wearing the same uniform he'd met Captain Hatwal in, sat in his old familiar chair, facing the freshly painted shark on the briefing room's large conference table. He didn't know who in the yard made sure the shark received a touch-up, but he was deeply appreciative of their attention to detail.

The holographic function of the NavPad displayed his dilemma in shimmering blue lights. Three midships and three ensigns were the entirety of his officer corps. Thankfully, someone at NavPer had thrown him a bone and sent a bright young engineering mind his way. Ensign Kai's jacket was replete with compliments and praise for his skills. Having him assigned to engineering was a no brainer.

As was Midship Marino's assignment to sickbay. While attending the academy, she'd completed every requirement for pre-med, and had her berth in Fleet Medical school guaranteed after she passed her final cruise. Very few midships received a slot at Fleet Medical before they graduated.

He pressed the call button on the table. "Sickbay, Captain."

After a brief moment, the line clicked. "Sickbay, Chief Pierre. What can I do for you, Skipper?"

Jacob inwardly sighed in relief. Whoever at NAVPER decided it was a good idea to send him a bunch of raw recruits at least had the good sense to keep experienced personnel in vital positions.

"We're short handed this cruise, Chief. I'm sending you a midship who, according to her jacket, is a very promising young doctor... once she actually attends medical school."

"Oh," Chief Pierre said. "I see, sir." The pause on the line spoke volumes. "I have Desper with me and a few spacers who served as EMTs. We'll get by."

Jacob appreciated Pierre's can-do attitude more than Pierre would ever know.

"Good man, Rob. Let me know if there are any problems."

"Sir? What about the XO?" Pierre asked.

What about the XO indeed? Jacob mused. "Right now, we don't have one. You'll know when I do if that changes. Captain out."

Two down, four to go.

A rap at the hatch drew his attention. Gunny Jennings stood at parade rest in the hatchway. Jacob smiled inwardly at how perfectly the rank suited her. He could have left her a sergeant and made do, but after her actions in Wonderland and Medial, it was clear she was someone special.

"Sir, Chief Warrant Boudreaux to see the skipper," Jennings said. Her formality wrapped around him like a comforting blanket. There were things, he decided, that made a place feel like home. Some of it was the ship, but most of it was the crew.

"Send her in," he said.

Jennings disappeared through the perpetually open hatch, and a moment later, Chief Boudreaux appeared.

"Skipper," she said.

"Have a seat." He gestured to the one next to him.

"The boat bay is just how I left it. Empty," she said with a grin.

"I'm hoping," Jacob said, knocking on the faux wood of the table, "we'll get a Corsair before we ship out next week." Tension built in his chest as he tapped keys on the NavPad to bring up a new PO's file. "This is PO1 Stawarski. He's certified on the Corsair, and from his file is more than qualified to fly her. What do you think?"

Boudreaux screwed up her face at the idea of someone else touching her beloved bird. She glanced at his scores, though, and shrugged.

"Sure, Skipper. In a pinch he could, but he won't need to," she assured him.

"Vivienne—"

Her face froze, and she held up her hand. "Stop right there, sir. If you're about to assign me to another ship, I'll pass. I've come to love *Interceptor*. I know eventually I'll have to go... but I'm not ready."

A lazy smile grew on Jacob's face. He was glad to hear her say that. He wasn't ready to lose her either.

"No, not at all. You're with us for a while longer. What I was about to tell you was..." He reached into his tunic and pulled out the soft velvet box that carried rank insignia and slid it across the table to her.

Chief Boudreaux raised an eyebrow as the box came to a halt in front of her. She cautiously lifted it before easing open the top and freezing.

———

Vivienne held the box out as if she were trying to avoid contact with her skin. A single gleaming silver bar reflected the briefing room light into her eyes. Fear squeezed her heart. Since she was a little girl, all she had wanted to do was fly. Some small rational part of her brain, the part she had listened to more and more since she lost her leg, told her she couldn't fly forever but she couldn't let go now.

She lifted the box up toward him. "No, Skipper." Her accent voice came out thick and full of conflicting emotions. "I appreciate the faith you put in me, but I'm an aviator, not a leader. I wouldn't know what to do with this... even if it came with a manual."

The captain looked at her. Really looked. His piercing brown eyes seemed to dive deep into her soul, and after a moment Vivienne looked away.

Shame replaced fear. He needed her. Needed her by his side, commanding the ship. She couldn't bring herself to say yes, even though it disappointed a man she desperately didn't want to disappoint. Boudreaux snapped the little box shut and slid it back across the table.

After Boudreaux exited the briefing room, Jacob settled back and ran his hands over his face. He was more than a little shocked she'd said no. Without an XO, they couldn't report allready to the squadron CO when it came time to ship out.

There were more urgent problems for him to deal with, though. Jacob shuffled his lack of an XO to the side, placing it in the "deal with it later" box, and pulled up his remaining crew to be assigned.

He would have two ensigns on the bridge. Lopez had more seniority, which placed him at Ops. Ensign Brown's marks at weapons put him in the top three percentile of the fleet, which suited Jacob just fine. The two men might be young, but they were good at their jobs.

At comms he put Midship Rugger. The young man's technical skills were first at the academy, and Jacob had confidence he would pick up the older ship's systems quick enough.

The last midship, Oliver Townsend, Jacob sent to damage control. Without an XO, they would need someone to at least coordinate and communicate. Townsend's scores showed a high degree of conscientiousness and extraversion, making him ideal for a position that required attention to detail and speaking clearly and concisely.

Jacob tapped the last key, sending the orders making their assignments official.

Then he paused.

Something about the new batch triggered a feeling in his gut. NavPer had sent them no one with real experience but they had something else. He pulled up each of the files and set them to display in the air above his NavPad. He didn't know what he was looking for, just that he had a feeling there was a connection.

"Son of a gun," he said as he put it together.

"You kiss your girlfriend with that mouth?"

Jacob jerked back at the sudden intrusion of a familiar voice. The last time he'd seen *Midship* Archer Ban was at graduation from the Academy. His blond hair was a bit longer than cadet short, but his trim waist showed he still kept in shape.

"Archer?" he finally managed to spit out.

"*Lieutenant Commander* Ban to you, *Mr.* Grimm," he said with a smile.

Matching his enthusiastic smile, Jacob pointed to the silver oak leaf adorning his uniform.

"That's *Commander* Grimm, *Mr.* Ban." There were several ways a superior could address other officers. Most were based on familiarity or command structure. Calling them *mister* or by their rank was interchangeable.

Archer let out a bellow.

"Well I'll be undone." He snapped to attention and brought his rigid hand up to salute. Jacob returned the gesture, playing out the scene to the satisfaction of both men.

"Are you my XO?" Jacob asked. For a fleeting second, he thought about how great that would be.

"Afraid not, old pal." He pointed to the circular emblem with a blazing fire in the center. Like *Interceptor*'s badge, the words "USS *FIREWATCH*" and "Ever Watchful" circled the fire.

"Your Hatwal's XO?" Jacob asked.

"Yep. I'm doing a visual inspection of each of the ships." He turned and wrapped his knuckles against the bulkhead, only to pull them away with an upraised eyebrow. "You sure this ship won't fall apart on you the first time we go through a lane?" His expression was only half full of mirth.

Jacob's hackles rose at the slight undertone of disrespect for his ship.

"She's the fastest destroyer in the fleet and she packs a mean punch. Even if the briefing room hatch won't close," he said.

"Good enough for me." Archer turned, leaned his head out into the passage, then back in. "Listen, I wanted to say how sorry I was about Pascal. I should have—"

Jacob held up his hand, interrupting his old friend.

"No need. It's hydrogen in the reactor. We hadn't spoken in a long time. Just because Pascal happened, didn't mean you were obligated to defend me. Then... or now."

Archer gestured to the chair closest to Jacob, who nodded and sat down. He placed his space-black watch cap on the table and looked Jacob right in the eye. Silence stretched out between them.

"If you're trying to see the real me," Jacob said, "it's not hard. I know what I must look like to an outsider. Can I offer you something to drink?"

"Coffee, if it's not too much trouble for your mess," Archer said.

Jacob leaned on the comm button. "Mess, briefing room. Can you send up a cup of black coffee for a guest?"

"PO Mendez here, sir. On it."

They chitchatted for a few minutes while waiting. PO Third Class Josh Mendez hurried in with a sealed cup of coffee and a chilled glass of orange drink.

"Here you go, sirs."

"Thanks, Josh. Good to see you're back."

"Good to be back, Skipper." Mendez hurried out. Jacob could only imagine the work the young man had to be doing to get the mess ready to go for deployment.

"Your crew seems to really like you," Archer said with a nod toward the departing PO.

"Some of us have been through hell together," Jacob replied. "Josh is a good kid. When I came aboard he was a spacer, now he's in charge of the mess. Actually got an award for making stew." While it was a fond memory now, their time almost starving to death on the way back from Wonderland wasn't.

"You trying to tell me something?" Archer asked as he sipped his coffee.

"Things aren't always what they seem, is all. I know you're here to find out about my records, and I wish I could tell you, but I can't. I can't even tell you why I can't, and I know that's got to drive Captain Hatwal crazy. I know it would me."

"My captain doesn't trust you. He thinks you've got some political connections that saved your butt and put you on a destroyer."

Jacob stifled a laugh. Archer wasn't wrong, it just wasn't as cut and dried as all that.

"No, I personally do not have those connections. Quite the opposite, really. After Pascal, my career was over... I just hadn't figured it out yet. The only reason they gave me *Interceptor* was because they needed someone disposable. It just turned out that I was the right man for the job and the admiralty, in their infinite wisdom, let me keep her."

Archer glanced around the room, his eyes lingering on the plaque on the wall with the attached ribbon.

"And that?" he asked with a gesture.

Not for the first time, Jacob wished his actions after Zuckabar were public knowledge. Wonderland was still classified, and the majority of the public didn't even know the Guild was anything other than a *persona non grata* corporation. As for their raid on Medial... well, the odds were that would never be declassified, at least not while Jacob was alive.

"I have an excellent crew," Jacob said. "That award was bought and *paid* for." His tone would brook no dissention. He'd lost too many men and women under his command to let anyone disparage his crew.

"I mean no offense. Give me something I can take back to Captain Hatwal to get him off your back," Archer pleaded.

"I wish I could, really. You know as well as I do that virtually every position in the Navy above shoeshine is based on prestige. No one likes a jacket filled with black lines. This is the hand I've been dealt, though. I get my own ship, I get to stay in the navy, and now I get to actually be part of the fleet instead of off patrolling some dead-end system. You knew me in the Academy, Archer. I'm still that man, even more so after everything I've been through. You can trust me to do the job. More importantly, you can trust my crew and my ship."

Archer looked, really looked, into Jacob's eyes for a long

while. The two men sat in silence, occasionally interrupted by the whoosh of air as the circulation system kicked in.

"That's not a lot to go on, but I'll see what I can do. This is his first squadron command, Jacob. He doesn't want to blow it. That's all. He's a good man too. Remember that."

Archer pushed the empty mug and stood. With a final nod, he turned to leave.

"It's good to see you, Archer," Jacob said to his friend's back as he walked through the hatch.

If Captain Hatwal didn't trust Jacob, then what would he do with him? Leave him behind? Five destroyers could bring a tremendous amount of firepower to bear on a single target. Hell, under the right circumstances, with surprise on their side, they could do enough damage to disable even a battleship. They would all be destroyed, but they had the firepower for it. While *Interceptor* was considerably lighter armed than the other four, she could still make the difference. No one could afford to leave a fifth of their force behind… he hoped.

Bells rang on his NavPad, letting him know it was seventeen hundred, time to work.

"Bosun, Captain," he said into the comm.

"Bosun here, Skip. What can I do?"

"We're going to have to pull some odd shifts. Are we blessed with deep pockets on Astro, Comms, and DCS?"

"One mike, sir." Through the comm, Jacob heard the bosun tapping away at his NavPad.

"Yes sir. We've got Oliv, Collins, and Tefiti returning."

Tefiti? If he was onboard, it was because he wanted to be. The man's skill at gravity sensors was nothing short of legendary. He'd have to push him, though, since Astro would be manned exclusively by POs.

"Have those three get together and pick out three ratings to train—"

Jacob lost himself in the mundane work of command. He loved every second of it, even the paperwork. Working with Sandivol, he would have the ship, at least on paper, manned and ready to go.

Except for an XO.

CHAPTER EIGHT

Captain Yousef Ali, of the light cruiser *Glimmer of Dawn*, watched the passive radar like a Medial Firehawk scanned for prey at night. The Consortium corvettes weren't supposed to be in the system, and his intel hadn't shown any official CN for at least six systems.

However, the Consortium Navy used corvettes in a way most used destroyers—for recon and screening. He had only seen them assigned to in-system patrols where the Consortium had planets, never beyond that... until now.

Yet, here they were, four of them cruising toward his position at the starlane, decelerating without any caution. They had no way of knowing Yousef and his four light cruisers were lying doggo at the entrance of the lane. If not for a very competent EW operator, Yousef wouldn't have even seen the ships. It was luck... or Allah's will. Either way, his squadron was about to get a kill.

They'd just returned from raiding Tein, and their holds were full of prisoners. From here they would travel to Medial, offload, and then come right back to do it again. The ships must have been sent to pursue them, not realizing he had seen them and waited in ambush.

Yousef loved his nation—he had faith in Allah—but this kind of warfare didn't sit well with him. In space, fighting other ships felt right. Attacking planets full of farmers and tourists seemed beneath him somehow. Ever since Caliph Hamid took control some twenty years earlier, though, things in the Caliphate had changed. Some for the better, and some, Yousef thought, for the worse. Thoughts he would keep to himself.

"Range?" he asked his EW officer.

"Eight-zero-five-two-zero-zero, mark," Lieutenant Wael replied.

Two more minutes and he could close the trap. Two of his cruisers were directly in the path of the frigates. His other two were a hundred and twenty thousand klicks on the flank. Once the enemy ships passed his first two, they would all open fire and catch the ships in a classic anvil. There was no where for them to go.

Dawn's bridge was quiet with tension as the range dropped. Yousef was more than confident in his state-of-the-art squadron. With their overwhelming fire power, they would make short work of the Consortium ships.

"Range, sir," Wael said.

"Fire."

Four light cruisers opened fire with turret batteries. At less than a hundred thousand klicks, the results were near instantaneous. Plasma impacted with the hulls of the ships and burned right through them. They never even had a chance to alter course. One second they were there, the next, all four were expanding clouds of debris.

His bridge crew celebrated and Yousef let them. Strangely, he realized, he was happy the ships were all destroyed. Why, he couldn't be sure. Was it because he didn't relish the idea of turning over survivors to the slavers of Medial?

Yousef's troubling thoughts haunted him as his crew celebrated. However, his duty always came first, and it was time to move on.

"Well done," he said. "Helm, set a course for Medial. All ahead full."

CHAPTER NINE

"And we're dead," Jacob said from the con. "Again." He collapsed into his chair more forcefully than he had meant, drawing sideways glances from his bridge crew.

Chief Suresh made no move. Her face didn't so much as flicker in the mirror as the computer pronounced their fate. Jacob felt the aggravation rolling off her. Captain Hatwal had given *Interceptor* engagement orders that made no sense whatsoever. Fly in a straight line at one hundred g's of acceleration. Do not deviate from his specified course. Pretend not to see anyone, no matter how early their own passive sensors detected the ships. Not exactly a challenging problem for a skilled coxswain.

On top of that, they were only allowed to return fire after they were fired upon. Which, Jacob noted, they weren't doing until *Interceptor* was under three hundred thousand klicks. No ship, no crew, no matter the training, could respond before their ship was torn apart in a torrent of fire at that range. It was just too close.

"Reset the sim," Jacob ordered.

"Same parameters, sir?" PO Oliv asked from Astro.

He sighed inwardly but did his best to keep his face neutral. "Yes, PO, thank you. The same."

Oliv went to work, making sure to follow *The Book* as she reset each system. Four times they had flown right into the enemy, only to be vaporized. Lost with all hands. He didn't even have time to call abandon ship. At least they didn't have to wear their ELS suits, which he considered the only saving grace to the bitter fiasco.

Ironically, if he had led the sim, he would have made everyone put them on, but he wouldn't have then punished one of his ships by virtue of who her commander happened to be.

"Mr. Rugger, can you get me a line to *Firewatch*'s CO, please?"

"Aye aye, sir," Rugger said.

Spacer First Class Felix Gouger sat in the secondary bench chair next to comms, assisting the midship with the ships older systems. Jacob noted how the rating gently pointed out the proper controls for the soon-to-be officer. Once again, his crew performed with the finest traditions of the Navy. It would be easy for a spacer to resent having to teach a midship how to do the job, but Gouger handled it with a high level of grace and professionalism.

Jacob's MFD showed the line connecting, and after a moment Commander Ban's face appeared.

"Captain Hatwal isn't available right now," Archer said.

Jacob pushed the ill thought he had out of his head. Surely Captain Hatwal wouldn't let whatever feelings he was having interfere with his duty? He nodded to his friend, letting him know it was okay.

"That's fine, Commander. *Interceptor* requests new parameters for the next engagement. We'd like to let the shark off the leash, if you don't mind," Jacob said with as much enthusiasm as he could muster.

Archer looked off screen, meeting someone's eyes Jacob couldn't see. He guessed it was Hatwal, who was listening and about to say no.

"Negative, Commander. Mission parameters remain in place. *Firewatch* out." The screen darkened, leaving an image of Jacob's face staring back. He wasn't surprised, disappointed, but not surprised.

"Sir," Oliv said from Astro. "We're all set. We can signal our readiness on your order."

Jacob spun his chair around to face the stern, holding his hand up with one finger to let Oliv know to hold on. Gunny Jennings stood at parade rest, not moving so much as a muscle outside the open bridge hatch. Her exactness to duty impressed Jacob, and he admired her following of the regs to the letter at all times.

To the letter...

Jacob opened up the message with the mission parameters again and reread them. He was sure he knew what they meant, but he needed to know the exact wording.

Commander Grimm, you are directed and required to participate in DesRon Nine exercise one-alpha. Interceptor *will proceed on course one-eight-zero mark zero-zero-one. You will accelerate at one-zero-zero gravities. You may not initiate fire. No course alteration is allowed, regardless of detection range, until after you're engaged.*

-Captain Ganesh Hatwal, commander DesRon Nine, USS Firewatch.

. . .

He couldn't open fire before they shot at him, but since they weren't running silent, he knew exactly where they were. Could he maybe... turn it around on them? Lord, what he wouldn't give for one victory. Something to hand his crew and show them they could do it. Crew shortages would be the least of his problems if the crew he had lost all hope.

He tapped a few keys on his MFD, pulling up the replay of the last four "battles." Since part of his orders were to ignore any "enemy" contact, the other four destroyers were essentially sitting still in space, waiting for *Interceptor*. With each battle, the second his ship crossed the three-hundred-thousand-kilometer mark, the rest of the squadron opened fire. If he knew when they were going to fire, and exactly where they were, then he could arrange a little surprise for them without breaking the rules.

"Astro, plot the course. Chief Suresh, execute when ready," Jacob ordered with his back still to the bridge. Orders were either a list of things that one could do or that one could *not* do. The way Captain Hatwal worded the orders made it clear they were a list of what to do, not an exhaustive list prohibiting other actions.

"Ensign Brown. Alert all weapons crews. Full combat readiness. I want us locked and loaded," Jacob ordered.

Ensign Brown, whose stout neck and shoulders showed he was from MacGregor's World, repeated the orders back with a voice like a bass guitar.

If Jacob's plan worked, his CO was going to be in for one hell of a surprise.

Captain Hatwal's command chair moved noiselessly as he slipped into it. On a larger ship, as the squadron CO he wouldn't also command a ship, but destroyers didn't have the luxury of a flag bridge. Instead, he let his XO handle the majority of the command of *Firewatch* while he focused on the fleet.

Grimm was a problem, Hatwal decided. The man's reports were late, his ship lagged in readiness, and then there was his dismal showing in the sims so far. They were on number five, and so far *Interceptor* had proved how little value she would be in a fight. *Interceptor*'s sole use would be to watch their back when they were in a contested system. The battered old ship would be a hindrance in a fight, and it certainly couldn't scout. No, the only thing it could do was lay in wait at a starlane and warn DesRon Nine if anything came through behind them. While he had set restrictive parameters for their behavior in the sim, he felt they were justified in order to teach their egotistical, glory-driven captain his place. Maybe if they walloped the ship a dozen more times, he would do as he was told.

Ganesh frowned at his own thoughts. Was he judging Grimm too severely? He thought back to every interaction he'd had in the Navy in his years of service. He couldn't think of a single officer who had so spectacularly screwed up as Jacob T. Grimm and then went on to have a career, let alone a command. The man had to have dirt on somebody, otherwise they would never have promoted him. On top of that, he was supposed to believe an officer with Grimm's record had seen combat twice, and won medals that were classified? It was much more likely he had a highly placed patron in Congress. Such was his Navy. As much as he hated it.

"Sir, *Interceptor* is closing right on time."

"Excellent, Mr. Moses. Tell all batteries to prepare to fire," Commander Ban said.

Ganesh felt a little guilty for the way he punished the ship and her crew. He was certain it needed to be done. This achieved two goals: it allowed the ships that would be doing any actual fighting to coordinate their maneuvers, and it would teach Mr. Grimm a lesson. However, he knew the effect it would have on *Interceptor*'s morale. It was an unfortunate necessity.

With *Interceptor* acting as the OpFor, that left him four ships, including his own. They were spread out in a classic box formation, each ship anchoring a corner a hundred thousand klicks from the other. Their bows were pointed directly at *Interceptor* and as soon it was in range, he would fire.

"Firing line, sir," Commander Ban informed him.

"Excellent. DesRon Nine, fire," he said as calm as could be.

All four ship's computers "fired" their weapons. At the same instant, alarms wailed on *Firewatch*'s bridge, signifying a hit.

"Damage control, what was that?" Commander Ban demanded.

More alarms wailed furiously as lights flashed, signifying hits. As one, all lights blinked and died. Emergency lighting clicked on. Consoles across the bridge strobed bright red, notifying them they were KIA.

"We were hit with a simulated Long 9, sir, then a MKXII torpedo finished us off," PO Yuval said from damage control, the stunned disbelief clear in his voice.

Hatwal fumed with impotent anger as more and more information rolled in. There was no chance Grimm had waited to be fired upon before returning fire. None. The range was such that he wouldn't even have time to give the order to fire.

Reports from the other three ships arrived moments later. The entire squadron was disabled or destroyed. *Interceptor* had escaped without a scratch.

Commander Ban let out a sharp barking laugh as the simulation master showed the outcome on the ship's main forward display.

"He technically fired after we did, sir. I told you, Grimm's a tactical genius. If anyone can figure out a way around a problem, it's Jacob T. Grimm."

Hatwal pressed his lips hard together and stiffly shook his head. Archer praised his friend, as he should, but genius or no, he disobeyed a direct order just to "win" the sim. However, Captain Hatwal wasn't sure what infuriated him more—that Grimm had disobeyed, or that he suspected Ban was correct?

Boudreaux remained at attention, along with the rest of the *Interceptor*'s officers and senior noncoms, while Captain Hatwal laid into their skipper. All her years in the Navy, she'd never heard a superior verbally berate a junior so. Especially not in front of his officers and senior enlisted.

When Captain Hatwal first came aboard, he accused the Skipper of cheating. When that didn't stick, he accused him of disobeying the *spirit* of the sim. What was the spirit? To plummet *Interceptor*'s morale into the toilet? If so, *mission accomplished*.

"And another thing, Commander, I resent the way your crew behaves. It is unprofessional for the ratings to address you so informally, as I have been told they do."

Boudreaux flinched from the hurt she saw in her captain's eyes. How a crew addressed their captain was an individual matter for ships, as long as they fell under the regs. For some officers, honorifics like "skipper" were justified, for others, a violation.

"Sir, many of my crew and I have been through some... extreme actions. It's perfectly normal for them—"

"Yes, yes, the redacted parts of your file. Are you going to stand here and insist to me that this *heap* of a ship has seen multiple combats and somehow won a Navy Unit Commendation?" He jabbed his finger at the smiling shark plaque with the aforementioned ribbon.

Boudreaux reached out and grabbed Chief Redfern's wrist as he involuntarily took a step forward. She shot him a look that told him to calm down. It was one thing to question a captain, another to insult the ship he served on and the men and women who paid for the award in blood. Most of their missions were secret, classified to only the top brass. The crew couldn't even talk about it amongst each other.

Which was gut-wrenching in its own right. There were few things a spacer loved more than telling stories.

"Sir—" Grimm stopped himself with a visible show of effort.

To Boudreaux, Grimm looked like he wanted to say something, anything, even the truth, to get Hatwal to back off.

Grimm glanced sideways at the assembled officers and POs. The line on his jaw went firm and he let out a breath. "Sir, I explained that to you already. If you wish to know more, you have to go up higher than myself to find out."

———

Rugger slumped down on the chair at one of the few round tables in the mess. The majority of them were bench seats, but a few in the back were swivel chairs and they were next to the vid showing the stars outside. With *Interceptor*'s size, there was no wardroom or even a CIC. It all had to be done a little differently than he had learned in the Academy.

"Hey, Travis," Mariposa said as she sat opposite him. "Why so glum?"

"You were in sickbay, so I suppose the pounding we took didn't really impact you."

She shrugged as she filled her spoon with creamy mashed

potatoes, eyes going wide for a second as she gingerly put it in her mouth. "Wow, good food for a tin can," she muttered. "I'll have you know we were part of the sim as well. Whenever the ship took a hit, the simulated casualties came in and we had to simulate working on them. Right up until the ship blew up and we had to do it all over again. Besides, we won one, didn't we?"

Travis moved the food around the plate. While he hadn't attended the meeting in the briefing room, the open hatch made it clear that he was on the wrong ship.

"Not really. The squadron CO came over and ripped Commander Grimm a new one for "cheating." We could hear it all the way in the bridge. I don't know about you, but I'm worried how being assigned on this ship is going to affect my career."

"You mind if I join you?" Ensign Kai said.

"No sir, be our guest," Mariposa replied.

Aiko slid in next to her. "You like being on the bridge, Travis?" he asked.

Before he could respond, three loud mouths entered the mess, led by Ensign Lopez. Travis had a feeling about the officer, the kind he got when he encountered a bully. He needed to keep his head down and not draw attention.

"Not really," Travis replied. "I'm on comms. I'm always on comms. I'd rather be working somewhere I haven't been before."

"With your test scores?" Mariposa said. "You aced all the EW courses. Of course they are going to assign you to comms."

"All the tests were on modern equipment. I feel like I'm trying to figure out how to drive my grandfather's aircar up there."

They ate in silence, only the clinking of glasses and hushed whispers of the crew permeating the room. Travis barely touched his food, though. The weight of what he witnessed pressing on his mind.

Why had Captain Hatwal's verbal tirade upset Travis so? Maybe it was because Commander Grimm didn't defend himself, or maybe it was something else. Something deeper. The rant felt personal. Like it was confirmation that Travis didn't belong in the Navy. He could never imagine being on the receiving end of such an assault and not crumpling.

"You deaf, Middy? I said these tables are for officers," Lopez said.

Confusion and fear swept over Travis. Confusion, because midships were officers. The lowest rank possible, but officers all the same. Fear, because Lopez loomed over him menacingly.

"Chill out, Lopez," Akio said. "Unless the *senior* officers are dining, these tables are for everyone."

Lopez glared daggers at the engineering officer.

Travis' chest tightened, and he desperately wanted to run away. Standing up too fast, he knocked his chair over, drawing every eye in the mess. As he scrambled to pick it up, he forgot his tray and spilled his food.

Lopez bellowed out a laugh, pointing at him.

Travis froze. He saw the food on the floor, heard Lopez laughing, and imagined everyone else in the mess was too. He couldn't take it, so he ran out of the mess, blowing by some chief with dark skin without so much as a hello.

From behind the serving line, PO3 Mendez eyed the interactions carefully. The crowd in the back might be officers, but they were the same age as he was, with less actual time on a boat and no combat experience. Lopez was a bully, plain and simple. Josh had seen enough of them back home to recognize one in uniform.

What he didn't know was what to do about it. Lopez's rank made a direct interaction impossible. He could tell the bosun, but at the end of the day, he would face the same problem as Josh. Short of going to the captain, he wasn't sure who to talk to.

"PO? Hello?" Chief Suresh asked, snapping her fingers in front of him.

"COB?" Mendez said without thinking.

"Food," she said, pointing at the serving line.

"Right. Sorry, Chief. I've got you." As he dished her, it occurred to him that the COB was exactly who he needed to see. "Chief, let me ask you something…"

CHAPTER TEN

Captain Hatwal closed the comm channel from the briefing room where he sat alone, the weight of the world fell on his shoulders and he wasn't ready. His new squadron had a long way to go before it was prepared for combat, and he still had the problem of an annoying, insubordinate officer with an ancient wreck of a ship holding them back.

Still, orders were orders. As of 0800 local, the Alliance was at *Alert Condition Two*. It seemed the Caliphate's determination to start a war, any war, was made of iron. The Consortium was under attack, and they needed all the light units the Alliance could provide.

They needed DesRon Nine.

"Ban," he said holding down the comms button.

"XO, go ahead?"

"Signal the squadron, change of orders. We're to depart for Praetor within the hour. All ships report readiness," he said.

"Aye sir, within the hour. Sir?"

"Yes?"

"As far as I know, NavPer still hasn't found an officer to XO

Interceptor. We could temporarily transfer one of our junior officers to him and—"

Ganesh's mood improved as he realized how to deal with the thorn in his side. "No. We're shorthanded as it is. We can't afford to spare anyone. Tell Mr. Grimm he's going to have to figure it out. If he's not operational in forty-five minutes, *Interceptor* will stay behind."

"If you're not operational in thirty minutes, Jacob, he's going to leave you behind," Archer said, his voice echoing in the empty briefing room.

"Thank you for the heads up," Jacob replied. Archer looked like he wanted to say something to his old friend but instead cut the line.

The screen went blank and Jacob leaned forward, hands clasped and pressed against his forehead.

Jacob was still reeling from the dressing down Hatwal had given him, and now this. As a CO himself, he understood the need to have respect of rank in uniform, but for Captain Hatwal to object to his people calling him skipper seemed harsh indeed.

The million and one things he needed to do before they could disembark flashed through his mind. The one thing he *had* to do, find an XO, was also the one thing he couldn't do.

If only Boudreaux had said yes. She was perfect for the position: she was within his ability to frock, and they could technically report ready without a dedicated Corsair pilot.

In twenty-eight minutes, he was going to have to report readiness. The last thing he wanted to do was tell his new CO he wasn't ready. Jacob decided he could spare two minutes, then call NavPer and demand an XO.

Glancing at the hatch to make sure no one stood outside the briefing room waiting for him, Jacob knelt down and prayed. His mother's faith had always outshined his own, but over the last few years, with all the death and destruction he'd seen, his faith had grown. It could have easily gone the other direction, embittering him to an uncaring God, but staying positive and exercising his faith had worked for him. Even if it was being tried at the moment with his new CO.

When he was done, he stood, feeling better if nothing else. It wasn't as if he expected prayer to solve all his problems, but often it brought clarity to his mind when he had a tough decision to make.

Jennings rapped on the bulkhead and caught his attention.

"Chief Boudreaux to see the captain," the Marine said.

"Come in," he said.

Boudreaux paused at the hatch. Hesitating for a moment before entering, she snapped to attention.

"Sir, if the offer is still available, I accept."

"Chief, you're literally answering my prayers," he said with a huge grin. He snapped to attention and returned the salute. "As you were," he said. Digging in his pocket, he pulled out the box, opened it, and took out the silver insignia. "These were mine, Chief. I'd be honored if you wore them?"

"Sir..."

He could tell she wanted to say something, so he gave her the time to find the words.

"When you no longer need me as an officer, can I go back to flying Corsairs, or is this permanent?"

Jacob gave her the most reassuring smile he could. "Viv, when we get back from this deployment, if you want to go back to being a chief, you absolutely have my blessing. However, I know you're going to be an outstanding XO. With your CO's recommend, you will be a shoo-in for OCS if you choose that route."

Her features softened and her eyes looked relieved. "Thank you, sir."

"Gunny, can you come in here, please?" he bellowed.

A moment later Gunny Jennings stepped in.

"Aye, sir?" she asked.

"We need a witness."

Jacob took Boudreaux's current insignia off her collar and replaced them with the single silver bar of lieutenant junior grade. He took a step back, snapped to attention, and saluted her.

"Chief Warrant Officer Vivienne Boudreaux, with the responsibility and trust invested in me by the president, Congress, and the Department of the Navy, I hereby frock you with the temporary grade of lieutenant, junior grade. With it comes all the responsibilities and authority of said rank. As an officer in the Alliance, you are held to a higher standard of duty and respect. Do you accept?" he asked.

"Yes sir. I do," she replied just as sharply.

With that formality complete, Jacob held out his hand to her, but she surprised him by hugging him. Not entirely appropriate, but it could be forgiven. Her head only came up to his diaphragm, and it was a stark reminder of how tall he was. Something he easily forgot for some reason. "One last formality. To the bridge," he said, gesturing to the hatch.

As Jennings led the way, Jacob noticed something about his gunny. She had the same level of alertness here, onboard, that she had when they were almost killed on Kremlin Station. It was like she had no off switch. Which, he had to say, he didn't mind. Considering she'd saved his life not once but three times during their voyages.

On the bridge, he snapped his fingers to get Rugger's attention. "Mr. Rugger, would you be so kind as to have the bosun join us up here?" he asked.

"Aye sir," Midship Rugger replied. He fumbled with the controls for a moment before managing to trigger the right one. This time, Spacer McCall sat next to the midship, and just like Gouger, gently guided the new officer in the right direction. Jacob noticed that not only did McCall take his time, but he let the midship fail before helping him. Jacob also didn't miss Midship Rugger accepting the help graciously.

"Bosun Sandivol to the bridge, Bosun Sandivol to the bridge," Rugger's voice rang out over the ship. It wasn't quite as confident as Jacob thought he should sound, almost coming out as a question rather than an order. He smiled and shook his head, glancing over at Kim to say something... *Right*, he told himself. She wasn't his XO anymore. He sure hoped she was doing well at command school. Those courses were tough.

Bosun Juan Sandivol clambered up the ladder to O-deck a minute later, slightly out of breath as he crossed the passageway to the bridge.

"You wanted to see me, Skipper?"

"Aye, Bosun. Sound the pipes, all hands, and prepare to record."

A moment later the pipes sounded, alerting the entire ship that they were to listen.

"All hands, now hear this," Bosun Sandivol said.

Jacob grabbed the mic from the overhead and keyed it.

"*Interceptor*, this is the captain speaking. Things in the Consortium are escalating and DesRon Nine has received orders to head out early. However, we can't depart without an XO." He paused for a moment to let that sink in. "Therefore, I have promoted Chief Warrant Officer Boudreaux to the temporary rank of lieutenant JG and have assigned her to be our new XO. She will be afforded the respect commensurate with her new rank." Jacob handed the mic to Boudreaux. "XO, get the boat ready for departure, if you will?" he asked.

She coughed once, took the mic, and keyed it. "All hands, this is the XO. Set Condition Yankee. Prepare ship for departure. Seal all exterior hatches and disconnect all moorings. I say again, Set Condition Yankee." She hooked the mic to the overhead and looked to Jacob for approval.

"You did good, XO," he said.

"Uh, sir...?" She looked around and stepped closer to him. "I'm not sure where I go from here."

"I've got you. Bosun?"

"Yes sir?" Sandivol said.

"Would you fabricate our new XO some appropriate uniforms?"

"Aye aye, sir. With pleasure." Sandivol marched off the bridge.

"XO, get down to engineering and make sure we're good to go for starlane travel."

"Aye sir. On the way." Boudreaux turned to leave, then looked back. "Thank you, Skipper."

He nodded to her. Once she left, he sat down in his chair. "Oliv, set us a course for the Gideon system and on through to Zuckabar."

"Aye sir, course for Gideon and on to Zuckabar," Oliv said.

"Mr. Rugger, get me the squadron commander, if you will."

"Aye sir, one moment." Jacob watched the young man search the console in frustration. After a too long interval and some help from McCall, Rugger got it. "*Firewatch* on the line, sir."

Jacob activated his MFD, showing Archer's face. "*Interceptor* reporting one hundred percent readiness. All positions filled."

Archer's smile widened to encompass his entire face. "I figured you could make it happen. I'll let the captain know. *Firewatch* out."

CHAPTER ELEVEN

"Who's that?" Travis asked his eating companion as a dark-haired Marine walked in. Their meal times matched, so Rugger and Marino had eaten together almost every day since they had come aboard. Since they unfortunately shared the same shift with Ensign Lopez, Travis started sitting on the other side of the mess from the officer's tables, not wanting to cause any trouble.

"She's a Marine. Other than that, I have no idea," Mariposa said.

The woman in question wore the gray-and-white shipboard uniform the Marine Corps favored, along with black combat boots and an uncovered head. The way she paused in the middle of the mess, as if she wasn't sure where to sit, made Travis feel for her. He didn't really feel like he belonged either. Intellectually, he was aware that he wasn't onboard to make friends, but damned if he wouldn't like some that weren't also midships or officers.

He decided that since she was a Marine, he could cross the streams. When her eyes wondered his way, he waved her over.

She had the taut, muscular gait of every Marine Travis had ever met. Her uniform's sharp creases could cut bread.

"Sir, do I know you?" she asked.

"Midships Travis Rugger and Mariposa Marino. Have a seat, Private...?"

"June. Private June. I'm not sure I'm allowed to sit with officers, sir."

Travis smiled at Mariposa and they shared a silent laugh. "We're more like proto-officers, or officers-in-training. And were like five seconds older than you. You're a Marine, so you can sit with us and we can talk without having to worry that we're accidentally messing something up. It's not like this is a wardroom; the mess is open to everyone so sit down."

June thought about it for a moment, brown eyes glancing around the mess. "Okay. But only because it's filling up in here and I'm hungry."

Travis scooted over so she could slip her legs into the bench seat. Once she was down, she started eating like a starving person.

"You don't have to hurry," Mariposa said. "Lunch is an hour. You can slow down and enjoy the food. I know the Marines like to be efficient, but that's actually very hard on your stomach."

June stopped, holding the spoon of beans in front of her like the idea of eating slower had never entered her mind.

"Sorry," she said, dipping her head with a sheepish grin. "I've been in school so long, I've forgotten what it's like to not have a DI breathing down my neck."

"Is this your first deployment?" Travis asked. He wasn't intending to make it sound like an insult, but from the way her cheeks reddened, he thought maybe he had.

"Yes. I joined nine months ago, right out of high school. I..." She looked around and lowered her voice. "I only turned eighteen a month ago."

"What?" Mariposa said. "You just turned eighteen?"

"What did you do to get here?" Travis asked.

June cocked her head at their confusion. "I graduated top of my high school on Blackrock. I didn't really want to go to college and my family isn't wealthy. I signed up with the Corps and with my scores I had my pick of schools."

Travis glanced at the silver badge with two lightning bolts crossing a shield above where her uniform said "MARINE."

"What school did you pick?" Mariposa asked.

"EOD," June said nonchalantly.

"You diffuse bombs?" Travis asked with stunned disbelief.

"And make 'em too," she said with an impish smile.

He glanced at Mariposa and they both smiled. The Marine might be young, but to have gone to such a school, she had to be one of the best. Which made Travis question why she was on *Interceptor*. The Navy wouldn't send her best people to her worst ship, would they?

"You're sitting in my spot, middy," Ensign Lopez said.

Travis groaned. "I thought you said the circular tables were for the officers?"

June's eyes went wide and she tried to stand up to come to attention.

"Oh, you have a guest, huh? What's your name, *private*," Lopez said, making her rank sound like an insult.

"Private Yanaha June, sir," she said after she managed to go to attention.

"Leave her alone, Ensign Lopez. We were just talking," Mariposa said.

"Stay out of it, Midship, or I'll have you on report," Lopez said.

As usual, Ensign Lopez had his two cronies with him: Ensign Brown and Midship Townsend. Brown looked like an apex bear in a navy uniform. The indifferent look he gave Travis terrified him.

"Listen, Ensign, she's just a private. Leave her alone," Travis said. He didn't know what he was doing, standing up to Lopez. All his instincts told him to duck and cover. However, June was only in the predicament because he invited her to sit with him.

"I bet," Lopez said, looking at his two buddies, "that Private June here could out pushup middy Rugger any day of the week? What do y'all think?"

That terrible fear in the pit of Travis' stomach welled up, tightening his chest and freezing his legs in place. He knew the rules; he was a midship, Lopez an ensign. Any lawful orders given had to be followed. Technically, Lopez could make him do pushups. Travis hoped to god he didn't.

"I think Travis here couldn't push his way out of a paper bag. I'll take odds on that," Midship Townsend said.

He didn't know why, but it hurt Travis more that the only other midship aboard had sided with the bully.

"Both of you take the position," Lopez said while pointing at the deck. He spread his arms, backing everyone up. The entire mess watched them, and with thirty spacers it was almost full. Unfortunately for Travis, there were no other officers.

With no real option, Travis got down on the deck, hands shoulder width apart, and feet together.

"Everyone," Brown called out to the crowd. "Count them."

Just as he was about to start, he heard heavy boots on the deck.

"Private June, get up," Gunny Jennings' voice cut through the room like a sonic boom. The crowd split, leaving the Ensign's entourage by themselves. June leaped up, falling into parade rest. Travis followed suit. "Excuse me, sirs," Gunny said as she walked by Ensign Lopez, Brown, and Midship Townsend to stand in front of June with her back to Lopez. "I told you fifteen minutes, no more. Get back to Marine country on the bounce."

"Yes, Gunny," June shouted. She snapped to attention, did a right face and double-timed it out of the mess.

Jennings, short as she was, imposed her will on everyone and everything around her. Somehow, without her even threatening him, Travis was terrified of the woman.

"I didn't dismiss her, *Sergeant*," Lopez said.

"*Gunnery* Sergeant," she corrected him. "She doesn't need your permission, sir. She's *my* Marine, not yours."

Lopez didn't find that funny, and he scowled. Travis stepped back, thinking the much larger ensign was going to make a bigger deal out of his authority being circumvented.

"Captain on deck," PO Mendez bellowed from the galley. Everyone leaped to their feet, snapping to attention.

Commander Grimm stopped halfway through the hatch with his NavPad in hand, stunned at the sudden announcement. Travis racked his brain, wondering if it was normal for the mess to go to attention when the Captain walked in?

"As you were," Commander Grimm said. He glanced over at PO Mendez and walked toward the circular tables. Once the interruption had passed, Travis realized that Gunny Jennings had vanished. He swore he would have seen her walk out... but she was gone.

———

Jacob found a seat near the bulkhead by the starfield display. Almost immediately, PO Mendez arrived with his ham and cheese sandwich and orange drink.

"Josh," he said in a whisper as not to draw attention. "What was that about?"

Mendez glanced back and forth, making sure no one was

too close and leaned in.

"Sorry, sir. It's just... there are some inter-crew personality issues. I used your arrival as a way to stem the tide, Skipper. I hope I didn't embarrass you."

Jacob leaned back, looking up at the PO. Once again, the young man had shown fine quality. It was a quick-thinking spacer who would use the CO's arrival in the mess as an excuse to break up a potential fight.

"I assume you have notified someone other than me about this?"

Mendez looked away for a second. "I asked COB what I should do and she said go to the bosun... but sir, it's an officer that's the problem and—"

Jacob held up his hand. "Say no more. I'll mention it to the XO and let her dig around. Thank you, PO."

"Aye sir, enjoy your lunch."

Somehow, Mendez always managed to find a way for Jacob to eat fresh food, even when the rest of the crew wasn't. This week, though, they were full up on stores and everyone ate well.

As he absently bit into a hot French fry, he mulled over what to do. When he first took on *Interceptor* there were problems, for sure, but he solved them quickly and decidedly. After that, they didn't really have time to develop personal beefs among the crew because they were too busy trying to stay alive.

This was a new experience for him, one he wasn't well-versed in. As the captain, he couldn't really get involved unless it came to a mast, and he'd made it clear to all his department heads, the Captain's Mast was a failure of command, not of the crew.

Sipping his orange drink, he pondered what to do and decided it would be best left to his new XO, since managing the crew was one of her responsibilities. He typed a quick message off to her and put the matter out of his mind.

Newly promoted Lieutenant (JG) Boudreaux held open the hatch to her new accommodations with one hand while she tossed her Navy-issue bags into the room one at a time. The final bag, a bright-pink hard container, was her only civilian accessory. She'd put off moving from the aviators' berth to her new quarters as long as she could, but now that they were about to arrive in Zuckabar, she didn't have an excuse anymore. The new Corsair and aviator were coming aboard from Kremlin Station and she couldn't hold the cabin any longer—it was close to the boat bay for a reason. She resigned herself to living on deck six with the Marines and the other officers.

Jennings arrived and picked up all four bags, two in each hand, and carried them the rest of the way into the cabin, placing them neatly on the top bunk.

"Unless the XO would like the bottom?" she asked without looking.

"No thank you, Gunny. Top is fine. And in here you can just call me Vivienne, or Viv."

Jennings nodded. The laconic Marine moved to the small desk with a built-in mirror and sat down. She gently undid the matronly bun she always wore on duty.

Boudreaux oohed, marveling at the intricate braid. She kept her own silky brown curls short because it made flying easier, but maybe if she were going to be a real officer for a while, she would have an excuse to grow them out.

"I had no idea your hair was so long. You're going to have to show me how you do that."

As Jennings finished, her blonde hair swished past her shoulders.

"Sure thing, XO. Anytime."

Boudreaux let the hatch close as she entered her new quarters. She couldn't complain—they were larger than her aviator berth. Sharing with another person, especially a person as respectful and no-nonsense as Jennings, wasn't going to be all bad. They had their own head and shower, a small closet, and the aforementioned desk. The bunkbeds were against the starboard bulkhead.

Her NavPad whistled the bosun pipes, signifying a new message. "I need to change that," she muttered.

"Lieutenant Yuki always had hers on silent. Once the captain figured out to send her all the paperwork, the thing never stopped making noise," Gunny Jennings said.

A knock on the hatch caught her attention before she could check the message. "Enter," she said.

It slid open, revealing Bosun Sandivol holding three more uniforms. "Sorry these took so long, ma'am. Tailor's Mate Barrack had trouble with the fabricator and there wasn't anyone from engineering available to assist. He got it all sorted, though."

He handed her all three without entering the stateroom.

"Thank you, Bosun," she said.

"Ma'am," he replied.

After the hatch shut, she examined the three uniforms. They were the ones she was least likely to wear aboard ship: her service dress whites, full dress, and the obnoxious mess dress.

"He's going to ruin me," she muttered, referring to the skipper.

Up until that moment, Vivienne Boudreaux had a carefree life, even under the rigors of the Navy. As an aviator and warrant officer, she had special privileges that weren't in the manual. But as an officer, she was just another number, bound by rules and regulations. She hung the uniforms in the small closet and collapsed on the bottom bunk.

She ran her hands through her curly hair before replacing

the watch cap. Her NavPad beeped again. "What now?" she said with a sigh, thumbing the device on. The screen lit up with a message from the skipper.

"Allison?" she said without looking up.

"Yes, ma'am?" Jennings replied flatly.

"Sorry, you prefer Jennings, don't you?"

"Aye ma'am."

Boudreaux briefly debated trying to convince the woman to call her Viv while in the cabin, but decided that if the stubborn Marine wanted to be formal, then who was she to make her change?

"Are you having trouble with one of the officers?" she asked.

"Ma'am?" Jennings turned away from the mirror, gathering her hair up in a pony tail and brushing it out. "I'm not sure what you mean."

Boudreaux glanced at the captain's note again. "PO Mendez reported some trouble in the mess. Ensign Lopez was involved..." She hoped her questions would get Jennings to open up.

"Oh, that. No trouble, ma'am. The ensign was under the impression my Marines were his to do with as he pleased. I disabused him of that notion."

Boudreaux seriously doubted that's all there was to it. Jennings' idea of "disabusing" someone usually involved her fists.

"If anything happens again, please let me know."

"I'm sure it will be fine, ma'am."

"Seriously, though. Let me know."

Jennings' brows furrowed for a moment before she gave the XO a nod.

Somehow, Boudreaux wasn't convinced.

CHAPTER TWELVE

PLANET BLACKROCK, ALLIANCE SPACE

Nadia's aircar circled the women's prison on the northern continent. Snow piled up on the basalt rocks that littered the area where the prison was tucked into the canyon wall. She waited on the ATC's authorization, trying to ignore the rapid-fire coilguns tracking her small, two-person vehicle.

"Lieutenant Commander Sara Mitchel, this is Blackrock penal One-Seven-Three, you don't have clearance to land. Please send your verification? You have thirty seconds to comply."

Nadia punched in the code her contact had fabricated for her. Sara Mitchel was her go-to cover ID for dealing with prisons. As a JAG officer, Sara had complete access to any military or civilian prison entrusted to the military. As far as covers went, it was dang near perfect.

"Codes accepted. We're taking control. Sit back and relax, Commander."

There was a reason Prison One-Seven-Three was located on

Blackrock. All military personnel passed through the planet's many schools. Army boot camp resided a few klicks south at Fort Yorktown, Marines trained on the Derna Archipelago, and the Navy at the Academy near Redwood City. If it weren't for the colonists who had come from old Earth's North American continent, there wouldn't be any civilians on the planet at all.

"Roger that, ATC," she replied.

Her car swerved, curving around into a descent onto an outstretched landing pad. The sleek vessel came to a rest and the door slid up, letting her exit.

Nadia wore her service dress whites, with all the pomp and circumstance of an important JAG lawyer. Unlike Fort Icarus, where the Army controlled the prison, DNI ran this one. The Department of National Intelligence, despite being the government's premiere intelligence agency, wasn't always on the same side as ONI.

Every ounce of her cover had to be perfect. She's spent the three-day trip over, making sure it all stuck. It had to be more than a cover. It had to be real. From apartments she rented on three planets to the time Sara broke her ankle on a date.

Above the landing pad, a technician watched as the computer ran her credentials and scanned her biometrics. The moment she stepped out of her air car, a dozen different electronic devices activated. Biometrics were read: fingerprints, thermal imaging, density of her hair, her skin was even checked against previous photographs and recordings to make sure it reflected light the same.

The technician frowned, making a grunting noise.

"What's the matter, Gizmo?" Agent Felicia Briscoe asked.

"I don't know... something." Gizmo was the name

everyone called him. He didn't mind. He had a knack for computers. The way he could read their code bordered on the mystical, at least to those around him. They almost spoke to him. This time, they were telling him something wasn't right.

There were multiple levels of searches he could authorize at his discretion. Level one looked at what they had on record locally. Level two went deeper, checking the civilian and military databases located on the planet and in orbit.

Level one came back authorized and he frowned again. It wasn't right, something about her *felt* off. He pulled up a still of Commander Mitchel as she exited her aircar.

She was gorgeous, no doubt, but that wasn't what triggered Gizmo. At least, he didn't think so.

"Gizmo," Agent Briscoe said, "you're not just keying in on her because you have the hots for her?"

He shook his head.

"You know me better than that," he said. Gizmo scanned her file again. From there, he ran her records through Naval Academy, followed by JAG school.

"Should I hold her?" Briscoe asked.

Gizmo wanted to keep running her IDs, hold her until he was sure, but in order to do that he had to have something solid to point at. Otherwise, he would end up looking bad.

"No, I'll keep looking though."

"Let me know," Briscoe said.

After an uncomfortable amount of time, the large door keeping Nadia on the landing pad flashed green and slid aside, letting her in. she held up her ID for the guard on the other side as she walked past.

"Commander Sara Mitchel to see prisoner Delta-Three-Three-Five."

A loud buzzer sounded and the next door slid open. Another guard, this one armed with stun guns and armor, led her through the maze of the interior of the prison until he showed her into an interrogation room.

She took her seat facing the door and put her anachronistic bag on the table. A few minutes passed—longer than Nadia thought should before the door opened. Two female guards escorted the Caliphate spy known as Daisy into the room.

Pure, spiteful rage boiled inside Nadia. She tried to keep it off her face, but the look of terror that passed over Daisy showed her failure.

Daisy opened her mouth to protest.

"As your *lawyer,* I advise you to say nothing until we're alone," Nadia said in as neutral a voice as she could muster.

Daisy looked between the two female guards and Nadia could see the battle playing out on the woman's face. Call for help? Cause trouble? Or comply? The guard shoved her toward the table.

Nadia frowned, standing as if she were going to protest the treatment of her client. The guard clipped Daisy's wrists to the table.

"You can leave now," Nadia said to the two women. They glanced at each other before leaving.

She worried about how the sight of the horrible woman made her feel. Could she even pull off the mission without finding a way to kill her? After the days of humiliation Nadia had endured at the hands of the Caliphate because Daisy, she wasn't sure she could keep from hurting her.

Nadia's devotion to her nation, to her Admiral, to her Navy warred with her desire for revenge. She'd satiated it somewhat with her mission on Medial, but with the woman in front of her, she wanted nothing more than to reach across the table and choke the life out of her. Daisy flinched and Nadia realized she had her hands clenched in fists.

But...

There was a corruption in her government, one they couldn't find without Daisy's help. And there simply wasn't another asset Admiral DeBeck had access to with the training and skill to pull off the mission. It had to be Nadia.

Instead of murdering her on the spot, Nadia took a deep breath and sat back down, activating her NavPad.

"Say your name for the record," Nadia said in a disinterested tone.

"Daisy Vogel."

"Your real name," Nadia insisted.

"I was recruited when I was four. That's the only name I've ever had..." A blue light flashed out from Nadia's pad, scanning Daisy instantly.

"We can talk freely now. For the next ten minutes, they're going to see and hear a conversation between lawyer and client. Since it is relevant, I'm here to tell you that your appeal was denied. Now, with that out of the way, how are you?"

With her emotions more or less in check, she took a moment to really look at Daisy. She'd lost weight, and the woman hadn't had a lot of weight to lose in the first place. Her previously curly golden hair was chopped short and matted against her skull. Taut skin pulled hard on her jaw and neck, and the bags under her eyes spoke of exhaustion.

Mentally beaten was the only way Nadia could think to describe her. Not that any poor treatment Daisy suffered would bother her in the slightest. As far as she was concerned, Daisy could die in a fire.

"I knew death would come for me soon. I just didn't think

they would send you. May I pray once more before you execute me?" Daisy asked with a trembling voice.

"We're not all that different, you and I," Nadia said. "We both sacrificed much for our countries. If my mother hadn't fled Caliph space during the Great War, I might have been you."

"Please, just kill me. I don't need a lecture about the mistakes of my life. I do that enough for myself," Daisy said, looking Nadia in the eye with a fierce gaze.

Nadia leaned back, a genuine grin on her face. "Oh, I'm not here to kill you."

"Then why are you here? To gloat? Can I go back to my cell?"

"What if I told you there was a way out of here?" she asked.

Daisy perked up, a glimmer of hope in her eyes. "What are you talking about? I won't betray my country if that's what you want. I see the error of my government's ways now, but I am still loyal to my people."

Nadia notched her respect up for the Caliphate spy. She wasn't sure she would be able to say the same thing if their positions were reversed. Of course, Nadia knew what the Caliphate did with their prisoners, first hand. In comparison, Daisy's treatment bordered on luxurious.

But after months of interrogation, she was certain there wasn't any information left for Daisy to give. "No, I'm not interested in your knowledge, just your skill. You're going to laugh, but I need your help."

Daisy did just that for a solid ten seconds before she realized Nadia was serious. "You need my help? With what? Prison soap?"

"A mole hunt," Nadia said. "Someone in our government is leaking information and we need to find out who it is and stop them."

"Do you think it's one of my people?" Daisy asked.

"Actually, no. I think it's more domestic than that. But..."

She glanced down at her NavPad. "Clock's ticking. I need to know now. Are you in or are you out?"

Daisy looked down at her hands, emotions warring on her face. "What do I get out of it?"

"A new identity and transfer to a minimum-security prison where you will live out the rest of your natural life."

Considering they would execute Daisy eventually, Nadia thought it was a pretty good deal.

"I want something more," she said quietly.

"You're not exactly in a position to bargain."

"I know, but still... I want your forgiveness."

CHAPTER THIRTEEN

NAJI SYSTEM, INDEPENDENT SPACE

Yousef double-checked his crew's work on his own screen. Satisfied, he nodded to his XO to give the order. Once his ships were moving again, he could look for what he considered more legitimate prey. The wreckage of the civilian ships they were currently sailing through did nothing to satisfy the warrior within him.

Though High Command was more than happy to have him do nothing but target cities and traders, Yousef wanted a challenge. *Glimmer of Dawn* was two hundred meters of lean, mean, fighting machine, and he had three other light cruisers as well: *Autumn's Favor, Courage of the Vanguard,* and *Yatağan Edge,* though *Glimmer* was by far the most advanced of the four.

Blowing civilian trains and bombing colonies from orbit seemed not only a waste of his time and talent, but ultimately of no real tactical or strategic value. He was a spacer, not an executioner.

"Sir," his XO, Lieutenant Ghazali, interrupted his reverie.

"Yes?"

"Message from the High Command, sir. Your eyes only."

Shifting in his seat, he pushed those thoughts and feelings down. This was his duty, and no matter how much he wished it would change, it wasn't going to.

"Helm, we have two starlanes to clear. Plot a course and send it to the squadron," Yousef said.

"Aye sir."

Naji's location three lanes from the cursed wormhole put it too far away for the Consortium to actively guard, but not so far they could risk moving freely through it.

"XO you have the con," Yousef ordered. He made his way to the small, one-man office off the portside of the bridge, where he could review the secret message. He prayed it wasn't more raids or civilian targets to attack. Sitting at his sparse desk, he placed his hand on the security reader.

Admiral Rahal appeared on screen. Surprise glued Yousef to his seat. The High Admiral of the Fleet had never sent him a message directly before. He jerked out his hand and paused the message before it began. The date listed the message as twenty days old. He wished the limited FTLC tech was more readily available, but they saved that for battleships and planets. Whatever message the admiral sent, it had to be important.

"This is either very good, or very bad," he muttered. Closing his eyes, he said a prayer for it to be the former.

"Captain Yousef! You have done your Caliph proud. What you do not know is that your missions these last few months have achieved their goal. The cowards guarding the wormhole have split their forces, leaving a paltry three heavy cruisers on station. We are sending the entirety of Second Fleet to smash them and take the asset for ourselves. We need your squadron to clear the path through Naji, Ocelot, and Taki, and then form up with us at the Praetor starlane. No advanced warning can be allowed to alert them. Embedded in this message are the exact time tables. Don't be late, Captain. We will catch them by surprise and crush them utterly. Allahu Akbar!"

The screen darkened, leaving Yousef grinning in the room by himself. Finally, a fleet action worthy of his skill. The time frame was tight, but he could make it happen.

"Bridge, Captain. Order *Vanguard* to head for Taki immediately, full silent running. Follow and observe any military ships at maximum distance with minimum risk to her if they are coming our way. I want to know of any possible danger before it happens. If we have to face enemy action head on, we'll have them flanked. Captain out."

With his light cruiser squadron, as long as he didn't have to face the Consortium heavy cruisers, who could possibly stop him?

CHAPTER FOURTEEN

PRAETOR, CONSORTIUM SPACE

Silence dominated the bridge as *Interceptor* passed through the event horizon of the wormhole into Praetor. In one instant, the view changed from a distorted image of a thousand-thousand galaxies to the comparatively *empty* view of the Consortium's farthest northern star system.

"Damn," Ensign Brown whispered.

Jacob, still in the throes of awe, decided to let the language faux pas go. This was only the second time he'd traversed it and he had no complaints. From the time they entered the wormhole in Zuckabar to the moment they exited, a single hour had passed on the mission clock. Yet, Interceptor had traveled nine hundred light-years. Nine hundred!

His MFD lit up with contacts as hundreds of commercial vessels waited in line to enter the wormhole. He'd never seen the system before—few in the Alliance had—but he was stunned at the level of infrastructure already surrounding the wormhole and the nearby planet. It reminded him of the stories he read about the mad rush to Alpha Centauri once the old

Terran World Gov had settled it. Not only did the population of the system explode, the facilities at the edge of the Sol System did as well in order to support the departing colonists.

"PO Collins, status?" Jacob asked.

"Yes sir. One moment," she said, distracted. "We're... we are in Praetor, confirmed."

Ensign Rugger turned to face him, one hand on his headset. "Sir, incoming transmission from Captain Hatwal."

"On screen," Jacob replied.

Captain Hatwal's dark feature filled the small MFD attached to Jacob's chair. While the captain hadn't rolled out the welcome matt, Jacob refused to think ill of him... mostly. If he started down that path, it wouldn't end well for him. After all, junior officers who feuded with senior officers didn't win. Not ever.

"*Interceptor* is one hundred percent ready, sir," Jacob reported.

"Good to know. We've been invited to dine with Rear Admiral Endo of the *Star Phoenix* at 1900 local. Full mess dress, Mr. Grimm, no exceptions. Hatwal out."

The screen blinked, and Hatwal's face vanished. Jacob leaned back, pondering the message. Hatwal had to be sweating inviting him to dinner, worried that his reputation would somehow impact the captain.

Maybe if he showed up in full mess and the Captain saw exactly what he had earned, what his crew had paid for with their blood, sweat and tears, he would ease up? Jacob didn't think that was a likely outcome. Most probably, the captain would be embarrassed by Jacob's appearance even more. No officer wanted to be upstaged by his junior...

That gave Jacob an idea.

He keyed the mic on his chair. "All Marines report to boat bay at 1830, full mess dress." If there was one thing that would take the heat off him, it would be his Marine platoon showing up in their outstanding outfits laden with metals they had won over the last several years, especially on Medial. Jacob wasn't the only one honored for his actions.

"PO Oliv, plot us a course to park with the squadron.

"Aye aye, sir. ETA five zero minutes," PO Oliv said from Astrogation.

"Excellent. Execute when ready," Jacob ordered.

"Helm, come about, three-seven-one, down bubble one-eight degrees ahead two-five gravities," Oliv said.

As Collins repeated back the orders, Jacob stood and headed for the hatch. He hadn't worn his mess dress in a while, and he needed to make sure it was up to snuff.

"Ensign Brown, you have the con."

"Aye sir, I have the con."

Jacob pulled gently at the collar of his mess coat. Service dress whites would suffice any situation and would be far more comfortable, but orders were orders. He just hoped that between the fruit salad on Jennings, Naki, and Owens' jackets, not to mention his XO, he would go unnoticed. If he could have swung it, he would have had Suresh come with them. Her uniform positively gleamed with service pride, not to mention the decorative sword she was authorized to carry. As it was, he was pushing it with a party of six.

Star Phoenix's massive interior dwarfed *Interceptor*. It was a glaring reminder of how miraculous it was that *Interceptor* had survived her engagement with the Caliphate heavy cruiser in Medial. Walking in the passageways of the Consortium beast brought home the knowledge that he would never command such an awesome machine.

Interceptor was his home, forever. He loved the little ship. Its speed and maneuverability had saved the day on more than one occasion, and he appreciated it. However, his dreams of commanding a ship hadn't stopped with just any command. Why join Navy if not to dream of battleships and fleets?

The lift opened onto a wide-open space filled with low tables decorated with soft, pink clothes that seemed to fall to the deck like petals. Two blue-skinned men wearing ceremonial black armor snapped to attention. For the life of him, he couldn't remember what the swords they carried on their backs were called.

"They're Tieshan Shudan, sir," Gunny Jennings whispered. "Consortium special forces. Kind of a big deal in the military world."

Jacob stepped forward, stopped, and saluted. He wasn't sure about the protocol for their ships, but it seemed the respectful thing to do.

"Commander Jacob T. Grimm, USS *Interceptor*, and guests," he said.

Both men bowed at the waist to a forty-five-degree angle. "It's an honor, sir. We will show you to your seats."

Beyond the two guards, a sea of people awaited. Admiral Endo knelt on a cushion at the head of a long, low table, his uniform as magnificently decorated as any Jacob had ever seen.

Jacob and his entourage followed the men. He thought they would lead him to one of the far tables where the other Alliance commanders knelt. Only Captain Hatwal was positioned at the table with the admiral. Even Archer knelt with the other officers. However, the two special forces men led Jacob right to the long table.

"Corporal Naki." The lead special forces man pointed to the place next to the admiral.

Naki glanced at Jacob. He had no idea how to respond, so he

just shrugged. Aft Naki, Owens, and then Jennings were positioned behind cushions with an empty place between them, which Jacob assumed was for a guest who had not arrived yet. Jacob was next, then Private June, followed by Boudreaux. Poor June looked nervous as hell standing next to her captain. Hardly anything decorated her mess dress, though the crossed lightning bolts of her EOD school were impressive to anyone who knew what they were.

Once everyone stood behind their cushions, Admiral Endo rose up and held his hands for attention. The tables were low to the deck, and the cushions were obviously for sitting on. While Jacob was happy to eat however his hosts wished, he hoped he didn't embarrass himself sitting in a way the mess dress wasn't intended for.

"Ladies and gentlemen, a call to order, please." A soft chime rang and all conversation vanished as the gathered group stood. "You may not be aware of the great service these guests have done for the Consortium, but I am," Admiral Endo said.

He turned and, one by one, bowed to the Marines, then to the empty place mat, followed by the rest of them.

The empty place for a missing man... a missing Marine, Jacob realized.

Jacob clenched his jaw, and he could tell Jennings did the same. It wasn't for a guest who had yet to arrive, but for Private Cole, who gave his life on Medial.

Once the Admiral had bowed to Jacob's crew, he said, "You are our honored guests. Please, eat."

Jacob knelt, then switched to sitting cross-legged on the cushion placed on the deck. He fidgeted for a minute, trying to find the right way to sit in a formal uniform designed for chairs.

"Sir," Jacob said, "you honor my crew beyond words and..." He glanced at the empty space between him and Jennings. "You honor Private Cole's memory. For that, you have my sincerest gratitude."

Admiral Endo bowed his head, opening his mouth to respond when Captain Hatwal interrupted him.

"May I ask what *great service* Commander Grimm has performed for the Consortium?" Captain Hatwal said, with barely contained derision.

"Not just Commander Grimm," Admiral Endo said. If he heard the negativity in Hatwal's voice, he ignored it. "This young man"—he clapped Naki on the shoulder—"is a hero to my family. A picture of him will forever decorate our ancestral shrine."

Naki's face turned a dark shade, but he managed to keep his expression neutral. He looked closely at the admiral for a second, and then his eyes went wide.

"Sakura... you're related to Sakura?"

"Hai. She is my grandniece. We were so very thankful to have her back, Corporal."

"I hope she is well, sir. The last letter I received was months old by the time I got."

"She is, son. And she speaks of you often. You should come visit when your duties allow."

"Interesting," Captain Hatwal said. "I wasn't aware of any operations the Alliance had in this part of the galaxy... before now, of course." Hatwal looked at the Marines, then Boudreaux, and finally rested his gaze on Jacob's uniform, almost like he was taking notes.

"Well, it's not my place to discuss Alliance military operations, Captain Hatwal. Just know that you have some of the bravest members of any military serving under you. My government doesn't hand out The Order of the Rising Sun to just anyone." He gestured at Jacob and Jennings, who both wore the star-shaped medal with the red ruby set in the center.

Jacob blushed, and even Jennings glanced away, uncomfortable at the unadulterated praise.

"So it would seem," Hatwal said with a thoughtful tilt of his head.

Admiral Endo frowned. "I'm afraid I'm not as familiar with Alliance medals as I thought, Commander Grimm. What is that one next to the order? Both you and Gunnery Sergeant Jennings have it, but the rest of your crew does not?"

Jacob glanced at Jennings, who returned his look with an empty expression. She was a gunnery sergeant; she knew it wasn't her place to talk about it.

"I'm afraid this won't satisfy you, sir, and I hope I'm saying this correctly. It's the Badge of Honor of the Bundeswehr. Beyond the name, I'm not at liberty to say. I know it sounds like something out of a bad vid, but we really can't discuss the details," Jacob said.

"No need to apologize, Commander. I've spent almost a hundred years in the Consortium Navy. I know what it means to serve."

Jacob blanched. A hundred years? "Pardon me, Admiral, but you look remarkably fit."

"That's because I am. The Consortium genetic treatments are some of the best in the galaxy."

The food arrived and Jacob sighed with relief that the attention would be taken off him and his medals. The admiral's staff served a kind of fried pastry that one of the men called, *Okonomiyaki*. Regardless, Jacob enjoyed the savory concoction stuffed with cabbage, fish, and rice with a sweet syrupy glaze. As they ate, two women served chilled sake, forcing Jacob to cover his glass when it was his turn.

"I mean no offense, but I don't drink," he whispered to the young woman in uniform. She bowed politely without a word and moved on to Jennings, who happily took the offered alcohol.

"I'll have his," Jennings told the server.

Jacob muttered something about Marines and slid his glass next to Gunny's and the server filled both.

"Forgive my intrusion, Admiral," Captain Hatwal said. "I couldn't help but notice that three heavy cruisers seemed rather... light, to guard the wormhole?"

Admiral Endo sipped his sake before answering. "I had nine, but the Caliphate Navy has shown no interest in the wormhole while heavily punishing several nearby systems that I must also protect. My Admiralty assumed, as you did, they would come right for the wormhole. That has not been the case. With over thirty systems they can reach, we had to decide on who to protect. Ultimately, I sent the other six heavy cruisers to safeguard our people."

Jacob understood all too well. In the time they spent patrolling Zuckabar, hundreds, maybe thousands, of Consortium citizens fell into the slaver's hands. There were days he felt like he was trying to fly an aircar by flapping his arms.

"Is that why you sent an official request to the Alliance?" Jacob asked without thinking maybe it wasn't his place. "With our light force, we can scout the nearby lanes and make sure there aren't any unpleasant surprises coming your way?"

Endo smiled, letting Jacob know he was correct. "Our heavy cruisers are powerful, but I can't send them to scout. If there's a fleet out there waiting to pounce on us, I would like advance warning. At the very least, we could hold them off long enough for the civilian shipping to escape through the wormhole or other lanes."

Captain Hatwal frowned. "What my commander is saying makes sense, but wouldn't you rather keep the concentrated forces here? After all, our battlegroup isn't far behind us. Once

Enterprise is on station, no Caliphate fleet would be foolish enough to try and take the wormhole from a Claymore-class battleship and escorts, even if she is a few years old."

"You are correct, Captain. I do believe once we are reinforced by your full battlegroup, there will be no conceivable way the Caliphate can take the system. If attacked before your battleships arrival, though, and I mean this with no disrespect, five destroyers will hardly make the difference against a force capable of overcoming my heavy cruisers."

"None taken, sir. I'm well aware of our force strength," Hatwal said.

Jacob tuned out of the discussion for a moment, losing focus on the world around him as he stared at the table. This was a new kind of problem for him. A strategic level beyond the immediate use of his ship. If the Caliphate were sending a fleet to attack Praetor, why not do it before the Alliance reinforced the system?

There were five starlanes leading into Praetor, making it a nightmare to defend. Two of them led directly deeper into Consortium space, one toward the Corridor and the route freighters used to have to use for travel to the Alliance. The last two had a bearing toward Caliphate space, though one of them was considerably farther away than the other.

Coming into the system from far enough out that there would be no hope of detection until it was too late made a lot of sense. Undoubtedly, the Consortium would have long-range sensor platforms with overlapping fields to prevent anything from slipping through unseen. Which left the closest starlane, Taki. Even if they managed to arrive undetected, they wouldn't get far before they were picked up. Though that wouldn't leave Admiral Endo much time to prepare if an overwhelming force appeared. Maybe five or six hours at most.

If DesRon Nine went through Taki and scouted the three

systems connecting to the Caliphate, they could make sure there was no surprise forthcoming. Five destroyers weren't a match for what the Caliphate navy could throw at them. Which was why destroyers were perfect for the mission. Anything they couldn't outfight, they could outrun.

"Sir," Naki spoke up, interrupting Jacob's tactical musing. "Might I ask why, with your Asian ancestry, some of your planets have Greek names?"

"We get that a lot," Endo said. "The Consortium's original settlers were from old Earth's Peloponnesian peninsula. They arrived seventy years before us and named many of the systems we now occupy."

"What happened to them?" Naki asked.

"They were ahead of their time, unfortunately," Endo said. "The medical technology to combat new diseases simply didn't exist, and they quickly succumbed to several new strains of flu created when human biology interacted with the new planets' eco systems. We keep many of their names and use them on some of our ships as a way of reminding ourselves how fragile life can be."

Jacob knew that first hand. He'd lost crew, people he considered friends, to the Caliphate and the Guild. A spacer's life was one of months of boredom followed by minutes of sheer terror.

And the Alliance wasn't even at war. How would that change when they were?

CHAPTER FIFTEEN

Invisible gravity waves spread out behind DesRon Nine as they patrolled the Taki system at a leisurely two hundred gravities of acceleration. Taki led from Praetor and had only a single exit besides the binary. The bent line formation DesRon used put the four advanced ships ahead, with nearly fifty thousand klicks between them, and *Interceptor* in the rear, a hundred thousand klicks behind with her towed array out.

In three-dimensional space, it was nearly impossible to cover all angles of attack, but it was best to keep any single ship from receiving the majority of incoming fire from the most likely angles. With one ship in the stern acting as both rear guard and scout, using her passive sensors inside the wakes, the chances of sneaking up on the formation were low.

Not impossible, but low.

Jacob stifled a yawn as his watch entered its fourth hour. It wouldn't do to set a bad example to the very young bridge crew he currently presided over. He rested his NavPad in his lap, absently tapping through paperwork that needed his attention, and sending everything else to Boudreaux.

Lopez manned Ops, and the ensign worked diligently,

managing the daily operations of the ship, if not a little formally. Something Jacob had noticed, especially with newer officers, was the mistaken notion that they were better or morally superior to those of lesser rank. It rarely lasted long. Officers who mistreated enlisted and noncoms soon found their lives a living hell, and he suspected the same would happen to these young ensigns.

Bosun Sandivol entered the bridge, bringing Jacob a much-needed refresh on his tea. While it wasn't quite eight degrees Celsius, it was recent enough to the last heat dump that his hands were cold.

"Thanks, Bosun," Jacob said.

"My pleasure, Skipper."

Jacob sipped, watching the bosun move around the bridge, checking on the junior enlisted who were shadowing the midships and new ensigns. Sandivol sidestepped Ops, almost like he hiccupped and walked right out the bridge. Jacob made a mental note to find out what that was about.

From his perspective, despite the business in the mess, Mateo Lopez seemed liked a fine officer. Then again... Jacob frowned. Looking around the bridge, he examined each of the officers, midships, and enlisted. McCall sat with Midship Rugger in a relaxed, friendly posture, whispering to the midship in a familiar but respectful way. POs Oliv and Tefiti were on shift together, along with Midship Townsend, who was learning from two of the finest Astrogators in the fleet.

At weapons, Ensign Brown, with his obvious McGregor's World build, sat quietly next to PO Mendez. Josh was a solid weapons operator and had trained under Lieutenant Fawkes. Not to mention actually operating the Long 9 in combat. Yet they weren't speaking.

Something was very wrong, and it was time to find out what.

"Chief Suresh, call up PO Collins and meet me in the briefing room, if you will."

"Aye sir," she said without looking up.

Jacob glanced over at PO Mendez as he stood to leave. "Josh, you have the con."

"Sir?" Josh practically squeaked. Jacob paused and gave him a hard look. "I mean, aye sir, PO Mendez has the con."

As Jacob exited the bridge, he could feel the eyes of the ensigns and midships on his back. They had to be wondering why he left a PO in charge.

Good, he decided, let them wonder.

After he seated himself farthest from the broken hatch, Jacob pulled up his NavPad, flipped on the holographic mode, and displayed the new officers and midships records. When he first came aboard, he'd formulated a theory about them. It was time to see if he was right.

"You wanted to see me, Skipper?" Chief Suresh said from the hatch. Despite four hours in The Pit, her day uniform's creases were immaculate, not a strand of hair out of place under her black watch cap. While the officers and midships took their dressing cues from Jacob, the enlisted had more stringent rules to follow. They either wore day uniforms—space-black multipiece tunic, trousers, and boots that were comfortable and practical—or work uniforms, which were essentially coveralls with enough pockets to hold what they would need while performing maintenance and other duties.

"Have a seat, COB," he said. She took the one farthest from him. "What's going on with the crew?" he asked point-blank. If the enlisted were having problems, they had two options: speak to their immediate supervisor, who would either solve the problem or run it up the chain, or see the COB in private. If the enlisted were acting jumpy around certain officers, and POs like the bosun were avoiding those same officers, that would cause a serious morale problem.

When she didn't respond immediately, Jacob leaned back and gave her the time to formulate her thoughts. It was a big call, and any good COB didn't want to bring a problem to the attention of the CO unless it was time to bring down the hammer.

She took her watch cap off and rested it on the table in front of her. "Gunny," she said.

Jacob assumed she was going to have Jennings close the hatch.

"Yes, COB?" Jennings appeared in the hatchway.

"Come in, close the hatch, and have a seat."

Without missing a beat, Jennings heaved the hatch closed with one arm, a truly impressive feat in Jacob's mind, since he couldn't open it with both.

He marveled at how the Marine managed to look like she sat at parade rest.

"At ease, Gunny," Jacob said.

"I am, sir."

Jacob glanced at Chief Suresh. "The podium is yours."

"Gunny, would you please tell the captain what you told me?" Her words were cool, collected, with no trace of emotion. It wasn't unusual, per se. Devi Suresh was one of the most professional ratings he'd ever had the pleasure of meeting. She was a shining example for the rest of the enlisted. Something about the way she spoke, though, put him on edge.

Jennings' eyes narrowed for a moment. "If it's all the same, Chief Suresh, I'd rather not. I don't think the situation calls for the captain to come in just yet."

"Humor me," Suresh said.

"Perhaps the XO could enlighten you on the problem, sir," Jennings said.

Jacob stifled his frustration as he dropped the palm of his hand on the comm button.

"Bridge, Captain. Can you have the XO join me in the briefing room?"

"XO to the briefing room, aye sir," Midship Rugger replied.

A moment later, the all-hands notification came out and Lieutenant Boudreaux was called. Not long after, the petite officer entered the room. Jacob pointed to the empty seat next to him, which she immediately took.

"XO, you want to fill me in on what is going on with the enlisted?" he asked.

Vivienne's lips pressed into a thin line before she spoke. "It's not the enlisted, sir."

PO Mendez had mentioned something to him about Ensign Lopez, but he figured it was just a fluke, not a long-term issue. Disappointment reared its ugly head in his heart.

"I want the three of you to look at these." He expanded the holographic images of each and every new crewmember, from enlisted to officer. "Take your time and tell me what you see."

Boudreaux leaned in, eyes scanning back and forth. Jennings and Suresh did the same. They all came up empty.

"I'm not sure, sir," Suresh said.

"Gunny, tell me about Private June?" Jacob asked.

"Excellent Marine, sir. It's her first deployment. Top marks in boot, signed up for EOD, which she graduated at the top of her class. Qualified expert in all three MP-17 tests," Gunny said with a hint of pride.

Jacob had noted as well that the Blackrock native was an above-average recruit.

"Viv, how about Midship Rugger?" he asked her.

"I looked at his jacket, sir. High scores in the academy, in the top one percent of electronic warfare students. He falls short in the physical demands, but not enough he didn't pass. If it weren't for that, he would have left as the number one student."

Jacob nodded, pretending to ponder what they were saying. "Let me ask you this: who is the number one cadet in his class?"

Boudreaux's brow's furrowed. "I don't know, sir. I would have to look it up and—"

Jacob's grin cut her off. "You should know, Viv, she's serving in sickbay. The number three cadet is down in DCS. Last year's top cadet, and the two years before that, are on ops, weapons, and engineering. Are you seeing a pattern?" he asked.

It wasn't often he figured out a puzzle before others, especially since he hated puzzles, but he took a moment to immerse himself in the satisfaction of having figured it out.

"How did we end up with this crop of officers?" Devi asked.

"It's not just officers," Gunny Jennings interjected. "If Private June is any indication, then it's probably just about everyone we received, isn't it?"

Jacob pulled up the files of every replacement they had. For once, his Hellcat ran with a full compliment and it looked like Admiral Villanueva managed to send him the very best.

"Why, though? Not that I'm complaining about good ratings and officers, sir," Devi said. "But why send us these now? Up to this point, they haven't cared one whit about *Interceptor*."

Jacob wished he had an answer for her. He suspected the Admiralty, or at least some of them, appreciated *Interceptor* more than they could broadcast openly.

"I don't know," he said, "But I think the bigger question is, what are we going to do about it? Whether they know it or not, these are the future fleet admirals and master chief petty officers. We have a duty to train them as such. Agreed?"

"Yes sir," they said in unison.

Instead of hitting the rack or relaxing in the rec room, PO Josh Mendez went to the mess after his bridge watch. There really wasn't much downtime on a ship underway. From the time he woke in the morning until lights out, there was always something to do. Sure, he could run down and spend half an hour watching movies or playing games, but he would much rather spend that time making sure his next shift went smoothly.

The mess was in the middle of gearing up for dinner. Josh had a number of spacers and apprentices under him, and they all were competent enough that he only needed to be there at the actual meal times. The rest of the time, he let Spacer Perch run the place, though Perch tended to only make hot roast beef sandwiches with spiced fries if Josh didn't plan the meals. That meant Mendez did the majority of the meal planning.

"PO," they said to each other by way of greeting when he entered the kitchen area. The mess deck itself covered the starboard side of deck three forward, while the port side had the majority of the long-term supplies, as well as the ship's store. (The only time crew wanted to buy novelty items was right before docking at home to give as gifts.)

"How are the stoves?" Josh asked. During *Interceptor*'s last battle, the mess had taken a direct plasma hit, wiping out the galley entirely. Utopia had generously replaced everything except the ice cream machine. They even managed a slight upgrade. The old galley stoves relied on magnetic induction, which meant they had to rely on limited heat and had very specific times they were allowed to cook. The new equipment included an industrial-sized vacuum fryer, laser cook tops, and his favorite addition, food savers. They could recycle much of the unused food into other ingredients, increasing *Interceptor*'s stores by a full three weeks.

That tech alone would have made a big difference when they were in Wonderland. Regardless of when they got it, he was glad they did. However, with every upgrade, there were significant downsides. Most of the starboard bulkhead was brand-new, which was where the electrical runs and supercapacitors were. About once-a-day power to the galley would simply turn off for half an hour, and there wasn't anything he or engineering could do about it. Somewhere in the new bulkhead was a fault, and the yard would need to cut open the bulkhead from the outside to find it. Not exactly something they could do while in transit.

"So far they're working," Perch said with a tired smile. "Dinner will be on time. I've got the watch meals ready too. They just need to be delivered."

Josh stopped and pounded him in the shoulder. "Well done!" Watch meals went to those who couldn't leave their post, even for a minute while on watch.

Josh stopped, looking around. Something felt off, but he couldn't quite put his finger on it. With no luck after a second of searching, he grabbed his apron and went to work.

CHAPTER SIXTEEN

TAKI SYSTEM

"Captain to the bridge. Captain to the bridge."

The alert klaxon woke Jacob from his slumber, shocking him so much he rolled out of his rack and onto the floor with all the grace of a drunken sloth.

"All-hands action stations. This is not a drill. Action stations," Spacer McCall's voice rang out through the whole ship, but somehow seemed louder in Jacob's stateroom.

"Ow," he muttered. Reaching up, he managed to slam the comm's button. "Bridge, Captain. What's going on?"

"Sorry to wake you, sir," Ensign Kai's voice came back. "We've got an unknown contact skirting the edge of our sensor envelope, sir. She's in and out, but Spacer Zach is on gravitics and he's pretty sure they're pacing us."

Jacob suppressed his initial reprimand for calling action stations when there was no immediate danger. He admired the kid's guts to call an alert instead of asking for permission. It showed initiative, and the last thing he wanted to do was step on that. Besides, the occasional unexpected drill wouldn't hurt the crew's efficiency.

"Notify the XO and call PO Tefiti to the bridge. I'll be right there."

Jacob jumped up, shed his night clothes, and dug out his ELS suit. It was a bit snugger than he remembered, which reminded him he needed to get down to the ship's gym and let Jennings beat the tar out of him for an hour or two.

A few minutes later, he strode onto the bridge, red helmet under one arm, and was pleased to see the crew had already donned their ELS suits.

"Captain on the bridge," June said in a crisp, clear voice.

Jacob paused for a moment, took a step back, and smiled at her.

"Private June. I've heard good things about you," he said.

June blushed as she snapped to attention. "Thank you, sir!"

He shook his head. *Marines.* "Welcome aboard *Interceptor*. I'm sure you'll do us proud. As you were."

June immediately dropped into a perfect parade rest. Jacob continued onto the bridge and waved for Ensign Kai to join him at gravitics. The small station next to astrogation had just enough room for one person to squeeze in between the ops panel and navigation.

Tefiti sat hunched over. One hand on his headphones as he listened to the drumbeat of space time. Spacer Zach waited patiently nearby and PO Oliv held astro.

"Did you want the con, sir?" Ensign Kai asked.

"Not yet, Akio. Let's see what the PO has to say."

A look of confusion crossed Kai's face as he followed the captain to gravitics.

PO Tefiti held one hand to the oversized headphones that were completely noise-canceling, allowing him to hear any hiccup in the ship's gravity detection systems lining the outer hull.

Lieutenant Boudreaux bound onto the bridge a moment later, her hair in a tight bun, a stain on her face, and wearing overalls.

"Sorry, sir," she said.

"What are you working on?" he asked.

"Helping PO Stawarski take apart the Mudcat's transfer-box to chase down a problem, Skipper."

"You can take the chief out of the boat, but..." he whispered to her.

"Aye, Skipper. True."

Tefiti looked up at one of his three screens, adjusted a digital slider, and pointed at the dancing line that looked like a lightning bolt bouncing around the screen.

"Definitely a gravcoil, Skipper," he said. "Low power readings. Could be a freighter or small warship. If they are following us on purpose, then they know about where our detection range ends—and that alone is enough to make them a problem. However," he said as he took off his head phones, "I don't have enough of a read to call them a contact if we're going by *The Book*."

"Well done, PO. Mac, secure us from general quarters. Resume Condition Yankee."

"Aye aye, Skipper. Secure from GQ, go Condition Yankee," Spacer McCall said from comms.

A few seconds later, Mac's voice rang out over the ship.

"What do you think it is, sir?" Ensign Kai asked.

"I hate to make any assumptions at this point." Jacob put one hand on the overhead grab bar and leaned into it. If he altered course to pursue, whoever it was would have more than enough time to go silent and disappear. "Range?" he asked.

"Roughly one-zero-million kilometers, sir," Tefiti said.

"They are skirting the edge, though, because every few seconds we lose contact with them."

"Oliv, can you plot me an intercept course? Something gradual... just enough to get us a few million klicks closer over time," he asked. "Ensign Kai, I have the con."

"Aye sir, gradual intercept course," PO Oliv said.

"Aye sir, you have the con," Ensign Kai said with relief.

"Hang tight, Akio. I won't need it for long."

"Yes sir," Kai replied. The brilliant engineering student stepped back next to the open hatch like he would bolt at a moment's notice.

Jacob took his seat, pulled up his MFD, and checked to see the distance between *Interceptor* and *Firewatch*. Not close enough for no lag, but close enough they could speak instead of sending messages.

"Mac, get me *Firewatch*'s OOD."

"Aye aye, sir. Connecting you now."

Jacob's screen blinked and a bright-eyed young woman who looked like she was in her early twenties appeared.

"Midship Brennan. How can I help you, sir?" the young woman's Irish heritage was obvious in her accent.

"I need to speak to Captain Hatwal, please."

"I'm sorry, sir, the captain has asked to not be disturbed."

Confusion clouded his next thoughts, making him think he'd misheard or misspoke.

"I'm sorry, Midship Brennan. I must have heard you wrong. I need to speak to Captain Hatwal, please."

Brennan's face fell and she glanced sideways then back at the camera. "I'm sorry, sir. You were very clear, but Captain Hatwal has asked not to be disturbed short of enemy contact."

Jacob clenched his jaw hard. Frustration boiled up inside him and it took everything he had not to take it out on the young midship, who already looked like she was afraid.

"How about Commander Ban? Can I speak to him?"

Relief covered her face, and she nodded. "Yes sir, one moment."

The screen flashed to show *Firewatch*'s badge rotating with the logo scrolling across the bottom.

"Did they just put you on hold, Skipper?" Boudreaux asked.

"I think so, XO. I..." Jacob caught himself. He was about to make a disparaging remark about his new CO but that wouldn't be a good look for him. No matter how bad his commanding officer was, there was no excuse to bad-mouth him. If he did it to the DesRon Nine's CO, then his ratings would do it to him. Every ship, his included, needed high morale to operate.

Boudreaux cocked her head to the side, lifting an eyebrow like she knew what he was about to say.

Thankfully, the MFD updated and Commander Ban's groggy face appeared as he rubbed one hand over his eyes.

"Commander Grimm, what's the emergency?"

"Not so much as an emergency, Archer, but more of a request." Jacob filled him in on what his people were seeing and his thoughts on the matter.

"Kudos to your gravitics team. That's a good catch. Let me get with our CIC and see what we can do. Send us the data and I'll let you know."

"Thank you, Archer. Grimm out." Jacob gave Boudreaux the order as he leaned back in his squeaky chair. Something felt off. In his gut. That feeling he had when things started to go sideways. Nothing he had dealt with up to this point could possibly challenge the five destroyers of DesRon Nine. At least not anything less than a Caliphate squadron.

Jacob reached over and activated the mission clock, giving him a timer from zero. He expected Archer to get right back to him with permission to alter course. The longer they waited, the higher the risk of an attack or the enemy ship bugging out.

He didn't think there would be an attack, but if that was an EW frigate or something like it out there, then they would do well to know they were being stalked sooner rather than when the torpedoes flew.

"Sir," Boudreaux said from the XO's station. Only in that moment did Jacob realize he'd ended up with two short XOs with very different body types. No one would ever mistake Boudreaux for a teenager the way Kim might have been. Still, he thought it was funny they were the minimum height to reach the overhead grab bar, and he ducked when walking through hatches.

"Go ahead, XO?"

"Isn't it a little uncommon for a squadron CO to... uh... be unavailable?" she asked, making sure to pitch her voice low. Even though he was sitting, they were eye level. He looked directly at her with a knowing gaze as an answer to her question. "Oh," she said. "Well, sir, permission to return to the boat bay?"

"Granted. I'll let you know if the situation changes."

"Aye sir."

Jacob mulled over the situation. In the past, he would have just rolled the ship to starboard and headed away at flank speed. It would force the contact to either take off or engage. Sitting on his hands doing nothing, though, gave whoever was out there the initiative. The tactician in him rebelled against the idea of letting the enemy dictate the terms.

After ten more minutes, when no communications returned, Jacob stood and gestured to Ensign Kai. "You have the con, Ensign. Call me if the situation changes."

"Aye sir. I have the con."

Gunnery Sergeant Jennings pounded the bag in front of her with all the might she could muster, pushing her muscles and lungs with the rapid blows. The impact of her fists echoed throughout the empty gym. Sweat dripped down her face, but she ignored the salty stinging liquid, lost as she was in her rhythm of practiced close combat punches, kicks, elbow and knee strikes.

"Not bad, for an amateur," a gravely voice said from behind her.

Jennings mastered her emotions, refusing to react to the man she'd expected to come see her. She'd never met Ensign Brown, but he was from MacGregor's World. Her homeworld. There was a reason she joined the Marine Corps at eighteen. She couldn't stand the people.

Men, and a few women, from every world in the Alliance had hit on her during her time in the service. Well, no one from Seabring, but everywhere else. The experiences ran the gamut from kind to cocky. Mostly, they were polite, if not always respectful. Not quite as nice as the captain, but none so rude and arrogant as the ones from her home planet. It was like her people took lessons on how to be obnoxious.

MacGregor's World had the worst atmospheric conditions for colonization of any planet in the Alliance. It was hardly suitable for human life to survive out in the open for more than an hour, let alone for building a thriving colony. The only way her people made it was by building their homes high up in the mountains and having lots and lots of children. More children than the traditional pairing of one man and one woman could afford.

Thankfully, her ancestors avoided the legally arranged marriage trap. With the consent of the child, such deals were made for financial gain, but only with a court's agreement. Mostly, young people were eager to get married and have kids, since the more kids they had, the more hands were available to work. However, despite modern medicine and nanotech gene-therapy to help the inhabitants of MacGregor survive, the hundred-year-old tradition of having multiple wives still existed. It was the norm, not universal, but more likely than not.

Allison Jennings had no desire to marry anyone, let alone be the fourth wife of some land baron and only see him when it was time to have children. She wanted to be exceptional. As long as she could remember, she wanted something more than children and a home. Maybe one day she would have those things, but it was so far away it might as well be nonexistent. And it certainly wouldn't be on MacGregor's World.

"Did you hear me, Gunny? Or do Marines not acknowledge senior officers anymore?"

There it was. The cocky, holier-than-thou attitude of her homeworld that she despised. Her muscle bunched from her back leg all the way up her side, transferring the energy into her left arm as she slammed the bag with all her power. Forty kilos of sand-filled leather leaped away and smashed into the overhead before it swung back down to Gunny's waiting hands. She steadied the bag, making sure it stayed still before letting go.

"Sir, regulations do not require me to interrupt my workout because you want to run your mouth." She grabbed her towel and headed for the women's head. Since everything on a Hellcat was a tight fit, she had to squeeze by Brown, who didn't move.

"Gunnery Sergeant, you will stand at attention when you speak to me," he growled. He stood ten centimeters taller than her but was short by any other measure.

Jennings glared at him square in the eyes, not an ounce of give in her expression.

"Sir, I will not. We're in the gym. Unless you have official orders for me having to do with my duties to the ship, or as a

Marine, you are just another POG. If you have a problem with me, see the *skipper*." Jennings knew she'd gone too far with the insult the moment she said it. She just couldn't help it.

His face turned red and his neck muscles distended.

"Like you said, we're in the gym. So how about a work-out?" Brown didn't wait for her to respond. His fist came up with whipsaw speed. He was fast and in good shape. Their shared heritage nullified her genetic advantage. However, Brown was in the Navy. He worked out, maybe even sparred on occasion, but his sole focus wasn't that of a killer.

Unlike Jennings.

She allowed him to graze her, spinning with the blow and robbing it of power. As she spun, she dropped her center of gravity and brought her leg around like a pendulum, slamming it into his ankles and dumping him on the floor with a loud *oomph* as the air burst from his lungs. Before he could recover, she was on his chest, one thumb over his eye, her other hand pressed like a knife against his throat.

"And that concludes today's unarmed combat class." She thumped him in the chest as she stood, leaving him on the floor, trying to recover his breath. She was in the shower when he finally managed to pull himself together.

CHAPTER SEVENTEEN

Nadia didn't like the situation she found herself in, running an op instead of being out in it. The suite on the fifteenth floor of the Ambassador Hotel directly across from the Capitol building allowed her to keep an eye on Daisy…

…while the Caliphate spy walked into the Capitol building armed with nothing but a smile and her wits. Not that Daisy didn't have plenty of both. And Nadia ought to know. They had been used against her to devastating effect.

The multiroom suite was packed with the latest surveillance and communications gear she needed to keep an eye on her erstwhile enemy and perform the mission. If she were being honest with herself, the incident on *Dagger* had mostly passed through her psyche. She would never be normal, though. It would never fully leave her. How could it?

The things she had done since—saving Kremlin Station, rescuing Elsa—those were important and they meant something. She would never have gotten to do those if *Dagger* hadn't happened. Not that she didn't wish it hadn't. She did. Every day. One of her goals, though, was to see the best in herself and others, even while maintaining her instincts of distrust.

Some days it was easier than others.

Today, she needed Daisy to infiltrate the new Capitol building and place a bug near Speaker Bradford. One that would hopefully lead them to whoever leaked top secret military information to him.

It wasn't like the Speaker couldn't have access to relevant intelligence, but his specific knowledge, and the fact that no one in ONI could account for how he gained it, was what mattered. If there was a leak, they almost certainly weren't just leaking that info to one person.

Her earpiece squawked.

"I'm approaching the Capitol building. How copy?" Daisy's sweet voice echoed in her ear.

"Roger five by five. Activate relay when you're ready."

Nadia held a mirror of Daisy's NavPad, but neither was stock. They were special prototypes created by ONI's R&D that never went into full use. A glowing holographic globe appeared around Nadia, and she stood in the center. It created a clone of Daisy's surroundings as if Nadia were walking into the building, not Daisy.

"Connection is green," Daisy said as she held up her NavPad to check the screen.

"Solid," Nadia replied.

Daisy fidgeted in the aircar as it descended toward the temporary parking slot behind the boxy Capitol building. Her nerves spiked through her stomach, and she resisted the urge to roll down the window. What was wrong with her? She'd prepared her whole life to spy on the Alliance for her Caliph.

Suddenly she found it nerve-racking? What would they do if they caught her? Sentence her to death?

"Your heart rate is spiking. You okay?" Nadia said in her ear.

"It's been a while since I did this," she replied. It had. For almost two years, she'd awaited her execution after each and every interrogation. They asked the same questions each time. *How many agents like her existed in the Alliance? What other operations were running? Who was her contact?*

One day, the questions stopped. All she had was her cell, and she readied herself for the eventuality she knew would come. Her death.

Instead, the last person she ever expected walked into her life: Nadia Dagher. At least for the time being, she was free.

The cab bumped to a halt. Daisy waited as the gull wing door opened, then carefully pulled herself out. Her knee-length dress swirled around her legs in the light wind as she made her way up the steps to the pillar shrouded entrance.

The Alliance had done a remarkable job rehabilitating the landscape after the orbital nuclear attack. Daisy tried not to worry about the residual radiation in the air, certain the Alliance wouldn't allow people in the area if it were dangerous. A laugh escaped her at the thought that people actually believed it was the Guild who had committed the atrocity.

Daisy pushed those thoughts away as she approached the first checkpoint. Scanners at the door compared the biometric security data on file with what was stored on her NavPad, and then evaluated her body's biometrics. Thanks to the ONI it all matched, and in less than a millisecond the light above the door turned green.

"That was the easy part," Nadia reminded her. "Don't worry, though. I promise, both the bug and our comms are undetectable by conventional means."

Daisy plastered her most playful smile across her lips and

walked through the doors. After all, she belonged there and had nothing to be concerned about.

"Walk through the tunnel, ma'am," an armed Capitol guard said.

What they referred to as "the tunnel" was actually a three-meter walkway surrounded by scanners that read every possible electromagnetic wavelength that could show her concealing any kind of dangerous or unauthorized device.

She stepped onto the moving walkway and lifted her arms out to her side, just as the picture indicated. The belt crawled along, transporting her at a snail's pace. At any moment, she was sure guards would burst in and bring her down.

"Calm down, Daisy. I'm not guessing, I know," Nadia said in her ear.

"How can you be so sure?" Daisy whispered back.

"Because if they catch you, they catch me, and I don't feel like being executed for treason so of course I'm sure."

"Fair enough."

At the end of the walkway, a sign flashed "Move Along."

"First bank, past the security booth, second elevator," Nadia said. "Look to your right and smile."

Daisy did just that, catching the eye of a heavy, older gentleman who was currently entangled in a conversation with a younger, sharply dressed man.

"Who was that?" Daisy asked.

"The older man is Congressman Bit Simmons. The younger is Perry Martin. Martin the Speaker's personal assistant and Simmons is a representative from Seabring. The same planet the Speaker is from."

"Is one of them the mole?" Daisy asked. The technology that linked them together also allowed Daisy to subvocalize her words and Nadia would hear them as if she spoke aloud next to her.

"Doubtful. Neither has high enough clearance. But I want them to remember you," Nadia said.

Daisy entered the first bank of lifts the same way she had the main door, using her NavPad for access.

"If you have total access, why do you need me?" Daisy asked.

"I'm known. No matter how carefully I planned, I could still run into someone who recognized me. And my reason for being there would be pretty obvious. The Admiral never imagined having to run a mole hunt in our own government. That's what DNI is supposed to do. Clearly they aren't."

Daisy pulled out her makeup compact and looked into the small mirror so Nadia could see her. She made eye contact and smirked. "You didn't know about me."

"You hadn't tried to infiltrate the government yet," Nadia said.

Daisy put it away, relishing the small victory. Perhaps the Alliance's vaunted intelligence apparatus wasn't what the Caliphate feared. If they were fighting among themselves, then it would be easy to seize control.

Or it would have been until that damn fool nuked them. Though they were still having internal problems, they seemed more united than ever.

The lift stopped and she stepped out.

"Turn left, straight down, second right."

She followed her instructions to the letter. After the second right, she came to a gallery that opened out onto the house floor, where several men and women in formal attire argued about trade levies.

"I thought I was infiltrating an office?" Daisy said.

"You will," Nadia replied. "Stand at the gallery and lean over." Suddenly the low-cut summer dress the ONI agent had her wear made more sense. Daisy fumed but couldn't outright complain, since Nadia was only using her the exact same way the Caliphate had.

Ten meters below, the house floor was half filled with attending representatives. Most of them were old and nodding off. She faced the seats, with the speaker's podium beneath her and to the right.

"Now what?" Daisy asked as she leaned over. The Caliphate ISB hadn't chosen Daisy by accident—they had picked her as a child and used genetic manipulation and painful surgeries to craft the *most desirable Alliance woman* according to their information. From her curly blonde hair, big eyes, and pale skin (of which she showed a generous amount), to her infectious smile, it was all designed, and very little of it was her. Daisy hardly remembered the girl she was before the surgeries.

It all worked together to put nearly every man into an instant state of diminished mental capacity. There were exceptions, of course; not every man was controlled by his base instincts, and for those she had her years of schooling in behavior control and charisma on command. At least she'd thought that until she realized how badly she had miscalculated Professor Bellaits. She shook her head, pushing that memory away and focusing on her mission.

Nadia didn't say anything else, just left her there to look around. A few of the people below noticed her. A woman frowned. One man grinned at her like an idiot. But she didn't have to wait long. Bit Simmons walked in and a guard led him to his seat, almost directly in view of Daisy.

"Clever," Daisy said.

"At least you have your clothes on," Nadia said. She expected the woman to resent the remark but was surprised.

"I'm truly sorry, Nadia. Truly. I was a—"

"Stop. Just look at Mr. Simmons and don't break eye contact with him."

As she followed her instructions she wondered if there was any way for Nadia to ever forgive her, or would she have to die to earn forgiveness?

———

With the three-dimensional interface, Nadia could see every inch of the house floor. It was perfect. There would be no real way to get Daisy close enough to Bradford to pull off what she was about to do.

For a second, Nadia was concerned Simmons wouldn't look up. When he finally did, he caught sight of Daisy and his lips spread wide enough to show his too-white teeth.

"Keep his eyes on you," Nadia said.

"Roger," Daisy replied.

Using Daisy's NavPad, Nadia shot a laser down at Simmons, striking him in the eye. The laser itself was harmless and invisible. Nadia knew the tech worked to build a molecular-sized surveillance device in a subject, but how it did that, she didn't need or want to know. Another abandoned project by ONI R&D considered too expensive for further development.

"I don't know how much longer I can hold his attention," Daisy said.

"Ten more seconds."

Her screen showed the nano-bot's status as the laser constructed it atom by atom. The device read one hundred percent just as the politician looked away.

"Done?" Daisy asked.

"Almost. Wave at him and leave. Go back the way you came and look for the door marked One-One-Five."

Daisy waved at the older man, winked, and walked away. The doors were clearly marked, making it easy for her to find where she needed to go.

This one was locked, though.

"Can you open it?" Daisy asked.

"NavPad," Nadia said.

She held the pad up against the electronic lock. Lights flashed for a few seconds, then she heard the lock click open.

"What are we doing here?" she asked.

"Find a place to put the bug I gave you," Nadia said.

It was a front office lobby. The main office was through a door behind the desk that was clearly for an assistant. Daisy looked around, trying to find an out of the way place. She went to the main office door, stood on the toes of her ten-centimeter heels, and reached the top of the door frame. The small bug detached from under her fingernail and deposited itself.

"Do you want me to go into the office?" she asked.

"No, I can't get you into his private office undetected. Now out you go, back to the lift. The last bug is for another office."

She had barely left the office when Bradford's young assistant walked around the corner. Her heart leaped, but he was so involved in his pad that he didn't notice her until she brushed by him. Her perfume and appearance drew him to watch her as she disappeared around the corner.

"Where am I going?" Daisy asked.

"Senator Talmage St. John's office."

CHAPTER EIGHTEEN

Ocelot's main sequence star burned bright in the viewer, even from seven hundred million klicks away. Small shadows orbited the star as the system's twelve planets all circled the sun like electrons around a neutron. A brilliant orange glow lit up the bridge, and Jacob couldn't take his eyes off it.

"You want a closer look, Skipper?" Chief Suresh asked. "We could do a gravity assist off of it."

"Sure, I'll just call over to Captain Hatwal and make it happen," he replied.

He tried to make light of the poor relationship he had with the squadron CO in a way that the rest of the crew would understand. It wasn't often they would get to see a less than stellar interaction play out with two superior officers, and how he behaved would set the tone for how they handled their own disagreements. If he flew off the handle or disrespected Hatwal, then they would too, and he wouldn't have that. His crew watched him, and whether he liked it or not, everything he said and did reflected on how they would approach their careers. He was their role model for how to be an officer, and he wouldn't let them down in that respect.

PO Tefiti swiveled to face him and made a motion for him to come look.

"What's going on PO?" he asked as he leaned over the gravitics panel.

"It's that contact again, sir. We're six hours out from Taki, and she just showed up on the screen. Once again just at the edge of range. I can't give you a definitive ID, but she's acting like a recon ship... watching and waiting."

Jacob clasped him on the shoulder. "Good man, PO. Keep trying to identify her. If there's a maneuver we can make that helps you hear her better but won't look out of place, let Chief Suresh know. As long as we stay in formation, we should be okay."

"Aye sir. Will do." Tefiti slipped the oversized headphone back on to keep listening to the drum beat of space-time. All Jacob remembered from his time at astro as a junior officer was the mad headaches he would develop after hours of listening to one beating drum that was indistinguishable from the next.

Jacob ran through the possibilities in his head. The ship was either a pirate or Caliphate navy. If they were pirates, though, he felt like they would have backed off. Of course, he was taking it as a given it was a ship at all. PO Tefiti had proven his skill time and time again, but even he had to at least acknowledge the possibility it was an anomaly of some kind.

He spied Ensign Brown stifling a yawn. Considering how early it was ship's time, they had to all be tired. Jacob clasped his hands behind his back and toured the bridge while he thought, making it look like he pondered the situation, but in reality using it as an excuse to examine the bridge crew and their emotional state.

Their files said they were all at the top of their class.

However, they certainly seemed to have some problems that needed ironing out. What Rugger and Lopez needed was a task to complete together. Something small, to give them focus. Sitting back down, he checked the clock.

Breakfast was in full swing on *Interceptor*. More than likely, PO Mendez was knee-deep in eggs and bacon. If he asked, Jacob knew the young man would drop everything and bring refreshments to the bridge. Jacob had a better idea.

"Ensign Lopez, Midship Rugger, why don't you two head to the galley and bring the bridge up some refreshments. PO Mendez will know what to send."

Rugger glanced at Lopez before jumping to his feet. "Aye sir," he said. Lopez quickly followed, and the two left the bridge. Jacob could tell they were none too happy about doing it together.

"Felix," Jacob said. "Contact *Firewatch* and put it on my screen."

"Aye sir, contact *Firewatch*. One moment."

Gouger spoke quietly into his mic for a second before turning and pointing at the command chair's MFD.

"*Firewatch*, Midship Brennan." The young woman's curly red hair peeked out underneath the black watch cap.

Jacob had to suppress a grin. The last time he called *Firewatch* he'd gotten the same midship. Was Hatwal sending him to her on purpose, or was it coincidence?

"Good morning, Fionna. I need to speak to Commander Ban or Captain Hatwal, please."

The surprise on her face at him using her first name made him smile. Brennan glanced to the side, her light skin reddening under his appraisal. She was obviously uncomfortable, and Jacob could guess why. Acting as an intermediator between two officers who were having obvious problems was a lot of stress for a midship.

"Is it an emergency, sir?" she asked.

"No."

"I'm sorry, sir, neither are available at the moment. I can take a message if you like," she squeaked out the last part.

Take a message? She could take a message? Jacob forced a neutral expression on his face, reminding himself this wasn't her fault.

"No thank you, Midship. I'll try again later." As if he were calling to order pizza and they were just too busy to take his order.

"Sorry, sir," she said as the screen blinked and was replaced by their current course and velocity.

Travis Rugger sild down the ladder behind Lopez, trying to keep up, but the larger man seemed intent on leaving him behind. That was fine with Travis. The only time Lopez noticed him anyway was to hassle or scowl at him.

The passageway outside the mess stood uncharacteristically empty. Travis had only ever seen the passageway and mess when it was near to bursting with hungry spacers. Probably because of when his shift allowed him down there.

Lopez turned right and went immediately for the galley. Travis went to follow when he spotted Private June and paused. She had her hands full of sealed meals and was trying to juggle adding four cups of coffee from the dispenser opposite the galley.

"Let me help," Travis said as he trotted over to her with what he hoped was a friendly smile.

June looked up and her face lit up. Travis felt the need to reciprocate. Something about her made his heart beat a little faster. In the Academy, there simply wasn't time for girls, and even if there were, relationships only complicated the already highly competitive atmosphere. At least for him. Plenty of his classmates seemed to have no trouble finding time for dating and hooking up. It just wasn't his area.

Travis placed each container on the top plate in the form of a triangle, allowing her to hold them in place with her other hand, then he lifted the final mug to the top, where she could use her chin to balance if needed.

"Thank you, sir," she said with a smile.

He wanted to tell her to call him Travis, but her being a private and him an officer made that impossible. How the heck were people supposed to even have relationships aboard ship?

"My pleasure, Ju—"

A roaring, deafening force slammed into Travis like a train. He crashed into June and the two spun through the air, over tables, and into the bulkhead, only to bounce like ragdolls off the coffee dispenser, then land face first on the deck. Several trays crashed around them, some landing on his back.

A deathly silence settled over the mess. Travis' face was a centimeter away from June's and his own shock and confusion reflected in her eyes. He couldn't hear anything but a loud ringing in his ear.

Heat flared to life hot enough to make him flinch, and a coil of fear wrapped itself around his heart as flames erupted from the galley door and service window.

June pushed on him and reality snapped into place. He forced himself up, standing with a hand against the bulkhead, only to find a cloud of billowing, acrid smoke filling the air. June grabbed his tunic and pulled him back down to the deck where she knelt.

"Thanks," he said between coughs.

He glanced at the mess hatch first, then the galley hatch.

The fire seemed to be contained in the galley for the moment, but if it spread to the mess, they would be in real trouble.

He tapped June on the shoulder and pointed at the mess hatch. "Hit the override, don't let it seal the room," he said. Fire protocol called to seal off the deck until the fire burned itself out, but there were crew stuck in the galley. They just needed a few minutes to rescue them.

She gave him a thumbs up and took off for the hatch, staying low to avoid the smoke. Travis grabbed the discarded coffee pods; the first one had burst, but the second was full. He broke it open and poured the scalding hot liquid on his hands. He winced, but once wet, he ran for the galley, staying as low as he could.

Through the ringing in his ears, he could hear alarms wailing. Fire encircled the hatchway to the galley, paint pealed and the plastic around the control panel bubbled and popped. He put his hands up to ward off the heat and that fear twisted around him again, freezing him in place.

His crewmates were in the galley. He couldn't let them die.

Travis charged in with his eyes mere slits to keep the heat at bay. A burned, bleeding, and blackened spacer fell into his arms as if pushed. Rugger grabbed the man under the arms and backed out, coughing the entire time. He stopped when he felt June's hands on his shoulders. She took over for him and he charged back in.

Fire roared, climbing up the bulkhead, and the smoke made it impossible to see anything. He tried to call out but ended up coughing. Another spacer stumbled into his arms and he yanked him out the same way he had before. Back into the fire he went, again and again, finding a stumbling, falling crewmember each time.

Agony, worse than anything he'd ever felt, flared through his hands and arms. From narrowed eyes, he saw his own skin bubbling and blackening as it burned. He wouldn't, couldn't, leave anyone in there to die, not like that. Not when he knew they were still alive and probably unconscious from smoke. He ripped part of his tunic and wrapped it around his hands to help shield them.

The next time he charged through the fire, he no longer felt any pain in his hands. A distant part of him knew that was bad, but he wouldn't stop. He tripped over something, fell to his knees, and lost his breath. Curling up in a ball, he knew he was about to die. Had he missed anyone though? Better he die than one of his shipmates.

Mist sprinklers came to life, spraying the galley, the mess hall, and the passage outside. Flames fizzled and popped as the ship's water supply flooded the compartments. Travis pushed himself up, unable to see clearly from the stinging smoke in his eyes. He found his way back to the mess and to where June leaned against the bulkhead. He fell against her and they both slid down to the deck, coughing and hacking between breaths of clean air.

June raised her hand in a fist, and Travis did the same, bumping them together heedless of the pain.

Seconds later, PO Desper charged through with her medical team to start evacuating the wounded.

CHAPTER NINETEEN

"It's safe to go in, sir," Chief Petty Officer Redfern said from the hatch. Jacob thanked the chief as he walked by. The chemical smell assaulted his nose, and he had to put on a breather just to keep himself from coughing.

Redfern followed him in wearing his firefighting gear—an ELS-F suit designed to resist heat and thermal energy while allowing the wearer to carry the thick foam they sprayed from a small cannister at their hip. The foam expanded fast, smothering the fire while absorbing oxygen and pairing it with a hydrogen molecule inside the foam, stripping the fire of needed fuel. What it left was a watery mess that was mostly immune to reignition.

"How many were in the galley?" Jacob asked.

Behind Redfern, Lieutenant Boudreaux pulled her ELS-F helmet off.

"Six, sir. Private June and Midship Rugger got five out," she said.

Jacob glanced at her, not wanting to ask, but he had to know. It was his job as the captain to speak for the dead.

"Who?" he asked. Somehow, he forced his voice to stay clear as he spoke, despite the tightness welling up in his chest like a hand squeezing his heart.

"Ensign Lopez, sir," she said, pitching her voice low.

"Damn," he muttered. He prepared himself, then headed for the galley to inspect the damage first hand. Five of his crew were in sickbay, with injuries ranging from light burns to medically induced comas so they would not feel the pain of their wounds. Having spent a week in a fluorocarbon tank for that exact reason, he knew how serious it was.

He choked back a cough. The fire had gutted the galley. Deck, bulkhead, overhead—all were black with soot. The flames had even been hot enough to melt the cooler hatch shut.

Chief Redfern pointed at the bulkhead that led to the outer hull. "We think the problem started in the new construction, Skipper. When we were in… in the last action, we took a direct hit here and the yard replaced the entire section. I can't say for sure until we pull her apart, but if I had to guess, I would say it was the supercapacitor that connects this part of the ship to the fusion reactor. If it overheated or grounded out, then all the energy stored would have to go some where."

Having enough power aboard ship wasn't nearly as difficult as storing and moving it. The MK III fusion reactor at *Interceptor*'s heart produced more than enough for the ship's needs, but moving and storing it required kilometers of cables, capacitors, and supercapacitors. If one part of the ship needed power immediately, it would draw it from a cap or supercap, depending on necessity.

"Sacre Coeur," Boudreaux muttered as she stopped to kneel at the charred outline where a body had clearly fallen. "How did Rugger and June survive in here?"

It was a fair question. Jacob examined enough of the galley that he was amazed anyone lived.

"How are our two heroes?" he asked.

"Rugger is in the tank. He suffered severe burns to his hands and face. June is in an upper body suit as the skin on her hands and arms regenerates."

"I've seen enough here. Chief, make sure everything is recorded, then get with Ensign Kai. I want a BDA ASAP and an estimate on repairs."

"Aye sir. Battle damage assessment and repairs. On it," Chief Redfern answered.

"Good man," Jacob said. "XO, you're with me."

He left the engineer to his task. The mess was on deck two, and sickbay was all the way down on deck five, forward of DCS. It would take a few minutes to navigate the ladders and passageways, something Jacob was happy for, since it would give him time to think. He hated that he lost a crew to a senseless accident, especially one they could have avoided if the yard had taken *Interceptor*'s repairs more seriously. He would note in his report how he felt, and add any data from Redfern's investigation to back up the claim.

Interceptor had undergone three major repairs in his time as CO, and each time he had fought with the yard. It was only a matter of time before something like this fire happened, and he wished to God he could have foreseen the possible problem sooner. Before Ensign Lopez paid the ultimate price.

Whether his ship deserved the resources for a refit or not had nothing to do with it. If the Admiralty wanted to continue deploying her, then the next time he was in port he was going to demand a full refit, even if it meant stepping down as her CO. *Interceptor* was supposed to protect her crew, not endanger them. Accidents like fires were a hazard in space, but one that was mostly avoidable. If it weren't for June's quick thinking in holding down the override on the main hatch, he would have lost six crew, not just one.

He slid down the last ladder, hitting the deck with a thump. Moans of pain mingled with hushed whispers emanated from the small room. Jacob stayed outside, not wanting to interrupt Midship Mariposa, Chief Petty Officer Pierre, or PO Desper as they worked hard to heal their patients.

"Captain, to the comms. Captain to the comms," Spacer McCall said over the nearest speaker.

Jacob glanced toward the for of the passageway by the long-term care unit. If he took the call right outside sickbay, he risked being a distraction. Boudreaux followed him.

He flattened the comm button with one hand, leaning against it as the weariness of the day sapped his strength.

"Go ahead, Mac."

"Sir, *Firewatch* wants an update. I have Commander Ban. Would you like to speak to him?"

"Thank you. Put him through." Jacob waited patiently while the signal connected.

"Commander Grimm, what's the status over there?"

All business then. Maybe Jacob imagined it, but he'd thought the two of them friends. Or perhaps he relied a little too much on perceived friendship. If Archer wanted a professional relationship, Jacob could do that.

"Fire in the galley, Commander. Five wounded and one KIA, sir. Ensign—"

"Sorry to hear that, Commander. Captain Hatwal wants to know your operational status?" Ban asked.

Jacob felt it was his duty to speak for the dead. Ensign Lopez's death demanded he stand up for him. However, he also understood that the mission came first and there would be time to mourn and report later.

"Sir, by *The Book* we should heave-to for an outer hull walk-down. The fire took place in the galley, which is—"

"I'm aware of where the galley is on your ship, Commander," Captain Hatwal burst into the conversation. "We can't afford to stop our mission every time your ship runs out of steam. Can you make the repairs underway or not?"

Jacob was well and truly stunned. Whatever he had done to Captain Hatwal, he was sorry, because there was simply no reason to be treated with such disrespect.

"On moment, sir." Jacob muted Hatwal and turned to Boudreaux. "What do you think?"

"There was a lot of heat in that fire, sir. The heat sink is still dealing with it. And if anything warped on the bulkhead, then we have a weak spot. I think *The Book* is right this time, sir. Gorilla suits and a walk down. It's too much of a risk otherwise."

He agreed with her, but he wanted to make sure she understood her job as exec, which she obviously did. They didn't always have to agree, but he always needed her opinion. Jacob hit the call button for the bridge.

"Mac, you there?"

"Aye sir," Spacer McCall replied.

"Ask Oliv how long we can stop acceleration and still catch up before they enter the next starlane?"

Oliv broke in from astrogation a few seconds later.

"At flank speed, sir, we can reach the starlane at about the same time as the rest of the squadron if we start accelerating in four hours and three minutes... mark."

"Roger that, Oliv. Well done." He turned to Boudreaux. "What do you think?"

"Sounds like a plan, sir."

Jacob reactivated the channel to *Firewatch*. "Captain Hatwal? My astro, PO Oliv, tells me we can make the starlane entrance at about the same time you do if we start now and do our walkdown. Would that be acceptable, sir?"

Static filled the air for a moment while Hatwal's line was open, but there wasn't a response.

"Fine," Hatwal said. "Don't be late. I don't want to be sitting with no acceleration at a starlane this close to Caliphate territory."

"Roger that, sir. We'll be th—"

The line clicked dead, leaving Jacob frozen halfway through his sentence.

Boudreaux scowled, "I don't get it, why is he such an a—"

Jacob stopped her right there, holding up his hand.

"Don't say it, Viv. Seriously. No matter how true it might be." He looked down past her and then guided her into the long-term care quarters. Once the hatch was shut, he faced her.

"As a warrant, you have a lot of leeway with how you treat people. And most service members, enlisted or officer, would treat you with respect," he said.

"If they knew what was good for them, sir. Otherwise..." She held up her hand up miming a Corsair and flipped it over with a big grin on her face.

"Exactly," Jacob said, glad she understood. "Your skill earned you that respect. It's not like anyone can just sit in the front of the Corsair and start pushing buttons and fly her."

Boudreaux rested her shoulder against the bulkhead while she chewed over what the captain meant.

"There's an awful lot of lights and switches up there to just start pushing buttons," she said.

One of the keys to being an effective officer was understanding human nature. Something Jacob was intuitively good at for his whole life. But it was also something he practiced. Knowing what people needed, wanted, and would do in any given situation had saved him more than once. Knowing himself that way had helped him even more.

"As an officer, though, the only thing that demands respect

is—" He reached up and pointed at her collar where the silver bar rested. "Your actions have to earn it, though. If you disrespect a senior officer, even if you feel it's perfectly warranted, then how will those of lower rank ever respect you?"

Understanding dawned in her eyes. She gave him a small nod. "Got it, sir. No matter what, keep it professional."

"Nailed it. Now, when you're alone in your cabin... swear into a pillow all you want," he said with a smile.

"Aye aye, sir. Permission to visit my cabin?"

"Granted. First, though, see to our repairs."

"Aye aye, Skipper."

After Boudreaux departed, Jacob decided to sit in the long-term care quarters for a moment and think about what he had told her. He would be lying to himself if he didn't acknowledge how angry the whole thing made him. The advice he'd given his XO was just as important, if not more so for himself. He was the captain, after all. Anything he did reflected on him, his ship, and the Navy as a whole.

"All hands. Now hear this. Prepare for full stop. Engineering, ready the Gorilla suits for exterior hull check," Boudreaux said over the ship wide comms.

With Boudreaux on the repairs, he needed to speak to Midship Marino about the wounded.

———

Midship Marino slumped in her office, which was really nothing more than a closet with a chair and a terminal. She wasn't ready for this. Two years of pre-med at New Austin Medical University didn't make her qualified to be a *doctor* on a destroyer or anywhere else. When she came aboard, she thought it would be a big fun adventure.

As nice as Chief Pierre and PO Desper were, she figured they probably wanted her out of the way. When the wounded came in from the mess, she froze. First the sight of their burned, bleeding bodies, then the smell.

Oh God, that smell.

She couldn't even go back to her cabin and shower.

"Ma'am, Skipper wants to see you," PO Desper said from the office hatch.

"Thank you, Petty Officer." One thing Mariposa had noticed shortly after coming aboard was how the veterans all called the captain *Skipper*. She'd heard rumors of some of the things they had gone through in previous deployments, but they were all pretty tight-lipped about their service.

Desper smiled. "You can say PO, ma'am. Or just Desper, I don't mind. Sickbay tends to be a little less formal. Don't want people stumbling over ranks and titles when you're trying to save lives, ma'am."

"Thank you, Desper."

Mariposa stood to go face the captain. It wasn't like she had done anything wrong, but she sure felt like she had. If she'd been a real doctor, maybe she could have resuscitated Ensign Lopez. Done something, anything other than seal his body in a suspended animation bag.

She did her best to straighten her uniform before exiting her cubby and finding the captain.

"You wanted to see me, sir?" she said once she stood at attention in front of him. She had to crane her neck uncomfortably to look up at him. As if he sensed her discomfort, the captain stepped back a meter to allow her a better angle.

"At ease, Midship. First, I want to tell you that Chief Pierre and PO Desper both speak highly of you and your performance. You were put in a tough position and you relied on your training and team to see you through it."

Saying "thank you" for being praised about how she responded seemed wrong. Ensign Lopez was dead. In the end, she decided a curt nod would suffice.

"Second, I want to know how everyone else is doing?"

Mariposa turned and gestured for him to follow her. "Midship Rugger and PO Mendez had the worst of it, sir. To be honest, there was a lot of soft tissue damage to all of them. I'm not sure how any of them survived." She paused, frowning like she had tasted something bitter. "June had second-degree burns on her arms and torso, and third on her hands. Spacer's Perch, Zach, and Rivera all had second and third-degree burns over their backs and legs. I've got them in ELS suits for the pain while the nanites do their best to rebuild nerves and skin."

She led him into the tank room. Unfortunately, they only had the one tank. Destroyers weren't big to begin with, and the sickbay was squeezed in between DCS and long-term care.

The captain shuddered at the sight of the tank. PO Mendez and Midship Rugger were unconscious as the full immersion tank did its job.

Mariposa purposefully looked away from the exposed bones of Travis' hands. Part of the process the nanites went through was to remove all the dead flesh before they started the rebuilding process. Half of Mendez's scalp was missing. The only reason they couldn't save Lopez was time, more than anything else. When the rescue crew got to him, there simply wasn't enough left to rebuild. The thought made her want to vomit all over again.

"Bravo Zulu, Mariposa," Grimm said.

"Sir, I'm not familiar with that order?"

Grimm gave her a tight smile. "It's Navy speak for 'well done.' You did more than anyone could have expected of you. Get some rest."

"Aye sir." Mariposa wanted to ask a question, and the captain seemed like the kind she could ask. After all, he came down here to check on his spacers first hand. "Sir, can I ask a question?"

"By all means," he said.

"Did he die for nothing? Lopez, I mean, sir. He was kind of a bully, but no one deserves to go out like that." Mariposa did her very best to keep her voice from quivering, but at the end of the day, she was barely out of her teens. Seeing a man reduced to burned chunks put her on the edge of breaking.

"That's the real question, isn't it?" Commander Grimm said. He put a hand on the tank as if he could feel the pain the men were in. "We have to believe the answer is 'yes' or we wouldn't be out here doing what we do. So yes, he died for something. There are people in this galaxy who want to see it all burn. They want humanity in chains and all the freedom we enjoy stamped out. I've seen this first hand. This is what we are out here for, Mariposa." He paused for a moment, looking up at something only he could see. "The Alliance. *This. We'll. Defend*. It means something more than just a job, just a service. If not, then we might as well just surrender and march into the slave stocks."

Mariposa's heart hurt for the pain in Commander Grimm's voice. His words inspired her; she stood a little taller, her burden a little lighter. She would never truly overcome Lopez's death, but maybe, just maybe, she would remember why he died. In that moment, she also came to understand something else about the ship she served on.

"Thank you, Skipper," she said.

Jacob's NavPad projected the view from Chief Redfern and Ensign Kai's curved displays, allowing him to look for trouble the two might miss on their own. It was also a decent way to pass the time as he plowed through his mountain of paperwork while sitting in the briefing room.

Part of him liked dealing with new people and seeing what they were made of. Part of him missed his old crew, like a lost friend. He'd been spoiled in a way, he knew that. NavPer thought they were punishing *Interceptor* by not letting anyone off, but in reality, they had created a tight group of spacers who would be friends forever. Since she started assigning them the best and brightest, it seemed that maybe Admiral Villanueva thought the same thing.

Jacob felt something he hadn't in a long time. He felt a lightness to his spirit. He felt hope. It wasn't too late for his Navy to turn things around and be the courageous institution it once was. They just needed someone to show them the way, and Fleet Admiral Villanueva was the woman for the job.

"Skipper," PO Desper called out to him. Jacob looked up from his NavPad; Desper stood in the conference room hatchway.

"What can I do for you, Prisca?" he asked.

From her haggard expression and the dark circles under her eyes, he could tell exhaustion hounded her. Yet when he said her name, she straightened up.

"I wanted to give you an update, sir. With the exception of Josh and Midship Rugger, everyone will be green lit for light duty in three days."

"Thank you, Prisca. Well done." He expected her to leave after that, but when she hung around for a moment, he thought maybe she had more on her mind. "Anything else? How's Lieutenant Johansen," he asked. "Did you get to see him before we departed Utopia?"

"Sir?" she stuttered. "How do you know about him?"

Jacob suppressed a mirthful smile. "It's not exactly a secret. Besides, it's my job to know about my crew. I take it, then, he's not what this is about?"

She glanced behind her for a moment, then back to him. "No sir. I wish it was. It's the way Ensign Lopez died, sir. I don't want to speak out of turn, but..."

Jacob motioned for her to come closer, and she did.

"What is it?" he asked when she stood next to him.

"It might be nothing... it probably is nothing." She looked pensively away from him for a moment.

"Prisca, anything you say will remain strictly between us, I promise. If you thought it was important enough to say something, I want to hear it."

"You see, sir, everyone Midship Rugger and Private June pulled out of the fire was badly burned, but they were alive. From what I can tell, the initial explosion caught poor Josh in the face and knocked everyone in the compartment down and then unconscious as all of the oxygen was instantly consumed."

Jacob figured that was what happened. He needed to wait for engineering's official report, though. "And?"

"And, sir, Ensign Lopez was the farthest away from the explosion and closest to the hatch. I just don't see how Midship Rugger could have missed him when he went in to pull them out. I didn't think anything of it, but then I heard some chatter about a problem between the two and, well, I hate to think this way."

Jacob's spine froze and a vise squeezed his heart. What she was saying was serious... beyond serious. How could he even contemplate it, though? Midship Rugger and Private June saved lives, but only Midship Rugger knew what happened in the galley after he charged into the fire.

"Thank you, PO Desper, I'll keep this between us."

"Thank you, sir."

After she departed, Jacob considered the situation. Ultimately, he would have to wait until engineering finished their BDA and gave him all the facts.

Redfern's Gorilla suit clamped around him like a vise. He didn't mind, though, since his ship and being out on the hull looking at the stars were two of life's biggest joys. As long as they weren't too close to a planet. Falling into the void didn't bother him near as much as falling when he could see the bottom.

"Anything, Chief Redfern?" Ensign Kai asked over their direct comms.

"Heat levels are nominal. No warping, or refracting. I think we dodged a bullet, sir," he replied.

Heat was the enemy in space. Quick to build up, difficult to release. Like most ships, *Interceptor* used carbon fiber conduits to channel heat into a heatsink installed under the keel. Once it had absorbed all it could, the ship dumped it into the gravwake where it shattered into the void, carrying the heat with it. For about an hour or two afterward, depending on the ship's level of activity, the interior could be downright chilly. Hence the watch caps and nanite temperature regulators in the uniforms.

"Time to head back in, sir. I think we're done out here."

"How long until they're back inside?" Jacob asked as he entered the bridge.

"Ten minutes, sir," Ensign Brown reported. His clipped way of speaking seemed even more tense to Jacob. As if he were forcing the words out.

"I have the con, Mr. Brown," Jacob said. He made a mental

note to speak to the young man. If he recalled correctly, Lopez and Brown were friends and he didn't want the Ensign to suffer in silence.

"Aye sir. Captain has the con," Brown replied.

"PO Oliv, is our course ready?"

"Aye sir. Chief Suresh has the updated course and—"

"Contact!" Tefiti interrupted. "Bearing two-one-zero mark three-zero-zero relative, range zero-two million kilometers. Minimal signature. Tentative ID as Bravo-zero-one."

"Condition Zulu, Mac. All hands battle stations," Jacob ordered. Bravo-zero meant possible hostile unknown contact, and until he was sure, he was going to assume it was hostile.

McCall slammed the button down, maintaining an even tone announcing Condition Zulu, battle stations throughout the ship.

"Tefiti, have they seen us yet?" Jacob asked.

"I don't think so, sir. No alteration to course, no power curve change. They're running silent, or close to it. I can't get an exact enough read on their velocity, but best guess... call it zero-eight minutes to weapons, range with a total engagement time of one-six minutes."

Eight minutes was tight. With his two engineers outside, he couldn't accelerate or they would be lost. Not that he would consider leaving any of his crew members, but especially not his engineers.

Jacob took his seat and hit the comms button. "Ensign Kai, we've got an unknown contact closing fast. I need you two back inside ASAP. Understood?"

"Roger, sir," Kai's garbled voice replied.

"Bosun," Jacob said, turning his chair to Ops. "Rig us for silent running."

"Aye aye, sir. Rig for silent running."

Another alarm rang throughout the ship. Crew ran from station to station, shutting down all nonessential electronics, from display screens to heaters.

"Ladies and gentlemen, suit up," Jacob ordered.

CHAPTER TWENTY

Jacob made sure he was the last person to close his helmet. With sickbay full of injured, his alert readiness took six minutes before the lights all turned green. Air hissed as his suit sealed. He took a moment to double-check and make sure he was good to go before giving Bosun Sandivol a thumbs up.

Interceptor was short on officers, and he was feeling it here on the bridge. Spacer First Class McCall manned comms, Gouger was on EW, and POs Oliv and Tefiti were his astrogation team. On the weapons side, Ensign Brown and PO Ignatius had their hands full.

"How long until they're back in?" Jacob asked Bosun Sandivol over his helmet comm.

"Two minutes, Skipper," Sandivol replied.

Two minutes. The mission clock had counted down from eight minutes the moment Tefiti registered the contact.

01:57:22

"Oliv, at their closest point, what will the range be?" he asked.

PO Oliv tapped away at her console. There were many variables to the question, and most of the answer, to be one hundred percent accurate, wouldn't really help Jacob tactically. What he needed was how close into the weapons envelope would they be.

"They must have followed us, Skipper. There's no way they are randomly on the same course. Tefiti?" she asked her partner without looking up.

"I concur. My best guess, sir, is it's the ship that's followed us since we entered Taki. They are accelerating at a very low level and keeping their emissions quiet as a mouse, but it's them. I would bet my rockers on it."

Jacob trusted the two POs implicitly. When Tefiti transferred to *Interceptor* back in Zuck, he already had a stellar reputation. Oliv's was only marginally less so, and that was only because of the five-year age gap. He was damn lucky to have them, and he knew it.

PO Oliv put a number up on his screen and he whistled in response. "That close?" Her estimate showed anywhere between fifteen and fifty thousand klicks. "When can we have positive confirmation on type and class?"

"Negative, sir. Their emissions are too low. I can't get a read unless we go active."

Jacob tapped the DCS button on his MFD, displaying a close-up image of Lieutenant Boudreaux's face.

"DCS, XO," Boudreaux said.

"Viv, what do you think?"

"Uh, not really my—" Boudreaux paused for a second. "Sorry, sir. I was about to tell you that's not my area, but I guess it is now. I hate to be the one to remind you, Skip, but we're not at war."

00:58:99

"I'm aware. If they're following us, though, then they're a

threat. I won't shoot a civilian ship, but if it's a warship… I won't risk ours."

"We can just do nothing. Let them pass us by?" she suggested.

If they did, they would gain knowledge of the enemy ship and be able to turn around and follow her. If it was an enemy ship. Just like the Alliance, the Caliphate Navy used destroyers for a lot of these kinds of missions. They would be no match for DesRon Nine if he followed her in, then signaled the rest of the ships.

"Let's try that." He closed the window. "Mac, how long till our boys are inside?"

"Chief Redfern, how long?" Spacer McCall asked.

Jacob heard both sides of the conversation.

"Thirty seconds, Mac," Redfern replied.

Jacob signaled Mac he'd heard.

00:35:41

It was going to be close. With the ship running silent, all her emissions were curbed. However, the two Gorilla suits would take upward of a full minute to enter the maintenance hatch. Enough time for a heat or light to glint off. Enough that the bogie might go active and spot *Interceptor* and then have the freedom to choose to fire or not.

"Ensign Brown, prepare a firing solution for all four turrets," Jacob ordered.

"Aye sir. Firing solution on all turrets."

"Chief Suresh, tilt twenty degrees to port to give us a clean shot."

"Aye sir. Two-zero degrees tilt to port," she replied.

00:05:99

"Chief Redfern reports Ensign Kai is entering the hatch, Skipper," Spacer McCall said.

00:00:00

Two things were about to happen. They were in weapons range, and the passive sensors were going to get a good look at her.

Tefiti sucked in a sharp breath. "Contact is now designated Tango-Lima-One. She's a light cruiser, sir. Tripoli class if the computer is right, and I think it is."

A light cruiser? If the Caliphate had them out here, then they were planning something big. A light cruiser following a destroyer squadron meant an imminent attack. A single LC, no matter how clever, couldn't take out five destroyers without more luck than most COs cared to operate on. Which meant she was part of a squadron waiting to ambush DesRon Nine.

"Give me a thirty-second heads-up when they're at their closest, or if you think they've seen us," he said.

"Thirty second warning or if detected. Aye sir," Oliv replied.

Jacob drummed his fingers against the chair's arm, the rhythmic pattern helping him focus. Attacking first would essentially be an act of war. No matter how justified he thought he was, he couldn't. However, if he gave up the element of surprise and was destroyed, then DesRon Nine headed into a trap. All of them would vanish, and the Alliance would never know what happened. Again, though, he had no *proof* they were hostile. Just the nagging feeling in his gut... and that wasn't admissible in court.

"Chief Redfern reports all hatches secure, sir," McCall said.

Jacob gave him an absent thumbs up, his mind grappling with the tactical problem.

He had to open fire.

He had to offer them the chance to surrender.

If the cruiser fired first, though, *Interceptor* would be destroyed. The moment they went active, the enemy would know exactly where they were.

What if they didn't go active? He could send a tight beam

directional message with instructions for them to leave their radar off, warning them that if they didn't comply, they would be destroyed.

It wouldn't eliminate the possibility of taking a hit, but it would mitigate it. He could certainly fire at the first sign of radar, and no matter how good they were—and he had to assume they were pretty good—they couldn't possibly lock on and fire fast enough to avoid destruction.

"I've got it. McCall, prepare a message for me. Don't send it until I give the order."

"Aye sir. Recording ready."

"Caliphate cruiser, this is Captain Jacob T. Grimm of the Alliance vessel USS *Interceptor*. I'm ordering you to heave-to. Do not activate your radar or any other sensors. If your turrets move, I will destroy you. Confirm receipt with an omnidirectional broadcast. Message ends."

"Got it, sir," McCall said.

He turned to Ensign Brown. "Austin, if they so much as twitch, don't wait for my orders. You fire."

"Uh, sir," Austin Brown replied in his gravely voice. "I can't just fire on them without a reason. The ROE is pretty clear."

Jacob suppressed a grin. "Don't worry about that. If they twitch, it's because they mean to fire." He watched the distance count down, faster and faster. Soon it would reach equilibrium, then start counting up. "Chief Suresh, hold the ship still. If we fire, though, flank speed, and don't wait for my orders."

"Aye aye, sir. Flank speed on weapons hot."

"Thirty seconds," Oliv said over the bridge-wide comms.

"Mac, send it."

"On the way."

Vanguard's bridge was neat and orderly, just the way Captain Farooq preferred. Every station shined, the deck freshly mopped, and all the uniforms worn to perfection.

Stroking his luxuriously thick beard, he leaned back in his chair and daydreamed about when he could return home. For six months they'd operated out on the rim, and he missed his wives and sons.

Raiding Consortium planets was fun. Especially when they got to partake of the goods before handing them off to Medial. However, the Alliance destroyers he shadowed presented another problem. The latest intel on Alliance fleet actions suggested they were well trained, possibly better than his own men. Still, they were *destroyers,* and he was part of a light cruiser squadron.

"Sir, this is odd," Hallal said from comms. "We're receiving a tight beam message."

"My screen." Farooq motioned.

"Caliphate cruiser. This is Captain Jacob T. Grimm of the Alliance vessel, USS *Interceptor*. I'm ordering you to heave to. Do not activate your radar or any other sensors. If your turrets move, I will destroy you. Confirm receipt with an omnidirectional broadcast. Message ends."

Farooq worked his jaw in shock. It couldn't be real. "Sensors... are you seeing anything?"

"Do you want me to go active, sir?"

"No, Allah, no. Just tell me what you see?"

The threat of imminent death sharpened Farooq to a point. If there really was an Alliance ship out there, then why bother with the message? Why not just shoot?

Because their foolish codes of battle won't let them shoot first.

The realization hit him and his grin spread to his whole face. The moment he had a shot, he would take it. Those Alliance cowards would never bring themselves to shoot a ship that wasn't already firing on them. They were in unclaimed territory. No one would ever know what happened to this silly ship. Only that it vanished with all hands.

Maybe they thought he would hesitate, but he knew it was a destroyer. He outgunned, out massed, and out matched them in every conceivable way.

"I think I've got something, sir. Starboard side, maybe twenty thousand klicks? It's faint, though. It might be nothing."

"It will have to do. Point our radar in that direction. Weapons, when we go active, open fire. Don't wait for a lock, best guess. Helm, prepare for evasive maneuvers." The more he spoke, the more his confidence grew. The Alliance captain should have just opened fire instead of warning him. Farooq wouldn't make that mistake.

Jacob's gut nagged at him, as though he'd made a grievous error. The more time that went by since his message, the less likely they were to surrender. Did they know all they had to do was not respond? Keep on their current heading and there wasn't anything he could legally do about it?

"Radar detected!" Oliv shouted.

"Fire," Jacob ordered.

Interceptor's four turrets were already pointing in the general direction of the Tripoli-class light cruiser. With their passive sensors doing the tracking, they had an iffy lock. The destroyer simply didn't have the time to go active on radar/lidar, lock on, then fire.

They had to shoot from the hip. As did *Vanguard*.

Four turrets fired as one, sending their twenty-millimeter rounds flying at the light cruiser. In order to maximize their hit window, they aimed at different points in space where PO Tefiti calculated the ship would be.

Vanguard's armored hull deflected the first round upward, gouging a furrow through her outer skin to the top of the boat. The second hit caught turret three just as it fired, causing the unstable plasma to explode, consuming the turret, six operators, and three meters of armored hull underneath. Her third round missed entirely, whizzing off into space and parts unknown.

The fourth slammed into the starboard armored plates of the bridge. The nano-hardened tungsten penetrator hit the armor, blasting into the inside where a fraction of the energy transferred to the atmosphere, instantly igniting a hellish firestorm that vaporized Captain Farooq and his entire bridge crew.

Chief Suresh slammed the throttle forward to flank speed the second she registered the turrets firing. A reaction that likely saved *Interceptor*.

Six turrets from *Vanguard* fired almost simultaneously at *Interceptor*, crisscrossing the space between the two ships with green plasma bolts. The light cruiser had less of a sure target, but her six dual turrets gave her more chances to hit.

The first two flashed behind *Interceptor* close enough they cast a pale green glow on the hull. Two more streaked above the bridge. Number five struck frame thirty-four, topside, vaporizing five centimeters of nano-hardened steel armor before spending its energy on the secondary computer node, turning it into a melted heap. Everything forward of the node lost main power as half the runs were severed in one disastrous hit.

The final plasma round struck deck four, frame thirty. Only five meters forward of *Interceptor*'s MKIII Fusion Reactor, directly into the fuel conversion chamber and only one meter above DCS.

Superheated hull plating exploded into the three-person DCS compartment. PO Hanz screamed like a banshee, his right arm engulfed by a spray of liquid metal, dissolving the entire limb.

Spacer Baker unbuckled, leaping to save his shipmate when a shard of armor the size of a person struck his seat. Boudreaux closed her eyes and waited to die, counting in her mind to five before deciding it was safe to look.

DCS was unrecognizable. Not a single screen had power. Half of Hanz's shoulder was stuck in a wall of metal that had cooled rapidly, leaving his left side trapped. Boudreaux couldn't hear anything over her own heartbeat pounding in her ears. She reached up and slapped the comms button on her suit.

"DCS, medical emergency. I say again, medical emergency. One casualty."

Baker activated Hanz's medical package, thankfully turning his shrill cry into quiet sobs of pain.

"Baker, you hurt?" Boudreaux asked.

"No, ma'am. I should be dead, but I'm okay," he said, his voice shaking.

She couldn't blame him. It happened so fast she didn't have time to be scared, but now that it was over, her hands shook and she wanted to vomit. The nightmare of Wonderland came back at her full throttle. The month of rehab she'd spent learning how to walk again gave her chills.

"DCS, Captain. Status?" Grimm's voice crackled over the suit comms.

"We're hurt bad, sir, but I don't know how bad. DCS is trashed. Rerouting to engineering and heading there now."

Boudreaux pulled herself out of her seat just as PO Desper and Spacer Whips charged in with an AG stretcher.

CHAPTER TWENTY-ONE

Rear Admiral Wit DeBeck tossed the white uniform cover he wore at the office onto the stiff leather couch of his small living room. Unlike many of his contemporaries who lived, or at least had lived, in or near the Capitol, Wit preferred a simpler home life. A small cabin up in the Horseback Mountains, almost a hundred klicks from the former naval HQ and now a full hour away from Melinda Grimm Naval Base, worked just fine for him.

He never married, though he certainly could have. Subjecting a poor woman to his life seemed more cruel than loving. Never knowing if he were coming home, never knowing where he might be. How could he do that to someone he supposedly loved? Not to mention all the lying he would have to do.

That was probably why he threw himself into his work. He saw his ONI operatives more as children than assets. He mourned when they died and rejoiced with their success.

The small cabin's front room acted as living and kitchen. Two doors led out, one to the bedroom where the bathroom was, and the other to the small storage room that was also set up as a safe room.

All he wanted to do was get his tired mind off work for a few hours and relax. He snagged a beer from the cooler, collapsed with a sigh on the couch, and activated the holographic entertainment center to watch his favorite movies. Wit's life consisted of high-stakes drama, life-and-death decisions, and down-to-the-wire actions. When he made mistakes, people died. Which was why the cheery opening notes of a romantic comedy springing to life on his HEC brought a smile to his tired face. No stakes. No tension. Just will they or won't they.

Cooper MacLeod crouched on the hillside a klick above the little cabin, watching as the lights flickered. His team of high paid mercs had inserted that morning, concealing themselves in the thick blue bushes that covered the hillside. They would wait a little while and let their target settle down before they moved in.

"Coop, why don't we move in now?" Hitch asked. Hitch was his second-in-command as well as their face. He bought all the supplies, weapons, and arrange transport. Sheela, his sniper, covered them from the opposite ridge. Brigs and Martin, twin brothers, handled heavy weapons and close combat. Lea brought up the rear, hiding five klicks away in a plasma-powered dropship ready to extract. The six-man team of specialists was a ridiculous number of people to capture one old paper pusher.

"I don't care how easy the client says this will be. We execute each and every mission as if our lives depended on it... because they do. Don't forget what happened on Vishnu last year. That's not how we operate."

Vishnu had gone wrong from the word go. It was only Cooper's slavish devotion to keeping his team safe that had gotten them out in one piece. Clients hired mercs for jobs they didn't want traced back to them, or as a diversion. Vishnu had been of the diversion variety. Of course, the client hadn't told them that. Another reason Cooper always demanded half up front. When the price was too good to be true, the client wasn't planning on paying out to the dead.

"Thirty minutes. Check your gear."

His earpiece squawked. "Incoming aircar," Sheela whispered.

Cooper swore silently. Their target was supposed to be alone. It was why they picked this spot.

Thirty seconds passed, and the aircar became visible as it descended from the night sky. Moonlight glinted off the canopy, and Cooper made out a mane of curly blonde locks as the light flashed over the transparent windscreen.

"What do we do?" Hitch asked.

"We wait."

Both forward doors opened and two women got out. Cooper eyed the blonde with the curly hair. She was on the thin side for his taste, but she was undeniably beautiful. The dark-haired one had a walk he didn't like, though. Something about her seemed off.

"Escorts?" Brigs asked, hefting his snub-nosed automatic rifle.

"On Alexandria?" Cooper said. Other planets he wouldn't bat an eye, but the so-called home of law and order?

"Man, they're everywhere money is to be made," Hitch replied. "The more illegal, the more they cost."

He supposed so, but he didn't want to assume. However, if they were escorts, then the lights should be going off soon and then his team could catch the old man with his literal pants down. Cooper smiled. Some days, things were just handed to him.

Nadia never took an eye off Daisy as they flew out to meet the admiral. The computer did the flying anyway, even if her hands were on the stick.

"I'm not going to betray you," Daisy said, breaking the long silence that had persisted since they took off from Anchorage Bay.

"You're not going to?" Nadia asked, keeping her tone even. "Or do you mean you're not going to again?"

Daisy frowned, her naturally pouty lips managing to somehow rob the expression of its seriousness.

"I didn't betray you last time. I had a mission to do, and I did it. Am I sorry I did it? Yes. Allah, yes. I am."

A hand clasped Nadia's heart; she wanted nothing more than to tilt the car to the side and shove the hateful woman out.

"Don't say that crap around me," she muttered.

Daisy shook her head. "It's not His fault that men are evil, Nadia. That's what I didn't realize before. I associated the worship of Allah with the evil men do, and I was wrong, just as you are."

Nadia didn't want to get into a religious debate with the woman. She bit back her retort and let the silence stretch on.

"Is that what you learned in prison?" she asked finally. "That the Caliphate are evil?"

Daisy stared out the window at the rising moon. Gray light illuminated the countryside as they flew over.

"People are flawed, Nadia. We make terrible mistakes, then try to find some rationale, some justification that will help our fragile minds deal with what we've done. You fight for the *good guys*. I'm the *bad guy*. It makes it easy for you to do what you do. After all, you're the good guy, right?" Daisy asked, looking over at Nadia for the first time.

Nadia was the first to admit she wasn't always comfortable with the job she had. Especially after Malia. Which was the entire reason she got out of the game the first time. Only to have Daisy drag her back in.

"What I do may be questionable, but I've never thrown someone to the wolves the way you did me. Three days, Daisy. For three days they—"

She clamped her mouth shut, cursing inwardly. All the emotions, all the helplessness and dread came back in an instant. She had lied to her therapists, the doctors, everyone. She told them she didn't remember. That the trauma was too horrible to recall. But she remembered everything. Including how much she focused her anger on the woman sitting next to her. After her action on Kremlin and later Medial, she'd fooled herself into thinking it would never bother her again. It might not cripple her, but it would always be an open wound.

"We're both victims, Nadia," she whispered. "Look at me. You look more Arabic than I do. Look what they took from me? I can never go home, never see my family again. I was a child when they started changing me. Brainwashing me to believe. They had such plans for me too. Plans I destroyed when I contacted my handler about Professor Bellaits' cursed wormhole." Daisy leaned her head against the window, a single tear slid down her cheek, catching the moonlight.

Nadia wanted to be angry at the girl. She wanted to kill her. Had since the moment they slapped that collar on her. Her anger, though, had nowhere to go. Her mother had fled Caliph space when Nadia was a baby, running from a cruel husband who only ever wanted her when it was time to bed.

Nadia grew up in the Alliance and she had choices. She

has chosen the Navy. She had chosen everything. Daisy hadn't. Until the moment Nadia offered her the chance to escape the death penalty, she doubted Daisy ever had any real choice. How many Daisies were there? How many women like Nadia's mother existed? How many men served in the Caliph military simply because they had never been allowed to choose?

A bitter taste filled her mouth, and Nadia was forced to swallow it. She had painted an entire people with one broad brushstroke, leaving out all the nuance and possibilities, letting her abject hatred color her perception.

"Well... I still don't like you," Nadia said sharply.

"As long as you don't like me, for me, and not because of someone else."

"Oh, I think you're a bitch. How's that?" she said with a smile, shocking both herself and Daisy.

"Okay then," Daisy replied with a hint of a smile.

The computer beeped, letting them know they had arrived. Moonlight shone through the clear night sky as the aircar circled in descent until it sat down outside the quaint log cabin. Both doors opened with a hiss of escaping atmosphere.

Daisy stood up, taking in a deep breath of the chilly air. "It's amazing up here."

"That's what he always says. I prefer my apartment in the city. Come on, he's waiting."

The cabin door opened and Admiral DeBeck waited for them, beers in hand, wearing a button up flannel with the sleeves rolled up showing his forearms. Nadia rarely saw him in civilian clothes. It suited him. He could have been a vid star if not for joining the Navy.

"Glad you could make it," he said as he guided them inside, closing the door behind them.

"This is only the second time I think I've seen you out of

uniform, sir," Nadia said as she sipped from the long neck of her beer.

Daisy sniffed hers, then quietly put it down on the counter of the small kitchen.

"This is a weird place to have a secret meeting," Daisy said. "Can't satellites see and hear us?"

The walls had no windows, but were decorated with multiple bizarre paintings. Nadia frowned as she looked at each one, shaking her head. The admiral she admired enjoyed images of animals dressed like humans and playing cards around a green table.

In response to Daisy's question, he pushed one painting of four dogs playing a card game aside and pressed a hidden button. Across the room, the refrigerator lifted into the ceiling, revealing a stairwell down.

"Now that's more like it," Nadia said. She downed her beer in one go, letting the cold refreshing liquid chill her throat. Sitting the empty bottle on the counter, she went down the stairs. Daisy followed her and the admiral took up the rear.

Lights blinked to life, illuminating the stairwell as the secret door closed behind them. Nadia estimated four meters down when they came to another door—one that opened automatically, revealing a circular room that looked like a replica of a CIC on a cruiser. A holo table in the middle, computers all around, and even had the same chairs found on most of the Alliance's older ships.

"Was there a sale at a space station?" Daisy asked.

"Not quite, my dear. I served aboard ship for a long time. I liked the aesthetic." DeBeck flipped a switch on the table, bringing up a map of the capitol building and surrounding area.

Three lights blinked to life, one for each of the bugs. The two in the offices were static, but the third moved.

"That's Representative Simmons on the move," Nadia said.

"Let's take a look." Wit manipulated the controls, and a screen opened, showing them what the congressman saw.

"Gross," Daisy said.

"He's just washing his hands," Nadia replied.

"He's not using soap," Daisy explained.

"Oh."

Bit Simmons exited the private bathroom, returning to the meeting happening in the Speaker's office. Bradford sat in a high-backed leather chair behind a large oak desk, both imported all the way from Seabring.

"Now, Mr. Secretary, you can see I'm being very reasonable." Though Bradford and Bit had the same accent, Bit couldn't help but wince at how much posher it sounded coming from the handsome young man. And as far as he knew, Bradford hadn't done any gene therapy for his age or appearance. Good looks and charm came naturally to him.

Secretary of the Navy Russo stood at attention in front of the desk like a first-year cadet. Bit marveled at how Bradford wove his connections and controlled the bureaucrats who controlled the government.

"I understand, sir, but at this point, to avoid building up is starting to look like lunacy. I can only logically hold off one more quarter. Then, if I don't give in to the Pzresident's demands, he can sack me and find someone who will. Frankly, I'm surprised he hasn't already."

"Let me worry about Axwell," Bradford said. "I need you to delay *Enterprise*'s departure as much as possible. We can't have the Navy starting another war. A battleship on the border with the Caliphate will do just that. This is why I got you this position, Russo. You're the best man for the job."

"Sir, I don't understand how delaying the ship will solve anything. One week or one month, I can't stop her from going. Fleet Admiral Villanueva has the pull to make it happen," SECNAV Russo said.

"I just need one more month to put the votes together among the new representatives and get them in line to vote the *right* way. The way that's best for our nation as a whole. Can I count on you?"

"I'll do my best. But the most I can guarantee is a week, maybe two."

"Do what you can."

Russo departed, nodding to Bit on his way out.

"He seemed adamant about it," Bit said.

"He always does. That's what military service does. Makes everything you say sound right. Speak loud enough and people listen, even if you're an idiot," he said with a nod to the door. The switch in his tone from commanding to condemning surprised Bit.

"Still, I'm not sure this is the best plan," Bit said, his voice wavering. "The Navy has presented some pretty damming evidence that the Caliphate was behind the bombing. They have also increased their attacks on Consortium planets and are clearly preparing to go to war with them." Bit chose his words carefully, hoping to have the desired effect.

Bradford shook his head. "What do we care if they go to war with another nation? As long as it isn't us. Besides, the concession package I'm preparing for reparations for kicking their ambassador and trade ships out of Alliance space will tie them to us financially. We will go from being an enemy to an ally."

"What if the ships we already sent trigger something?" Bit asked.

"A handful of destroyers? They won't pose a problem for us."

Bit found himself nodding along with Bradford. The young man was everything Bit had hoped he would be when he started shepherding his career.

Nadia had heard some damn stupid things in her life, from the POs on her first ship sending her looking for a box of grid squares, to someone trying to convince her that people had evolved beyond violence. This, though, took the cake.

"So they nuke the capitol and we're going to pay them for it?" Nadia said.

"Can't you show someone this info and stop them?" Daisy asked.

Wit sighed, shaking his head.

"We've obtained it illegally and we aren't authorized to spy on our own government," Wit explained. "Besides, his argument sounds reasonable. It's not like he's doing anything illegal. He could even argue that going against popular opinion proves his incorruptibility."

Nadia's visioned tunneled as she zoomed in on the problem. She pushed her emotions to the side, bottling up her frustration and contempt for these elected jackasses as she tried to solve the puzzle.

If Bradford was a well-intentioned fool, then he was blind to the reality of the situation and nothing he said or did would be relevant to the actual facts. He would act how he would, regardless of any response or new information. Like a robot with limited, pre-programmed reactions.

She looked at Daisy. The girl's gorgeous hair, her ski-slope nose, even her hourglass figure, were all designed to make her the ideal Alliance woman. Someone people would listen simply because she was beautiful. Then there was her charisma. The girl had it in buckets. Everything she said was the right thing. When Nadia and she had verbally sparred back on Dagher, she had only known something was wrong by how perfectly Daisy said and did the little things.

The little things.

"Oh God," Nadia said. "Bradford is one of her." She pointed at Daisy.

The lights vanished, and the trio was plunged into darkness.

"What happened?" Daisy asked.

"EMP," Wit said. "It's the only way the power would be shut down." His calm demeanor while he scrambled around in the darkness was exactly what Nadia had come to expect from the old man.

The total blackness prevented her from seeing anything, but she felt his presence a moment before he pressed the cold metal grip of a pistol into one hand, and glasses into the other.

She slipped the glasses on and suddenly she could see again. A three-dimensional wire frame of Daisy and Wit glowed before her. The room's walls and furniture became visible too.

"What kind of pistol is this?" she asked.

"CP-9, the latest and best. Internal targeting display links with the glasses, it won't fire if you point it at a friendly. Just make sure you know what is behind your target. They fire armor-penetrating coil rounds."

"Oh," Nadia said.

She looked at the gun and a box popped up over it, showing her twenty rounds in the mag and one in the chamber. Heat levels, power charge, everything. It wasn't her beloved chemical-fired pistol, but it would do in a pinch.

"I'll go up first," Wit said. "Nadia you follow me, go left. Daisy, go right. We'll sweep the room and engage any tangos present. If none, we'll fall back to the bedroom and engage them as they enter."

Nadia clicked the safety off, cracked her neck, and headed for the stairs. "I like your plan, except you're bringing up the rear. Daisy, on me."

"Might I remind you I'm an admiral?" he said with a level of annoyance reserved for cadets.

"Yes, which is why I'm not letting you go first. You're too important. Get onboard or stay down here."

"Wait, you want me behind you with a gun?" Daisy asked.

Nadia stopped at the base of the stairs, not realizing what she had asked. She didn't second guess herself.

"Can I trust you?"

"Yes." Daisy's one-word reply filled Nadia with a confidence she didn't expect and didn't have time to ponder.

"Here we go."

———

Cooper inched the front door open. He liked using EMP grenades since most power doors failed safe, not secure. Wouldn't want people trapped in a home during a fire.

He swung it open, going low, covering the room with his H&L V-12 stun shotgun. Hitch stood behind him, the same gun shouldered.

Brigs moved in, immediately turning hard right and then back again as he swept the room with his short-barreled rifle. Hitch went in next, hard left and mimicking Brig's pattern.

"Clear," Brigs said. They wore state-of-the-art night vision in their contacts, allowing them to see in the dark.

Cooper was supposed to go in next, but his gut nagged at him. No one was on the couch, and unless the bedroom had amazing sound dampening, nothing was happening in there.

Unless the old man had already finished. But then, why hadn't the girls left?

"Cooper." Martin tapped him on the shoulder.

"I know," he whispered in reply to Brig's twin brother. He usually didn't ignore his instincts, but he needed the money this job brought in. And his squad of killers was more than a match for one old man and a pair of hookers? Right?

———

Nadia knelt next to the two-centimeter crack in the secret door. It would swing open silently, but she didn't want to charge in blind; she wanted to scope the lay of the land first. While the opening didn't allow her to see the entire living room, some vision was better than none.

Movement caught her eye, but it was outside the range of the limited cone she could see. Daisy knelt behind her, one hand on her shoulder.

A man moved across her vision. Fast and in a low crouch, carrying a rifle that gave off a lot of energy. She only caught a glimpse as he passed through her field of vision, but to her, he moved like an experienced operator.

She waited. Two more crossed behind him, then disappeared toward the bedroom. Were they a hit team? Why come for the admiral?

The bedroom door opened with a bang. Nadia acted. Throwing up the secret door-refrigerator, she charged out. Daisy would cover her back if there was anyone else in the room she hadn't seen.

Three commandoes squared off with their backs to her. One was already in the bedroom, the other entering, and the third was turning just as she came out. His eyes went wide and he opened his mouth to shout a warning.

Nadia fired. The smooth snap of electricity filled the air as the coils discharged, sending a ten-millimeter disk flying toward her target at two thousand meters per second. The big man took it in the chest, slamming him against the cabin wall. The structure shuddered from the impact.

Daisy was behind her, and the snap of electric discharge filled her ears. One more went down, with half his head missing. The third took cover behind the bedroom door and fired back. A blue bolt of energy shot past her. The skin on her arms shriveled and her hair stood on ends where it passed.

"Stun guns," she yelled as she dropped to one knee.

Daisy screamed behind her, followed by the thump of something heavy hitting the floor. Nadia didn't have time to look or worry. She placed the reticule at knee level, half a meter to the left of the door and fired. Two rounds blasted through the wood and struck home on the other side.

The man screamed as he fell face first onto the admiral's hardwood floor. He tried to bring up the rifle. Nadia charged across the room, kicking it out of his bloody, shaking hands.

She only had a second to pause when a huge mass crashed into her back, smashing her into the wall. Instinctively, she breathed out with a sharp cry to avoid her lungs collapsing.

"We only need the old man alive," the brute said.

Nadia managed to glance back at him for a second. He was huge, but his right arm was completely severed, blood spurting out where his elbow used to be. Daisy had hit him at least once.

Her gun hand was pinned between the wall and his bulk, with one of his arms wrapped around her neck. She brought up her knees, scrambling with the toes of her boots for some kind of traction, and pushed off the wall. His brute strength refused to let go of her neck, but she forced him to take a step back, freeing her arm.

He swung her around to slam her back into the wall. Nadia

pushed the gun against his wrist and fired. The loud snap next to her ear deafened her, but she was free. Falling to the floor, she tucked and rolled, coming back up with her gun cradled against her chest.

The big man hadn't moved. He stood looking between his missing arm and missing hand, mouth agape. He let out a primal roar of an enraged beast and charged straight at her.

Nadia fired one last time, taking him between the eyes, splattering gray matter all over the admiral's paintings.

Everyone was down. Daisy twitched on the floor from the stun round. Admiral DeBeck slumped against the wall.

"Admiral?" she said.

CHAPTER TWENTY-TWO

Globs of smoke filled the bridge from fried circuits experiencing feedback from the incinerated computer node.

Jacob swallowed hard, trying to generate saliva, reassuring himself he was still alive. He had to force himself to unclench his hands from the command chair. There were people on his ship who needed his help. He didn't have time for gratitude or guilt.

"DCS, Captain. Status?"

Boudreaux's voice came back broken and garbled, a sure sign the comms were fully on the suits and not being rerouted by the ship's computer. "We're hurt bad, sir, but I don't know how bad. DCS is trashed. Rerouting to engineering and heading there now."

"Juan, cycle the bridge and clear this smoke," he said. No matter the damage the ship suffered, the suit comms would almost always work. It was one of the reasons the Navy invested so heavily in the ELS tech.

"Aye sir." Bosun Juan Sandivol's voice was slurred, and Jacob felt his pain. The hit the ship took had shaken the crap out of them. Smoke cleared from the bridge as the Bosun cycled the air.

"Oliv, anything on your panels?"

"No sir. No power. I can't see anything."

The light cruiser could be out there. *Interceptor* was still alive, though, which meant he'd at least hurt them. His crew needed to get their systems back online, then they could figure it out from there.

Jacob leaned his head back for a moment, waiting for the smoke to clear.

"Sound off. Everyone okay?" he asked over the bridge comms.

A chorus of aye-ayes returned.

He unlatched and stood, stretching away the discomfort. When the plasma rounds struck, they disrupted gravity long enough for the crew to get bounced around, which was exactly why they harnessed.

Jacob went to each station, physically checking each of his people, making sure they were actually okay and not suffering from shock and unable to report an injury.

"Engineering, Captain. Status?"

"Sir, Ensign Kai. I'm, uh, still trying to put things together." The young man sounded flustered and out of breath.

"Akio, it's okay. Take a deep breath. Get the checklist out and follow procedure. Report as soon as you have something. Clear?"

"Aye aye, sir."

The bridge hatch scraped open half a meter and Jennings poked her suited head in. "The hatch to deck one is sealed, sir. We must have taken a hit there."

"Roger that, Gunny. Thank you," Jacob said.

"Bridge, engineering. Redfern here. Sir, we can get emergency power going here in a second. I'm routing it to the bridge. If any of your panels are damaged, stand clear."

"We're good, Redfern. Shaken, not stirred."

"Roger that, Skipper. Power in the three…"

Screens flickered to life and a collective cry of victory echoed from the bridge. "Huzzah, Chief, well done," Jacob said.

"No rest for the weary, sir. We'll have that status for you soon. Engineering out."

Jacob stepped across the bridge to PO Oliv, leaning over her and holding onto the grab bar on overhead.

"What have we got?"

"She's out there, sir. Trimming to stern by eighteen degrees. There's a lot of debris… the radar's having trouble seeing a clear picture."

He patted her shoulder and turned to Tefiti. "Anything on grav?"

"No sir. She's dead in space. Not a peep."

"Austin, power to weapons?"

No response.

"Ensign Brown?"

Jacob crossed the small bridge in a few steps and knelt next to the ensign's station. Brown shook his head, blinking several times as he strived to recover.

"Sorry sir, I… one moment."

Jacob gave him a thumbs up. "It's okay, Austin. Deep breaths. You're okay."

"Yes sir. Thank you. Turrets have local control, but the central computer guidance is down at the moment."

"Contact the turrets, have them target the ship as best they can but hold fire. Do not fire… unless they look like they're going to fire at us. Then, by all means."

"Aye sir, target but don't fire unless there is a definitive threat."

The briefing room felt empty with just him, Boudreaux, and Bosun Sandivol in attendance. He had to peel Boudreaux out of engineering to update him—the rest of his department heads were too busy doing actual repairs to stop and give a report. Jennings had her place by the door, as usual. Sometimes Jacob wondered if she ever slept.

He would love for everyone to stand down and take off the ELS suits, but with multiple hull breaches, they couldn't take the chance. The best they could do was restore atmo to the places that were confirmed safe, and let the crew take their helmets off in shifts—mostly in the boat bay where they could congregate and eat their e-rats. Emergency rations weren't his favorite, but until they repaired the galley, it was what they had. Calorically dense bricks, they tasted as flavorful as real bricks, and were just as hard to chew.

"Why don't we start with what's working." Jacob suggested.

"Aye sir. Engineering gives us the green light on the grav-coil, emergency power, thrusters, weapons, and comms. The computer is at two-thirds efficiency, and they have a crew rerouting the lines to bypass the damaged node."

Jacob tapped away at his NavPad, making notes in the holographic projection of the ship that hovered in front of him. Angry crimson slashes marred the blue wireframe holo of the ship, just forward of the bridge as well as the main reactor. They had come very close to dying. Too close. The first four shots missed only because Chief Suresh acted as quickly as she did. One more second of acceleration, though, and the last shot would have taken out the reactor instead of just the fuel conversion chamber.

"And the enemy ship?" he asked.

"That's a little more complicated. Their course currently has them diverging from us at about a rate of one hundred klicks an hour. From what we can tell, they have no power and they're trimming to stern and rolling to port. I don't know how we did it, sir, but we kicked their butts."

"Surprise, XO. The most powerful weapon in any military arsenal. If they had known we were there a moment sooner, I doubt we would be alive to have this conversation."

Jacob zoomed the holo in on the fuel conversion chamber where the crimson deepened. "Tell me about that," he said, gesturing toward the damaged section.

"Yes sir. Chief Redfern and Ensign Kai are working on their BDA now, but from what I've seen, the conversion chamber is a total loss. We got lucky, though. Engineering, Fusion, and the fabricator are all a hundred percent. As soon as we have main power back, we can make real repairs."

Jacob was about to ask another question when the intercom interrupted him.

"Captain, Chief Redfern, sir. I've got some bad news."

"Lay it on me, Chief."

"You're going to need to come down to the fuel converter, sir. It's best I show you."

Fuel conversion happened between the slush deuterium tanks and the fusion reactor on deck four. Six large, pressure-sealed, reinforced and armored tanks carried all the slush deuterium the ship would need.

In an emergency, the gravcoil aperture could be opened to maximum and they could skim planetary atmo and pick up new hydrogen if needed. However, since the Navy believed in redundancy of everything, running out of fuel rarely happened.

Even though each tank was only about the size of two large men, they carried enough deuterium to power the ship for a year. The deuterium wasn't the actual reactor fuel—they refined their own metallic hydrogen by smashing the atoms together with a diamond anvil.

Jacob, Chief Redfern, and Ensign Kai knelt next to the jagged hole leading into the conversion chamber.

"What am I looking at, Echo?" Jacob asked Chief Redfern.

They all had their helmets on. He could easily see out into space through the two-meter jagged hole burned into the side of the ship.

Chief Petty Officer Redfern pointed to the blackened, melted remains of the DAC.

"Well, Skipper, what you should be looking at is the DAC. The diamond anvil cell. It's what compresses the deuterium into metallic hydrogen that fuels the reactor," Redfern said. "But as you can see—"

The entire chamber looked as if it were ground zero for a thermal grenade.

Ensign Kai pointed along the port bulkhead, tracing the path of the blast with his gloved hand.

"The plasma hit there, burned through the armor, and out the other side, taking the DAC with it."

Jacob looked through the hatch, first up at the overhead, then down at the deck where the blast had flowed down into DCS along with molten metal, nearly killing PO Hanz.

"How long to get the conversion chamber back up and running?" Jacob asked. Without it, they only had the fuel in the reactor and the lines running to it on the fusion side of the bulkhead.

"Uh, about a day for the repairs, sir. That's not the problem, though."

"What is?" Jacob asked.

Kai looked to Redfern and the chief just shrugged.

"Tell it to him straight, sir. He's not going to punish you."

Kai nodded, clearly unfamiliar with an understanding CO, or maybe just anxious as he fulfilled a role he didn't have the experience for.

"We can run the fabricators with the power we have left and repair the room and replace the armor." He pointed at the bulkhead as he spoke. "We can make a few parts for the other systems that are down, but the actual anvil, the diamonds that smash the deuterium together? We can't make those. It's like the gravcoil. Too dense."

A cold hand of dread wrapped Jacob's heart and squeezed. The reactor would run for the time being, but eventually it would fail. Once that happened, they would run out of air to breathe. There were few things spacers dreaded more than suffocating out in the black of space.

They couldn't notify the squadron without giving away their position to the rest of the cruisers he had to assume were out there. Not to mention the one enemy ship he was certain of. No help would come.

"Chief, tell me we have reserves," he asked.

"I wish I could, sir, but no. The odds of a direct hit on the DAC are so small that the cost of having spares is greater than the benefit according to BUSHIPS," Redfern said. "It accounts for a fifth of the cost of building the ship."

Jacob's heart sank along with his head. He needed a plan. Some brilliant maneuver to get his crew out of this, but nothing came to mind.

Staying low to avoid the jagged metal of the ruined overhead, he stepped into what used to be the conversion chamber.

"Careful, sir," Ensign Kai said. "Some of those pieces are deceptively sharp."

It didn't look any better from the inside. Jacob turned a full circle, inspecting every meter, looking for something that would spark an idea.

Nothing.

He examined the damage closely while he let his mind work the problem. From inside the room, he could see the two meters of hull and five centimeters of armor the plasma had burned through. The light cruiser had killed his ship. Not instantly, but dead was dead. And he couldn't call for help because the enemy was still out there somewhere.

There was another ship out there.

"Chief... I have an idea."

Even through the ELS suit Chief Redfern recognized the expression on his captain's face. It was the same look the skipper had when they dropped into the thermosphere of Wonderland and hid from the enemy while they repaired the ship. Whatever the captain was thinking, Redfern knew it was going to be inventive, if not down right crazy.

"No offense sir, but you're as crazy as she is," Boudreaux said with a nod to a grinning Jennings.

"It's not crazy, ma'am," Gunny Jennings said. "It's improvising. Adapting. Overcoming the obstacles. The captain would have made an excellent Marine, ma'am."

Jacob could think of no higher compliment a Marine could pay him. He knew he could count on her support, and he felt that pride in his bones.

"Can we do it, though? Akio, do Caliphate ships use the same tech?" Jacob asked.

Ensign Kai looked very much put on the spot. His cheeks darkened as he flipped through his NavPad, researching the answer on the fly.

"I can't say yes with a hundred percent guarantee, sir. I don't know how else they could deploy ships for more than a month at a time without it, though. So yes, they must have an anvil aboard. After we get that, we can make whatever modifications we need."

"That's settled then. Jennings, take your team. Get with Chief Redfern and have engineering send two people who can recognize the parts we need. We're also going to need someone who speaks the language to translate, and—"

"Private June speaks three languages, sir. One of them is a Caliphate dialect," Jennings said.

"Outstanding," Jacob replied. "Get it done."

"Semper Fi, sir."

CHAPTER TWENTY-THREE

Gunnery Sergeant Jennings, Corporal Naki, Lance Corporal Owens, and newly minted PV1 June geared up in silence. The three veterans kept an eye on the new Marine, making sure she geared up in the right order.

Jennings appreciated that June had graduated at the top of her class, but they were in the real world, not a class. Nothing trumped experience.

Space Armor went on in phases. The soft, padded armored Marine ELS suit, followed by the hardened armor and helmet that made them look more like medieval robots than armored people.

"Gloves last, Private," Naki said as he watched her attempt to put them on first.

"Yes, Corporal," she said with the stiff inflection of the new Marine.

Once they were geared up, Jennings went over each of them, making sure they were locked in tight.

"Well done," she said, slapping each one on the helmet in turn.

Even with the added bulk and height of the suit, Jennings

was short compared to the one point eight meter Naki. No one in her squad, though, doubted her lethality.

The double hatch opened to the boat bay, where a long line of spacers wound around the room as they waited for their e-rats or found nooks to eat in. The Marines marched right through the crowd, which parted quickly once they noticed.

It hadn't taken long for the grapevine to learn of the ship's dire condition. Jennings got more than a few "Give 'em hell" shouts on her way to the ship.

The side doors to the Corsair were open and as she climbed in, her radio squawked.

"Gunny, I'm Petty Officer Stawarski. I'll be your aviator this evening. Let me know when you're buckled in and we'll kick this bird."

"Roger that, PO," she replied.

Instead of forty seats, the center of the dropship had been cleared out to make the hatch on the keel easier to reach. She assigned each Marine a seat around the hatch, then took her own at the front.

"PO, we're waiting on our engineering contingent, then we're good to go," Jennings said.

"Roger that," he replied. "I'll start the pre-flight."

Mechanical whirs and clicks filled the cabin as the pilot went through his checklist. In the past, this was the part where she would fall asleep until arriving at the drop point, but she was the gunny now. She was in charge.

"Okay Marines, I want it smooth and by the numbers. The computer says Tripoli's have a crew of three hundred. That's three hundred against four."

"Five," Chief Redfern broke in over the comms.

The lanky engineer climbed aboard from the side hatch, a toolkit in one hand and a pistol-configured MP-17 strapped to his hip.

"I thought the captain said two engineers?" Jennings asked.

"Can't spare two. And I'm really the only one who knows how to do what we need to do. So get me there, keep me alive, and get me out."

Jennings pointed at the seat she wanted him in. "Stawarski, we're ready. Lift off ASAP."

"Roger tower."

Alarms warbled through the boat bay, signaling all personnel to stand clear of the yellow and black lines painted on the deck around the massive boat bay doors. After ten seconds, the ships Richman field snapped into place and the doors dropped open like a storm shutter. The Corsair hung above open space, ready to go.

Stawarski's voice crackled over her suit comms. "Drop in three..." when he hit one, the ship lurched out into space passing harmlessly through the Richman field holding in the atmosphere.

"Marines," Jennings shouted into her comms. "You *will not* puke in your helmets."

"Oorah," they shouted back.

PO Rupert Stawarski gulped audibly as *Interceptor* disappeared from his aft cameras. Two weeks before, he'd spent his days ferrying supplies from Kremlin Station to the new Marine base on Zuck Central. A relatively easy run, all things considered. With the black in front of him and the *Interceptor* vanishing behind him, he suddenly longed for the milk runs he'd spent his evenings complaining about.

Oliv updated his course via laser pointed at his ship. He had every faith in Oliv, but not so much in himself. He was flying blind, with only his computer to tell him where to go. They couldn't turn on radar or lidar. Passive only. If he was off even a half a degree, his ship could fly off into the black and never come back.

"No pressure, Rupert. No pressure."

Somewhere in the trip, Jennings dozed off. Her intel briefing from the XO estimated at least two hours, but it could take longer. She was just happy to be in her space armor instead of a Raptor strapped on the wings.

"Gunny? Can you come up here, please?" PO Stawarski said over the comms.

Jennings' eyes snapped open, alert and ready.

"On it."

The cargo section of the Corsair was easy enough to move around in, but once in the nose, things got tight fast. She didn't think she could climb the small ladder to the cockpit, let alone fit in the second seat wearing her armor.

Instead, she took the third seat below where the EW tech sat. "Go ahead."

"I should have found it by now, Gunny. But I got nothing," Stawarski whispered as if other people could hear him, even though it was just the two of them on comms.

Jennings bit back the first thing that came to mind. Navy types were sensitive, and she had to remind herself to be more like the captain. "Take a breath, Stawarski. Tefiti would have warned us if they moved. It's out there. Where are we on time?"

He audibly took a breath, letting it out slowly. "Two minutes till we're at Rubicon." The point at which they were to return to the ship. The mission wasn't without risks. They could very easily become lost and *Interceptor* wouldn't be able to help them without exposing herself.

Jennings wasn't a radar tech. She didn't know much about how the ship's systems worked, so the best she could do was guide Stawarski.

"What about other ways to detect them?" she asked.

"What do you mean?"

"You tell me," she countered.

Seconds passed while he thought it through. Jennings stifled a yawn, not worried in the slightest.

"Well, I supposed I could pop the FLIR on. It's not really meant for space, but if they're close enough it would pick them up. Should I?"

Jennings wanted to laugh at the situation. Here he was, a Navy petty officer asking a Marine gunnery sergeant how to fly a Corsair.

"Yes," she replied.

She moved out of the way of the EW panel and returned to her seat with the rest of her Marines.

"Got it," Stawarski said over the ship–wide comms. "Bearing three-three-two, range eight hundred klicks. Dang, Gunny. Way to go!"

Jennings ignored the looks from her team as she settled into an equipment check.

Jacob hated waiting. Every time he sent people off his ship, the man-of-action inside of him demanded to go with them. Like some kind of damn-fool hero from a vid.

That wasn't who he was, though. Captains of naval warships didn't charge into battle with the grunts. With very few exceptions, leaving the bridge to go on shore parties was a big no. He was lucky he hadn't gotten into more trouble for boarding the mining platform in Zuckabar, even though there were extenuating circumstances.

At least on the ship he could do some good. With engineering's limited power for the fabricators, they were forced to triage what needed repair first. He was elbow deep in the heatsink exchange, fixing the linkage that powered the transition when a new heat synch loaded into the absorber.

Resting on a small catwalk in a compartment barely two meters wide and only one-point-five meters tall, he dragged a hand across his forehead and leaned back against the bulkhead.

"Captain. Ensign Brown here. Do you have a minute?"

Jacob glanced up out of pure habit. It didn't make a difference, but somehow, being in the bowels of the ship, it seemed right to look where the person was talking from, even if he couldn't see them.

"Of course. Come down to the heat exchanger. I'll be here for a while."

"Aye sir. On the way."

Jacob lost track of time, trying to align the correct linkage when a thick hand grabbed the cable and easily pulled it into place. Jacob took advantage and tightened down the cables and secured them to the hardpoints.

Jacob sat back, one arm resting on a raised knee, with his head dipping low to look at the man. "Thanks, Austin. What can I do for you?"

"Sir, it's... Permission to speak freely?"

"Of course."

"Mateo and I were friends, sir. Ensign Lopez, I mean. I want to know why he died?"

Jacob knew no answer he could give would ever satisfy that question. It was one spacers had asked for as long as the service existed. He imagined men and women asking that same question throughout time in the aftermath of thousands of battles and millions of dead.

"That's a big question, Austin. Have a seat." Jacob gestured to the catwalk.

Ensign Brown hopped down, shaking it with his mass before finding a way to sit.

"I understand, sir, but he died and I don't see anyone being punished for it."

Punished? It hadn't occurred to Jacob to punish anyone. They hadn't even completed their preliminary investigation before the light cruiser was on them. As far as he could tell, though, it was an accident. A preventable one, but that was a matter for the yard on Utopia.

"I'm not sure I follow? We know what caused the explosion... there wasn't any fault on the crew's part. No one in the galley could have stopped what happened. The malfunction happened in the bulkhead, installed by the yard after our last battle."

Austin shook his head.

"That's not what I mean, sir. I heard that... I heard that Midship Rugger left Mateo in there to die. To burn alive."

Jacob's face tightened and he tried hard not to grimace. The ship's grapevine spread speculation like fact, regardless of the veracity. It pained him, though, that someone would spread that particular rumor with no basis. Or at least, very little evidence at all.

"No one can know what conflagration Midship Rugger and Private June faced. Have you ever been shot at?"

Brown's face flinched at the odd turn of the question.

"Uh, no, sir. I haven't."

"I have." Images of the hell he, Jennings, and Naki had faced in the warehouse shot through him. He hadn't really thought about it in some time. One second they were having a cordial conversation, the next people were trying to kill them. "You know what I did the first time it happened?"

"The first time, sir?"

Three times, Jacob realized. He needed to stop leaving the ship.

"I tripped over my own feet and broke my nose. My point is, our training helps, but dangerous things happen in the life of a spacer. Don't judge the actions of others until you know all the facts, and maybe not even then. I understand there was some beef between the two of them, but I don't think, not for one second, that anyone in the Navy would leave a spacer to die in such a horrible way. The fact that he went back in so many times says he wouldn't. Understand?"

Jacob saw the confusion and frustration on Ensign Brown's face. Like Jennings, he wasn't great at hiding his emotions, but unlike Jennings' stoic nature, Brown seemed to show much more. Maybe it wasn't McGregor's World so much as it was her being a Marine.

"I think so. I'll try to reserve judgement until the report comes out. If Rugger did do it on purpose though, he'll face justice, right?"

"Of course. But like I said, Austin, I think you'll find that it was just an accident."

After the wide man left, Jacob got back to work on the heatsink, trying to keep his mind off his Marines, who were certainly facing danger at that very moment.

CHAPTER TWENTY-FOUR

Superheated beams of plasma splashed off the bulkhead Jennings had ducked behind. She didn't see how many men were barricaded down the passageway, but from the beams turning metal into water, there had to be at least three, maybe four.

Jennings cursed their luck. Tripoli's were three hundred meters along the keel. Her Marines had entered through the bow at the only emergency airlock they could find to override, and they'd barely boarded the ship when they took fire. The Caliphate ship was damaged, but her crew seemed very much alive.

"Owens, you okay?" she asked.

"Yeah," he muttered. He'd taken a plasma beam right in the chest, partially melting his armor and knocking him off his feet.

"June, yell at these guys to surrender," Jennings ordered.

"Yes, Gunny," she replied. June stepped up next to Jennings and shouted something in their language.

A hail of green plasma filled the passageway in reply.

"Don't say we didn't try," Jennings muttered. "Grenade,

anti-personnel." She pulled the palm-sized cylinder from her belt. "Proximity detonation."

She turned and hucked it as hard as she could. It bounced off the overhead and right over their makeshift barricade. She spun back around just as it detonated. Hundreds of four-millimeter BBs shredded the men and ricocheted, expending their energy on the bulkhead.

"Go," Jennings yelled.

Rifle pressed firmly into his shoulder, Naki charged around the corner. Jennings dashed out right behind him, going far to starboard while Owens and June protected the engineer.

Naki was over the barricade first, putting two rounds into the first man he saw. Jennings followed, firing, and dropped a second who had somehow managed to survive the devastating attack.

The other two had taken the full brunt of the grenade and weren't easily confused with living persons; their heads and torsos were shredded beyond recognition.

"Clear," Naki said as he repositioned his rifle and moved down the passage. Jennings dropped in behind him, covering port. June, Redfern, and Owens brought up their six.

"Suggestions on which way to go?" Naki asked.

"We need to find a reactor. From there I can find the anvil," Redfern said.

"Reactor. Got it. June, you speak their language. What's that sign say?" Naki asked, pointing with his off-hand while maintaining his rifle.

"Deck Four, life support, maintenance, and lift, that way," she said, pointing to the port. "The other way is barracks and the armory."

Jennings didn't want anyone coming up behind them, but at the same time, her force was small enough that splitting up was a bad idea.

"Owens, June, stickies. There and there." Jennings pointed at the intersection behind them. The two Marines activated grenades to act like sticky bombs, slapping them on either side of the passageway intersection and setting them to detonate on proximity.

"That should keep our six clear for a few minutes," Owens said.

The Marines spread out, not walking down the center, but alternating port and starboard. Owens lagged behind, acting like overwatch.

They came to a series of hatches marked with life support where the passageway curved around.

"The lift should be next," June said.

"Okay, hunker down and stay here. I'll take a look," Jennings ordered.

She had expected more resistance, to be honest. Other than the damaged turret and the wrecked bridge, the ship seemed lightly damaged. Unless, of course, they had abandoned ship. The Marine pushed herself up against the bulkhead and inched her way down the passage while straining to detect enemy combatants.

"Shh," she overheard. She might not speak their language, but that was a universal sound.

An explosion behind her rocked the ship as someone tripped their booby trap.

A man yelled, and booted feet came running down the passage. She didn't have time to think, only react. Pushing off the bulkhead she pointed her rifle toward her target. When they appeared, she squeezed the trigger. The MP-17 spewed out deadly silicate shards while she followed her momentum to the next bulkhead, then down on one knee, firing all the while.

Two men went down in a mess of blood and bone as hyper-accelerated silicate slivers shredded their unarmored suits. The remaining four overran their dead crewmates and were on top of Jennings before they even realized she was there.

Jennings leaped forward, slamming her rifle butt into the chest of the first one. He fell back with a yelp, taking her rifle with him. Stepping back, she brought up her arm to shield her side as she drew her bayonet from the other. A hard blow bounced off her helmet. She lunged sideways, shoulder checking him and driving her bayonet deep into his throat.

More yells in their language as she turned and tossed the man she just killed into the remaining three men and charged right behind the body. Her armor slowed her down, but she wasn't slow. A blow landed on her torso. One of them fired the plasma rifle at point blank range, hitting her shoulder with a hiss of melting armor.

Jennings snap kicked the first one, swiped her bayonet along the next one's arm, and backhanded the third. While the one she kicked recovered, the other two leaped at her. She tried to dodge, but the armor wasn't designed for hand-to-hand as much as ranged combat.

They pushed her into the bulkhead, raining blows on her head and shoulders. One pulled a wicked looking serrated blade with a glow around the edge and an ear-splitting hum. She recognized that sound—a vibroblade.

She was in trouble and she knew it.

Lifting her free leg, she wedged it against the bulkhead and shoved with all her might. A primal growl from deep within her roared out as she pushed off, slamming the two men into the far bulkhead. The humming blade clattered against the deck.

A plasma beam struck her thigh and she grimaced in pain as her skin burned underneath the armor. Jennings flipped her bayonet over and hurled it at the one with the rifle. Twenty centimeters of nano-hardened steel, sharpened to a killing edge, lodged in his throat, ending his life.

Off-balance from the throw and falling sideways, her helmet banged off the deck and the two men were quick to punch her, trying to keep her disoriented.

One climbed on top of her, straddling her chest as he pulled another blade, yelling as he lifted it into the air. His head jerked and he fell backward as a silicate round punctured the faceplate of his suit.

The last one turned to run and three rounds caught him in the back, splashing the deck with his blood.

June appeared, rifle covering the passageway while Naki helped her up.

"Thanks," Jennings said.

"Got your six, Gunny," Naki replied.

They heard Owens covering them, his MP-17s sounding like a discharging battery when he fired.

"Gunny, contact rear, six hostiles. Falling back to you," Owens' voice crackled over the comms.

Jennings recovered in a flash, retrieving her rifle and charging down the passageway to the lift.

"You sure engineering is this way?" Naki asked.

Redfern shook his head. "No idea. It's not back that way, though." He jerked his thumb behind them.

Owens backed around the corner, firing as he retreated. Green lines of electrostatic plasma flashed around him, scarring the bulkhead.

"Owens, June, thermite," Jennings ordered.

They both pulled grenades and hurled them down the passageway. The diminutive weapons exploded in an inferno of twenty-two hundred degrees Celsius, filling the corridor with acrid smoke and the screams of the dying.

The lift appeared around the curved passageway.

"Why build them in curves?" Owens asked.

"Who knows? The interior of a ship has a lot to do with

culture. As long as it doesn't exceed the area of the gravcoil, then anything can go," Redfern replied.

"Owens, hack it." Jennings pointed at the lift. "Naki, June, six. Redfern, stick to me."

"This will teach me to volunteer myself for a boarding party," Redfern muttered.

"They have next-level encryption, Gunny. Maybe the XO, I mean Lieutenant Yuki could have, but it's beyond me," Owens said.

"Plan?" Naki said over his shoulder.

"Thermite's not going to hold them for long," June added.

Jennings cracked her neck. A million scenarios flashed before her, all ending with their death or enslavement. She pushed those down and refocused. They had seconds to act. She was good at making decisions, right or wrong. The anvil was near the fusion reactor. Reactors were important and protected.

"Ship this size is going to have two reactors, right?" she asked.

"Yes," Redfern replied.

"We go down, then. They're three times as big as *Interceptor*. Three hundred meters long and eighteen decks, yes?"

"Up, Gunny. They count from the bottom, not down," June said.

"Roger that, Private. Up then. Owens, burn the hatch."

Omar Assad hated the position he was in. As a junior lieutenant, he shouldn't even be in command. With the captain dead and the other officers not responding, he was all that remained. All he wanted to do was wait for rescue. Something he doubted the fifteen enlisted behind him would allow.

"Lieutenant, there are reports of fighting below," Raqib First Class Zafar said.

"Intruders? From where?" Assad asked. All he knew was the ship went to alert and then all hell broke loose. They were in the middle of nowhere, following an Alliance squadron around. Who would have even fired on them?

Zafar held one hand over his ear to hear better. "It sounds like"—he looked up at the lieutenant, face screwed up in anger—"Alliance Marines, sir."

So it was the Alliance who attacked them. Cowards. What was he supposed to do? That's what the soldiers were for. "Alert the security teams to converge on them. We can't have them running around. How many?"

Zafar relayed the question and raised an eyebrow. "They are saying a dozen at least."

Assad was only a lowly junior lieutenant, but even he knew Alliance destroyers didn't carry that many Marines. "Not possible. Tell them to deal with it." He could send some of his men to help, or have them patrol his deck. His engineers needed time to reroute the control runs to take auxiliary command of the ship.

"Why are they here?" he asked Raqib.

"I don't know, sir. Blow the ship maybe? Or prisoners?"

If they were there to blow the ship, then they would be coming right for Assad. He glanced behind him through the open hatch where the massive fusion reactor sat. If the idiots in engineering could get aux running, then they could just take off. Once they were underway, the Marines would have to surrender. They would never be going home.

"Security team requests reinforcements, sir," Raqib Zafar asked.

"Negative. They are going to have to deal with it. Zafar, take the men here and set up an ambush. If they are coming for the reactor, we must defend it at all costs!"

Private Yanaha June was almost positive this wasn't the normal first deployment activity. She floundered behind Gunny Jennings, trying desperately to keep up with the shorter woman.

"Which way," Jennings barked.

June glanced at the signs, trying to make sense of the dialect. She spoke Caliphate, which was a mix of half a dozen old Earth dialects, including Farsi and Arabic, but there were generations of lingual drift and not everything made sense to her.

"Two lefts and a right, I think," she said.

Jennings turned to her, the dented, scorched armor a stark reminder of the fight she had barely survived.

"You think?"

"Gunnery Sergeant, it's not a one-for-one translation. There's nuance and I'm guessing on some of it."

"Do your best," Jennings said.

"Oorah, Gunny," June replied. A sense of relief filled her. Half of her anxiety came from fear of being yelled at. Even though the enemy was trying to kill them, it seemed secondary to the yelling.

"Charlie Mike," Jennings ordered. The gunny took the point, followed by Naki, Redfern, June, and Owens.

June traversed her rifle back and forth as they moved steadily down the passageways. The Alliance would have set up ambushes at every intersection, but the Caliphate seemed to want to overwhelm them with surprise charges. The blackened streaks on Gunny's and Owens' armor proved their failed tactics. The space armor, as they called it, was saving their collective butts.

Jennings held up a closed fist, followed by her patting an

imaginary dog. June racked her brain, trying to remember what the second one was when everyone else crouched down. She followed suit.

Her offhand under the barrel fidgeted, and she had to force herself not to move. Should she move more to the bulkhead? She took a half step left when something whistled by her head. The explosion slammed her into the deck face-first, and she flopped onto her back.

"Contact rear," Owens reported over the radio.

Somehow, they had managed to shoot a grenade at them. June stared up at the overhead, eyes unfocused as she tried to make her fingers work.

"You hurt?" Naki asked as he fired his rifle with one hand and held out his other to her. She grabbed it and he pulled her up.

"No, Corporal, I don't think so," she said.

"Good. Owens, suppressing fire and let's get out of here."

Owens switched his MP-17 to hypervelocity, and a stream of death shot down the passageway. June's throat tightened as two men were cut in half, blood and entrails spraying the deck.

"Don't puke," she muttered as she tried to take deep, calming breaths.

"Keep going," Jennings shouted.

June charged behind the engineer and Jennings, while Naki and Owens laid down covering fire from behind.

She passed a hatch and slid to a halt, pointing.

"Reactor, that means reactor!" June shouted in glee. She hit the button to open the hatch. Jennings shouted her warning too late.

Plasma beams reached out to June in slow motion. Redfern leaped for her. The first beam struck above the angled visor, deflecting the beam up but knocking her back a step. The next hit her chest, the hardened armor absorbed and dissipated the plasma before it burned a hole through her. The third beam deflected off her shoulder armor. The fourth electro static plasma beam struck the soft armor below her collar bone and burned all the way through her and out the backside.

Redfern tackled her, knocking her down as a fifth beam burned past so close it singed his ELS suit.

"June," he shouted.

Private Yanaha June let out a blood curdling scream of agony and curled up into a ball, trying to desperately block it all out.

"How bad is she?" Jennings asked from her position beside the hatch.

"Bad," Redfern said. "The armor deflected the kill shots, but she took one in the chest. The suits nanites might stabilize her, but she's in a lot of pain."

"I... can take it. No pain meds. I can do it," June said, her voice shaking as she clenched her jaw.

Jennings nodded. Damn fool private should have waited. No matter how good she was in class, this was the field, and mistakes like that cost lives. Hopefully not this time.

She pulled a grenade from her waist. "Flashbang," she said. "Proximity detonation."

A green light flashed on her HUD, letting her know it was ready. She heaved it around the hatch. More plasma rounds burned through the air the second they saw movement.

Light a hundred times brighter than the sun, and a sound like a sonic boom filled the compartment. As soon as it detonated, Jennings charged in, firing as she went left. Naki followed, going right, and the two Marines shot everything that moved as they swept their weapons toward the center.

A man leaped over the makeshift cover and ran right at Jennings, a grenade huddled against his chest while he yanked the pin. Time slowed down and Jennings could see everything in exquisite detail. He was an officer, young and handsome, but the fear and hatred in his eyes was as ugly as it came.

Jennings leaped forward, gun butt slamming him in the jaw, sending him into a spin. She dived after him, smashing into his shoulders and knocking him down, riding him to the deck.

A muffled boom echoed through the room. Jennings lifted into the air before collapsing back into a puddle of the man's own innards.

"Redfern, get in here," Jennings yelled.

He entered, dragging June behind him. She held her rifle in her only working arm. Owens followed, still firing out the hatch.

"Owens, close and weld," Jennings ordered.

"On it." The hatch banged shut, and Owens whipped out his small torch and placed the end against the side. Sparks flew as it welded.

"Naki, cover the other one," Jennings said.

"Rog." Naki leaped over the terminal and past the reactor to train his weapon on the hatch.

"Redfern, where to?" she asked.

He let go of June to look around the large compartment. The pulsing fusion reactor dominated the center, with pipes and conduits running through the bulkheads and overhead to the reactor.

"I'm looking! It's usually a double-thick conduit, reinforced and leading into the top of the reactor."

The main hatch started to glow as the enemy used a torch to cut through. Jennings figured they had five minutes. Speed was their ally, getting stalled aided their enemy.

There were three pressure hatches leading from the fusion

room. The one they came from obviously led to the enemy. The other two were dogged and sealed. They didn't have time to cut both open.

"Chief, any other way to tell?" Jennings asked.

"It's a fuel chamber. It should be reinforced to withstand explosions," Redfern said.

June pointed with a shaking hand toward the hatch leading to the stern. "That one. See the struts? They're designed to push an explosive force around them and away."

Jennings leaped over to the hatch and banged on it with a fist. "Owens, burn it. June, rig this thing to blow on my signal." She pointed at the reactor. "When we leave here, I want this ship and everyone on it dead, got it?"

"Yes, Gunny," June said. The private got to work, using her two remaining grenades for a makeshift bomb. "Chief, can you place it for me? Top of the reactor?" she said.

"You got it."

Redfern grabbed the makeshift explosive, leaped up a meter to hang on to the lip of a pipe, and placed the bomb three meters up against the reactor.

Owens' torch flared to life, and metal ran in driblets off the reinforced hatch. It was a race to see who could burn through a hatch faster. Owens versus the Caliphate.

Jennings hated races.

CHAPTER TWENTY-FIVE

Jennings mentally prepared herself for another fight—possibly the last one she would ever have. The enemy were almost through the hatch leading to the passageway.

"Naki, Chief, June, line up and take cover." There were plenty of consoles and metal housings to hide behind, though nothing that would last long against sustained plasma fire.

Redfern helped June to her feet and guided her behind a solid console she could rest against and fire her weapon.

Jennings slung her weapon, grabbed two of the bodies, and dragged them in front of the hatch. At the very least, the Caliph spacers would stumble over their comrades when they came through.

Marines used MP-17s because they wouldn't damage anything vital on a ship. Any hardened armor could stop them, but wearing armor like that was cumbersome and not something regular spacers moved around in.

Hiding behind a pump housing, though, she wished for something more substantial. With a coil rifle, she could kill the first person through the hatch and ten of his closest friends stacked up behind him.

Flame leapt out from their side of the hatch as the torch cut through, showering the dead bodies with sparks and lighting them aflame. Jennings' visor dimmed automatically, protecting her from the sudden burst of light.

"Ten seconds," Owens yelled over the radio.

The torch stopped and the Gunny saw a helmeted head peak through the hole.

It disappeared. Not thinking, just acting, she leapt over the housing, grabbed her last grenade. "Hi-ex," she shouted as she thumbed the detonator. There was no time for more instructions. The number three appeared on her HUD and counted down in milliseconds.

Jennings reached the hatch just as the torch resumed, showering her in superheated embers. She jammed her hand through the hole and dropped the grenade on the other side, yanking her hand back just as a tremendous thump resonated through the hull. Fire and debris shot through the small hole.

She spun backward, hitting the bulkhead before falling to her hands and knees.

"Done," Owens shouted. He heaved up his foot and kicked as hard as he could. The hatch clanged as a square hole big enough for June to crawl through fell out the other side.

Redfern ran over, sticking his head in and looking around.

"Bingo!"

He helped June crawl through, groaning as she was forced to move her wounded torso and shoulder. She disappeared into the black of the other room.

Jennings dusted herself off and joined them.

"How long to remove the anvil?" she asked Redfern.

"Maybe ten minutes. It's quite small. Do you think you can hold them for that long?" She turned and leveled her gaze straight at him.

"Forget I asked," he muttered.

The hatch hissed, sliding open only part way, jammed on some of the jagged metal Owens had left behind. It was enough for all of them to squeeze through.

Jennings brought up the rear, then closed the hatch. She picked up the metal piece and jammed it back into place as best she could.

Owens used his torch again, welding the pieces back on.

"That ought to hold them for a few minutes. Get to work, Chief."

"Yes, Gunny." Redfern put his tool box down next to the anvil housing and went to work.

"Charlie One-One, this is Bravo Two-Five."

"Go for Charlie," Stawarski's voice came back. Jennings breathed a quiet sigh of relief for the clear frequency. No jamming from the Caliphate meant they were still disorganized.

"We've encountered heavy resistance. I don't think we can make it back to the hatch. Dust off and loiter. Will send instructions as needed."

"Say again? Dust off and loiter?"

"Roger."

"Charlie One-One, dust off and loiter, roger," Stawarski said. She thought he sounded a little shocked. It was going to take time to break in their new taxi driver.

"Okay, Naki, Owens, find us a way off this heap," Jennings said.

"Is something wrong with the hatch?" Owens asked, pointing back the way they came.

Jennings fast walked to the Lance and smacked him in the helmet. "The dozen or so bad guys who want us dead?"

"Oh, right," Owens said sheepishly.

"What about a lifeboat? They have to have those, right?" Naki asked.

"Go find out," she said to the two men. They snapped to and

said, "Semper-Fi," in unison. There was another hatch opposite the one they entered and they moved through it cautiously.

Jennings knelt next to June, where she'd propped herself up against the bulkhead.

"What have we learned?" she asked the private.

"Don't open hatches and stand in front of them like a brain-dead moron."

"Good woman," Jennings said. "It's okay to screw up. What doesn't kill us makes us smarter." She leaned over and gingerly checked the part of the armor the plasma beam had cut through. Private June either had incredible luck or bad luck. Jennings wasn't sure. The beam hit right where the hardened armor and soft armor met. She leaned the girl forward and examined the exit wound. The nanites had dispensed a sealing foam to protect the raw skin underneath. As she watched, bits of blackened dead flesh seeped through the foam to fall off on the deck.

Goosebumps broke out along her arms just watching the little buggers progress. They wouldn't last much longer, though. They had enough resources to stabilize and do some repairs, but unless they got June back aboard the Corsair soon, her condition would start deteriorating.

"How bad is it, Gunny?" Private June asked between clenched teeth.

Jennings paused for a moment. Cole's face popped in front of her and his dying breath played out in her mind's eye. She had let him die or, at the very least, couldn't save him. Marines died and that was a fact. She wished more than anything she could go back and make some decision that would save him, or June. But no one controlled anything. Not in life and certainly not on the battlefield. Gunnery Sergeant Jennings would move heaven and Earth to save her Marines, but she knew she couldn't save them all.

"Bad," she said flatly. "But you'll make it. Watch the hatch," she said.

"Oorah," June replied in a weak voice.

Jennings made a quick search of the room, looking out for any other possible avenues of attack. "How long?" she asked Redfern as she returned to the main hatch.

Chief Redfern had the housing off. He slipped on a pair of tinted goggles and reached into where the anvil presumably rested.

"Just another minute," he said absently.

Jennings kept an eye on him while she knelt next to the hatch leading to the reactor and placed one gloved hand on it. She felt tiny vibrations from the other side.

"Bravo, status?" she called to Naki over the comms.

"Alpha, I think we've located one of their life boats. I'll secure the RP and send Charlie back to guide."

"Roger," she replied. "Chief?"

Redfern lifted two silver-painted square containers out of the guts of the device he worked on. "Got it. This will get the old girl back in the fight."

"Help June. I got your six," Jennings said.

Redfern stowed the anvils in his toolkit and dashed to assist Private June, who was attempting to stand on her own. Jennings couldn't see her face through the visor, but June's vitals warbled on her HUD. Alerts flashed, letting Jennings know the private was in a tremendous amount of pain and on the verge of going into shock.

A thud from the hatch vibrated the room, forcing Jennings to step back. She toggled her selector switch from "full-auto" to "Hyper-Velocity." Her MP-17 would vomit silicate shards at an insane cyclic rate, emptying the entire 500 round magazine in just a few seconds. Not ideal for sustained firefights, but it would make the enemy think twice about following them.

Gunny Jennings crouch-walked backward, using the three-sixty camera to navigate across the compartment as she kept her MP-17 on the hatch like a laser.

Sparks flew as timed breaching charges burned through the hatch in a span of moments. Redfern and June were already out. Jennings leaned against the exit hatch, switching her overlay to ultrasound. While her helmet couldn't see through the heated smoke, the ultrasound spotted a human-sized target entering the compartment, followed closely by a second, then a third. From their outline, she knew they weren't wearing hard armor.

She took aim, letting out her breath and reciting the ancient Marine mantra: "Slow is smooth, and smooth is fast." At the end, she squeezed the firing stud. The nearly silent weapon spat five hundred silicate shards through the men. They didn't have time to scream as their bodies were perforated, and only their bones held them together as their innards painted the men behind them—who did have time to scream in horror.

Jennings fell back, slamming the hatch shut and manually dogging it.

Her comms squawked. "Alpha, Delta and the package have arrived. Waiting on you," Naki said.

Jennings turned and ran, pumping her legs full speed as she dropped the empty mag from her rifle and slammed home a new one.

"Charlie One-One, Bravo Two-Five. Home in on our transponders and pick us up," she said.

"Roger, Bravo Two-Five, where is the airlock you're going to use?"

"Negative airlock, just home in."

Electrostatic plasma beams whined past her. Jennings leapt forward, hitting the deck on her chest and sliding forward as she spun.

Two men in combat armor stood twenty meters away,

adjusting their aim to nail her. She fired first, taking the one on her right in the chest and stitching a pattern up his torso. The silicate rounds sparked and ricocheted off his hardened armor.

"Crap," she muttered. Rolling hard, she dodged return fire that scorched the deck behind her and gained her feet. A beam sliced by her helmet, then a second traced a line up her back and sent her stumbling forward.

"Bravo," she said, out of breath. "Launch, launch, launch." She ducked sideways into an open hatch, narrowly avoiding the next beam. Her armor warbled, alerting her to malfunctions and impact areas. Alison Jennings took a deep breath, forcing it out through her nose, the agony with it.

She flipped through her rifle's available configs until she found the less-than-lethal settings. Nanites went to work, reconfiguring the weapon until it had a ten-millimeter barrel.

"Let's see you stop this." Her ammo count changed from five hundred to twenty. However, instead of firing silicate shards, she would shoot ten-millimeter solid slugs, capable of knocking a grown man down.

Kneeling, she ducked out of the cover of the hatch and fired a three-round burst at the first guy. He didn't even dodge, thinking his armor made him invulnerable to her weapon. He was right; just not the way he thought. Fired at a much lower velocity, the weighted rounds struck like a hammer, hitting him in the head and flinging him backward to land with a crunch, his legs in the air.

The second one fired, his beam reaching out in slow motion as Jennings pushed herself to move faster. The plasma hit her arm, burning through her soft armor and melting skin and muscle. She fell in a heap into the passageway, out of sight of the enemy.

Pain lanced through her, so bad it clouded her vision. She

clamped down on her jaw hard enough she worried her teeth would crack.

She breathed out through her nose again, forcing the pain down. Her HUD flashed more warnings, including a timer that would administer pain meds if she didn't override the sequence. If she was going to die, she was going out on her terms, not loaded up with pain killers.

Cradling the rifle in her good arm, the gunny heaved herself up and waited for the assailant to stick his head out.

A small black object the size of her palm flew past her head and toward the Caliphate.

"What the—"

The explosion took her by surprise and she ducked her head back. Strong hands grabbed her shoulder and Naki was there, pulling her toward the lifeboat.

"I told you to launch," she yelled at him.

He tapped his helmet with one hand in the universal sign of failed comms.

She could only grin as he guided her to escape. Today wasn't her day to die.

They rounded the last corner. Owens, down on one knee with his rifle shouldered, covered their six. Redfern and June were in the small lifeboat and strapped in.

Naki pushed her down into the crash chair next to the engineer.

"Buckle her in," he ordered. Redfern didn't argue.

Two Caliphate spacers charged around the corner, firing plasma rifles and trying to cover the distance. Owens fired twice, taking each one down with precision and alacrity.

"Get in here," Naki said. Owens fell back immediately. Once everyone was in, Corporal Naki hit the emergency launch and the lifeboat rocketed away from the ship with a spine-bending nine g's of thrust.

"June." Jennings grunted her name through the pain. "Blow it."

Private June struggled for a moment to reach the panel on her forearm, then pressed the activation button.

Two Caliphate spacers guarded the fusion reactor while engineering officer Ramzi looked over the housing, trying to figure out what the infidels had done to his ship. They couldn't figure out why the raiding party had sabotaged the anvil. The light cruiser had two of them, making it was a pointless mission. Sure, they had killed a few crew and delayed repairs for a few hours, but ultimately achieved nothing.

Still, Khan's concern they had damaged his reactor had him searching the dangerous device from bottom to top. A light flashed from the top of his reactor near where the main fuel line entered. He suddenly wished he'd started at the top.

Stasis fields inside the pressurized grenade housing dropped, and high-nitrogen energetic materials suspended in a hydrogen-rich gel collided. Eight cubic meters of metal housing exploded inward on the fusion reactor. An instant later, super-heated plasma burst forth in a runaway reaction that filled the engine room with screams of agony before the reactor overloaded and turned into a miniature sun, consuming the ship and the three hundred remaining crew.

CHAPTER TWENTY-SIX

Wit DeBeck nursed a wicked headache with a bag of ice. He only wished there was a bag for his wounded pride. The big mercenary had dispatched him handily. A single blow sent him flying against the wall. Clearly his assailant had mods, but it still hurt his ego. Wit had been a spy for a long time, and too much of that was sitting behind a desk. He'd even let his regenerative treatments lapse, and truly felt his biological age at the moment.

The last man had died of shock before they could treat him. Five minutes later, a drop ship screamed through the valley, stopped at the opposite ridge, then vanished off to the south. Once they were sure the area was clear, Nadia and Daisy dragged the bodies out of the cabin and stashed them in a thicket a hundred meters downwind.

The cabin was a mess. Blood everywhere. Holes in the walls. It looked like a horror vid.

"How did they know about this place?" Daisy asked as she carefully washed the blood and grime off her hands in the kitchen sink.

Nadia glanced at him, wanting to know as well.

"Clearly, I hadn't hidden it as well as I thought."

"Daisy, can you check the admiral's aircar for trackers?" Nadia held out her NavPad; the girl took it without question and exited the cabin.

Nadia had surprised Wit with how willing she was to work with the spy, then again when she trusted Daisy to watch her back. Nadia had always shown a high level of intuition, an innate ability to judge character. From her own report, she had known something was wrong with Daisy before the agent revealed herself. She just hadn't acted soon enough.

"What is it?" he asked.

Nadia knelt next to him, pitching her voice low.

"Bradford is a Caliphate agent," she said.

The words registered. He just couldn't wrap his mind around them. It was one thing to find a spy among the population, but to imagine one among the highest seats of power? Bradford had a presidential campaign in the works for the next election. If he truly was a Caliphate agent and became president... the Alliance would be finished.

Wit shook his head.

"For that to be true, DNI would have to either know, or be so incompetent as to be unthinkable."

"He says and does the right things to have the media eating out of his hand. I bet anything he left the planet well ahead of the attack on the Capitol."

"A lot of congressional members return to their homeworld between sessions. It doesn't mean he knew." Wit wanted to refute her claims, because if they were true, then DNI wasn't the only people bad at their jobs. "All the Seabring politicians were off planet. It was dumb luck, not malice. You need more than that to prove your claim."

She grabbed a chair and massaged her neck, gazing off to the distance as her mind connected the dots.

"He's been the prime voice of dissent since he joined Congress. He's smooth, has all the media attention, and everyone seems to bend to his will." She looked out the door where Daisy had gone. "Just like her. I can't prove it right now, but if you let me off the leash, I will. I swear."

"How?" he asked. Wit didn't disagree with any of her logic, but it wasn't like he could open an official investigation on a sitting congressman. Even if he wanted to, ONI didn't have the authority. He was already so far off-book with his current mole hunt it was likely to cost him his career.

Nadia glanced at the door, making sure Daisy's task continued to occupy her. "Daisy," she said. "There's no way they can know she's out. Her contact in Zuckabar is long dead, and everyone involved in the actual mission—" Nadia's jaw went hard and Wit saw the pain in her eyes. "I'm the only person who knows. If Bradford is a deep-cover operative, and it makes sense they would send more than one, then she can find out for sure."

At that moment, Daisy walked back in and handed Nadia back her NavPad. "However they found him, it wasn't with a tracker. Does anyone else know of this place?"

Nadia slipped the device in her jacket pocket, then held her cybernetic arm out to the admiral to help him up.

"Yes," he said, not taking his eyes off Nadia as he stood. "It's in my government files, but you would need high-level clearance to access them."

"What kind of clearance?" Daisy asked.

"The congressional kind," Nadia told her.

"Do you think it's one of the men we tagged earlier?" she asked.

"One of?" Wit asked.

Nadia turned away, going back to the secret door and pushing it open.

"I put a device in St. John's office. I don't know him and you seem to trust him. He could be on their side as well."

Wit let out a low whistle. Was he really getting so old as to miss these things? Of course, Talmage could be a traitor. Anyone could. But those who positioned themselves close to him as invaluable allies? They required extra scrutiny. Instead of relying on his more official channels to make sure of their loyalty, he should have had Nadia do it.

But dammit, Talmage had done things a spy wouldn't normally do. Risking his position and status to help Wit and Noele for one. Which, he mused, is exactly the kind of risky maneuver a good spy might try. A plan formed in his mind. It risked much, but he needed to know who he could trust and who the mole was.

"Okay, here is what we're going to do..."

As he explained the plan, the astonishment was plain on their faces.

CHAPTER TWENTY-SEVEN

Jacob stifled a wince as Jennings and her Marines reported in. They were all injured in some way and obviously exhausted, but the Gunny and Private June looked like they had gone ten rounds with a spider-bear and lost.

"Once we were secure in the life boat, I ordered June to blow the ship," Jennings said, finishing her report.

Jacob looked over the written and visual reports as she spoke. ELS and space armor recorded everything the user said and did, making it easy to verify all statements. Not that he doubted the factuality of Jennings report, but she had certainly left out some details. For instance, she stated in her report that second contact with the enemy involved six combatants, two of whom she killed with her knife when it turned to close combat. Her dry statement left out the details of the life-and-death struggle—one he planned to make sure was rewarded. All of them deserved medals for what they had accomplished.

He would never again doubt the need for Marines to have several weapons. In fact, he made a note to authorize *Interceptor*'s Marine contingent to carry whatever weapons they deemed mission-necessary aboard ship.

"Chief Redfern and Ensign Kai are hard at work installing the new anvil," Jacob informed them. "You completed your mission and performed spectacularly. Well done. Dismissed."

The Marines came to attention as one, did a left face, and marched out of the briefing room.

Jacob ran through the vids at double speed one more time, making note of anything he might have missed the first time. While he was thrilled they weren't going to be stuck in the middle of nowhere until they ran out of power, the appearance of the light cruiser left him with several troubling and unanswered questions.

Why were they following DesRon Nine?

Were they alone?

And most of all, what was he to do?

Once engineering had the anvil installed and the conversion chamber repaired, they could move out. The question was, what next?

If he sent a signal to the squadron, it could be intercepted, and at their current range, it would take hours to reach them and he wouldn't have any guarantee it would. If the enemy intercepted the message, they would know where he was and could ambush him accordingly.

Boudreaux poked her head in, taking off her watch cap to run a hand through her curly hair. "Sir? You wanted to see me?"

"Come in XO. I need to break down our situation as I see it and I need your help to figure out what to do next."

Boudreaux slipped by the unused seats and sat down opposite him.

"I forgot to ask, and forgive me if it's improper, but were you and Lieutenant Bonds able to say a goodbye?"

"Yes sir," she replied with a wide smile. "Though he tried to cut it short. Wanted to impress his new captain with how on top of it his Marines were, but I convinced him otherwise. How about you and Commander Dagher?" she asked.

Jacob had a sudden flash of the last time he'd seen Nadia, her long hair blowing in the wind as she boarded her aircar for the spaceport. Watching her leave, his heart had felt like it would burst, not knowing when he would see her again, or even hear from her.

Had a month really gone by? Life in the Navy wasn't easy on relationships, even if just one person served. Heaven forbid, as in the case of Boudreaux and Bonds and himself and Nadia, they all served.

"It's been awhile since we've had time to spend together. Also, and keep this between us, her whole shtick as an officer was a cover ID. I think she's back to being a CPO."

Boudreaux let out a musical laugh.

"That figures. She certainly sold me."

"Me too. Now, let's focus on the problem at hand. DesRon Nine is five hours ahead of us. It's doubtful our light cruiser worked alone. Somewhere in this system or the next are two to four more light cruisers. More than a match for our squadron. We can message our sister ships and hope the signal doesn't get intercepted, or we can run silently to avoid detection until we're close enough to send a message in the clear. What do you think?" he asked.

"Why not"—she cocked her hand like a gun and pretend-fired toward the bow of the ship—"just run at flank speed to catch up?"

Jacob had asked himself that very question.

"If we knew for a fact the LC was alone and not part of a squadron, we could. After all, no one can match us for speed. However, we don't know they were alone and..." He gestured for her to put it together.

"And if they have escorts in-system, then they would know

we destroyed their ship and come right for us. We would end up leading them to DesRon Nine."

"At which point they would obliterate our squadron. We only won this fight because we had the universe's oldest weapon on our side."

Boudreaux's obvious confusion amused Jacob, and he couldn't keep the mirth from his face as she struggled to figure out what he meant?

"I'm not Christian, so I'm not sure what—"

"No, no, that's not what I meant. Surprise, Viv, we had surprise on our side."

"Oh, yes sir. Surprise. Which, if we go flank speed, we won't have in the next encounter."

"Which brings us back to our problem. Send a signal or run silent?" He wasn't testing her. Jacob had weighed the pros and cons of each decision and came up even. They both had advantages and risks. When he needed help coming to a decision, running things by his XO was exactly the thing to do.

"I say we run silent, sir. Make best speed, and when we're much closer, we can send a signal. Until then, we would just be sitting ducks," she said. "Or worse, lead them right to our squadron like you said."

"I think you're right. If we keep it to under two hundred gravities, we should be undetectable past ten million klicks. That's still a wide margin, but better than nothing. Okay, we've got our plan. I want you to execute it."

She jumped up into attention, "Aye aye, sir."

Chief Petty Officer Devi Suresh wore many hats aboard ship. As the coxswain, she was responsible for flying as well as training others on the ship's helm. As the highest ranking, longest serving non-commissioned officer aboard, the captain had seen fit to make her COB as well. Which gave her the additional duty of overseeing all the enlisted on the ship and acting as a go-between for them and the officers.

Since *Interceptor*'s size didn't permit many of her crew to be hyper-specialized, Devi also wore the Master-at-Arms hat when needed. Something she shared with Bosun Sandivol when possible.

In the case of the galley fire, engineering had collected the relevant details, Sandivol went through it and made sure it was accurate, and it was her job to figure out what happened and make any recommendations to the skipper as needed.

Stellar cartography's holographic facilities made the investigation a lot less time-consuming. Camera's in the mess and galley recorded everything, but she wouldn't normally even see the footage unless something was reported. Crews who are spied on by their superiors don't perform well when they know they're constantly being watched. A little eyeballing went a long way toward keeping them in line... no cameras needed.

Holo-cameras built into the bulkhead flared to life, building an exact replica of the mess one minute before the explosion.

She smiled as she saw Rugger make a move on June. Nothing too overt, but obvious to her. He seemed genuine and polite, not throwing his rank around. As long as he stayed that way, it would be fine if they saw more of each other. As long as they weren't in the same immediate chain of command, it wouldn't ruffle many feathers. Though, there were always the traditionalist who didn't want any relations between the sexes aboard ship. She almost spit out her coffee at that thought. You didn't put men and women together aboard ship, in the prime of their life, experiencing life-and-death situations, and then say "no sleeping with each other." The best they could do was keep the personal and professional separate.

Keeping the camera on them, she turned to the galley as Ensign Lopez walked through the hatch. His face wore a frown and he generally seemed unhappy as he barked at Josh Mendez for coffee. Devi turned the volume up.

"Where's the cream and sugar, PO?" Lopez said.

Devi grimaced. No true spacer took cream and sugar in their coffee.

Josh pulled mugs down in rapid succession, lining them up for the Ensign to deliver.

"I've got the sugar, sir. Cream is in the main fridge, to your right," Josh said over his shoulder.

Lopez opened the bulkhead-sized metal hatch that enclosed the refrigerator and stepped in to find what he was looking for.

She froze it as the timer counted down to the millisecond when the explosion occurred. She had wondered why the ensign hadn't succumbed to the blast wave like the others had —the walk-in cooler protected him.

With both videos lined up, she started them at half speed. As June and Rugger recovered from the initial explosion, the galley cameras were clear. Mendez, Perch, and the other spacers were on the floor. For half a second there was no fire, then flames erupted from everywhere as the flammable materials caught in the oxygen-rich environment.

Lopez stumbled out of the fridge, one hand over his face. He took a step toward the hatch, but as he did, he saw something and changed course deeper into the galley.

There was simply too much smoke and fire for her to make out exactly what happened next. She saw Rugger go in and then out with Mendez. "Wait a second," she muttered to herself. Rewinding, she went back to just after the explosion. Mendez was on the floor and Rugger could have certainly picked him up, but there were other downed crew between them, not counting Lopez. He would have had to go all the way to the back of the galley, six meters in fire and smoke, to find Josh and bring him out.

Then she watched as Travis dragged Perch out. Rugger rescued the spacers in the reverse order of their distance to the galley hatch.

Closing down the image from the mess, she expanded the galley until it filled a three cubic meter area. Rewinding the footage, she went back to the moment before the explosion happened. Lopez was in the fridge, and Mendez was definitely at the far end, away from the hatch. Running the view at one-quarter speed, she watched for even the tiniest clear moment where she could see what had really happened.

For several hours, Chief Suresh watched over and over as Midship Travis Rugger pulled the spacers out of the fire, saving their lives. Each time he cleared the galley hatch, Private June would take over and drag the wounded out into the passageway. The entire event lasted less than two minutes from the explosion until the mist sprayers activated.

When she got to the point her eyes ached from watching, she decided there wasn't anything more to learn. She knew what happened, or at least had excellent evidence to make the case. She just hoped that everyone involved would accept her finding.

CHAPTER TWENTY-EIGHT

Jacob wanted to convey the seriousness of what he was about to do, which meant wearing his high-collared, service dress whites, complete with red combination cap sitting on the conference table in front of him. These occasions were the only time he wished he had his own office with a desk. Though he felt the shark on the table brought a sense of esprit de corps to the meeting.

"Bring them in," he said.

Chief Suresh and Bosun Sandivol marched Ensign Brown, Midship Rugger, and Private June into a line on the opposite side of the shark-emblem-painted table.

"Detail reporting as ordered, sir," Suresh said.

"Stand at ease," Jacob ordered.

"Detail," she said as sharp as a knife, "stand easy."

The three crew members dropped to at-ease. Technically, they should be at parade rest, but he didn't want them freaking out and thinking they were in trouble. How much trouble could they be in if he had them at ease?

"Ensign Austin Brown, Midship Travis Rugger, and Private Yanaha June, I brought you before me today to announce the official finding of the galley fire. Ensign Brown, though you were not there, I thought you would like to represent your friend in this ceremony."

"Thank you... Uh...ceremony, sir?" Brown asked.

Jacob heaved himself up and came around to stand in front of the three.

"Ceremony. You see, Austin, we were all wrong about Ensign Lopez and Midship Rugger. Chief?"

Suresh snapped to attention. "It is the official finding that Ensign Mateo Lopez, as an officer and as a member of *Interceptor*'s crew, conducted himself in accordance with the finest traditions of the Navy. Ensign Lopez gave his life rescuing the spacers trapped in the galley during the incident. After several rescues, he succumbed to both his wounds and the smoke, and died a meter before reaching safety."

"Sir?" Midship Rugger asked when she was done. "I never saw him, sir. Not once. I would have gotten him out if I had. I swear."

"I know, Travis. When you were in the galley, did you pick the spacers up off the floor, or were they already making their way out?"

"As I stated in my report, sir, the crew members were walking under their own power... oh no." Rugger's sudden realization hit him like a slap in the face. Jacob's heart ached, knowing there was one more man in there, one more just a meter from safety.

"It's not your fault, Travis. Mateo did what I would hope any member of my crew, or the Navy for that matter, would do. Despite any differences you had, he did his duty and saved lives. Just like you."

Jacob pointed to the XO as he stepped back.

"COB?" Boudreaux asked.

"Detail, atten-shun!" Suresh barked.

The three snapped to. Jacob could tell they were still processing the dreadful news.

Lieutenant Boudreaux marched to a stop before Ensign Brown and held out a small black box and flipped the lid open. Inside, a gold medal with the Navy's logo emblazoned on the surface rested on top a black velvet interior. A blue, gold, and red ribbon held the medal in place.

"Ensign Brown, on behalf of the United Systems Alliance, I appoint you the solemn and holy duty of delivering this Navy Medal for non-combat heroism at great risk to Ensign Mateo Lopez's family. To report to them how he saved lives at the cost of his own. How he upheld the highest standards of duty, honor, and courage. Do you accept?" she asked.

"Aye aye, ma'am," he said.

Boudreaux handed him the box. Took a single step back and snapped a salute which the ensign promptly returned.

"Your turn, sir," she said as she moved to stand next to Jacob.

Jacob stood before Rugger in the way Boudreaux had just done. "Midship Rugger..."

The rest of the ceremony only took a few more minutes. When it was over, both Ensign Lopez and Midship Rugger were awarded the Navy Medal, and Private June the Marine Corps medal for heroism not related to enemy action or combat. Technically, they would have to be approved by the Department of the Navy, but he was confident they would back his decision. He may have overstepped his authority a smidge, but ship's morale was at stake, and with them so far from home, it could take months to get official approval.

After they were dismissed, Jacob slumped against the conference table, one hand resting on the shark-nose emblem. He hated losing people, no matter the reasons or the acts of valor they may have performed. The golden medal would be a poor comfort to Lopez's family in the long, cold nights. He hoped, though... No, he prayed... that those he saved would take it upon themselves to make sure Mateo's family was cared for.

It was the right thing to do, and in his mind, that meant the only thing.

Ensign Kai looked down at the open conversion chamber. It was tight, and only Chief Redfern's nimble hands fit inside the little box.

"I thought it would look more hi-tech," Kai said.

"You would think, sir." Redfern nodded his head toward the fusion reactor. "We have panels wide-open on the reactor, cables running on the floor, and optical wiring attached to the overhead with zero-g tape. *Interceptor* is held together with spit and baling wire."

Kai moved the bright light to the side to better illuminate the detailed work Redfern attempted. "It's larger than I thought."

"That's what she said."

Kai did a double take, dropping his head and putting a hand over his face. "Okay, Chief, ha-ha. Let's focus on the work." He couldn't help but blush as Redfern grinned merrily.

"Aye sir. I couldn't resist. We're just about done."

With few exceptions, the technology for fusion reactors was virtually the same throughout the known systems. Slush deuterium provided a reliable, and more importantly, stable form to convert to metallic hydrogen, which the reactor actually used. However, the DAC the Caliphate used measured ten cubic centimeters larger than the Alliance version, forcing them to jury-rig a system to hold the anvil in place.

"Ready for the molecular binder?" Kai asked.

"Yes sir, right where I pointed out earlier."

"You think it's going to hold?" Kai placed the tip of the applicator on the contact points and squeezed out the binding agent that used nanites to alter the molecular structure to create an unbreakable bond.

"It should, but let's pray we don't get into serious combat," Chief Redfern said.

CHAPTER TWENTY-NINE

OCELOT SYSTEM, DESRON NINE, USS *FIREWATCH*

Sipping his coconut milk and lassi in his ready room, Captain Ganesh Hatwal mulled over the reports provided by the three destroyers flanking *Firewatch*. Since they had exited Praetor, the unknown contact had consistently and steadily followed them... right up until *Interceptor* dropped back to repair the fire damage. He hated to admit it, but *Interceptor*'s sensors were far more efficient than the rest of the squadron. He told himself that was why he'd placed the ship in the stern. How did a forty-five-year-old ship have better passive detection ability than his brand new one?

In truth though, Commander Grimm upset him. His mere presence threatened to tarnish Ganesh's first command. He glanced at the little mirror he kept on his desk, adjusting the tiniest imperfection on his uniform. He'd spent years working toward this goal. Allowing an outside force beyond his control to ruin it proved too much for him.

But...

Had he let his pride get in the way of doing his job? Maybe

his concerns, regardless of ultimate motivations, *were* reasonable. Jacob Grimm's reputation appeared to be one of reckless abandon, not to mention his obvious political ties. No spacer in the Navy went from senior grade lieutenant to full commander in under three years unless strings were pulled. Admittedly, Grimm had stayed a little longer as a junior grade, but that didn't make up for the huge leap.

Everything he'd heard about the man put him off. Yet, Grimm acted respectful in his manner and reserved in his opinion. And by all accounts, his crew worshiped him. There were two presentations of the commander: the one in his jacket, and the one Ganesh met. One of them lied. He desperately wanted to believe the deceit came from Commander Grimm, but the more he investigated the situation, the more he knew it wasn't true.

Ganesh commanded a squadron on the verge of a war. There were few more prestigious positions he could want. His ship outgunned and out-massed *Interceptor* four to one, yet that Hellcat destroyer and her captain made Ganesh feel small and shallow.

"Bridge, have Commander Ban join me, please."

"Aye aye, sir," Midship Brennan replied.

Ganesh waved his hand over the visual display of his NavPad, turning the page on Grimm's career. An enormous amount of the man's career from the last three years consisted of dates, commands, and blacked out lines. Either he was one of the most decorated *secret squirrels* to ever wear the uniform, or he was such an embarrassment the brass blacked out his history in an effort to hide their shame.

Then, of course, there were the medals. A Navy Cross, a Silver Star, and the two foreign awards that weren't even in his computer. He had to rely on what he could dig up about them from public sources. The Consortium medal was for meritorious service by outside military personnel. As far as he could find, no one else in the Alliance had earned one in two hundred years.

The other medal seemed to be from the Iron Empire, but that was ridiculous. If not for the fact that Jacob's Marines were all decorated as such, Ganesh would have thought Grimm picked it out of a brochure. The idea of an officer wearing fake medals registered as more plausible to him than the Iron Empire awarding an Alliance Navy captain one.

His hatch beeped and Ganesh waved for it to open.

"You wanted to see me, sir?" Archer Ban asked.

"Yes, come in and sit, Archer."

Archer did just that, sitting stiff and proper. Which somehow annoyed Ganesh even more. Mostly because it highlighted his own bad behavior. Archer's report on Grimm's crew and the way they revered their captain came out of a desire to show the commander's quality, and Ganesh had turned it into an avenue of attack.

Ganesh looked down at his file while his XO remained perfectly still. As a man, Ganesh needed to face this head-on. He looked Archer dead in the eyes before speaking.

"Am I wrong about Grimm?" he asked. Perhaps he wanted to rip the bandage off. Just have his XO tell it to him straight.

Archer's shoulders twitched, and the officer seemed to deflate ever so slightly. "Sir, are you asking, or are you *asking*?"

Ganesh thought about it, and decided he really did want to know his second officer's opinion. "You have permission to speak freely, Archer."

"Thank you." Archer sucked in a breath and proceeded to speak before Ganesh could change his mind. "If you pardon my language, sir, you've been a horse's ass about the whole thing."

Shock froze Ganesh in place. A good ten seconds passed before he could even blink. He reminded himself he'd given the commander permission to speak freely. He just hadn't expected that much freedom.

"You care to explain yourself, *Commander*?"

"Sir, yes I do. What exactly do you think Jacob Grimm did that was wrong? Refuse to resign? Would you? I know I wouldn't have. He was put in a terrible situation, everyone—me included—turned their backs on him, and he didn't have the dignity to resign and save the Navy a black eye? I call BS, sir. That man has given more to this Navy, more to earn the respect of his peers, than any man alive. And what did you do? You've berated, disrespected, and ignored him... sir. If you want to know what I think, that is."

"Don't hold back, Archer. Tell me how you really feel," Hatwal said with a level of mirth that surprised even him.

Archer visibly relaxed, and Ganesh respected what the man just risked, standing up for his friend. Another CO would hold it against him, regardless of the order to speak freely.

"I get it, sir. From the outside he's a screwup, or worse, some politicians pet. Neither of those would square with the cadet I served with. He got up early and went to bed late. No time off, no leave. He read the manuals, the history books, and then some. If not for him, I would never have passed Astro-navigation. I just don't see how the media's depiction of him, the Navy's grapevine, or his duty history line up with the reality. No. The only answer is that Commander Jacob T. Grimm is one of the finest naval officers of our time, sir. Anything else you've heard, or anyone has heard, is either a lie or sensationalized."

Ganesh pushed back from the table, giving Archer's comments the consideration they deserved. Speaking to a superior the way he did could seriously dampen his career, yet here he was, telling Ganesh the opposite of what he wanted to hear. He wanted to know that he was right, that

Grimm was a screw-up with some unknown patron protecting him.

It just wasn't so, though. Looking at the matter with the cold logic Archer had splashed on him, Grimm's official history in the naval jacket made no sense. No patron, no matter how powerful, could maneuver a Navy Cross. Considering the numerous decorations for valor and duty, did all his crew have the same patron then? Even the ship had an award.

"Damn," Ganesh said, in full violation of the regulations against swearing. "Help me out, Archer, what do we—what do I—do about it?"

"When he rejoins DesRon Nine, officially make him the squadron XO as you should have. I've already spoken to Novak"—Ganesh flinched from the knowledge that his people plotted behind his back—" and she understands. It's the right thing to do, sir. It will also garner you the respect and admiration of the enlisted who already know who and what Commander Grimm is."

Of all the things Archer had said to him, that one surprised him the most. "Explain?"

"Sir, I know you mean well. But *Interceptor* has a reputation among the NCOs that officers only dream of. People want to serve on her. Did you know that Commander Grimm, at great risk to himself, personally pulled a wounded Marine behind cover? Or that he saved the governor's wife on Kremlin by taking a maser blast to the back? I had to dig around for this info. My guess is it's in the blacked-out part of his jacket. I had to part with a case of good bourbon back on Kremlin for this information. The NCOs protect him and didn't want me using this against him. When a crew knows their captain will risk his own life to save them, they will risk anything for him, sir."

Ganesh glanced down at the official file on Grimm, waving his hand over it, rapidly looking for any indication of what

Archer revealed to him. It wasn't there, yet he knew his XO wouldn't lie to him. That realization left a sinking hole in the pit of his stomach.

"I have been a horse's ass, haven't I?"

Archer grinned ruefully in agreement. "Don't worry, sir, we all have been at one point or another."

Ganesh looked deep inward, took a long breath, and let it out slowly. Along with the air, he let out the pride, anger, and resentment he'd steadily entrenched himself in since taking command.

That was that. As soon as *Interceptor* rejoined DesRon Nine, and before they entered the next starlane, he would make Commander Grimm his XO of record. Then he would need to go about building a real squadron. Perhaps even invite his new XO over for dinner to propose some ideas.

CHAPTER THIRTY

"Let me go over the plan once more time," Daisy said, trying to reassure herself that it would work. "You want me to approach the Speaker of the House, the de facto third-in-command of the System's Alliance, and tell him I'm a Caliphate spy?"

Nadia leaned back in her chair and plopped her boots on the table, an annoying, braggadocios grin plastered on her face. "Yes."

"Oh." Daisy leaned against the door jamb of the small apartment overlooking the Capitol Building. Their idea bordered on insanity in her mind. Even if he was a Caliphate agent, she had already told them she wouldn't betray her people. She had no special codes to contact him, no secret handshake.

"I know what you're thinking." Nadia said. "You are wondering how, right?"

"There is no way to do it. Even if I wanted to help you, I simply don't have a way to do it," she said.

"Here's where it's really cool. We're going to fake an attack on him at home, pretend to be Caliphate agents bringing him in to end his mission. We'll tag and bag him. Bring him to the safe house and fool him into thinking we're Caliphate. At that point, he'll tell us what we want to know."

Daisy shook her head. "You're insane. He'll never fall for the ruse. For one, we're women. He's going to know something's wrong when we don't have a male agent with us. My deep cover status wasn't ever intended to be revealed until such time as I had political power. He will be the same. He won't break cover for two women."

"You're right, of course. Which is why I'm bringing in a ringer. A man who owes me some favors."

As if she had planned it that way, a knock from the door next to Daisy made her jump. She moved across the room, putting the counter between her and the door.

"What is this?"

Nadia leaped up and let in a dark-haired, dark-skinned man of about forty. She took his hand and they shook enthusiastically.

"Ms. Dagher, it's a pleasure to see you again."

"Rashid al-Alami, meet Daisy. My partner on this op."

Rashid bowed to her.

"An honor to meet you." He turned to Nadia. "Now, how may I repay you for your sacrifice?"

Something had obviously happened to Nadia since Daisy had last seen her. How had a man with the accent of the Caliphate Capitol come into her debt?

"I need to trick someone into thinking we're ISB, or at the very least, Caliphate agents. The time you spent on the outside of your law could be invaluable—"

"And I am a man, and you will need that if you're to be believed." His tone robbed the words of any offense. "My answer is, of course, yes." He bowed again. "Is this something we can do over the weekend, or will I need to take time off from the Bureau of Linguistics?"

Daisy couldn't believe her ears. Rashid came from the homeworld. How could he so easily agree to help the Alliance? "Why would you do this?" Daisy asked. "I don't know who you are, but I know your accent. Why?"

Rashid examined Daisy the way a father might look at his daughter. "Because, miss, when the Caliphate navy betrayed me, executed my parents, and sold my little sister into slavery, they also showed me they are honorless dogs. Nothing would make me happier than to bring them down."

"Are we all on the same page?" Nadia asked. "Daisy? Rashid?"

His reply was immediate. Daisy's took longer.

On top of a five-story apartment building a dozen klicks from the Capitol, Lieutenant Bonds knelt next to the dark-haired agent, a long-barreled X-34 sniper rifle cradled in one arm. He liked the look of the neighborhood, suburbs butting up against the city in a mix of commercial properties and private homes. Not the kind of homes a Marine could afford; they were all top-notch, made from stone and wood, with picket fences and massive yards. And thankfully, far enough away to have escaped the devastating nuclear attack.

"Is this why you needed me and Clarabelle here?" Bonds asked in his deep baritone, gesturing to his rifle.

"According to Jacob, you're trustworthy and willing to step a tiny toe outside the line for the good of the service."

"As long as the *good of the service* is done by Oh-dark-thirty. *Enterprise*'s new Admiral is fired up to be underway, like if we don't leave now we might never. My company is shipping out in the morning and I don't want to be out all night or rotting in jail for murder."

"No murder," she assured him. "I just need two tangos taken out at exactly the right time. Which calls for precision shooting of the Marine variety." She fished out a magazine with yellow tape wrapped around the base and handed it to him.

Bond grumbled. He wasn't sure about "India" as he knew her. But the skipper (and for him, only Jacob was afforded that grand title) vouched for her in a manner of speaking.

"Okay, lady, but if this all goes south, I'm pleading ignorance." He checked the rounds inside, two of them, before slamming it home. "They look normal."

She grinned at him, her black-out suit shimmering around her face, making only her lips, nose, and eyes visible. "They're supposed to. If it goes sideways, I'll be dead. Now, when you see the door open, shoot the women, then the man. After that, bug out."

"You sure you don't want me to cover your exfil?" he asked.

She shook her head, pulling the suit all the way over her face and vanishing in front of him. Her muffled voice came from the air for all he could tell.

"If we need you after that, it won't matter. Thank you, Bonds, I appreciate it."

"Semper Fi, ma'am," he said, though he couldn't be sure she was there any longer.

Because of his size, and how uncomfortable the rooftop looked, Bonds found a nice corner to lean against to fire from the seated position for both comfort and stability. The sun vanished below the horizon, casting the world in deep shadows. He adjusted his scope for night vision, making his target appear as a bright spot.

Shooting was both an art and science. The computerized scope handled the science, leaving the art to Bonds. Lifting the rifle up, he braced the buttstock against his shoulder, then lowered his whole body into a crouch, where his elbows fit snugly in the soft flesh of his inner thighs. The long-range tactical scope lit up the night, telling him exactly where to aim.

Eight hundred meters stretched out from him to the target's front door. No easy shot in the best of situations, and this wasn't one of those. The advanced scope showed him firing at a thirty-degree angle above his target. He moved the center of fire down a tick. Once he knew exactly where to shoot, he opened his left eye and slowly let the area around him phase in.

"Gabriel in position and ready," he said over the comms. He thought the callsign fitting, being the avenging angel and all.

Bradford's home sat at the end of a long row of houses. His protective detail handled his life at the office, but he used private security for his home. A decision he was most likely going to regret. With the admiral's help, Nadia had his detail delayed. The last shift left ten minutes before normal, and the next shift would arrive ten minutes late, giving her and her team a twenty-minute window to get him and get out. More than enough time. The only complication would be the precise shooting, but she had no doubt Bonds could handle it.

She met up with Daisy, who wore a similar suit and, as cliché as it was, hid in the bushes next to the house.

"What if he varies his routine?" Daisy asked her once she settled.

"It's highly unlikely. We've watched him long enough. If he was going to change it up, he would have by now." The streets of the suburbs were a mix of ground traffic and aircars. For logistics, especially deliveries, ground vehicles just made more sense. They ran on the city's electric grid or their own fusion batteries and could carry a lot more weight than an aircar.

Right on time, lights flashed over the house as the speaker's aircar flew down the street to hover in the landing way before setting down with a soft thump.

The door opened and Speaker Bradford stepped out wearing an impeccable suit, as if he had walked off the set of a movie. Nadia knew he was supposed to make her swoon, or put her at ease, and the knowledge made her blood boil.

"Get ready," she whispered. Daisy moved right while Nadia circled left behind the aircar. The plan was simple. The moment he opened his door, Bonds would shoot his wife, then him.

Bradford opened his door, and just like every other day that week, his wife waited to greet him.

The air cracked from the supersonic bullet as it zipped by, striking the woman in the chest and flinging her backward. The Speaker was too stunned to move, and the next bullet smashed into his back, sending him sprawling toward his wife.

Nadia and Daisy rushed in before the bodies hit the ground. Daisy had the aircar open and went to work reprogramming the computer for an automatic flight across the continent so anyone looking for him would start there.

While Daisy did that, Nadia grabbed Bradford's feet and, with a grunt, dragged him past Daisy to the curb just as Rashid arrived with a ground cargo hauler. Rashid leaped out, took over the job and flung Bradford up and through the sliding door into the interior.

As Nadia dragged Bradford's wife down the walk, Daisy finished and the aircar shot off into the atmosphere, vanishing over the horizon. Once both packages were in, Nadia climbed aboard, snatched the adhesive tape, and went to work securing them.

"Daisy, jammers. They're both bound to be low-jacked," Nadia spoke in her mother's tongue.

"On it," Daisy said from the passenger seat, also in Caliph. Electronic countermeasures built into the van sprang to life, hiding their activity from prying eyes.

They were perfectly aware the bullet that hit both Mister and Mrs. Bradford had different doses of sedative. Specially designed to disintegrate on impact, the bullets felt and sounded real, but they delivered a neurotoxin that was absorbed through the skin, rendering the target instantly unconscious. Unless, of course, the assailant wanted one of the targets to be semi-lucid and hear the language spoken.

CHAPTER THIRTY-ONE

NAJI SYSTEM: STARLANE TO OCELOT

Vanguard was overdue. Captain Yousef Ali's gut told him something was wrong, even though logic told him the ship probably had a communications issue. Or better, had found a worthy target for them to hunt and was just waiting for the right time to break free and make their rendezvous.

"Comms, any word?" he asked, knowing it was superfluous, but his anxiety gnawed at him.

"No, my captain, no word."

"Astro, anything?"

"Negative, sir. Screens are clear."

If *Vanguard* was going to show, then he would need to meet them in the next system over. On his charts it was but a series of numbers, but the Consortium maps called it *Ocelot*. A foolish name from a foolish people. It was the last system before Taki, before recognized Consortium space. The idea had been for *Vanguard* to patrol it for traffic and, if any targets were found, to return to the formation where they would pursue and destroy said targets.

If they ran into anything big, which was doubtful, they could claim the neutrality of Ocelot. All the while completing the order given to him and clearing a path for the fleet to follow.

"Prepare for starlane entrance then. Leave a buoy in case we starcross with *Vanguard*." In some rare occurrences to ships would cross a starlane going in opposite directions. The buoy would provide *Vanguard* with the necessary instructions if that happened.

"Yes sir, programming buoy… buoy away."

"Excellent. Proceed to starlane."

Admiral Rahal circled the luxurious bridge deck of *Glorious Crusade* as they approached the Naji System starlane. By now, he noted, his forward element would have cleared Naji of any surprises and moved on to Ocelot. Starlane transits were the most nerve-wracking of any operation. All the ships had to come to a complete halt leaving them sitting ducks. The screening units would advance and if the way was clear, a scout would be sent back.

He hated thinking he could be a sitting duck on both sides of the lane, but the scout had just arrived, letting him know Naji was devoid of any observable hostile ships.

Then again, if there was a force out here large enough to take on his fleet of battleships with eight heavy cruisers, six light cruisers, and four destroyers, they deserved to win. He frowned, a shimmer of worry crossing his mind before his confidence eradicated it. He only had two light cruisers with him—the other four were deployed ahead to clear the way. Still, four light cruisers, in an order of battle with as much tonnage as he had, wouldn't make or break a victory.

Maybe he should have sent the destroyers, but he wanted to make sure his screening units could handle whatever came their way. It was just... he looked at the tactical plot, tracing the outlines of overlapping fields of fire. The missing light cruisers left entire chunks of his stern practically unguarded. His enemy would be ahead of him, though, about to be taken by complete surprise. A death knell sending them straight to Jahannam hellfire. They wouldn't have time to out maneuver him, they would be dead.

He checked his intelligence again. The ISB showed just three Consortium heavies. While their ships were technological marvels, giving them an advantage, they simply couldn't stand up to the volume of fire he was about to bring to bear.

As long as they remained hidden and no one knew about their course, they couldn't be stopped. It was Allah's will... and good planning.

CHAPTER THIRTY-TWO

Petty Officer Josh Mendez knelt in the reconstructed galley, hand on the spot where they had found Ensign Lopez's body. He hadn't felt the explosion. One second he was pouring coffee for the bridge, the next he woke up in sickbay with no idea how he had gotten there or what happened, until PO Desper told him. The galley itself looked brand new. The only trace anything had ever been wrong was the fresh patch where the explosion had rent the bulkhead.

The next time, he told himself, the next time he would supervise the refit of the galley himself. Even if it meant he didn't go on leave and see his parents. Guilt gnawed at him about how he'd reported the ensign's behavior. The man was still wrong in his treatment of the midships and Private June, but in the end, he acted with courage and honor. Josh wasn't going to waste that sacrifice.

He pulled out his NavPad, logged into his private account, and changed his life insurance policy on the spot. Twenty percent of it would go to Lopez's mother if anything happened to Josh. Once they were back home on New Austin, he would make sure to visit them as often as he could, and provide whatever resources they needed if it was in his ability. Josh's mama and abuela had a baby boy thanks to Mateo Lopez. If it was the last thing he did, he would pay it back with interest.

"PO, you have a second?" Midship Rugger asked from behind.

"Yes sir," he said, dragging the back of his arm across his eyes. "Just thinking about what to make for dinner."

"I didn't like him much," Rugger said suddenly, voice barely above a whisper.

The sudden confession tickled Josh's curiosity. Why tell him? "He did seem kind of a jerk."

Rugger's soft smile was both mirthful and sad.

"He saved all of you, you know?" he asked.

"Desper told me. I don't remember anything, not really. Just a lot of pain, then waking up next to you in the tank."

"I won't forget him," Rugger said. "Not ever."

"I'm going to give his family money whenever I can, or whatever they might need. It's the least I can do."

They stood together, their own private moment of silence, neither one in a hurry to leave. It was only broken when spacers started lining up to eat.

———

Jennings wrinkled her nose as she and her Marines entered the mess, where an acrid smell like rotten eggs brushed at the edge of their senses and fought a losing battle against Josh Mendez's culinary skill.

With the situation with Lopez resolved, albeit in a grizzly manner, Gunny Jennings authorized her Marines to eat in the mess again. However, they would dine together or not at all.

Afternoon watch was an hour in, and lunch had settled down. Eight spacers occupied the mess, and that suited

Jennings just fine. She wasn't there for conversation, just chow. She was also still in a fair amount of pain from her ordeal. Nothing was permanently damaged, but the plasma burns itched as the nanites painstakingly repaired her tissue. Thankfully, they were covered in pressure bandages.

Though both of them were considered unfit for duty, Private June got the worst by far. Her arm was held firm in a sling covered by a pressure seal for protection during the healing process.

They were supposed to be taking computer courses and reading books during duty hours. Private June most certainly did those things, but Gunny Jennings wasn't one to sit around for any reason, not even pain. Not even if it was worse than the time she stood in front of the maser to protect Lieutenant Yuki. Or the time she got shot through the stomach with a coil gun. This time, she felt like meat tenderized with a tank.

"Gunnery Sergeant?" Ensign Brown said from behind her.

Jennings' spoon froze perfectly still halfway to her mouth, not a drop of Mendez's stew wasted. All she wanted to do was eat, not get in another sparring match with Brown, physical or verbal. Why couldn't the rest of her people just stay on McGregor's World and leave her alone?

"How may I help you, sir?" she asked as politely and respectfully as she could.

Naki and Owens froze as if they sensed something wrong.

"May I speak with you in private?" he asked.

Jennings weighed her response and chose the one that would make it clear to him what she thought. "I can't spar right now, but if you want to wait a few days, I can continue your hand-to-hand lessons."

Naki pressed a hand over his mouth to choke back a laugh. Bits of stew leaked between his fingers. Owens turned to cough.

"No, Gunny, I would like to explain myself. If that's okay

with you," Brown said. He glanced at the three Marines who sat at the table with her. He clearly knew they were aware of what she had done.

Jennings wasn't much on recriminations. She slightly regretted telling her squad how she downed Ensign Brown without breaking a sweat. She had meant it as an educational moment, about how skill and training can defeat a larger opponent, but maybe part of her intended it as a brag.

"Rec room, ten minutes. I want to finish my chow, sir," she said without looking up at him.

"See you there," he said.

The table stayed silent until he was out of the mess.

Naki spoke first. "Damn Gunny, you don't play."

"Apply nanites for burn," Owens said with a grin as he and Naki bumped fists.

June didn't respond to the playful teasing; she just continued eating, not really engaging with the table. The life of a Marine was one of skill, discipline, and training, broken up by seconds of sheer terror and death-defying action. Only after such moments came the time to process, and June had two such events on her first deployment. It would be a lot for anyone.

Jennings' first op out of infantry training was like that. A bunch of smugglers had taken hostages on a mining planet not unlike her homeworld. They were frontier types, trying to make a living. Her squad happened to be in the vicinity and had moved in to assist. She'd thought it went well, thought they saved the day, until she realized they hadn't. It wasn't her fault, but she could have been better, faster, more skilled. After that, she decided if she truly wanted to be the best, then her life needed a singular focus on all things Marine. She didn't have family she wanted to visit, nor desire for relationships, and while she did enjoy drinking and dancing, she only allowed herself that time in small doses. The rest of her time she spent training. Spent fighting.

Jennings put the spoon down, her appetite vanishing along with Ensign Brown.

"Finish your grub, then back to work," she said. "I want all our equipment checked and ready by 1900. Copy?"

"Copy that, Gunny," Naki said.

"June, finish the book about small unit tactics I gave you and start on the captain's list." Many captains would put out lists of literature to read. Most of it, Jennings thought useless. However, the captain had a sharp mind for strategy and tactics.

"Aye, Gunny," Private June said.

She got to the first ladder and suppressed a groan as she slid down to the next deck, landing with a thump and almost crumpling on the spot. Why had she told him the rec room? Mess was on deck two and rec on six. She had to navigate three different ladders and walk half the length of the ship. She just should have told him to wait out in the passageway. The lift beckoned her, and no one would question her need to use it, but she would die before entering one while conscious.

By the time she reached the keel, her body ached and she fought each step to avoid trembling. If he wanted a fight, she was in no position to defend herself. Not that it occurred to her to notify the COB or anyone else. She was a Marine. She solved her own problems.

This time of the "day" aboard ship, the rec room stood almost empty. Spacers Perch and Zach occupied the sofa, perusing the ship's stores of physical graphic novels. A stack of unread books was next to them, and they argued amongst themselves about which one was better this week. Entertainment aboard ship was at a premium. Arguing amongst themselves about the superior medium made them almost as happy as consuming the videos and books the library had.

On the opposite bulkhead, Brown stood next to the digital "porthole" that showed a view of space just above the gravcoil.

"Perch. Zach." They both looked up when she said their names, and she nodded at the door.

"Roger," Perch said. He thumped Zach, who didn't seem to get the message, on the shoulder. Perch hopped up, grabbing the floppies and placing them back in the secure shelf as he headed out, followed by Zach a second later. The hatch hummed shut behind them.

Jennings let the silence stretch on, perfectly happy to wait. She hobbled over to the beverage dispenser and ordered coffee. When the beverage emerged, she cradled the hot cup and sipped the bitter drink. She leaned against the bulkhead, giving her worn out body a chance to rest.

The stars outside didn't move, but the eerie distortion from the prow of the gravcoil caused a warping and shimmering effect she found mesmerizing.

"You don't know who I am, do you?" Brown asked.

Of all the things she thought he would talk about, that wasn't on the list. She wracked her brain for his name or face, but nothing came to mind. He was younger than her, but not much. They hadn't served together before. She was sure of that.

"Should I?" she asked, perhaps a bit sharper than she intended.

"Yes," he said. With his hands clasped tight behind his back, he turned around. "We were engaged to be married."

"What?" she asked. She put the coffee down before she spilled it. Jennings had known from a young age that she would not remain on her homeworld. At fourteen, the offers started coming in, but she rebuffed them all. Her lineage made her a target and so she won the game by not playing. She hadn't even dated. A giggle escaped her at the thought of Brown expecting to marry *her*.

"My grand father loaned your parents the money to start their shuttle business." Brown said. "The agreement included your hand in marriage." His face flushed, and Jennings thought maybe he realized how ridiculous he sounded hearing his words out loud. "The day we were supposed to come and formally complete the arrangement, your parents told us you had joined the Marines. I realize now that you never intended to go through with the deal."

She did recall some fuss about the way her parents had gotten the loan to buy their first cargo vehicle.

"Never intended? Brown, I never *knew*. If I had, I wouldn't have agreed to it. I'm sorry my parents swindled your grandfather, but that has nothing to do with me."

The venom in her voice surprised even her. Brown took an involuntary step back. Jennings wanted to control her temper, to let the heat and anger seep out of her like silt through a grate, but she couldn't quite manage the inferno and continued, "You've been holding on to that for a decade? Ensign, I don't mean to be disrespectful— check that, I do. *Over my dead body*. I left McGregor's World to get away from people like you. I hate that place, *hate it*. I hate who everyone expected me to be. I hated how my life had one outcome. I hated all of it. I'm never going back and I'm certainly not going to marry you for some *illegal* deal made when I was a child."

Jennings debated her next words. She'd already said more in the last five minutes than the last five days. No, it was enough. She spun on her boot heel and headed for the hatch, her anger temporarily washing away her aches.

"Wait," he pleaded.

She turned around, managing to regain some control.

"What?" Her question had a bite reserved for idiotic privates who didn't know what end the MP-17 fired from.

"I'm sorry. I now realize that... I was stupid. I joined the

Navy for much the same reason you joined the Marines. To get away. When I saw you it just, well, it's hard for us—hard for me—to shake how I was raised. I'll do better."

That she understood. His acknowledgement allowed her to let her anger fall away, leaving her back in control.

"Good." As she turned to leave, a thought occurred to her. "Seriously, though, your hand-to-hand sucks. You're making us look bad. Join me three times a week and we'll sort it out."

It was the closest she could come to accepting his apology.

CHAPTER THIRTY-THREE

Lieutenant Boudreaux bounced up from engineering, checking off the latest task on her list while she made her way to the mess. Chief Redfern and his crew had done an outstanding job of rebuilding the galley in the short time they had, no doubt staying up through the night to make sure the crew didn't have to eat cold food for more than a day.

She glanced in, noticing the two dozen enlisted, noncoms, and officers at the tables. The quiet hum of the ship was replaced by the clinking of glasses and flatware, and the dull murmur of conversation.

Viv ducked through the mess into the galley and waved at PO Mendez.

"Chief? I'm sorry, I mean XO. Anything I can get you?" he asked. His fingers flew across the cutting board as he chopped up a mix of vegetables.

"Just making sure everything is running smooth. Any problems?"

"No, ma'am. Everything is five by five."

She took one last look around and double-timed back out to the main passageway. Her NavPad showed her list; she tapped "check on mess," and flicked it off her pad. From there, she dodged around the line forming in the passageway, past the food storage, by the forward magazine storage up to the hatch leading to the Long 9. She stuck her head in.

PO Ignatius waved at her. "XO," he said.

Two spacers had the coil assembly open, running magnetic resonance scanners over the exposed coils. While the coils didn't have to be replaced as often as rails would, they still needed constant maintenance. Even a single coil with a different polarity could cause a disaster when firing the 9.

"Can I talk to you for a moment, PO?" she asked.

"Aye ma'am." Ignatius hopped down from the gunner's seat to the deck where the hatch was and slid out.

"PO, I need to switch up the Long 9 crew rotation."

"How so, ma'am?"

Boudreaux showed him the hole they had on the roster. With Ensign Lopez's unfortunate death, they needed an officer on ops. Which meant moving Brown to Ops, leaving weapons without a first watch.

"I've got two POs qualified for weapons—you and PO Mendez. The captain has him in the galley and we're inclined to leave him there."

"As he should, ma'am. That kid can cook."

"Agreed. Which means I need you up on the bridge for first and third watch."

"All right, ma'am, I think I can do that. Who's going to have the Long 9 during battle stations if I'm on the bridge?"

She pulled up two names: Mendez, and PO Collins.

"I wanted to leave that to you. You've got the most seniority. What do you suggest?"

He mulled it over for a moment before tapping on Mendez's name. "He's already familiar with the hardware. Not to mention, Collins already plays double duty. Better to leave her than shuffle the deck too much."

"I agree. Thank you, PO."

"Yes ma'am. See you on the bridge."

Boudreaux stopped at the next ladder, sending her recommendation off to the captain before sliding down to deck three on her way to make sure the new anvil functioned as expected.

Jacob glanced at his NavPad as the latest report came from Boudreaux. He didn't think she realized how efficient she was as XO. Yuki was a fine officer and would make a great commander, but she struggled with paperwork the same way Jacob did. Boudreaux had no such struggle. She ran an effective, clean system for dealing with both hardware and crew issues. Her latest resolution wasn't one he would have thought of, but simple and elegant all the same, and would work until they could get reinforcements.

"COB, how are we looking?" he asked.

Suresh eyed him through the mirror. "Quite good, sir. One hour and zero-four minutes to destination."

"Rugger, time to secure communications?" he asked.

This was their big issue. They had to be close enough to DesRon Nine to send secure communications without giving away their position. The last thing he wanted to do was to lead an enemy light cruiser squadron right to the destroyers. So far, they had managed to remain undetectable and not seen any signs of other ships.

"Five minutes and change, sir," Rugger said.

Five minutes until they could send a brief message alerting DesRon Nine to the danger.

His instincts said pull back and prepare for an attack.

However, the roll of a destroyer squadron was that of recon and screen. He could assume an attack was imminent all day long, but they needed solid intelligence.

Jacob pressed the button on his MFD, activating the record feature. He leaned in close to the pickup. "Captain Hatwal, embedded in this message is my report on an encounter with a Caliphate Navy light cruiser, name unknown. I suggest battle stations and silent running from this point forward. Grimm out."

He keyed in his report, including all the information from the battle and the recommendations for awards in case *Interceptor* didn't make it back. Jacob double-checked his work, making sure he included the necessary details to support his position.

"Time sir," Rugger said. Jacob finished his communiqué, saved it, and gave Rugger a thumbs up.

"Send it."

"On the chip, sir. Sending."

CHAPTER THIRTY-FOUR

Nadia sealed the last magnetic cuff that secured Bradford to the metal chair. He couldn't move or see. The last image in his mind was his wife being shot. Part of Nadia rebelled against the cruelty she inflicted, but it was squashed by the surety that he was a Caliphate spy.

After one last check, Nadia stepped into the bathroom where her recording equipment sat ready to capture the confession in perfect fidelity. She signaled Rashid to begin.

The door to the safe house slid open and Rashid and Daisy walked in, arguing in the Caliph language, which was a mix of several old Earth dialects.

"We were ordered to round up all agents for interrogation. I don't care how close you were to your objective, *Kafir*," he said, using Daisy's code name.

"I understand, but how am I supposed to return to cover when you've blown it so?" Kafir asked.

"You're not. All missions are canceled. ISB has changed the operation."

Nadia had mulled over the wording they would use. Having the son of the Caliph, she hoped, would be one such situation, and they would be correct in trying to free him using whatever they could.

Rashid strode into the room where Bradford sat, and ripped off the hood. Daisy knelt and undid the cuffs on his ankles.

"It seems an awful waste to torpedo my mission of ten years because a VIP got himself captured," Daisy said.

Bradford's sweat-streaked face looked down at Daisy, then up at Rashid and back to Daisy.

"What do you want with me?" he said in the common language of the Alliance.

Daisy glanced past him to Rashid.

"Do not speak to her. I want your full report," Rashid said.

Nadia had to hand it to Bradford—when Rashid told him not to look at Daisy, he didn't even flinch. Either his acting was world class… or he really didn't understand them.

Bradford turned awkwardly in the chair to Rashid, then back to Daisy.

"I don't understand what you're saying. Please let me go, you don't know who I am. I'm very powerful," he said slowly, as if that would penetrate their language barrier.

"Don't speak to her, speak to me," Rashid said again. He came around, shoved Daisy out of the way, and looked hard at Bradford. "Enough with the games. We broke your cover to find out where the Caliph's son is. Now speak."

Bradford glanced between the two, eyes squinting as if he couldn't tell what he was supposed to do.

Nadia's stomach sank, and a queasy, not quite nauseous feeling started to seep through her. The cameras did more than record. They also showed biometrics, heart rate, temperature, and brain activity. All of it saved to her NavPad, where a sophisticated algorithm analyzed the data and told her if he was lying or not. So far, he was telling the truth, and his body and mind were in distress. He could be a top-notch agent, though. If she pushed him harder, he might crack.

"Rashid, up the ante," she said through the private comm they shared.

The former Caliphate navy captain gave her a subtle nod and backhanded Bradford. Daisy's head snapped up at the crack of flesh. Rashid's boldness surprised Nadia.

Bradford wailed and blubbered. He sobbed like a child, begging for his life. He offered up every secret he knew without hesitation.

Nadia couldn't quite keep up with what he was saying, but his vitals were all over the place, his heart beating so fast she worried he would have a heart attack.

Something was very wrong. This pathetic person was no double agent.

"Calm him down," she told Daisy.

Rashid stepped out of the room, leaving Daisy to work her magic on Bradford. She soothed him, whispering in his ear as she took a rag and started dabbing his face.

"It's going to be okay," she said. "Listen, our missions are over. We need to focus on getting off this planet and back home—"

"I don't speak your language!" he shouted. "You killed my wife, kidnapped me, and now you keep speaking like I'm one of you. Tell me what is going on!" He jerked the chair up and down before collapsing as much as the restraints would allow.

Nadia glanced at the NavPad, desperately hoping it would show his deceit.

TRUTH, it read.

Away from his sycophants and niceties and outside of the protection of society his true character was revealed. Between his rapid eye movement, shallow breathing, and intense pulse, it all pointed to one thing. A man in terror. Maybe he could fake some, but her NavPad would detect any mechanical or biometric oddities.

"For what it's worth, Nadia," Rashid said after he closed the door, "I don't think he's lying."

Nadia fidgeted, cracking her knuckles. "I agree, which is a problem. Because if he isn't the spy, who is?"

Wit couldn't be anywhere near Nadia's black-on-black operation, so he picked the one place everyone expected to see him: his office. It wasn't like he didn't have a million things to do, and he was expected to show up at 0600 anyway.

The Department of National Intelligence insisted on using electronic intelligence, and the other military intelligence branches took their cues from them. Not Wit, though. His real knowledge came from people. He had a dozen operatives working at any given time, and that was just the ones on the books. Nadia was his star deep-cover asset. He didn't have as much power as others might assume, though he certainly played it like he did.

Many of his assets were layered throughout the known nations, from traders who occasionally sold information, to long-term, deep-cover agents who lived under cover. His job demanded a maestro, and he played the part to perfection.

Right then, though, the most important operation of his career was taking place and he couldn't be anywhere nearby. If Nadia turned out to be wrong, she would have to face the consequences on her own.

His NavPad squawked, interrupting his thoughts.

"Admiral, you have an unscheduled visitor, sir. Senator St. John is here to see you?"

St. John? Wit leaned back, an unusual feeling in the pit of

his stomach. He had no plans to meet with Talmage. Nor did he have a reason to.

"Send him in," he said. Wit reached over and pulled the top drawer closest to his side open and pressed his thumb against the biometric security clasp. Cold steel dropped into his hand, and he made sure the old but reliable chemical-powered semi-automatic was ready.

His door opened and Talmage entered, looking in a state fit to be tied. At first, Wit thought he must have dressed in a hurry, but it only took him a moment to realize the man had either slept in his suit or hadn't slept at all.

"Wit, we have a problem," he said, coming to rest in front of the desk, palms down on the hard surface.

"What's that?" Wit asked, eyes carefully examining the senator.

"Agents from DNI came to my home last night and showed me a bug that was planted in my office. They then searched my home, Wit. *My home,* and they found several more. I sent Eva back to New Austin on the first flight while I tried to figure out what's going on."

Had Nadia planted more than the one she told him of? Clearly, the man was distraught, and rightly so. DNI could be intimidating to anyone, even a powerful senator.

"What else did DNI tell you?" he asked.

"That they don't know where they come from, but that they were manufactured locally. I need to know Wit. Was this you?" Talmage bore into him, demanding the truth.

Truth wasn't something Wit was used to dealing in. Half-truths, partial-truths, but not the plain truth. "The one in your office, yes. The others, absolutely not. Where did you make your plans for Eva from?"

Talmage nodded to himself as if he'd expected the answer.

"I took her to the spaceport myself and bought the tickets in person. She's on a shuttle up to the transport now. I'm certain she's safe... well, safer than here. Why, Wit?"

"You play the game, Talmage, you know how it goes. Moves and countermoves. If it helps, I never believed you were a traitor. We were just hedging out bets."

Talmage St. John sank into the stiff-backed guest chair, deflating a little as some of the stress was removed. "Okay, I understand that. Never play cards with a man you don't know. You can't tell if they're bluffing," he said. "But why me? Why my home?"

"I don't gamble," Wit said. The curious metaphor seemed the perfect one for interrogation as well. "I really hate to lose. Two nights ago, a merc unit attempted to capture me in my home up in the mountains. They failed. We surmised that Rep. Bradford was behind the attack. My team is currently examining that possibility. It seems logical that if they were going to come after one of us..." Wit let the unspoken statement hang.

"Then they would come for all of us. It's not exactly a secret that I've helped ONI and the Navy. Clear the board in one move. Why didn't they come for my family then?" Talmage asked.

"Probably because they were dead. Notice how I'm still here and not in a safehouse under questioning and torture?"

"Oh. Right. Good point."

Wit played idly with his NavPad. There was only one answer. "They have to be making a play for our guest, but he's locked away in the depths of Fort Icarus." Wit stopped as Talmage slapped his hands together.

"I think he is here. In the city, I mean. DNI requested a funds increase for *prisoner management* when they moved several inmates from Fort Icarus to an unnamed offsite facility. It's the kind of request we get often at appropriations, and usually just rubber stamp."

Wit had made more than a few of those kinds of requests in

his time; he tried not to be bitter about DNI getting theirs rubber stamped. The Navy had to fight and claw for every solar dollar.

"Do you think someone in DNI is assisting a prisoner escape?" Wit asked.

"They don't have to know that's what they're doing. They might not even know who they have."

Wit thought it through for a moment. Why bring Imran to Anchorage Bay? They could and were interrogating him just fine at Icarus. "There's just no reason for him to be here other than to let him go. I can't wrap my mind around DNI being knowingly involved in this."

"What about a deal?" Talmage said. "It's crazy, I know, but with the ambassadors officially gone, then having him there to make a deal would be all they could do? Right? If the appropriate authorities gave it their approval—say the SECNAV and Speaker of the House—DNI would go with it."

Wit wanted to say it was absurd, but he'd seen too much like it. "A deal then. And they let him go. Who though?"

"Bradford. Everyone knows he's planning a presidential run. What better way to announce it than with a peace deal? He could push through a ratification tonight if he needed to. He has the votes. On both sides."

"Okay. Then where?" Wit asked.

"Only Bradford would know. Too bad we can't ask him," Talmage said.

Nadia put down the NavPad and considered the message from Admiral DeBeck. They were in a gray area, surrounded by deep shadows. Technically, the Speaker of the House had the authority to propose treaties for ratification. However, the diplomatic corps were charged with the negotiation of treaties. Politicians normally became involved only after all the ground work was complete.

Bradford could propose a treaty with the Caliphate, but doing so with a prisoner of Imran's importance *could* be seen as a violation of the Constitution. Until it was ratified as a treaty, it would be colluding with an unfriendly foreign power. Especially if it were negotiated in secret without the knowledge of the Diplomatic Corps, the ambassador to the Caliphate, or President Axwell.

She turned to Bradford, who was still mag cuffed to his chair. He'd long since stopped crying, only occasionally sniffling.

He wasn't a spy, or a traitor, just a self-serving politician who had technically broken the law. Nadia's entire job description involved technically breaking the law. Except her breaking the law could save the Alliance, while what he did would doom it.

The sun crept up over the distant horizon, lighting the sky with pinks and yellows. Anchorage Bay came alive with the sunrise, filling the streets and air with commuters. Time ran short and she had to decide.

"Bradford, listen. What I'm about to tell you is very important and it may just save your life, do you understand?" Nadia said as she walked into the room the congressman occupied. Daisy and Rashid flanked her.

"You speak common?" he asked.

"Obviously," she said. "Where are you releasing Imran?"

Bradford shook his head. "How do you know about that?"

"We're the ISB, Congressman. I don't know who you were dealing with, but you're not releasing the Caliph's son to the Caliphate, but navy agents in disguise."

"No," Bradford said. "No. I made sure. I checked with DNI. You're lying."

That confirmed DNI was involved. How could her government be at war with itself?

"Every step of your operation has been guided by ONI." Nadia knew she was taking a risk, playing on Bradford's fear of the Navy. A fear he had pretended for so many years that he now believed it himself. "It has all just been a way to get Imran out in the open in order to assassinate him. If that happens, there will be no peace. We will destroy you down to the bedrock."

"No, no, no! That's not what we wanted. We had a deal. He goes back and we get a non-aggression pact."

TRUTH, her NavPad informed.

Everything Nadia understood about the Caliphate told her they would never honor a NAP. If they did, it would be for a very short amount of time. Just long enough for them to conquer the Consortium and then they would turn on the Alliance.

"We put our own people on the slavery block, Bradford. What makes you think we care about you?"

"Why negotiate for a treaty, then? Surely you must see the benefit of having us as an ally?"

"We wanted our Caliph's son returned. What lies would you tell to see your president's daughter brought home? You kidnapped our citizen and tortured him, and now you're going to get him killed," Nadia said. She turned around and threw her hands up in the air.

"Wait. I don't want him dead. I wanted him free—as proof that we're reasonable and trustworthy. A gift to your mighty Caliphate. The Navy did what they did without our permission. Please, we can still salvage our treaty."

Nadia stopped at the door hesitating. She choked down bile from Bradford's retched begging. If he really understood the

Caliphate and the ISB, this would never work. He would know that having a female agent speaking for a man would never fly. She played on his prejudice, though, his willing blindness.

The paths she sometimes took to find the truth twisted around her like shadows—to the point she didn't always know the truth from the lies. He really had made a deal with the ISB to free Imran Hamid for a real non-aggression pact. Nadia also knew without a doubt that the Caliphate would never honor such a treaty.

"I want more than just Imran's location. Give me something else I can take to my Caliph?" she said.

"What more do you want?" he asked.

"Promise me that once you are president, you will concede the wormhole and Zuckabar to us as reparations for your arrogance in the last war."

Bradford looked down, his eyes rapidly darting back and forth as he worked through it.

"If you honor the deal we already have to help me get elected, then yes, I'll do it."

Nadia used every ounce of her self-control to keep her face neutral.

"Deal. Now, where were you meeting him?"

Bradford told her, he told her *everything,* and the more he said, the less Nadia could believe.

CHAPTER THIRTY-FIVE

ANCHORAGE BAY INTERSTELLAR SPACE PORT

Besides the large monument gleaming in the center of the city and the vast amount of new construction, it was almost impossible for Nadia to tell the city had ever been destroyed.

"They really bombed it from orbit?" Daisy asked.

"I wasn't here. I was in Zuckabar on another mission. When I returned, this was all craters and death," Nadia said as she banked the aircar around to the north. She glanced at Daisy. "You don't believe me?"

Daisy shook her head. "No, I do. I just don't want to. In a way, I'm glad you blamed the Guild. If your government had decided to declare war, your people would have been behind them in a way I can only imagine. It wouldn't have been enough to just defeat the Caliphate in battle. You would have wanted blood."

Nadia hadn't thought about it that way, but she supposed Daisy was right. People—regular, everyday people who were the life blood of her nation—were angry. Angry at the Guild, but mostly they were angry at the Caliphate. She didn't know anyone who actually believed the Caliphate story that they were framed by the Guild.

They were all bound by rules. If the president decided to go to war anyway, then he wouldn't be the president anymore. She hated the politicians who were blinded by their own agendas, greed, and arrogance, but she had to accept that her not liking the decisions they made did not make them Caliphate agents.

Like Speaker Bradford.

As misguided and naïve as he was, he thought he was doing his best for the nation. From his perspective, he saw the Caliphate as an unstoppable empire waiting to swallow them up. He was afraid of them. Afraid the Alliance would cease to exist. His solution was to broker a peace deal.

She couldn't fault him for wanting to save the Alliance, but she could fault him for willfully ignoring what the Caliphate actually was. They might say the words and act out the trappings of religion. They might even swear by it. But at the end of the day, they were bullies and tyrants. All they cared about was their own power and position. It wasn't like the Caliph himself would run a suicide mission with an advanced prototype ship. No, that was for other people. The difference between the Alliance and the Caliphate was simple.

The Alliance looked to help and grow the prosperity of others. The Caliphate, only themselves. At least that was how Nadia saw it.

"Aircar zero-four-niner, this is Spaceport ATC. Please change course to one-three-seven, descend to two-zero-six meters."

Nadia pressed the comms switch. "ATC, this is aircar zero-four-niner, requesting emergency clearance to land at the interstellar gates. Authentication code, Alpha-one-mike-bravo."

Seconds passed while ATC checked her code. She didn't change course.

"They have gun turrets tracking us. You know that, right?" Daisy asked, her face pressed up against the glass to look down.

"I know. My codes are good... I think."

"What do you mean you 'think?'"

"I mean, if DNI is involved, they might have pulled my clearance."

"All that's holy," Daisy muttered as she yanked on her crash belt. "You could have warned me."

Nadia shrugged. "Wouldn't change our plans."

"Aircar zero-four-niner, ATC. You are cleared to land at requested point. Do not deviate from current course."

"Roger, ATC. Four-niner out." She glanced over at Daisy. "See?"

"I see you're more of a thrill seeker than I am."

The aircar slowly descended toward the terminal. The spaceport's external shape looked like a snowflake, each arm a different terminal, with the spikes being the landing pads for shuttles to the ships in orbit.

"That's the one," Daisy said, pointing below.

"Got it." Nadia maneuvered the car to rest gently on the designated landing spot. She reached past Daisy into the glove box and pulled out two dull-gray pistols in black magnetic holsters. "This one's for you."

Daisy held the pistol gingerly. "You're giving me a gun?"

Nadia stopped and looked at her hard for a long moment. Did she trust the former spy? She must, since her instinct was to arm her. Had she forgiven her?

At some point during the last few days of working with her, Nadia *had* forgiven her. She, of all people, knew the value and power of a lie. She could no more hate Daisy for what had happened to her than she could hate the collar they had placed around her neck. Both were tools—forged by evil, used until needed, then discarded.

"Yes. I... I guess I have."

Daisy lunged forward, engulfing Nadia in a hug that pulled at the spy's heart. She hadn't expected such a show of emotion, but it felt right. Her own sense of resentment over what had happened to her and over her betrayal vanished with the embrace. For the first time in a long time, she felt light. Light enough to float.

"Enough of that," Nadia said in a thick voice. "Let's get going."

"What's the plan?" Daisy asked as she pulled the gun from its holster. A holographic display popped up, showing her where the pistol aimed and its general status. The readout showed twenty rounds in the magazine and one in the pipe.

"We go in, locate the detail with Imran, call the admiral, and get the whole thing shut down. If he escapes, we lose our only leverage. No matter what, he doesn't leave this planet."

The two women exited the car into the stiff wind of the spaceport. Set right up against the ocean, the smell of brine mixed with jet fuel filled Nadia's senses. She slipped the pistol into the small of her back, making sure it was clipped on. Once Daisy was ready, they beelined for the entrance.

Two security men wearing spaceport uniforms and armed with advanced body armor and stun rifles waited for them.

"Agent Dagher?" the taller of the two said.

Nadia pulled her NavPad out for verification. Once they were sure, they opened the door for her.

"Stay on our six. Shoot at who we shoot, got it?" she asked.

"Aye ma'am. Are you seriously going to have a shootout in the spaceport?" the younger of the two asked.

"Only if we must," Nadia said. "The man we're looking for" —she tapped a key on her NavPad and Imran's face appeared—

"is very dangerous. We *must* stop him from boarding a shuttle. I don't care who you have to shoot, or who the people he's with say they are, he cannot leave this planet. Understood?"

The older man, whose name badge read "Peck," gripped his rifle and nodded. "With the clearance you provided, I'd shoot myself."

"Hopefully, that won't be necessary," Daisy said.

"Move out," Nadia said.

Admiral DeBeck tapped away frantically at his own NavPad, desperately trying to route a call to the battleship in orbit while his aircar roared toward Anchorage Bay.

"You sure this is a good idea, Wit?" Talmage asked. The senator looked down at the ground a kilometer below and swallowed hard while holding the grab bar above his head with white-knuckled ferocity.

"No. But it's all I got." He managed to hit the right sequence and his NavPad lit up. "USS *Enterprise*, this is Admiral DeBeck. Come in."

"Ensign Culvert, sir. Uh, why are you calling on this channel?" The young woman's voice sounded distorted. *Enterprise*'s current high orbit, just shy of Utopia, meant a half second delay.

"Ensign Culvert, I need to speak to your Marine contingent commander ASAP."

"Aye sir, one moment." To her credit, she didn't hesitate. The NavPad provided the clearance she needed to know she was speaking with the real Admiral. "Sir, Captain Lepke isn't aboard ship. I have her XO, though, Lieutenant Bonds."

"That will do."

The line clicked over several times before a deep baritone

filled the volume. "Lieutenant Bonds speaking. How can I help you, sir?"

"Bonds, you have enough Marines aboard to do a combat drop?" he asked.

"Yes sir, I do. Forty-five heartbreakers and lifetakers, sir."

Despite the seriousness of the situation, Wit found himself smiling at the Marine's answer. There was something comforting about that level of commitment.

"I want a combat drop at Anchorage Bay International Spaceport, interstellar departure terminal. The agent-in-charge on the ground uses call sign *India-One-Five*. No shuttles are to depart, no personnel are to leave. I want a complete lockdown, understood?"

"Lockdown the terminal. India's in charge. Understood, sir. We'll be in the air in ten, and on the ground ten after that."

"Get to it. DeBeck out."

Static filled the line for a moment before it died.

"Marines at a civilian spaceport, Wit? What if Alliance citizens are caught in the crossfire?" Talmage asked.

Wit DeBeck answered with the grave authority of a man with only one goal. "Senator, I'd order an airstrike if it meant that man didn't get off the planet."

"All right then," Talmage said.

Imran Hamid cracked his knuckles in frustration. They had assured him Speaker Bradford would be waiting and then he could depart on a private ship heading for Consortium space. From there, it would be easy to find his way back to the Caliphate, and not long after, he would lead the fleet that conquered this pathetic planet filled with infidels. Of course, he left that part out of the proposed treaty. As if any treaty signed by infidels were valid.

Their government had provided three plain clothed gents to deliver him to the treat signing.

"Sir, the VIP is on his way," the DNI agent-in-charge said.

"Good," Imran replied. They had him in a private room, off the terminal, sitting in an uncomfortable hard-plastic chair.

The door opened and an older, heavy set man Imran didn't recognize walked in.

"Congressman Simmons. We were expecting Speaker Bradford," the AIC said.

"Change of plans," Simmons said.

"Sir, I'm afraid we can't alter the—"

Simmons raised his hand suddenly, pushing it flush against the agent's neck. Blood sprayed across the room as the vibroblade sheared the man's head from his body. The elderly statesman's other hand carried a pistol and he fired, hitting the second agent in the throat with a beam of coherent light that burned a hole in him.

The third agent was bringing his gun up when Simmons fired the final time, killing him with a single laser shot to the heart.

The sudden violence and explosion of blood left Imran stunned. "Who are you?" he finally managed to spit out between clenched jaws.

"My Caliph, I am a deep cover agent, *Alzalam*. I am here to get you out. ONI agents are on their way here to kill you. I have a ship standing by, but we must go now."

As the head of the ISB, Imran was well aware there were several deep cover agents throughout the major powers of the galaxy. What surprised him was how old this one was.

"How long have you been here?" Imran asked as he held his wrists up.

Simmons ran his pad over Imran's exposed arms, finding and neutralizing the tracker the Alliance implanted in all their prisoners. "Forty-four years, my Caliph," he said. "I am ready to go home."

"Lead the way!"

Nadia cursed at how many people crowded the terminal, the vast majority headed for the wormhole and Consortium space beyond. Suddenly, for the first time in anyone's life, traveling to an entirely different culture was relatively easy and risk free. Of all the opportunities the wormhole presented, tourism had never even crossed her mind.

"Spread out," she said over the comms her impromptu team shared. "The DNI agents should be a dead giveaway."

"India, security just messaged me and said DNI agents are using a private room on the west wing. Turn left at the next section, straight through to the other side," Peck said.

"Roger," she replied. She and Daisy kept their weapons concealed, but the two men behind her had their rifles slung against their chests, hands on the grips.

She followed the directions, moving past a group of college students double-checking their bags while a professor droned on about staying together. They were at the far end of the terminal arm, where it was crowded with passengers waiting to board.

The door she wanted was ajar. Nadia pulled her pistol, moving to the far side, while Daisy mimicked her on the other. Using her foot, Nadia nudged the door a tiny bit and glanced in. Blood dripped from the walls and ceiling and she counted three dead. A standard DNI protection detail.

"He's in the wind," Nadia said. She glanced around. The

only way he could have gone was back toward the main building. She pointed in the direction she wanted and Daisy immediately moved out.

"You two," she said to the security men. "Go back the way we came and head for the main building parallel to us. Do not engage without calling me first, got it?"

"Understood." They took off, running for the other major hall.

Nadia fell in behind Daisy, hustling through the crowd, doing their best to keep their weapons out of sight.

"What do you think happened?" Daisy asked.

"I think he never planned on signing any treaty, and if we hadn't done what we did, Speaker Bradford would be dead right now."

Nadia felt a sense of urgency. If they lost Imran, it would be a huge blow to their efforts, not to mention removing their de facto protection. No matter what, even if she had to kill him, she couldn't let him leave the planet.

She hustled, pushing past people while scanning every face, every movement, trying to see everything at once. Was she too late? There had to be thirty thousand people in the spaceport, a quarter of which were in the interstellar terminal.

"Ladies and gentlemen," a pleasant voice announced over the speaker, "due to circumstances out of our control, all interstellar departures are delayed. Please be patient while we work to resolve the issue."

A wave of complaints swept through the spaceport as everyone in the terminal stopped to look up and listen. Everyone but the two men a hundred meters away, who didn't care if their flight was delayed.

"Daisy, there," Nadia pointed.

"I'll go left," Daisy said as she vanished into the crowd.

Nadia stepped up her pace through the crowd, pushing people out of the way. "Move. Get out of the way!"

It seemed the more she tried to clear them, the more people crowded between her and Imran. Someone stepped in front of her, and she shoved them with both hands, knocking them on their butt.

Imran turned, caught a glimpse of Nadia, and their eyes locked. She didn't need to be a spy to see the hatred in his countenance. Raising her pistol with both hands, she aimed carefully, then growled in frustration. There were just too many people in the way for her to risk shooting.

Imran grinned, pointing at her then ran his thumb over his neck like a knife before disappearing through a doorway.

"India One-Five, this is Charlie flight, call sign Cobra. How copy?" a deep baritone voice asked in her ear.

"Cobra, you handy with a sniper rifle?" she asked.

"Only when pretty brunettes ask me," he replied.

Bonds, she thought. Lucky her. "What's your ordnance situation?"

"I've got one Corsair loaded for bear and CAS. Where do you want me?"

Nadia glanced around. She was heading south—that was about all she knew.

"Head to the south side of the interstellar terminal. Dissuade any vehicles from lifting off. Deadly force is authorized. Weapons free."

"Weapons free. Roger that, ma'am."

CHAPTER THIRTY-SIX

To Jacob's great relief, the rest of the squadron sat silent at the entrance to the starlane. He was only aware of their presence from the laser relay connected to *Firewatch*. It allowed for secure communications; as long as an enemy ship didn't pass through the laser, they would never know it was there.

"Marta, time to full stop?" he asked.

PO Oliv glanced up from her panel, hand hovering over the calculator as she read off the running numbers.

"Three minutes, eight seconds... mark," she said.

"Thank you."

Jacob pulled at his ELS suit, performing the suit Tango, the little dance male spacers did when the connection to the plumbing didn't quite fit. Thankfully, no one laughed the way they would have if he wasn't the captain. Once he finally got it in place, he strapped himself in like the rest of the crew, who were at action stations for the starlane entrance.

Ten minutes earlier, he had received Captain Hatwal's response. He had to listen to the whole message three times to make sure he understood it right.

"That's quite the story. I've got CIC going over your findings, and I have to say, Commander Grimm, well done to you and your crew. I would like to have you aboard *Firewatch* to dine as soon as we are in the next system. Please send my compliments to your tactical officer. Also, my condolences on the loss of your crewman. I looked over the criteria for the awards and I support it one hundred percent."

What had changed? Something must have gotten through to him. Either that or Captain Hatwal had a stroke while *Interceptor* was off fighting for her life.

"Ensign Brown, sound the pipes. All hands prepare for transit," Jacob ordered.

Brown fumbled through the unfamiliar ops station before finding the right keys to press. "All hands, lockdown and prepare for transit. Notify your department heads immediately if you need assistance."

Jacob watched the forward radar array showing *Firewatch, Tizón, Kraken,* and *Sabre* floating two thousand klicks apart with their apertures fully open, waiting for *Interceptor*'s arrival to jump.

"Rugger, send *Firewatch* my compliments and let Captain Hatwal know we're on schedule and we'll be right behind them. No need to delay for us."

Commander Archer Ban looked up from his screen to Captain Hatwal in the command chair. The new destroyers were big enough to house multiple chairs for the crews and Archer had to admit, it was nice to sit for his watch instead of stand.

"Sir, *Interceptor* sends her compliments and says they'll be right behind us if we want to jump."

Archer noticed Captain Hatwal relax a little in his chair. It was tough for the newly promoted captain, trying to get everything right on his first deployment in a, frankly, crap sandwich of an assignment. They weren't at war with the Caliphate, couldn't fire first, yet, if the telemetry Commander Grimm sent over meant anything, the Caliphate had no such compunction.

He couldn't quite suppress a grin, though. How the hell a forty-five-year-old destroyer beat a light cruiser was beyond him. That was one for the records and would have the boys at NavTac hitting the books for weeks trying to come up with some kind of name for the maneuver.

"That sounds like a plan, Commander. Order them to follow at best speed. Comms, the word is given. Transit."

"Transit at best speed, *Firewatch* out," Commander Ban said. The screen blinked out of existence a moment later, replaced by a three-dimensional representation of the volume of space the ships were transiting from.

Jacob lifted his helmet above his head. "Ops, drain the can."

"Aye sir," Ensign Brown said. "All hands, helmets on, helmets on, helmets on. Draining the can in two minutes."

There were a multitude of reasons to have atmosphere in the ship, from psychological to physical health. Even something as simple as eating was nigh impossible while wearing an ELS suit. There were also a multitude of reasons *not* to have atmosphere; any situation, no matter how safe or dangerous, was made infinitely riskier by the chance of a hull breach when atmosphere was present.

Condition Zulu, both action and battle stations, was almost always accompanied by draining the atmosphere. Regulations stipulated draining the can upon entering and exiting starlanes. Jacob liked following the regs, no matter how trivial. It gave him a good feeling in the pit of his stomach when he could check the box on his reports, indicating all standing regulations were obeyed. Except when there were no regulations that covered his situation. Something that seemed to happen often aboard his ship.

His MFD updated from Astro, showing the stern aspects of the squadron. USS *Tizón* disappeared first, flashing off the screen as the gravity of the starlane took hold. *Kraken* and *Firewatch* leaped forward together.

USS *Sabre* remained, floating at the transit point as *Interceptor* grew ever closer.

"Rugger, signal Captain Carlos and let him know we stand ready to assist if there's a problem," Jacob said. It was rare, but there were a few issues that could creep up with a gravcoil that a ship's engineer wouldn't notice until an attempt was made to enter a starlane.

"Interceptor, this is Commander Carlos. We're fine, just lost lock on the lane for a second and—"

"Gravity wake incoming!" Tefiti announced over the bridge comms.

Witnessing a ship exiting a starlane wasn't the exciting event it sounded like. One second space was empty, the next it wasn't. Space being space—large and empty—the chances of hitting another vessel, even in a busy lane, were almost nonexistent.

Crews lived and died in the "almost" part.

Three Caliphate light cruisers sped down the lane, appearing in an instant. One of them, unfortunately for *Sabre*, slammed into the Alliance ship as velocity neared zero. With five times the mass of the destroyer, the light cruiser imparted more energy into the vessel than she could withstand.

While the cruiser deflected off the collision, leaving a long furrow in her starboard bow and bleeding atmosphere and fuel, *Sabre* came a part like she'd been hit by a planet.

Hull plating shattered, and her starboard side turrets exploded inward, blasting through the ship, rending metal and flesh like so much confetti. By some miracle, the fusion reactor didn't go critical, but what once was a fighting ship had become a collection of parts and people floating in space, in an expanding cloud of death.

Silence deafened Jacob's bridge. *Interceptor* was two thousand klicks away, but she might as well be on the other side of the galaxy for all she could do to stop *Sabre*'s destruction or help her surviving crew. Anguish filled his chest at the sudden and unexpected loss of life. Reality snapped back at him fast, though. If he didn't act now, his crew would be next.

"Con, twenty degrees down bubble, flank speed!" he said in a hurry.

"Aye sir, twenty-degrees down bubble, flank speed," Chief Suresh replied calmly.

"Weapons to standby," Jacob ordered.

PO Ignatius put one hand on the console while he ran down the checklist. "Weapons hot in thirty seconds, Skipper," Ignatius said.

The entire ship felt the motion as Suresh pushed the throttle all the way forward. Gravity roared through the coil, gaining strength as it reached the stern, which pulled on the crew while the secondary coil did its best to keep the crew oriented toward the deck.

"Contacts designated Bandits One through Three, Skipper," PO Tefiti said.

Several numbers appeared on Jacob's MFD. Velocity, angle of attack, and distance all climbed rapidly, but not rapidly enough. In thirty seconds, his ship would only hit a hundred and sixty-seven KPS and put barely twenty-four hundred klicks between them. If the light cruisers opened fire, there would be next to nothing Jacob could do.

With *Interceptor* heading down and away from the enemy ship's bows, accelerating into their blind spot, he hoped to buy them more time.

CHAPTER THIRTY-SEVEN

Alarms warbled all over the ship and his bridge crew tried to inform him all at once what was happening. Yousef had eyes; he could see *Yatağan Edge* trimming forward as she left a wake of debris behind her. What she had hit wasn't as clear.

His own ship, *Glimmer of Dawn,* and the third cruiser, *Autumn's Favor,* were unscathed.

"Was it an asteroid?" he asked.

"No sir," his helmsman replied. "I think there was another ship in the lane waiting to depart and *Edge* hit her as she decelerated."

Yousef shook his head at the improbability of the event. Had the Consortium mined the lane?

"Sir, *Edge* needs immediate help. Should I launch search and rescue?" Lieutenant Ghazali asked.

"Yes. Sound collision and prepare for search and rescue."

The XO went to work, speaking rapid fire as he organized the ship to lend aid to their damaged squadron mate.

Something didn't seem right to Yousef, though. He checked

the scope on his own screen and they had hit a ship. There wasn't enough left of it to scrape off a boot, so they would never know who it was, but he could guess.

Whoever it was, the debris field looked large enough to be a destroyer, but no bigger. If there was one tin can, then there were more. They didn't travel alone, but in packs.

"Battle stations!" Yousef yelled.

"Contact," his astrogator blared out. "Bearing one-eight-zero mark two-four-four and accelerating, range, one-eight-seven kilometers."

Yousef blinked at how close they were. Practically on top of them.

"Belay search and rescue. Helm, bring us about, pursuit course, maximum acceleration. All sensors to active."

It took them a little longer than he expected to get their bearing, but they did. Jacob watched as one of the light cruisers broke formation and began maneuvering to come about and pursue them.

"We're being painted, Skipper. Active radar and lidar," Oliv said.

"Comms, switch to active ECM. Let's see if we can blind them."

"Aye sir," Midship Rugger said. "Active ECM."

"Weapons are hot, Skipper," PO Ignatius informed him.

He wanted to fire. With every fiber of his being, he wanted to fire. To rain righteous fury down on the bastards who killed *Sabre*. They weren't at war, though, and as far as he could tell, it had been an accident. The fact that another Caliphate ship had fired at him didn't change the situation. Until there was a formal declaration of war, or hostile action from a pursuing ship, he couldn't fire. Those were the rules of engagement, whether he agreed with them or not.

Jacob let out a breath, leaning back in his chair and consciously relaxing his muscles. He forced his mind to clear and let the adrenaline go. Instincts made bad decisions. Great for warnings, but bad for strategy. If he opened fire, *Interceptor* would be dead. And worse, when the rest of DesRon Nine returned to investigate, they would be destroyed as well. He needed a plan that saved all the remaining ships and foiled whatever the Caliphate had up their sleeve.

He prayed they would render aid to his fallen shipmates. No one deserved to be left in the black to die alone.

"Status?" he asked.

"Velocity approaching five-zero-zero KPS. Distance to tango, twenty-two thousand klicks," PO Oliv said.

"Rugger?"

"ECM at max, sir. They can see us for sure, but they can't know precisely where we are."

"Weapons?"

"Their EW systems aren't up yet, skipper. At this range I couldn't miss, not with three targets to hit," PO Ignatius said.

"I know, PO. I know. We're not in a shooting war... yet. As much as I want to, we can't open fire on them. We just can't. However, if they start shooting at us, do not hesitate to fire back. Focus fire on the damaged one. If we must go down, let's do the most damage we can. Suresh, run true for as long as you think you can get away with it. The more velocity advantage we can build, the better. If the shooting starts, though, maneuver as you see fit."

"Aye aye, sir," Ignatius and Suresh replied simultaneously.

Jacob leaned as far forward as his straps would allow, placing his elbows on knees and bowing his head for a quick prayer. He really needed help to get his crew out alive. Once done, he depressed the comm switch on his MFD, not wanting to disturb Rugger from his EW by asking him to do it.

"Now hear this, all hands, now hear this," he said. "This is the captain speaking. While trying to exit Ocelot, we encountered the remainder of the squadron the previous light cruiser belonged to. By now you've heard of *Sabre*'s loss. Keep her crew in your thoughts and prayers. In this moment, though, we need to focus on our jobs. They haven't opened fire yet, and every second we pull farther away from them. We need those seconds, and many more, if we're going to make it. Trust your training, trust each other, and trust in *Interceptor*. Captain out."

―――

Ensign Akio Kai looked up from his terminal, pausing his scan of the fuel regulator flow system to listen to Commander Grimm. Chief Petty Officer Redfern said the captain liked to keep his crew informed. Which was wildly different from his last station, where he went six months and never once heard the CO.

For a moment, he'd forgotten they were pursued by a light cruiser. The thought should've filled him with fear. On paper, destroyers were designed to escort merchants, to provide screening elements for fleet actions, and maybe to fight small ships. Cruisers, even light cruisers, out massed and outgunned them, and were able to fight while sustaining far more damage than a destroyer ever could.

Yet they had already faced one and emerged victorious.

The fact that the damage sustained in the brief exchange was repairable, and that there were no casualties could be chalked up to luck, but Akio wasn't sure that would be accurate. In his experience, as limited as it was, luck only played a part once all the real work had been done. Grimm set them up to succeed before the first shot was fired, and that was something he admired in any person.

Yousef focused hard on his screen. The little ship had first appeared clearly, but was now a fuzzy mess behind a solid wall of ECM.

"Sir?" Ghazali asked. "We're ready to fire. All we need is a couple of solid hits and they will have to surrender."

"I know, XO, but if we miss, that ship gets away with proof that we opened fire first. We can't afford that. No, I'm going to play this one cool. I won't fire until he does, or until I know we can shoot him down without risking our operation."

"At their current acceleration, sir, they're going to outrun us and leave weapons range in roughly one-five minutes."

"They're running the wrong direction. Even if they do get away, our fleet will be through the starlane before they can make it to Taki. Does the computer have an idea what they are?" he asked.

"No sir. We can't see past their jamming, and the gravwake is close enough that we're having trouble narrowing down the pattern. CIC says they can have a tentative ID in five more minutes. All we can say for sure is she's a destroyer."

Yousef certainly wanted to fire, but he needed more information first. "Any sign of *Vanguard*?" he asked his XO.

"No sir. Not yet."

That struck Yousef as strange. In the confusion of arrival and the collision, he'd forgotten *Vanguard* was supposed to be here waiting for them. Unless... unless they were following these ships at long range, per instruction. But why didn't they show up the moment *Glimmer* arrived in system? They could have obliterated the fleeing ship and not left any trace.

"Sir, do you know why they're not firing?" Ensign Brown asked.

"I can't say for sure, Austin. If I had to guess, though, and I suppose I do, it's they are trying to maintain the fiction of no conflict. If they don't fire and we do, they can blame us as the aggressor. If they knew we were already fired upon by one of their ships, this would be all over. As it is, we have a chance to create as much distance as we can before they realize they have to destroy us."

With the immediate threat subsiding, he had to figure out what they were going to do next. They couldn't run in a straight line forever.

"Tefiti, is she the same class of ship as the other one?"

"Yes sir, Tripoli class."

"What's their maximum acceleration?" Jacob asked.

"No more than four-three-zero, g's sir. Which they are doing now. It's not enough, though. We will still break contact in..." Tefiti glanced over at Oliv, who showed him the numbers. "Zero-eight minutes," he finished.

Eight minutes.

"XO," he said, "if you were them, and you knew you were about to lose me, how long would you wait to fire?"

Boudreaux looked up from her panel. "Not much longer, sir. Plus, they can't chase us for long. As soon as they figure out there are more ships heading down the starlane, they will either go after them, or set up to ambush them when they return to find out what happened."

Jacob figured they would wait for his squadron to come back. It hadn't occurred to him that they might reverse course and go right down the lane after them. He had to keep them in Ocelot and away from the starlane.

Which meant he had to give them a reason to stay. Just not an obvious one. He couldn't fire on them, and he certainly couldn't let them fire on him. He pulled up a map of the system, with its massive star and planets that orbited it like electrons. *Interceptor*'s current course sent them out to the far reaches. Even if he wanted to turn tail and run back to Taki and then Praetor, he couldn't.

"Oliv, plot us a course to come around. The second we're out of weapons range, I want to turn toward the systems center and see if we can't bring ourselves back around in a wide loop."

"Aye sir. Plotting course," Oliv said.

Interceptor's maneuverability might prove enough to let her essentially circle back and shadow their pursuer. With her small hull and low profile, once he broke contact, they could run silent and wait for the other ships to return. At least give DesRon Nine a fighting chance.

He had to hand it to his opponent. Not firing showed how much the Caliphate captain understood the Alliance, and understanding the enemy was the first step to victory. In a weird sort of way, Jacob would almost have preferred it if the man had immediately opened fire. This captain, though, was cunning, and a cunning enemy was ten times as difficult to trick.

"Three minutes, sir. Still no sign they are going to fire," Oliv said.

———

Turret One's computer showed a perfect silhouette of the chasing Tripoli-class light cruiser. PO Collins deliberately took her hand off the firing controls, just to avoid any possible accident. The light above the digital targeting screen burned crimson, which meant safeties on, no firing.

She wanted to fire... probably more than the Skipper did. Her leg ached in the morning, every morning. The four months she'd spent in a fleet hospital learning to walk again while the vat grown nerves reattached had been hell for her. She was thankful, of course, thankful that she could accept a vat grown replacement, that she didn't have to have a machine leg or, God forbid, a prosthetic.

The memory of the battle in Zuckabar with the Guild ships woke her up in cold sweats, her mind perfectly recreating the last moment of Spacer Teller's life, with Spacer Alvarez slumped against the bulkhead, his body broken and bleeding.

She blinked hard, pushing it all away. There was no time for that, no time for recriminations or regret. She did her duty. They all did, just like the captain. Today would be no different. Maybe some of them died, maybe not, but regardless, they would live or die doing their duty with honor. A certain kind of pride filled her, the kind that only came from real accomplishment, from being a part of something great and meaningful.

"If we're going to fire, sir," Ghazali said, "now is the time. Twenty more seconds and they will be out of reliable range."

Yousef pondered his opponent. The man had played it remarkably cool. Neither of them wanted to open fire, neither of them were willing to make the first move. That showed an advanced tactical acumen in his adversary.

"Helm, bring us around, full reverse. Let's get back to the lane."

"Aye aye, sir, full about."

His XO frowned, watching the tiny ship fade from their scope. "I don't like it, sir."

"Neither do I, but we are as bound by our rules as he is by theirs. Besides, whether we kill him now, or the fleet destroys him when they move through, doesn't change what Allah wills. We recover our damaged ship and head to the next starlane, trapping him behind us. He's one destroyer, hardly a threat to the fleet."

CHAPTER THIRTY-EIGHT

Nadia burst through the door and down the stairs, two steps at a time.

"Daisy, heading down and south. I think he's going for the private terminal," she said.

She didn't have time to ponder the lack of response. The underground area Imran had retreated through was a maze of turns and tight tunnels, requiring her to clear each corner before moving, while her quarry could run unimpeded.

"Cobra, how copy?"

"Good copy. No targets yet." Cobra's voice crackled with interference.

"Swing over to the private terminal. Make sure nothing takes to the air," she ordered.

"Roger. Cobra copies."

She ducked under a pipe that obscured a long straight tunnel, with several more pipes at the end. She frowned, stepping back behind the corner. The tunnel was long enough that it would expose her for a solid ten seconds while she ran the length. The pipes at the end were big enough to conceal a man, and she wouldn't have any way to hide from fire.

Nadia dropped her head around the corner for three seconds, then pulled back. No fire. She did it again. Still no fire. The spy took several large gulping breaths, filling her muscles with oxygen, then darted away, running flat out down the corridor as fast as her legs would take her.

With every step, she expected fire from the corner ahead. She made it to the end, sliding over the pipe to find another corridor just as long heading off to the east.

"Dammit," she muttered. It was going to take her forever. "Daisy, where are you?" she asked over the comms.

"I got turned around. I'm with the two security men. We're proceeding on foot to the private terminal. ATC says there's a shuttle in preflight that isn't responding to calls to shut their engines down."

Nadia leaned against the wall, pulling out her NavPad to see the distance between her and the private terminal.

"I'm five minutes out. Cobra, locate that private craft and lock them down."

"Roger that, India," Cobra replied.

Daisy hustled along with the two security guards as they led her through the private section of the terminal, avoiding the crowds. She gripped her pistol in one hand, holding it down by her leg as they jogged.

She'd hoped Nadia would stop Imran before Daisy reached him, because now she had a decision to make. She'd told Nadia that she wouldn't betray her people, and she meant it. Whether Imran lived or died, she didn't care. He was as worthless as the Caliph—a thought that would have sent shards of discord through her just a few years before.

However, that was before she realized that her people were

more important than their leaders. If Imran escaped, he would wage war against the Alliance. As horrible as it sounded, it would just be a *political* war.

If Imran died at the hands of the infidel, then the Caliph would use it as an excuse to wage a *holy war* against the Alliance and the Consortium.

In a holy war, the Caliph could whip the population into a frenzy. Hundreds of millions would die needlessly. The Alliance would never be able to secure Caliphate planets without inflicting massive casualties. Daisy couldn't let that happen, even if it meant letting Imran go.

"That door," Peck said with a jab of his finger.

Daisy hit it with her shoulder, banging it open. Bright light from Alexandria's sun assaulted her, along with the roar of plasma engines and the acrid smell of burning fuel.

She spied them almost instantly, two hundred meters away, running full speed for a needle-shaped ship. A ship fast enough that if it got airborne, they would never find it.

"Target located. He's running for a ship," Daisy said over the comms.

Nadia found another gear. Knowing there wasn't anyone ahead of her waiting in ambush, she ran full speed through the service tunnels until she found the exit.

"India, Cobra, I've got a SK-54 jump ship powering up on the tarmac. Two targets fifty meters out. How copy?" Cobra asked.

"Cobra, India, do not let them board. I say again, do not let them board the ship."

"Roger that."

Lieutenant Bonds held onto the grab bar above the side hatch of the Corsair as it hummed open. Behind him, Private Reynard hooked a line to his harness to keep him from falling out.

"Down there," Bonds yelled over the scream of the plasma engines. The pilot swiveled the dropship around sideways, with Bonds facing the two men running for the ship.

He shouldered the MP-17, set it to heavy-support mode, and clipped it in to the hatch harness. The two men fleeing across the tarmac stopped as the Corsair flew past them, banked, and came level just above the needle-shaped SK-54.

Bonds waved at them, holding one hand out in the universal gesture of stop.

The older of the two, a man who looked vaguely familiar, raised his hand as if to fire. Light flashed through the air as the small laser pistol discharged. The beam missed Bonds but struck the tail of the ship.

"Does he think he can hurt us with that?" the pilot asked over the comms.

"I have no idea, but I know I can hurt him with this," Bonds replied. With one hand on the grip, and the other holding the weapon steady, Bonds let out a burst of fire that spattered the tarmac ten meters in front of the two targets.

He didn't have to kill them, just delay them long enough for India to catch up. The old man fired again, aiming for the cockpit. The pistol lacked the power to penetrate armor, but it startled the pilot enough that he banked the ship away from the shot.

"Hold on, coming back around," the pilot's voice crackled over the radio.

Nadia shot out onto the tarmac, pushing herself harder than she ever had. Her breath came in ragged gulps and her legs burned with acidic intensity.

The wail of plasma engines echoed over the spaceport. Cobra's Corsair lifted up and banked, turning its nose away.

"Daisy, where are you?" she asked.

"Fifty meters north of the jump ship. I can see the Corsair, but not Imran. Nadia, listen to me, I know you want to stop him, but if you kill him it will be worse than if he escaped."

"He's not leaving this planet, Daisy. You copy? He's not getting off this planet."

She dodged past a baggage carrier that blocked her view of the jump ship. Its needle shape spoke of speed and maneuverability. A small ladder extended down from the belly to the ground.

While the Corsair banked around, Simmons and Imran ran for in the open. Nadia dropped to one knee, gripping her pistol with both hands. She inhaled deeply, sighting on her target as she let out her breath, counting down from five, then squeezed the trigger. The gun barked as the chemical propellent sent the five-point-seven-millimeter round speeding toward its target.

Bit Simmons screamed and fell, his body spasming from the impact. Imran continued running toward the jump ship, leaving the old man to his fate.

Nadia changed targets, putting the holographic pip over Imran's back. She hesitated, Daisy's warning echoing in her mind. A surge of anger demanded she squeeze the trigger and kill the bastard. Her finger switched to the guard.

"Dammit," she muttered. Leaping up, she ran to catch him.

"Cobra, if that ship tries to take off, you shoot it down," she said over the comms.

"Roger," Bond's voice crackled back at her.

Imran hit the ladder and started climbing. Nadia was fifty

meters away... less than ten seconds. Her ribs ached and her legs were burning.

Imran's feet disappeared into the ship. Daisy banged into the ladder from the other side, swinging around and climbing up after him. As Daisy vanished into the interior, the ship's engines roared, plasma struck the tarmac, and the ship lifted slowly into the air.

"No," Nadia yelled. The ladder was still down, and she leaped for it, her hand hitting the last rung. She held on, dropped her pistol, slapped her other hand on the ladder, and pulled herself up.

Daisy was there, hand out, grasping Nadia's wrist to help her up.

"India, you're on the ship. Shoot it down?" Bonds asked.

With Daisy's help, Nadia managed to make it to the interior just as the hatch started to close, almost bisecting her.

"In..a, y..... in the ..ip, .ow copy?" Bonds' voice came over distorted and broken.

"Hold fire, Cobra. Hold fire," she said. "I'm not sure they can hear me."

Daisy pointed toward the front of the ship.

"It's not that big. He's got to be in the cockpit with the pilot."

They took up sides on the hatch, Daisy with her pistol out. Nadia reached for the small of her back, pulling a wicked looking fifteen-centimeter, double-edged blade.

"Ready?" she asked.

Daisy nodded.

Nadia hit the override on the hatch and it slid open. Imran froze, half strapped into the copilot seat while the pilot worked the controls. They both charged in. Daisy grabbed the pilot's head, pressing the pistol to his temple.

Imran pulled a sleek, deadly looking SMG from beside the

seat and jammed it into Daisy's side while Nadia pressed her blade against his throat.

"Land," Daisy ordered the pilot.

"Do no such thing," Imran barked.

Nadia wanted to yank the knife along his throat. "You're only alive because I will it so," she said with gritted teeth. "You lose."

Daisy jerked the pilot's head with her pistol.

"Land," she ordered.

The pilot glanced sideways at Imran.

"You will have to kill us. Then we will see how long your empire of lies lasts," Imran said.

Nadia was prepared to do just that.

Daisy kicked Nadia in the side, sending her flying into the bulkhead, her knife clattering away.

"I'm sorry," Daisy said.

"Ha, even my traitorous spy knows that..." Imran trailed off.

"Allahu Akbar," Daisy said. She shot the pilot in the head, splattering the controls and windshield with his brains.

The jump ship's nose dived forward, the ground rushing up. Imran screamed, letting off a burst from the SMG that caught Daisy full in the chest.

The jump ship lifted into the air, nose angling down for a moment before the engines roared to life and it shot out away from the airfield.

"What do we do, sir?" Private Reynard asked.

"Follow them. Chief," he said over the comms to the pilot, "do not lose that ship."

"Rog," the pilot replied. The Corsair's pilot rotated the engines and spread the wings, gunning the thrust, sending the dropship in pursuit. Corsairs were fast; they had to be to reliably break orbit in planets with gravity up to one-point-five g's. They weren't purpose-built for speed, though.

Light, fast, and maneuverable, SK-54s were racers, not troop carriers.

"She's pulling away, sir. There's nothing I can do about it. Want me to open fire with the ten-mike-mike?" the pilot asked.

Bonds balled his fists in rage. He wanted to shoot the damn thing down, but India was aboard. Her last orders were to hold fire.

"Give me a shot, maybe I can wing 'em," Bonds said over the radio.

"If I bank, you've got one shot. Ready?"

"Do it," Bonds ordered.

He leaned forward into the harness, gripping the MP-17 firmly, but loose enough to maneuver. The drop ship banked suddenly, bringing the hatch around, then tilted his side down. For a split second, the SK-54's silhouette appeared, and Lieutenant Bonds finger hovered over the trigger.

The SK-54's nose pitched down and drove right into the ground, gouging a furrow as the Corsair roared by. Bonds blinked, not having fired even once.

"What happened?" the pilot asked.

"I don't know. Bring us back around!" Bonds yelled. "Call search and rescue."

CHAPTER THIRTY-NINE

Interceptor prowled through space, silent as the shark on her nose. Though it wasn't required, even her crew moved around her decks in hushed whispers.

Jacob sat in his command chair, pulling at his collar as the heat inside the ship built up. For twelve hours they had run silent, not so much as an errant electromagnetic wave had departed the hull.

"You sure about this, Skipper?" Boudreaux whispered from his side. Even though they were in an elevated state of readiness, they weren't in ELS suits. Jacob felt that any risk of combat was foreseeable enough that his people would have time to don them if needed. They were already uncomfortable enough with the rising heat.

"No, but we can't let them out of our detection range and we can't engage them," he said. Once the light cruiser had pulled off, Jacob used *Interceptor*'s speed advantage to turn toward the only possible destination; Taki's starlane. Worst case, he decided, he could get to Praetor on the double and bring back help. He fully expected the light cruisers to remain at their current location and wait for DesRon Nine to return.

However, to his surprise, the light cruiser formation immediately set out for the Taki lane. Either they didn't realize there were destroyers behind them, or they didn't care.

He wasn't sure which bothered him more.

Worse yet, they hadn't picked up a single emergency beacon from *Sabre*.

Interceptor sailed ahead of the light cruisers by more than twelve million klicks, skimming their detection range and only accelerating for short periods of time to avoid detection. The cruisers, on the other hand, were at flank speed and gaining velocity with every second.

"Astro, what's their minimum distance going to be?" he asked.

PO Oliv didn't take her eyes off the scope. "Eight million klicks, sir. Close enough that if they went active, they would have a fair chance of picking us up."

Eight million. They could be seen, but not fired upon. If they were seen, *Interceptor* controlled the rules of engagement. She could run away, essentially, and there would be nothing the tango could do to stop her. They could take up a position at the Taki starlane and try to stop *Interceptor* from returning to Praetor, but whatever mission they were trying to accomplish would not succeed.

"What do you think they're doing out here, Skipper?" Boudreaux asked.

It was a good question. Taki was nominally Consortium space, Ocelot wasn't. They could be here without risking a territorial violation.

"Causing trouble," he said with a grin.

Jacob pulled up their info on the Tripoli-class light cruisers. They had an operational range much greater than *Interceptor*, and they were much closer to Caliphate FOBs out in the black. Three-hundred-plus crew, multiple weapon systems, dropships—they weren't as big as the heavy cruiser they had faced in Medial, but that didn't mean *Interceptor* could win another in a fight without extraordinary amounts of luck.

Luck they had already used to take one out. He wouldn't get the chance on another.

On their first engagement, every advantage that favored destroyers had favored him. In a straight up fight, regardless of the kind, *Interceptor* would lose. Unless...

"I see that look," Boudreaux said.

"Look?" he replied.

"Yeah. The 'I have a crazy idea' look. The one you're wearing right now."

Jacob pulled himself away from the screen to stare at Boudreaux. He thought he carefully masked his emotions, making sure the crew only saw the unflappable captain.

"Marta," he said, looking over at PO Oliv. "Do I have looks?" he asked, fully expecting her to answer honestly.

Oliv glanced at her CO, one eyebrow raising slightly as she thought over her answer.

"I think wise POs don't comment on a captain's looks... or lack thereof, Skipper."

A slight grin played across his face. His bridge crew was very astute.

"Okay, maybe I have some looks—"

Chief Suresh snorted.

"Skipper," she said, looking in the small mirror they shared, "you have exactly two looks. Everything is fine, and 'some crazy stuff is about to go down.' Sir."

"Okay, okay," he said, holding his hands up. "I surrender. I have looks. Well, in this case, Viv, you might just be right. If they had a specific or unique mission in Ocelot, why would they beeline for the Taki starlane?"

Boudreaux examined the tactical screen showing the LC's current velocity, trajectory, and probable destination.

"Their mission is in Taki—"

"Or Praetor," Jacob said.

She shook her head. "Why would they go to Praetor? The Consortium has three heavy cruisers there that would make short work of their squadron."

Jacob had wondered that himself. The fact that they didn't stay and guard the lane to Naji and that they broke off from their engagement, meant they weren't concerned about the destroyer or what they left behind them, only what lay ahead.

"They could be going to Taki for an ambush. Hoping to catch one or two of the HC's if they come through the starlane," Jacob said. He looked at her expectantly, willing her to think like an officer and solve the tactical problem.

"I don't think so, Skipper. They would never know if it was just one, or all three, or even more coming through. Once they engaged, they would be too far from their line of retreat to escape. Unless everything went perfect, they'd be dead," she said.

"Well done," Jacob said. "That's what I was thinking too. That only leaves why they're really here, doesn't it? Because if they don't care what's behind them, they either have more ships on the way, or they're not heading for Praetor."

"They have to be, don't they? Heading for Praetor, I mean. It's the only thing that makes sense."

Jacob leaned back, drumming his fingers against the leather arm of the con.

"I think so. I think, and I can't be sure, mind you, but I think this is a forward screening element of a task force or fleet," he said. Leaning toward Boudreaux, he dropped his voice. "If they have a fleet coming up behind us, then the squadron should be able to evade. Only poor *Sabre* will be lost... and us."

Boudreaux put one hand on the con and leaned down to her captain. "How do you figure?" she asked with a matched volume.

"Because the second they go through from Taki to Praetor, we're going to have to follow. As soon as we're in system, we have to warn the Consortium, and in doing so, give our position away. There's just no way around it. If we don't warn Admiral Edo, he won't have time to prepare—"

"And if we do warn him, we'll be broadcasting our location to a fleet practically on top of us," she said.

"Got it in one, XO. This is it, Viv. The first engagement of the war we've tried to avoid for so long. If we succeed, we die. If we live, we've failed. Not much of a choice, is it?"

―――

"Starlane exit in three..." *Firewatch*'s XO counted down while Captain Hatwal focused on not puking. He hated puking. Not that he knew anyone who enjoyed it.

Minutes passed, and he managed to avoid looking like a fool. Once he was able to breathe and speak again, he ordered his ship ahead slow, making sure to clear the lane just in case.

"Sir, we've got a problem," Lieutenant Ban said.

"What is it?"

"Only *Tizón* and *Kraken* have arrived, no *Sabre* or *Interceptor*."

Ganesh pulled up the plot, cloning the radar systems on his station. Only three ships, his included, showed up.

"Astro, push out radar and lidar to maximum resolution. Maybe they drifted in the lane?" Ganesh ordered.

Was it unheard of? No. Rare, though. Occasionally, ships would enter the starlane at a wrong angle, or some stellar phenomenon could push them out a degree or two. When the distances were measured in light-years, any variation, even a tenth of one degree, could result in millions of kilometers off course.

"Nothing, sir," Ensign Marlin said.

"Strange. Maybe *Interceptor* had a malfunction and *Sabre* decided to wait for her?" Lieutenant Ban said.

"Maybe. Helm, let's come right." He tapped a few keys on his plot, making sure he had it correct. "Two-three-zero. Ahead one-zero gravities for zero-five minutes."

"Aye sir," his Coxswain said.

Ganesh frowned, wondering why he'd been so hard on Grimm. Yes, the man had a reputation, but if he'd taken ten minutes to get to know him, then maybe he would have realized what an outstanding officer he clearly was. If it weren't for actually reading the report of what went down between his destroyer and the light cruiser, Ganesh wouldn't have believed it. The man had a knack for surviving situations he shouldn't, and bringing his ship along.

They waited ten minutes as they accelerated away from the starlane. Ten minutes more than the other two ships would logically need, yet nothing.

"All stop," Ganesh said.

"Aye aye, sir." *Firewatch* and her consorts decelerated until they came to a stop relative to the starlane.

"What the devil is going on?" Something nagged at Ganesh. A feeling he couldn't ignore.

"Sir," Ensign Marlin said from Astro. Her watch cap fit snugly over her ears. The crew still wore their ELS suits but had placed helmets on the racks behind their chairs and donned watch caps.

"What is it?"

"I'm picking up something distant... like an incoming ship, but it's weak. I've never heard anything like it," she said.

Ganesh unstrapped and moved to stand over her. "Show me," he said.

"Aye aye, sir." With a tap of a few buttons, she showed the raw feed. Lasers in the hull vibrated as gravity waves passed through them, which the computer translated into sound. The line on the scope jumped and danced to the beat. Natural gravity had a regular beat that never changed, but this jumped up and down irregularly.

Almost like they were seeing multiple sources?

"Set Condition Zulu, battle stations. All hands, rig for silent running!" Ganesh yelled. "Order *Tizón* and *Kraken* to do the same."

A chorus of aye-ayes followed as Ganesh returned to the captain's chair. It was no wonder Ensign Marlin didn't recognize the signature. How often did they see fleet-sized gravity signatures from warships?

He just hoped they'd moved far enough away to avoid detection, and that whatever delayed *Sabre* and *Interceptor* would keep them for a little while longer. If they appeared amidst that fleet, there wasn't enough luck in the universe to save them.

CHAPTER FORTY

Jacob's ELS-garbed command crew gathered around the conference table, their sweat-streaked faces wearing dour looks as they placed their helmets on the shark-emblazoned table and took their seats. They were tired. He was tired. Three days of continuous alert status would exhaust even the best crew, and he had the best. His officers on the other hand... other than Boudreaux, were still learning.

Boudreaux sat opposite of him, taking up the usual seat of the XO. He didn't really think of it as *divide and conquer*, but it helped maintain order, especially when things were tense. The particular seating arrangement also allowed for more fluid conversation and made it easier to see who was involved and who wasn't.

Which was useful since Jacob and Boudreaux were the only ones doing the talking. Ensign Brown and Kai sat silently next to each other. Midships Rugger and Marino sat quietly on the other side. PO Oliv, PO Ignatius, and CPO Sandivol were also in attendance. Jacob had a feeling they would speak more, but they were trying to encourage the junior officers to be involved.

As the captain of a destroyer and an officer in the Navy,

Jacob appreciated what Admiral Villanueva was trying to do for these young officers. They would be around for a long time and their influence would shape the Navy for a generation. Right then, though, he just wanted his old crew back. It wasn't fair of him to wish, but he did.

"How's sickbay?" Boudreaux asked Midship Marino.

"Fine, ma'am. Chief Pierre and PO Desper have been a great help. We had two spacers in yesterday with upset stomachs. No one else has reported a problem, so we think that's taken care of."

"Engineering?" Boudreaux said, leveling her gaze at Ensign Kai.

"Ma'am, all ship's systems are one hundred percent. Chief Redfern inspects the borrowed anvil after every ten hours of operation; so far no problems, though the fuel mixture is slightly off from what we would normally use. He thinks it's because of the DAC's size difference. Theirs are larger than the ones we use, but it doesn't effect operations of the reactor in any appreciable way."

In a way, at least from a managerial standpoint, sickbay and engineering were easy compared to Ops, which accounted for seventy percent of the ships personnel and systems.

"Ensign Brown?" Boudreaux asked.

"Ma'am?"

"Anything to report in Ops?"

"No ma'am."

Jacob glanced at Boudreaux and nodded, letting her know to dig further.

"What I mean, *Ensign,* is please give us a status report. It's important for everyone aboard to know what's going on in each department, as any one of us might be required to take over at any given moment."

Brown's eyes opened a little bigger, and he squared his

shoulders. "Sorry, ma'am, of course you're correct." He took a deep breath. "With Bosun Sandivol's help, we've taken care of the issue we had with crew rotations…"

Jacob half listened to the report. It was important for him to know, but it was more important for them to talk. Oral reports and communicating with other officers was ninety percent of command. These kinds of meetings also built comradery.

However, he also had a tactical problem to solve, and he needed to get through that as well. They were two hours behind the light cruiser squadron, keeping them on passive while *Interceptor* coasted toward the starlane entrance to Taki.

Did they go through when they arrived? Wait to see if the rest of DesRon Nine returned? If he was wrong, and the LCs were meeting a fleet in Taki, he needed to follow them immediately or he would lose his chance to warn Admiral Endo.

If he did follow them and there was a fleet behind, he risked being flanked and destroyed before warning the admiral. The entire situation seemed like lose-lose.

Of course, it wouldn't be the first time.

"So yes, while there are still some ruffled feathers from the shuffling, I think the new crew assignments will work, Ma'am," Ensign Brown finished.

"I think that's everyone, Skipper," Boudreaux said.

"Thank you, XO." Jacob looked down at his NavPad, trying to think of a way to broach the subject without killing morale. "We have a problem, people, and I need input. There are no wrong answers here. Ahead of us is a light cruiser squadron. What are they doing? They may be a screening element, or lone wolf. All we know for sure is that they are heading for Taki, next door to Praetor. If they stay by themselves, they aren't a threat to anyone but us… so we can put that aside for the moment."

Using his NavPad, he pulled up a holographic representation of Taki, highlighting the two starlanes in the process. The situation, he decided, was even more dangerous because of the short transit time between Taki and Praetor. A slow ship could cross Taki in twelve hours, and transit to Praetor four-five hours after that.

"Why don't we just follow them, sir?" Ensign Brown asked.

"Because, Austin, if there are enemy ships behind us, we will be trapped in Taki. It only has two lanes. If there is an impending attack, our priority is to alert Admiral Endo, then disrupt the attack, in that order. If we are destroyed before we can alert them, we die for nothing."

He hoped Austin understood. Seeing tactical situations both from an immediate perspective and a strategic one was a valuable asset in an officer.

"I don't really see as we have a choice, Skipper," Midship Rugger said. He stopped, realizing he'd spoken familiarly, but Jacob waved for him to go on. "Uh... we have to *know* if there is a fleet. We can't guess, right?"

"Right. We have to know. And if there is one, we need to be able to warn the admiral. That's the mission now," he said.

"Skipper," Ensign Marino said. "We should wait here and see if there is a fleet... or if DesRon Nine returns."

"There is always the chance that ships were able to sneak past us while we were on the other end of Ocelot, but it doesn't seem likely, does it?" Jacob asked.

Boudreaux agreed. "It doesn't, sir. Even if they were going full stealth, that's a lot of ships to hide."

"Everyone agree, then? We wait to see if anyone follows them?" All heads nodded. "Okay then, set Condition Yankee and give the crew break from ELS."

Jacob felt like it was the right call, but something nagged at him. A feeling that no matter what he did, he would have somehow made a mistake he couldn't correct.

PO Collins' watch didn't start for a few minutes, but she wanted to be early to speak with Chief Suresh. It was always good for the coxswains to be on the same page when it came to the operations of the ship.

She tucked her NavPad into its pocket on her thigh as she started climbing the ladder to the O-Deck, expertly maneuvering herself to the top deck while holding her coffee. The sealed cup wouldn't spill, but she didn't want to drop it.

Naki stood at the top, waiting for her to finish transition. He reached out offering his hand. She took it and his strong grip pulled her up the rest of the way.

"Thank you, Corporal," Collins said.

"You're welcome, PO."

Collins pulled out her NavPad and resumed looking at charts as she entered the bridge. She paused for a moment, looking up to take in the bridge. Second watch was about to end, and she felt the restlessness of the crew waiting to be relived.

She went to The Pit to kneel next to Chief Petty Officer Suresh. "COB."

"Jen, you're early." Chief Suresh said after looking at the time.

"Aye, COB. I wanted to ask you about the readings on the gravcoil. They're showing stress under acceleration…"

The two coxswains spent a few minutes going over the logs, and then Chief Suresh unbuckled and stretched. "All yours, Jen. Enjoy."

"Thanks, COB," she replied.

The Pit's chair felt like a second home to Collins. Unlike the rest of the chairs in the ship, The Pit was more like a molded couch, reforming and gripping the user like a long-lost friend.

Chief Petty Officer Suresh was a solid eight centimeters taller than her, so Collins found the controls to change the setup. The seat moved forward half the distance and the pedals and HOTAS adjusted the other half, so that she could comfortably reach what she needed.

She held the stick on her right and the throttle on her left, running them through their tests. Once the computer showed full function, she ran through the self-checks on the thrusters. Each watch ran through the list for their own department, and any discrepancy would be reported immediately. There was little to no chance of a system failing in the five seconds it took most watch stations to shift over, but the Alliance Navy had learned long before that ship safety required crew vigilance. Having a system fail during a watch could go unnoticed, especially if the ship was in port or laying doggo, but the chances of that failure going from watch to watch was mitigated by the checks.

Green lights flashed on her NavPad, signaling the completion of the maintenance. "Skipper, I have the helm. Operations are nominal," she said.

"Aye, PO. Helm is yours," he replied.

One by one, the rest of the watch reported the same thing. Aboard ship, watches were secondary to normal duty, though PO Jennifer Collins preferred her time in The Pit to any other duty she had. Flying the *Interceptor*, even when mundane, filled her with purpose and joy she never thought possible. She'd joined the Navy as a weapons tech mate and worked on the coilguns for the first couple of years. One day, she had a chance to stand watch in The Pit. She never looked back. Her secondary position was still with the coilguns, but flying was her passion.

"Uh, sir," Spacer Alderman said from Astro. The young man had the gravity receivers over one ear while fiddling with the equipment.

"Yes, Alderman?"

"I'm picking up something weird, sir." Weird was hardly a technical definition. "It sounds like an echo?"

Collins watched her captain in the mirror that allowed them to see each other. He leaned forward, linking his MFD to Alderman's station, and his face went from interested to stone cold.

"Set Condition Zulu, all hands to battle stations," Grimm said.

The lights turned red and the klaxon sounded. Collins cracked her knuckles and neck, knowing things were about to get tense.

She was ready.

CHAPTER FORTY-ONE

Interceptor was seven million kilometers from the starlane entrance, with its nose pointing at the incoming signal to reduce her radar cross section. Radiation from the Caliphate fleet reached out to her but was unable to find her hidden among the stars.

"Everyone stay calm. With our gravcoil off, we're just a hole in space. Roger?" Jacob said to his crew. They wore their ELS suits with helmets racked on chairs. He wanted to be ready for combat, but not make his crew feel overly stressed.

"Roger," they answered as one.

Tefiti arrived, relieving spacer Alderman, who was more than ready to let someone else sit at gravitics.

"Ryan," Jacob said as the young man hurried away. "You did good, son."

"Thank you, sir," Alderman replied. He practically ran off the bridge.

"Tefiti, when you're ready, give me a ship count please," Jacob asked.

"Aye aye, Skipper," PO Tefiti replied.

Jacob cloned the passive sensor station on his MFD,

watching the gravity waves, heat sources, and radar emissions formed around the starlane entrance to Taki. All Jacob saw was a mass of signatures that he couldn't begin to sort out. However, between PO Tefiti and Ensign Brown, he was certain they could give him a solid read. It hurt, having so many officers pull double duty on the bridge, but that decision was above his paygrade. His job, besides survival, was to train them to be the best. Better even, if he could.

One by one, the mass emissions took shape and individual ships appeared, each one with a tag denoting suspected type. Tango-Lima was for light cruisers, the Tripoli-class ships like the ones they had already faced. Then there were the Tango-Hotels, which were heavy cruisers. Jacob swallowed hard at the memory of the one they fought in orbit above Medial.

He reminded himself they weren't spoiling for a fight here; it was recon only. Once they were back in Praetor, they would relay the information to Admiral Edo and give him the heads-up on what came his way.

Still, as Tango-Hotels continued to appear, he already suspected what the admiral would do: bug out.

Then the death knell appeared.

Tango-Bravo.

Battleship.

Jacob leaned back in his squeaky command chair, one hand rubbing his jaw at the sight of that monster.

"So it's a battlegroup, then?" Jacob asked.

"It looks that way," XO Boudreaux said from her position down in DCS. "One battleship, eight heavies, two lights, and..." she paused while the computer and Tefiti marked the rest. "Four destroyers." Boudreaux looked up from her station into the mirror she shared with Jacob and smiled. "I don't want to be your XO anymore. Maybe a transfer?" Her soft tone robbed the words of any bite.

"Granted. Would you like to get off now?" he replied with a mischievous grin.

"At least we know the Caliphate's plan, Skipper," she said.

"Agreed. This is war." Jacob understood the weight of his words, and he hated having to say them. No fighting person wanted war. At least no sane person. In this case, it was unavoidable. The Alliance had bought as much time as they could to even the power dynamic of the two forces, but in the end, it would be more up to strategy than numbers.

On screen, the images grew in strength. The longer they held them on passive sensors, the more reliable the identification became. He watched the Caliphate fleet form up at the starlane entrance. The battleship was in the middle of a globe, while the heavy cruisers orbited the ship over its central axis, with the light cruisers and destroyers forming a wedge along the ecliptic in front of it.

In 3D space, where threats could literally come from any direction, traveling in a globe formation made sense. Especially to protect a battleship whose armament would decide the outcome of any major battle.

"Tefiti, see if you can pin down classes on those ships. Anything at all will help," he said.

"Aye sir. On it."

Caliphate ships tended to be larger and more heavily armored than their Alliance counterparts. These ships were probably no different. However, if he was reading the screen right, the heavy cruisers' signatures were those of a previous class. Not the newest Sayaad-class, but the older Djinns. Not that an older ship meant they were weak. The two light cruisers popped up as Tripoli's, just like the one they had already fought.

The four destroyers were an afterthought, because the killing power was in the battleship. All the other ships were there to take fire and defend the battleship against torpedo attacks. Something about their formation struck him as odd. He pondered it, looking at their ship layout from different angles.

Then it hit him. The light cruisers were arrayed toward the front, so the flank was practically wide open. If the light cruisers they'd already seen were part of the fleet, and it was a good bet they were, then they would fill in the stern.

"Gravwake. They're entering the starlane," Tefiti said.

The first of the destroyers disappeared, followed by the light cruisers a moment later, then four of the heavy cruisers. A second later, the battleship went. Last of all, the remaining four heavies disappeared.

"They're all gone, sir. Negative contacts," Tefiti said.

"Now we wait," Jacob said.

Theoretically, he could follow them in and emerge undetected in the middle of the fleet on the other side, but the last thing he wanted was to emerge in the middle of an enemy formation. The anomalies detected by gravitics worked better at a distance. Maybe they wouldn't detect his gravity signature if he was right on top of them, but even a millisecond radar burst would show them, and *Interceptor* would be vaporized.

"Should I have the crew stand down?" Boudreaux asked.

"Go ahead and set Condition Yankee, XO. Ensign Brown, you have the con," he said. Jacob exited the bridge and walked to the briefing room just a few meters away. The short walk let him stretch his legs and circulate his blood. He needed to think.

It was a sure bet that if he had tried to warn Admiral Edo by taking *Interceptor* through the starlane before they detected the fleet, his ship would've been destroyed. That was the good news, he decided.

They knew exactly what they were up against, and exactly where they were heading. What did he do about it? As usual, the briefing room hatch stood open. Far easier to leave it so than constantly fight with the broken mechanism. No matter how many times engineering came up to fix it, the hatch stubbornly remained inoperative. Almost to the point that Jacob suspected someone was sabotaging it for luck.

He took his usual seat at the back and sank down in the chair, eyes losing focus on the shark emblem dominating the table. The cartoon shark had a fresh coat of paint. "USS INTERCEPTOR" on top; the ship's motto, "First to Fight," in the middle; and "DD-1071" along the bottom.

Every ship had their mascot and motto. Esprit de corps was important in the military, and especially the Navy, where crews spent months, sometimes years, on the same ship. While they were a long way from the days of surface ships where the only entertainment was an occasional movie and whatever books they could scrounge, there were still months of boredom aboard. The shark represented an idea, one the crew could rally behind.

Jacob keyed the comms button. "XO, join me in the briefing room, please."

"On my way, Skipper," she said.

He called down to the galley and asked Josh to bring up some drinks, which the young man did before the XO arrived. As PO Mendez departed, Lieutenant Boudreaux entered, still wearing her ELS suit.

"Haven't changed yet?" he asked.

"No sir. As you haven't," she replied.

Jacob admired Viv's leadership skills. Seeing her in her ELS suit after they had all changed out would signal to the crew that she was working hard and hadn't had time. The same went for him.

"Touché." He sipped his orange drink while she took her seat. "Viv, I have an idea I want to run by you."

"Go ahead."

Jacob transferred the plot data from Astro to his NavPad and activated the holographic feature. The starlane flared to life, along with the enemy fleet.

"We know their battlegroup is full strength—"

"Minus one light cruiser. Let's not forget that," she said.

"How could we? Now, they entered the starlane in this formation. It stands to reason then, that this is their preferred battle formation."

"Since you approach a lane like you're going to battle," Boudreaux said.

"Correct. What if, and this is a bit iffy, but what if we could follow them in, wait for them to transit to Praetor, and then *immediately* follow them through? If we can do it fast enough, and I mean fast, then we should appear while their sensors are still recalibrating. We would have a window to stay undetected."

His XO chewed it over, pulling out her NavPad, interfacing it with his, and manipulating the image to look at it from different angles.

"I don't see how we could, Skipper. We would have to be right behind them in Taki all the way to the lane. I just don't see how we could do that."

Jacob looked at the map and sighed. She was right. There wasn't any way to enter the lane fast enough after they transited. Even if they went into Taki ASAP and used flank speed, they would overrun the enemy fleet or be detected and destroyed.

"Wait a second," Jacob muttered. He rewound the video, watching the ships arrive at the lane. Two light cruisers arrived first, followed by the heavy cruisers and destroyers, and last, but only by a minute, the battleship.

"What are you thinking, sir?" Boudreaux asked.

"I'm thinking they are all traveling at the battleship's max accel. Which means they aren't using all their thrust. If we wait two hours to make sure we are out of range of their sensors, then go in and hit flank speed, I think we can catch up to them and time our arrival *without* ever being detected. What do you think?"

It was bold, he knew. Fortune favored the bold. But even if it worked, it would still be risky as all hell leaving them next to a battleship.

"I think it will work, sir. I can run it by PO Oliv if you like. Get her input on the course?"

"Do that and get back to me. We're on the clock."

"Aye aye, sir."

———

Interceptor lined up to the starlane, her gravcoil aperture opening wide to lock onto the gravity manifold. They would have downtime after entering the lane, six hours at least. He could make sure the crew was rested and well-fed before they emerged into possible combat. On the outside, he looked like the unflappable captain, and he knew it. He'd mastered his outward appearance long ago. Except, apparently, for when he had a crazy idea.

Internally, though, his gut churned. His crew was important to him. He hated the idea of losing any of them, but he knew, even if they pulled off this crazy stunt, he *knew* some were going to die.

As a captain, it was his job to command the ship, to ride her into the storm and rule the fate of spacers. For that privilege, he answered to the president and to God. One he could disappoint, the other he could not. He preferred not to let down anyone. Other than the enemy.

"Okay people, on your toes and here we go."

"Uh, Skipper," Tefiti said from Astro. "I'm picking up something on one-eight-zero relative. It's a gravwake."

Oh no, Jacob thought. Was there more to the enemy fleet that he hadn't waited long enough to discover?

"How long till we can transit the starlane?" he asked.

Tefiti answered, "Not soon enough, sir. They're going to be on top of us in ten mikes. I... wait one."

Wait? Jacob wanted to reach out and throttle the man, but he stifled his reaction. As they knew all too well, seconds counted when transiting.

"PO?"

"Hang tight, Skipper," Tefiti said. His eyes were closed and he focused on whatever he was hearing. "They're not Caliphate ships I'm hearing... I think... Sir!" Tefiti swiveled in his chair, a smile splitting his face wide open. "It's *Firewatch* and DesRon Nine!"

Noticeable relief flooded the bridge; Jacob could hardly blame them for showing the same rejoicing emotion he felt. He slumped back in his chair, letting out the breath he'd held for the last half minute. DesRon Nine had returned. That would quadruple their minuscule chances of success, but only if he could convince Captain Hatwal of the importance of warning Admiral Edo.

So far, he hadn't been able to convince Hatwal of anything. He prayed this time would be different.

CHAPTER FORTY-TWO

Jacob didn't like being aboard *Firewatch* for the transit to Taki. He did understand Hatwal's reasoning: the odds of them emerging into an enemy fleet were low. If the Caliphate navy's plan was to attack Praetor, he could hardly argue that they would stick around the starlane in the system *before* their target. Even though Boudreaux was capable enough to command *Interceptor*, otherwise he would never have chosen her for XO, he still didn't like it leaving his ship.

Still, as he looked out the digital porthole to his ship five hundred meters away, he yearned to be aboard her. From the outside, she looked in bad shape. *Firewatch*'s position off her portside showed the external damage to the fuel conversion chamber. Just a few meters down and they would have lost sickbay.

They had survived that encounter by pure luck. From what Jennings reported, the light cruiser was mostly intact when the Marines boarded her. A lucky hit had destroyed the bridge, and they were in the midst of their own repairs when Jennings' strike team had arrived.

He shook his head, remembering his reaction as he read her

report. That crazy Marine seemed determined to get herself killed in combat. He hoped and prayed she never did. Gunnery Sergeant Jennings and Corporal Naki were special to him. They had been through thick and thin together, and as long as he was alive, he would do everything in his power to shepherd their careers.

If they didn't get themselves killed on some damn fool idea of heroics in the meantime.

The ready room hatch slid open and Captain Hatwal, Lieutenant Commander Novak, and Gustav marched in, sans their XOs, who they left in command of their ships.

Gustav approached Jacob instantly, holding out his hand.

"Good work against that Tripoli," he said.

Jacob returned the handshake. "Luck, really. Destroyers have no business punching above their weight."

"Don't I know it. Still, damn fine." He patted Jacob on the shoulder before taking his seat.

Novak remained characteristically silent, only giving him a slight nod, which he returned. It was something, at least. An acknowledgement of his existence, he decided.

"Damnable bad luck on *Sabre*'s part," Hatwal said. "I watched the recording and read your report, Commander Grimm. You did the right thing. There was nothing else you could have done."

Jacob wasn't sure he heard right. His last communique with Captain Hatwal had seemed odd to him at the time, but this was almost like a different person.

"I only wish I knew if the Caliphate stopped to do S&R, sir. When we returned to the area, we did search for beacons, but we came up empty."

The assembled commanders' grave looks told him they knew exactly how he felt. No spacer wanted to leave friend or foe alike in the black to die. Jacob boxed those feelings away. He had come uncomfortably close to just that on his last tour. Some experiences left marks that were deeper than scars... and ten times as dangerous. More than once since his near death in an ELS suit, he'd awoken in the middle of the night, drenched in sweat, with the beeping of the low oxygen alert ringing in his ears.

"Understood. I brought you all here to go over Commander Grimm's strategy. I want to hear your opinions on it before I give my own. Commander Novak, as the squadron XO, why don't you go first?"

"Aye sir," she said. "I'll be blunt." She looked at Jacob. "It's suicide. I don't think any goal we achieve will be worth our lives or our ships. We will die, and no one will be the wiser, sir."

"I appreciate your candor," Hatwal said. "Commander Gustav?"

Gustav folded his prize fighter hands in front of him. "I agree with Commander Novak that it's suicide." Jacob felt his chest tighten. Had he miscalculated his tactical acumen that badly? "But we will achieve the goal. Admiral Endo will be warned of the attack, all of our logs and data will be transmitted to him, and the Alliance will know of the Caliphate Naval offense on *Interceptor*. Which was an act of war. There are twelve hundred people on each of those Consortium heavies, thousands more working on the infrastructure around the wormhole. Four hundred lives for thousands seems a bargain, sir."

Jacob glanced Gustav's way, and the older man gave him a wink. He was right. The math was solid.

"My understanding, Commander Grimm, is your astrogator has plotted a course that will end with us coming to the Praetor starlane within thirty to forty-five minutes of the Caliphate fleet's departure. And your supposition is that when we arrive in Praetor, we will have enough time to send our warning to Admiral Endo... and possibly escape?"

"When it was just *Interceptor*, I fully didn't expect to escape, sir. I still don't. However, four ships are better than one. If we go flank speed upon arrival and broadcast the alert in a tight beam at full power using our long-range antennae, I don't see how the Caliphate could react in time to stop us. Maybe one or two ships, but all four? I've seen their ship handling first hand. They've spent too much time fighting freighters and raiding civilians. We can do it."

"Yes," Novak said. "Maybe. That's a big maybe. And who dies, Commander Grimm? Me? My crew? For what? A chance we might succeed at warning of an attack? We aren't at war with the Caliphate, nor are we going to be. I say we wait, go through when it's safe, and enter the wormhole back to Alliance territory. If they want to send an invasion force at that point, that's on high command."

Jacob was flabbergasted. How could an officer in his Navy think that way? It was borderline cowardice as far as he was concerned. Run? Abandon their allies? Hide when they could fight? When they could achieve a tactical and strategic victory?

"Hold on, Commander Novak," Jacob said, fighting to keep his emotions in check. "Are you suggesting we do *nothing*?"

She sliced her hand through the air like a knife. "No. I'm suggesting we don't spend the lives of our crew like chips at a gambling table."

Jacob understood the desire to protect one's crew. It was noble and good, in any commander. The opposite was an unforgivable trait, and he prayed no captain in the Alliance had that. However, it wasn't a waste. They would save thousands, maybe millions, if they succeeded.

"Captain Hatwal, sir, if we succeed, Admiral Endo will have one place to retreat to. Zuckabar. From there, he will send our message to the fleet. The rest of our battlegroup may already be on the way. At the very least, three heavy cruisers added to the ships at Zuckabar may be able to hold the Caliphate off long enough for the *Enterprise* to arrive. Once that happens, they can retake Praetor. If I'm right, and I think I am, this is the beginning of the Caliphate of Hamid's war against the Consortium, and by extension, us. Their first step has to be severing the connection between the Alliance and Consortium forces. It's the only thing that makes sense. Don't you see that?" he asked.

"I don't see that," Novak said. "All I see is an officer looking for another medal and a chance to get killed."

As the argument raged, Ganesh Hatwal chastised himself. This was his fault. His pride and indignation at Grimm's assignment to his squadron had permeated down to Novak, the squadron XO. He'd only confirmed her suspicion of him when he made her the squadron XO instead of Grimm, who should have had the position by virtue of his rank.

Those feelings permeated his command and made his officers unwilling to trust Grimm and the *Interceptor*. It was all his fault. Time to fix it, time to make it right.

"That's enough," he said, rapping his knuckles on the conference table. "For the record, Commander Grimm's performance in a difficult situation has been exemplarily"—surprise appeared in Novak's eyes—"as is his plan to warn Admiral Endo of the invasion. Our job isn't to decide whether we will do our duty, but how we do it in order to give our ships and crews a fighting chance. Let's get to work."

Jacob wasn't sure what he'd done to turn Captain Hatwal around, but he was glad of it. Excluding a direct order, he couldn't just let the people in Praetor, and eventually Zuckabar, be slaughtered and taken into slavery. It just wasn't in him to do nothing. He would never know what drove his mother when she decided to stay aboard her ship, rescuing trapped spacers and carrying them to the escape pods one by one, but he suspected it was something akin to what he felt. Duty wasn't some existential idea, some vague philosophy in the ether. It was real. He could do no less than his absolute best to fulfill it.

"My basic plan remains the same, sir. However, with four ships all appearing at the same time and immediately lighting off our drives, we will confuse them. Our sensor logs show the formation they use to depart and arrive in a system. We can take advantage of the confusion by running at flank speed, broadcasting our warning. As soon as we're sure our message has made it through their EW, we trigger our ECMs and slam down an electronic curtain on them. Shooting at everything we can as we go will add to the chaos. Even if luck isn't on our side, some of us will make it through... and we will have warned the fleet."

Captain Hatwal nodded as Jacob elaborated, giving him hope that the man agreed.

"That sounds good, Commander Grimm. Here is what I want from all of us. Let's make the plan even better. No arguing over the strategy. This is what we're doing. What we need now is to make it airtight. We *must* warn Admiral Edo, and we will do it while saving as many as our own people as possible. Understood?"

"Aye aye, sir," the three commanders said as one.

"I may have something, sir," Commander Gustav said. "We have the new MKIV EW warheads for our torpedoes. Normally, because of the limited number we can fire, we would mix them in a one-on-one engagement. However, if all four ships launch a volley at once, before we light off our drives, then it will have them second-guessing their sensors. It might buy us a few minutes of confusion."

Jacob hadn't thought of that. It was a solid idea. He would have loved to use them in Wonderland.

"We can add to that," Commander Novak said. "*Kraken*'s comm suite has the latest EW package. She has twice the capability of any destroyer. We can blind them, for sure. If we tie in all the ships EW to her computer, we can increase the efficiency by thirty or forty percent. It's what they designed her for."

"That's excellent," Jacob said.

"There is a drawback, though," Novak said. "In this kind of operation, we should all head in different directions, force them to split the fleet. However, in order for the EW link to work, we will need to maintain a formation no farther than ten thousand klicks from *Kraken*."

That revelation sobered them. SOP for a destroyer squadron against an overwhelming force was to break formation and run a starburst. If the enemy wanted to pursue the destroyers, they would have to break up their own formation, and since that was where the power of a fleet lay, no commander would want to do that. However, it also meant with DesRon Nine running tight, shots fired by the Caliphate meant for one ship could end up hitting another.

Jacob double-checked the numbers on his NavPad; *Interceptor* was faster than any of the other ships, and he would have to throttle her back to keep with the squadron. However, with their comms tied together, they could manage point defense more efficiently as well as the improved ECM. *Interceptor*'s chances alone were superior to the rest of the squadron, but if they stayed together, it increased all of their odds of survival.

"That will make *Kraken* the center of our formation,

Commander," Jacob said. "I think it's a solid plan, sir. I would suggest putting *Kraken* at the tip of the spear. That way, we can defend her and maintain our best chance of escape."

Captain Hatwal looked Jacob in the eye and nodded. "Let's go with that, from there I want..."

The rest of the meeting was about the logistics of what they wanted to do and how to get through Taki undetected. Jacob paid attention to the specifics, but part of his mind wandered. They'd spent so much time trying to delay the war, so much effort into holding it off as long as possible... and now it had come, whether they wanted it or not. Part of him had hoped the war never happened. There was always the chance the Caliphate would collapse or undergo a revolution. After all, what sane person willingly started a conflict that would cost millions of live? There were times it was necessary, or even desirable. When the list of injuries and crimes swelled to the unimaginable, when the threat of war became the threat of genocide, the time had come to act. Failure to do so would cede the initiative to the enemy and, in doing that, could cost their people everything. But it still had to be the very last resort.

He didn't advocate a first strike; that moment had passed when the Caliphate bombed Anchorage Bay. But once the war was on, Jacob prayed with all his heart the politicians and bureaucrats would allow the military to fight and win. After all, it was the military who were going to do the dying. His spacers who would wake up for the rest of their lives with nightmares and cold sweats, hearing the screams of their dying comrades forever echoed in their ears. His Marines would have blood on their hands no soap would ever wash off.

God, please let us make it through this. By whatever grace you can provide. Please.

CHAPTER FORTY-THREE

Nadia awoke with a burning pain in her chest. Fog filled her head for a moment, then it all crashed in on her. Daisy. The ship. Imran! Her eyes flew open and she struggled to make sense of the scene in front of her.

Admiral Wit DeBeck stood at the foot of her bed, a grim look on his face.

"Oh no." Her words were slurred. Whatever medicine they gave her for the pain made her mouth feel like it was full of cotton balls. "He escaped?"

"No," Admiral DeBeck said. "No. He was killed on impact."

Nadia felt a surge of satisfaction at the news. The man deserved death. Worse, if there were such a thing.

"Water." She held out her hand, grasping with her fingers.

DeBeck moved to the small table beside her and handed her a full glass.

Cool water cleaned her mouth and washed away the dull sensation. She blinked again, forcing herself to sit up more.

"Then we succeeded," she said.

"No. Not quite. With him dead, the Caliphate will certainly

launch an attack now. Which might work for the best, but in the meantime—" he turned and pressed a button, activating the holovid to show the news.

Pictures of Imran flooded the Alliance News Network. However, they weren't victorious celebrations of the head of ISB being killed, but questions about who murdered him, and why?

"I don't understand? He wasn't murdered."

"It was very public, Nadia. We're a covert agency, not law enforcement, and certainly not assassins. I rely on you because you're quiet and clean. ANN is all over the crash, they're calling it the worst diplomatic disaster in a century. Speaker Bradford is out there claiming Imran visited in secret to cement a non-aggression pact and was murdered by Navy separatists. Congress is falling all over themselves to vote all kinds of concessions to the Caliphate."

Nadia balled her cybernetic fist and crashed her head back down onto the bed. No matter how much evidence they accrued, no matter the blatantly obvious facts, the damn politicians always found a way to screw it up.

"Daisy died for this, Wit. She gave her life to keep us from going to a holy war. I didn't kill him. He died in the crash while trying to escape. My NavPad can verify that."

Wit's rigid stance and cold shake of his head told her what he was going to say before he said it. "It doesn't matter what's on your NavPad. We can never officially release that information. It would blow your cover and show us in a poor light. What am I supposed to tell the president? I authorized you to kidnap the Speaker of the House? What's done is done."

"What about Cobra?" she asked.

"The Marine who provided CAS is already out of the system. The *Enterprise* battle group left for Praetor ten days ago."

"Ten days?" Nadia bolted upright, hand flying to her head as dizziness overwhelmed her.

"Take it easy. You suffered a severe head trauma. They put you in a coma to assist in healing. But yes, you've been out for ten days."

Ten days or a hundred, it didn't matter anymore. It was out of her hands. Daisy died for nothing. Her mission, all the corruption she uncovered, meant *nothing*.

"Is there anything we can do?" she asked. Pleaded really.

"We lost this one, Nadia. Let's hope we don't lose the next one."

Wit smiled down at her, a soft, almost fatherly smile. She'd known the man her entire career and she'd never seen him look at her like that. Almost as if he was saying goodbye.

"I have to go. While you recover, I want you to review your mission and make a full report. After that, get better. Maybe see some farmland?"

The admiral left her to contemplate her failure, but Nadia refused to sink down that dark path. There had to be a way. A sitting member of Congress had been a Caliphate spy who killed DNI agents. They had recordings. Evidence. She'd seen them with her own eyes. The admiral, though, said they couldn't release it and... had he tried to tell her something?

All the evidence she had was stored on her NavPad. And it was damning, irrefutable proof. But she had been out for ten days. Surely ONI would have scrubbed it in that time? She glanced over to where her ubiquitous device sat.

Surely Admiral DeBeck didn't leave it here with all that sensitive intelligence, right? She asked herself.

Nadia reached over and thumbed the display. Her mind reeled at what she saw but she kept her expression carefully neutral, just in case. There was no way DeBeck had left all the intel on her NavPad by accident. He would know she couldn't just leave the matter be.

Nadia Dagher glanced at the holovid and did the math. Her career, possibly her freedom, versus the truth.

That was math even she could do.

CHAPTER FORTY-FOUR

Jacob exhaled slowly, forcing himself to relax. The last of the blips vanished from their passive sensors.

"Full reverse. All hands brace," he ordered.

Spacer McCall called out the warning over the ELS suit radio network.

As one, all four destroyers flipped over and powered their gravcoils to maximum. The math was tricky, but his star astrogators, POs Oliv and Tefiti, had figured it out. By accelerating at flank speed, well, flank speed for DesRon Nine, they pushed their maximum velocity to the limit, then killed their drives. A risk in of itself. Without active acceleration, they had no gravwake to clear small debris from the front of the ship. At seven thousand kilometers per second, even a relatively small particle could damage the ships.

However, they had to kill their drives in order to avoid detection by the enemy ships, especially where the enemy lined up to enter the Praetor starlane. At that point, their gravcoils were down and their detection apparatus was at its most sensitive.

Once they confirmed the enemy had gone through, they lit

their drives up for maximum deceleration. They would end up a full hour behind the Caliphate, but it couldn't be helped. It might even prove advantageous, since an hour wasn't long enough for the enemy fleet to reach the wormhole, but more than enough time to clear the lane.

Interceptor bucked and shook as she cavitated on her own gravwake, her velocity steadily falling as she did so. They had a plan and were executing it. There wasn't much more he could do other than pray.

Deep down, he felt a surging excitement at the coming conflict. It swelled inside him like an ocean's current. He wasn't happy to be going into the jaws of death, but there was something about having a specific goal, an outcome, that filled his spine with steel.

Part of him, though, hoped that when they came through the starlane, the Caliphate Navy ships would be gone and DesRon Nine could transmit their signal without the need for a fight. Not because he was afraid, but because people would die. Killing, or dying, was a last resort, no matter the reason. However, if it came down to his people or theirs, he would do what had to be done.

"Five minutes to full stop, sir. We'll be in the lane twenty minutes after that," PO Oliv said.

"Drop the heatsink, Ensign Brown."

"Aye sir, dropping the heatsink."

Boudreaux switched through her damage control screens, checking each compartment, crewmember, and station. In a way, she had more access to the ship than the captain did. With its three screens, two interfaces, and numerous readouts, her station was akin to The Pit. With a tap of a button she could pull up any compartment, see any crewmember's life signs, or show any damage to the ship.

There were limits, though, which was why there were three people assigned to DCS at any given time. Spacer First Class Baker sat buckled in his repaired chair, checking on the crew, making sure they were nominal. PO Hanz, newly released from sickbay but still missing one arm, worked the screens as best he could, running down the checklist for the ship's systems.

Boudreaux switched her comms to Hanz. "You okay?" she asked.

"Aye ma'am. It's a little weird, mind you, but I'm good to go. Midship Marino assures me I'm a solid candidate for regen back home, and that I have nothing to worry about. Of course, she's not the one with a hand that itches like crazy but no actual hand to itch."

"Affirmative. Hang in there. Let me know if you need anything."

"Aye ma'am. Will do."

Boudreaux marveled at his chipper attitude. When she woke up after losing her leg, they had told her the same thing. Her mood hadn't been quite as upbeat as Hanz's though. For her, it felt like the end. It took a month to regenerate, and five more in rehab learning to walk again.

She shook the morbid thoughts away and went back to work, making sure the ship was ready for combat.

"All hands," Spacer McCall announced. "We're in the starlane. Time to exit, three hours. Maintain Condition Yankee enhanced. That is all."

Private June sat on her bunk in Marine country, elbows on knees as she stared at the bulkhead. What had she gotten herself into? *Interceptor* was her first deployment and she had almost died twice. Once in the galley during the fire, and another time boarding an enemy ship in deep space. Neither of those were on the recruiting poster.

Twice!

It was like something out of an animated vid she watched as a kid. Though her hands and forearms were fully healed, she had several streaked scars on them that would only go away with regen.

"I'm only eighteen," she muttered. "What am I doing out here?"

Her torso looked like a yellow-and-purple onion, and a patch on her chest covered the hole as it healed. One deployment and she already had scars she would bear for the rest of her life. And she wasn't even thinking of the physical ones.

People had died by her hand. Men were cut in half in front of her. The screams of the ones who burned alive under the thermite grenade she threw would haunt her until she died.

She needed to talk to someone.

They were in the lane and they had time... at least a few hours before they would resume combat stations. She triggered the comm. "Midship Rugger, Private June."

"Go for Rugger."

"Can we talk?"

The line opened, but static filled it for a second.

"Uh, yes, Private. Meet me in the rec room?"

"Yes sir. Five minutes. June out." She killed the line. Rugger was just the person to speak with. He was nice to her, he was not quite an officer, and he wouldn't make fun of her for being emotional. In truth, she wasn't sure the other Marines would, but Gunny was such a robot when it came to things, she didn't think she could confide in her.

Travis shuffled down the passageway toward the rec room, not sure what to expect. June was undeniably beautiful, but he knew he needed to focus and stay on point. He outranked her, even if he was just a midship.

Strictly speaking, and he had double-checked the regs, they could be romantic. However, the NavPer guidelines strongly discouraged interpersonal relationships aboard ship. They didn't forbid them, but only because the Navy would spend more time punishing people for breaking those regs than actually doing the job of the Navy.

He shook his head, pushing any romantic thoughts aside. She was an eighteen-year-old girl; he was twenty-two. They were on the same ship, so things were bound to happen. Feelings were bound to be formed. He tried to push those feelings aside, still... his thoughts lingered a little too long on her curves.

"Focus, idiot," he muttered as he walked through the open hatch to the rec room.

June stood at the far end, her stark white ELS suit silhouetted against the gray hull. Her black hair was twisted in a tight bun, and her arms wrapped around her chest as if she were hugging herself.

He paused at the hatchway. On the one hand, she stood in such a way as to catch his breath. On the other, he instantly understood that he'd misread her call. There was an intense sadness about her. He wasn't exactly the most socially savvy guy in uniform, but even he could pick it up.

Travis rubbed his bare hands against his suit, drying his sweaty palms. He took two deep breaths and slowly exhaled to calm himself. He grinned inwardly at using his naval combat training for something wholly unrelated.

After his heart stopped racing and his mind calmed, he

approached. "Private?" he asked with a note of concern in his voice.

June turned to him, showing her tear-streaked face. Once he stood beside her, she leaned in close.

"Everything okay?" he whispered. He chided himself for such a stupid question.

"I think I made a mistake," she whispered. "I don't want to be a Marine anymore."

Her confession shocked him into silence. He wanted to say something, anything. After a too long silence, he finally spat out, "Why?"

June didn't look at him, just stared into space as if the answers to her problems could be found in the empty void of starlane travel.

"When the fire happened, were you afraid?" she asked.

He didn't even have to think about how to answer. "Yes." With a sigh, he relaxed, leaning against the display. "I've never been so terrified in my life, to be honest."

She looked at him, eyes going wide. "You didn't show it."

"Training, I guess. We run a lot of fire drills. When I came out of the healing tank, I certainly had a lot of time to think about it. Yeah, I felt it then."

His answer seemed to satisfy her for the moment.

"Were you?" he asked.

She shrugged, her suit making it an oddly restrictive gesture. "I... yes. But I thought, this is normal to be afraid. It was a fire, after all." She showed him her burn-streaked hands. "When we get back to a fort or base hospital, I can have the skin regenerated and the scars will go."

He showed her his hands as well. They were a mottled brown of burned skin and fresh pink. There was only so much they could do aboard ship. However, once they were back in civilization, he could have the skin regenerated good as new.

"If it was *just* the fire, I would be okay. But then we boarded that ship and... did you read any of the reports?" she asked.

"I'm commo, June. I read all the traffic," he said with a half smile.

"Then you know bad the fighting was. Gunny Jennings, she went hand-to-hand with four of *them*. She killed two men with a knife, Travis. A *knife*. This is the 30th century. I shouldn't be fighting with a knife, let alone on a vital mission with the fate of the ship in the balance, depending on me knowing how to kill a man... with a *knife*."

He'd known about the close combat. Everyone onboard knew Gunny Jennings' record as a stone-cold badass. The reports of her killing Caliphate spacers in hand-to-hand combat were legendary. However, it was one thing to read the account in a clinical report, another to see it and live through the trauma.

"She's seen combat before, though," he said.

"Yeah, they all have. Except me. That was my first time." She looked at the port. "I killed people. When I'm alone in my rack, trying to sleep, I can hear them screaming as they burn alive from the thermite grenade I threw. I was shot, beaten, blown up... and yeah, I lived." She looked down at her hands, not sure what to say.

Travis felt wholly unprepared to deal with her trauma. He had never seen any close combat, nor was he likely to. He did take some elective psychology classes, though, and he thought saying something was probably better than saying nothing.

He put a comforting hand on her shoulder as he remembered human touch could ground a person. "June, I can't begin to understand what you went through aboard the Cali ship. However, I know this. When that explosion happened in the galley, and you and I pulled those men out, that fire was going to happen whether we were there or not. There are men alive who wouldn't be if you hadn't acted."

Travis mentally leaped to the next thing, not giving her a chance to make an excuse as to why it didn't matter. "What you and the Marines pulled off on that cruiser was the same thing. If you hadn't been there to guide them, they would have all been killed, and us as well. You saved the ship, June. You saved all of us."

She glanced up at him, then to his surprise, buried her face in his chest and wrapped her arms around his waist. She let out a sob, then another, and very quietly, she wept.

CHAPTER FORTY-FIVE

APPROACHING PRAETOR

"Five minutes to exit, Skipper," PO Oliv said.

Five minutes until they were in the middle of an enemy fleet that could, and most likely would, wipe them off the map. A cold fist of fear wrapped around Jacob's heart. He closed his eyes for a second and pushed it down, until only his calm remained. "Travis, all hands please."

"All hands, aye," Midship Rugger replied.

The comm in his helmet clicked and he knew the next words out of his mouth would be heard by every man and woman serving aboard *Interceptor*. He'd prepared for the moment, Lord only knew he'd given a variation of the speech several times before, but his mouth still dried and he struggled to come up with the words.

Boudreaux looked up at him from DCS. He gave her a slight wave to tell her he was okay.

Jacob unclasped his harness and stood, needing to move to make his brain work, then began: "I never understood why we're an 'Alliance' and not a single nation. We are many planets, peoples, and traditions, bound together by the bonds of family. We are stronger than any single people could ever be, because, through our individual hardships, we have worked together to build something greater than ourselves.

"No person on this ship is worth less than another. We are all citizens. Marines, spacers, officers... crew. Like the diverse peoples that make up the Alliance, we are stronger together than apart. Our ship, our destroyer, our *Interceptor,* is like the Alliance. Powered by the bonds we have formed together. The bonds that bring us closer than friends, closer even than family.

"Years from now, when you're telling your children, your grandchildren, hell, maybe even your great grandchildren, the story of today, you will tell them of heroism. Stories of skill, of courage, of sacrifice. Maybe from you, maybe from your shipmates. We will tell them how we fought to survive. How we fought for each other, and how we fought to get home.

"You will tell them these stories because you will be alive to do so. Because we are going to make it. Because we will break through the Caliphate fleet and warn Admiral Endo of the impending attack. And when we're done, we will join the admiral in saving millions of lives in the Praetor system.

"A very wise man once said, 'there can be no greater sacrifice than to lay down one's life for another.' Saving lives is what we're about. The Alliance Navy has fought pirates and oppressors for hundreds of years. We will continue to do so this day, and we will be victorious."

Jacob paused for a moment, letting the words sink in, letting his crew feel the impact in their hearts.

"Stick to your training. Trust the spacer beside you. Duty, courage, honor." He pondered adding anything else as he sat back down in his squeaky chair. "Good luck. Captain out."

He glanced down at Boudreaux; she held her thumb up,

along with a big grin. Sometimes, he managed to get things right.

"Ten seconds to exit," PO Oliv said.

"Weapons hot. Get ready to fire the decoys the moment the order comes through."

"Aye aye, sir, weapons hot," PO Ignatius said.

Exiting a starlane wasn't pleasant, though some people were able to manage better than others. Not for any reason Alliance researchers had ever discovered. It had nothing to do with any physical or genetic component. The Alliance had spent billions trying to find why some people puked while others could manage to keep their food down.

Jacob hadn't puked since his first time as a midship. He found that if he forced his eyes open and focused on a specific point, like the back of his coxswain's helmet, he could resist the urge.

Gravity surged, and for five seconds, every person aboard felt like they were flying upward through the air, leaving their stomach behind.

Then it was over.

Jacob breathed deeply in through his mouth and forced the air out of his nose, fighting the nausea for another thirty seconds. "Status," he said with a thick voice over the bridge comms.

One by one they checked in all clear.

"Multiple contacts, all bearings. We're right in the middle of them, sir," Tefiti said.

"Comms, link us to the squadron. PO Ignatius, status?"

"Linked up, Skipper," Rugger said.

"All crews reporting ready, Skipper," Ignatius replied.

"Open the outer doors," Jacob ordered. "COB, prepare for squadron flank speed." *Interceptor*'s top acceleration was more than the rest of the squadron, so the shark wouldn't be running at flank for her.

"Outer doors opening," Ignatius said.

"Squadron flank ready," Chief Suresh replied.

Jacob's heart thudded in his ears. He was glad the ship had no atmo; it made the crew safer and solved a multitude of problems. He just hated the way he felt isolated in his suit, as if they were all fighting alone.

Seconds crept by. The computer updated the contacts, one by one tagging them with their probable class based on their size and power output. They had gotten lucky. The Caliphate fleet was running silent, with no radar, no lidar, no acceleration. Just floating at the starlane exit, waiting for the signal to begin their attack.

They were planning to run into Praetor from the closest lane, mere hours from Endo's fleet. He'd been right, and it broke his heart to know all the people that would die if they failed.

"Oliv, any sign they've seen us?" Jacob asked in a hushed whisper, as if a loud voice could give them away.

"None yet, sir. No EM radiation hitting the hull. Ensign Kai has locked our own emissions down tight," she said.

Their biggest concern had been being spotted due to the gravity event coming out of transition, but the Cali fleet had to have missed it because of their proximity. They were looking forward, not back. If they had seen DesRon Nine, they would have fired.

"Captain Hatwal on the comm, sir," Rugger said.

Jacob tapped his helmet and Rugger put him through.

"I knew what to expect," Hatwal said, "but being in the middle of it is something else."

"I completely agree, sir," Jacob said.

"I've got the battleship, three-five-five mark three-three-one. Range... five-zero-seven klicks!" Tefiti said.

No wonder the Caliphate hadn't seen them yet; they were practically docked.

Hatwal's face stiffened as his astrogator relayed the same information. At that range, the decoys might not be as effective. The farther from the source an ECM was, the more effective it was. With them being on top of the enemy fleet, it might let the more powerful ECCM cut through it.

Commander Novak and Commander Gustav also appeared on screen, dividing it into three.

"We could still split up," Jacob said. "Launch our decoys and go starburst." Starburst meant scattering the formation in all directions, looking like a star.

Hatwal shook his head.

"Commander Novak's EW suite is far more advanced than any of ours, and is still our best chance at making it out of here. Once the torpedoes launch, we run."

Looking at the plot, Jacob held up his hand to interrupt. He tried to keep "the look" off his face; the look his crew accused him of having when he came up with a great idea. "Sir, the battleship... she's right there," he said. "Practically spitting distance."

"Our turrets can't penetrate the armor and our torpedoes are loaded for decoys," Hatwal reminded him.

"I know, sir. But, if we fire the torpedoes and then immediately follow it with a Long 9 barrage, we could disable, or at least distract them. It would buy us time."

In a typical fleet engagement, at least according to *The Book*, they would never be this close to the enemy. Certainly not facing off against a battleship.

Jacob glanced at Oliv, making sure they still were undetected. She gave him a thumbs up.

"I like your plan, Commander Grimm. Very bold. Novak, on my signal, activate the ECM. At that point, the entire squadron will fire torpedoes, then hit the battleship with their Long 9s. Then we get the hell out of here." He finished with a grin, but Jacob could tell everyone was as nervous as he was. They were skating on thin ice.

"Aye aye, sir," he said.

―――

PO Mendez squirmed in the unfamiliar gunner's chair. With PO Ignatius stationed on the bridge overseeing weapons, Josh was in charge of the Long 9. Spacers Perch and Zack worked below him, ready to lift the nine-kilogram ship-killer the moment it arrived.

"Load," Josh ordered as the light turned green on his console. In milliseconds, the computer ran a self-test check on the system. A single misaligned coil could severely diminish the power of the weapon... or even damage the ship. Therefore, the nine-kilogram tungsten-penetrator wrapped in a nano-reinforced steel shell wasn't loaded until the moment before they needed to fire.

The two spacers lifted the round from the arm and slid it into the opening.

"Close," Josh said.

Perch pressed the button that sealed the hatch on their end of the compartment.

"Raise the next round."

Zach activated the mechanism to raise the follow-up shot. It wasn't necessary to immediately prepare the next round, but Josh liked to follow *The Book*. The supercapacitors supplying the energy to the Long 9 took a full minute to recharge. He wanted to be ready if the captain needed a second shot.

―――

Yousef disagreed with Admiral Rahal about the disposition of his forces. As a cruiser commander, he felt guarding the fleet's six was important. However, when his superior officer told them to scout ahead, he scouted ahead. Albeit at the slowest acceptable acceleration.

"Status?"

His astrogator answered: "I'm getting some funny gravity readings, sir. I'm not sure what to make of it."

That was odd. Gravity's predictability was one of the things that made it useful.

"What do you mean?" Yousef asked.

"Well, sir, if I didn't know better, I'd say several ships just exited the Taki starlane behind us. But that's not possible since the fleet would pick them up."

"Gravity disruption? Maybe caused by the wormhole?" Yousef asked.

"Negative, sir. It came from the wrong direction."

"Range to fleet?" he asked.

"Four million klicks, sir."

They were far enough out that they couldn't just turn around and go back. He could, though, send them an alert.

"Comms, notify fleet of the disruption. Odds are they already know about it, but let's be cautious."

―――

Admiral Rahal sipped his hot drink from the comfort of his flag command chair, watching his crew perform their tasks. He didn't mind the waiting. Eager for combat, he wasn't. It would come all too quickly, and he didn't feel the need to rush headlong. Which was why he sent his light cruisers ahead.

Rahal frowned. Three light cruisers where it should be four. The loss of *Vanguard* perturbed him. Ships didn't just *disappear*.

Vanguard was following the destroyers the fools at the Consortium had sent to scout the area. All they had managed to do was hide from his fleet. They were trapped behind him. Once he crushed the heavy cruisers protecting the wormhole, he would send his light units to deal with the stragglers.

"Sir, message from *Glimmer of Dawn*. They're saying ships may have exited the starlane behind us. I don't understand."

Exited the starlane? From Taki? That wasn't possible. They were exactly where they were when *they* exited the starlane... unless the destroyers had somehow managed to hide their emissions, or their proximity to his ships didn't allow for time to pick up the grave wake.

"Red alert, fleet to battle—"

Admiral Rahal's warning came too late. Sixteen of the Alliance's most advanced MKIV EW torpedoes exploded onto the screen, broadcasting a decoy signature that looked exactly like the destroyers.

Almost simultaneously, four destroyers fired their Long 9s mere milliseconds apart. Since the ships were in a tight formation, the rounds flew a trivial few klicks apart. Traveling at a third the speed of light, the penetrators barely had time to discard their protective casings before they slammed into the stern of the Caliphate battleship.

A battle wagon armed with thirty-two turrets, twelve forward plasma rails, eight torpedo tubes aft, and sixteen forward, *Glorious Crusade*'s starboard side held more firepower than the entirety of DesRon Nine. And though she wasn't the Caliphate navy's most advanced battleship, she was a kilometer long, five hundred meters tall, and two hundred and fifty wide, with eighteen centimeters of nano-reinforced armor wrapped around her.

None of which helped in a surprise attack.

Nine kilograms of tungsten fired from *Firewatch* blasted

through stern armor plating above *Crusade*'s portside torpedo room. The penetrator continued, bursting through several compartments and turning eighteen men to ash before its energy was spent, thirty meters in.

Kraken's slug hit twenty meters to the right of *Firewatch*'s. Six compartments and twenty more crew died in an instant, vaporized by the blazing ball of tungsten that burned like a miniature sun as it carved through *Crusade*.

Tizón's round hit far below, slamming into the stern plate at a ninety-degree angle, a lucky shot that sent it into a main horizontal lift. Fifty-seven crew were incinerated as the projectile traveled half the length of the ship before blowing into the Immortals quarters and wiping out an entire company of infantry in the middle of preparing for battle.

Interceptor's missed the hull entirely, but it wasn't an accident. Josh Mendez had local control of the weapon; coordinating with Chief Suresh, he pointed the ship at the enemy gravcoil. Such called shots were practically impossible in the heat of battle, but the *Glorious Crusade*'s proximity, combined with the time they took to line up the shot, allowed for it.

The round slammed into the stern gravcoil, exploding on impact with the hyper-dense material, sending superheated fragments of tungsten and gravcoil through the ship's coils, obliterating a third of them and leaving her without propulsion.

"Punch it," Jacob yelled as the ship stopped shaking from the recoil. "All turrets, open fire."

DesRon Nine leaped ahead, following their decoys at five hundred gravities of acceleration, firing twenty-millimeter turrets, spreading out their fire to limit the chance of return fire zeroing in on them.

"We have good hits on the battleship, sir," PO Ignatius said. "I think we disabled her." The shock in the PO's voice was duplicated in Jacob's mind.

"Well done, PO," Jacob replied.

"Active radar and lidar, ECCM. We're being tracked," PO Tefiti said calmly.

"Drop rear decoys as needed," Jacob ordered Rugger.

"Aye, sir, as needed."

Captain Hatwal appeared on the MFD. "All ships, link EW."

Rugger didn't wait for an order; he had pre-programmed his console to link with *Kraken*'s and he slammed down on the button.

The battle had commenced. The question now became, could they survive?

CHAPTER FORTY-SIX

Stable bolts of plasma lit up the stern screen, shifting color as they approached. The deadly shot flashed by DesRon Nine as the Caliphate fleet fired at the decoys that were slowly spreading apart in the hopes of buying the four ships more time.

"Decoys have one minute left on the clock," Commander Ban said.

Hatwal nodded. "Order all ships to launch another salvo."

"Sir, that will be all of *Interceptor*'s decoys and half of the remaining for the rest of the squadron," Commander Ban informed him.

Though he appreciated Ban's reminder, Hatwal was well aware. Unfortunately, it couldn't be helped. They just weren't far enough away from the fleet to allow the decoys to expire. Another three minutes and they would be out of range of the heavy cruisers and they could relax a little.

A very little.

"Have *Interceptor* move ahead of the formation and we'll shield her signature," he said.

"Aye aye, sir."

"...take the lead when the next decoys run dry. *Firewatch* out."

Jacob agreed with Captain Hatwal on the decoys. With the exception of the disabled battleship and the eight heavy cruisers who could never catch them, the Caliphate ships responded quickly, accelerating after them. Two light cruisers and five destroyers were on their flank.

They'd managed a few hits with the turrets as they accelerated out of the enemy fleet, but nothing significant as far as he could tell. The enemy ECM still clouded their own screens, and Jacob prayed their message had already made it through. But they couldn't count on it.

"Astro, do you have a solid read on those ships?" he asked.

Oliv sent the information to his MFD.

"Aye, Skipper. Two Tripoli-class light cruisers designated Tango-Lima One and Two. Followed by four Khan-class destroyers designated Tango-Delta One through Four. They are staying together, which means we're pulling away," Oliv said.

While five versus four wasn't good odds, it surprised him that the enemy would limit their acceleration.

After the initial barrage, and the confusion that must have followed, DesRon Nine had a solid seven minutes of acceleration before any of the other ships gave chase. In three more minutes, they would be out of range of the heavies and only have to worry about the pursuing force.

Which is what worried Jacob. He knew they had more light cruisers than what followed them. At least three more. Where were they?

"PO Tefiti, do either of those LC's match the signatures of the ones we identified when *Sabre* was destroyed?"

"One moment, sir. I'll double check."

The mission clock counted down toward when they would be clear and able to broadcast their warning, as well as fan out to avoid incoming fire more easily. Two minutes. They just had to hold on for two more minutes.

PO Ignatius signaled him from weapons.

"This will be the last of our decoys, Skipper, but they're ready to launch."

"Launch as directed, PO," Jacob replied.

A moment later, the ship shuddered as all four forward tubes fired as one. They ran silent and true until they came even with the previously launched decoys. As the originals ran dark, their fuel and energy expended, the new decoys took over, giving them a near seamless transition.

So far, the enemy hadn't seen through the deception and continued to fire on the decoys.

Admiral Rahal's eyes didn't leave the plot as the enemy decoys sped away from his fleet. The light screening units chased after them, but unless he was willing to let the destroyers engage alone, they weren't going to catch them.

They didn't have to, though. They only had to chase.

While he didn't know *Glimmer of Dawn's* exact location, she was ahead of the enemy, out there waiting. The signal Yousef sent had come too late, but his fleet was relaying the information they had back to Captain Yousef Ali. He would be maneuvering his ships to intercept and destroy the infidels.

Like he should have the first time.

Rahal cursed his rotten luck. *Glorious Crusade* would take nearly a day to repair. Until then, she had no propulsion. The rest of the damage, while significant, wasn't nearly as painful as the broken gravcoil.

In hindsight, he shouldn't have sent any ships. If the screen hadn't gone after them, his heavy cruisers and the *Crusade's* own batteries could still be firing. Not that he blamed himself. The hits his flagship took were catastrophic, and he had acted on reflex.

In the end, though, it wouldn't matter. Those ships would be destroyed well before they could alert the Consortium forces guarding the wormhole. Even if they somehow managed to warn them, it was eight heavy cruisers versus three. There was no math there. Despite the Consortium's slight tech advantage, his ships would obliterate them. It would briefly leave *Crusade* relatively undefended, but that was an acceptable trade to him. Once the light units dealt with the fleeing destroyers, they would return.

"Comms, signal Captain Masud. Order him to take his squadron and advance to the wormhole. All ships that aren't Caliph flagged are considered valid targets. Once he's dealt with the Consortium fleet, he's to take and hold orbital infrastructure. We don't want to start from scratch out here." He turned to his private panel and held his thumb on the reader. Reporting to high-command via the FTLC panel would take time, but he had to. And he would follow the report up with a victory.

―――

"Skipper?" PO Tefiti said. "The heavies are on the move. Their course isn't exactly the same as ours, but they are heading for the wormhole."

Miraculously, none of DesRon Nine had sustained any damage in their flight; in thirty seconds, they would be beyond weapons range of even the light units that pursued them.

"Keep an ear on them as best you can, PO. If they present a problem, don't hesitate to let me know."

"Aye, aye, sir."

The enemy fleet commander's decision to dispatch all his ships puzzled Jacob. Why would he risk leaving his crippled flagship defenseless unless he knew the light elements would return soon? Either he was planning on calling them back or...

"Travis, get me Captain Hatwal, asap."

"Aye, aye, Skipper. One sec."

Hatwal appeared on screen, stress obvious on his helmeted face. "Go ahead, Commander."

"Sir, we have a problem. I think the missing light cruisers are ahead of us."

Hatwal's eyes widened. Everything had gone so perfectly up to that point. They had survived the impossible and were minutes away from warning Admiral Endo of the attack.

"Explain," he said.

"We've observed a total of six light cruisers, sir. One we destroyed. There were only two with the fleet. That leaves three unaccounted for. The fleet commander back there just sent his heavy units for the wormhole. He wouldn't do that unless—"

"—unless he expected more ships to return." Hatwal looked down at his plot, examining the situation with a tactician's mind. Something Jacob appreciated. Despite their initial friction, once Hatwal re-oriented himself, they worked well together. "There could be more support units behind him?"

"I hadn't thought about, sir. Yes, there could. However, they have three light cruisers unaccounted for. If he sent them forward to screen, then we're running right for them."

Hatwal frowned, thinking over Jacob's logic. When he could find no fault, he sighed. "Commander Ban, signal all ships, starburst in five mikes. Once we're clear, all ships are to immediately broadcast the message warning Admiral Endo. Understood?"

"Aye, aye, sir," Ban said from off screen.

"Good catch, Commander. And good luck."

"Thank you, sir. And you as well."

The screen went dark, leaving Jacob with his own reflection and a problem to contemplate. He hated the idea of leaving his squadron behind, but *Interceptor* would surely outrun them.

Yousef grimaced at the report from *Crusade*. Generally speaking, destroyers didn't engage battleships. They could never get close enough to begin with. This time, though, it seemed the Alliance dogs got lucky. Or maybe it was something else?

"Ghazali," he called to his XO, "Can we see through their jamming?"

"No sir. Whatever they're using is twice as effective as anything we have on Alliance capabilities. I'm surprised they have the power on such small ships. Once we've destroyed them, it may be worthwhile to do a detailed search of the wreckage. Council Research Division could benefit from it."

Yousef nodded more to himself than the XO. In a perfect world, they could do that. But by the time he finished pounding those ships into oblivion, there would be nothing left.

"Range?" he asked.

"Three million klicks and closing."

"Maintain silent running. I don't want to fire until we're right on top of them."

The plot updated, showing a yellow circle around DesRon Nine. To the stern, just outside the circle, the seven ships of the Caliphate Navy pursued them. Technically, they could still fire, but outside that circle the chances of hitting were so small as to be practically zero.

Ahead of them, a blue dot represented when the decoys would burn out and the four ships would be forced to starburst. The ships wouldn't alter their heading by more than twenty percent, since doing so would cost them far too much forward acceleration. Two of the ships would go "down" and away from each other, and the other two would go "up" and away.

Interceptor and *Tizón* would pair and head above the ecliptic. Five million klicks after initial separation, they would change course again, away from each other. The entire time though, every ship would broadcast the warning to Admiral Endo. No matter what happened, they had to warn the Consortium heavy cruisers.

Jacob prayed they wouldn't run into the light cruisers before they split.

"One minute to Point-Sierra, Skipper," Oliv said.

Just one more minute.

"They're in weapons range now," Yousef's XO told him.

Yousef experienced something he wasn't used to; concern. At least one of the destroyer captains over there was good. Better than Yousef expected. If he opened fire and somehow failed to destroy them now, destroying them later wouldn't do him any good. He would find himself on the wrong end of a sword aimed at his neck.

"Let's wait. We will have a better look through their jamming at six-hundred thousand. I don't want to miss. When we can see, focus fire on the largest of the ships. That should be the commander. We'll switch targets as they're eliminated."

"Yes, sir. Fire at six-hundred thousand."

The mission clock counted down to zero and the order came through: All ships break formation. The decoys vanished off their screens, and only Commander Novak's ECM from *Kraken* protected them.

"Chief Suresh, up bubble fifteen degrees, maintain acceleration," he ordered.

"Aye, aye, sir. Up bubble fifteen degrees and maintain."

Interceptor's nose pitched up and the numbers showing the distance between the ships of DesRon Nine rapidly expanded.

"So far, so good," Boudreaux said over the comms.

"Weapons fire, three-three-zero mark three-four-zero. Danger close," PO Oliv shouted.

"Evasive," Jacob ordered as he pressed forward against his harness.

Eighteen turrets opened fire, sending thirty-six bolts of stable plasma flying through space aimed right toward *Firewatch*. Like the rest of the squadron, the Griffin class destroyer was already on alert. In part, thanks to Jacob's warning.

Firewatch rolled to port, changing course by five degrees. The bolts missed her entirely.

"Contact. Correction, multiple contacts. Designation Tango-Lima, One through Three. Dead ahead, six hundred thousand klicks and closing at a slow rate, sir. They were waiting for us," Tefiti said.

Jacob grimaced. They were already in weapons range. If Jacob hadn't issued his warning, that opening barrage would have destroyed them. "Roll the ship. All turrets open fire."

With their computers still linked, the four ships opened fire with their twenty-millimeter turrets, sending a salvo of nano-steel wrapped tungsten penetrators toward the newly detected light cruisers.

It was a knife fight. One they were ready for, but incapable of winning.

The Caliphate ships accelerated in the same direction as the destroyers, but their initial velocity started lower, allowing DesRon Nine to "catch up" to them. With the engagement on, the light cruisers accelerated to flank speed. No hits were scored on either side.

"Sir," Travis said. "They're jamming us hard. The only thing keeping us in contact with the other ships is our laser."

That was a problem. With the heavy cruisers accelerating, they couldn't afford to get into a prolonged fight with the light cruisers. Every second they didn't warn the Admiral was a second he wouldn't have to evacuate his people.

Jacob watched the range decrease far too slowly for his liking. Another barrage of plasma appeared on screen. If only he could accelerate and—

"Are they targeting *Firewatch* only?"

"Aye, sir," Oliv replied.

How could he use that against them? Obviously, they believed *Firewatch* was the command ship, and they were right. Taking it out first would make sense, as did focusing fire on a single target. After *Firewatch* and *Kraken* were destroyed, the enemy could turn and chase down *Interceptor* and *Tizón*. No one would survive, and no warning messages would be sent. Jacob couldn't let that happen.

As he raced through his options, *Firewatch's* luck ran out. Twin bolts smashed into her prow, vaporizing armor and sending molten steel into her interior, killing fourteen crewmembers and wounding another ten. Her acceleration dropped as debris trailed off behind her.

Kraken's course shifted, attempting to cover *Firewatch*, but it was only a matter of time before a hit crippled her.

"Travis, get me Commander Gustav, please."

"Aye, aye, sir. One second. *Tizón*'s commander is on the line."

"Yes, Grimm?" he asked.

"Commander, I'm going to engage those cruisers. When I change course toward them, I want you to change course away from them. After ten minutes, change course again. If you're still not clear of the jamming, run silent until you are, then commence broadcast. Understood?"

As the newly appointed squadron XO, Jacob had the authority to issue such an order. Gustav didn't have to like the order, but he did have to obey. With the plan Jacob was building on the fly, this would guarantee *Tizón* made it out alive to warn Admiral Endo. Maybe guarantee was too strong of a word, but it would improve their odds considerably.

"Understood." Almost as if Gustav sensed Grimm's plan, he nodded at him before killing the connection.

"Chief Suresh, bring us down bubble ten degrees. See if you can't point us in the general direction of one of those tangos," Jacob ordered.

"Aye, sir. Ten degrees down bubble. Does the captain have a preference for which one?" she asked.

Jacob glanced at the plot. The three tangos were in a tight formation, no more than a thousand klicks from each other. The enemy ships had all the time in the world, and *Griffin* had almost none.

"Starboard side, Tango-Lima Two," he said.

Interceptor shuddered as the ship altered course, her gravity contending with itself for a moment, leaving the crew feeling as if they crested a hill.

"What are you thinking, sir?" Boudreaux asked.

"That we give them another target to shoot at."

He knew she understood exactly what that meant. *Interceptor* could take a lot of punishment; hopefully she could take enough.

CHAPTER FORTY-SEVEN

Captain Yousef Ali leaned back in his command chair, smiling as one of his turrets caught the largest of the destroyers.

"Excellent job, weapons. Keep focusing fire. Let's spread out a little and see if we can't pin them in a crossfire. Increase distance by…" he glanced at keypad as he tapped in the numbers, "Twenty-thousand klicks. Helm, take us up two degrees. We should be able to box them in then."

Faithful crew acknowledged his orders and it filled him with pride how they efficiently went about their duty. It wasn't as if the destroyers couldn't hurt them, but at five hundred thousand klicks, the evasive maneuvers they performed were enough. So far, they had sustained a few glancing blows, but nothing debilitating.

Another bolt struck the large destroyer. Someone on the bridge cheered, and he couldn't blame them. He didn't just have more turrets, his were more powerful, designed to fight other cruisers with thicker armor. Something nagged at him, though. He honestly thought the fight would end after the first few hits.

These Alliance destroyers were tougher than his navy intelligence had realized.

However, the end was inevitable.

"Okay Devi, just inch us over a little bit. We're nothing to pay attention to here out in the black. Certainly not anything three big, bad cruisers should be afraid of."

"Aye, sir," she replied.

"PO Ignatius, cease fire on all turrets, but standby the Long 9."

"Aye, sir. Cease fire all turrets, stand by the Long 9," PO Ignatius confirmed.

Jacob desperately wanted to go flank speed and rush to the aid of *Griffin*. But doing that would surely tip his hand and he needed to close the distance. Was he really considering going one versus three against light cruisers? If *Griffin* were destroyed, then *Kraken* would be next. Their starburst plan hinged on escaping *before* an engagement. Once the enemy engaged, he had to change the plan. After all, if none of them escaped, no one would warn Admiral Endo.

The enemy commander acted with nerves of steel, waiting until torpedoes would be less effective, even dangerous to fire, and then slowly easing them into main gun range to finish them off.

Well, Jacob thought, *two can play at that game*.

"Devi..." he swallowed hard, knowing he might be about to condemn his crew to death, but he also knew he had no other choice. "Let the shark off the leash."

"Aye, aye, Skipper."

Interceptor lunged forward, her gravcoil pounding out a wake behind her as she topped out to five-hundred and sixty g's. Far more velocity than the other destroyers in the squadron could make.

"Five minutes to range," Ignatius said.

"Travis, you're an EW wizard. Let's see what you got," Jacob said.

Midship Rugger put his hands on his console and went to work.

———

Captain Hatwal gripped the side of his chair with white knuckled ferocity. His ship was beaten; he knew it, the crew knew it. The smart thing to do would be to flip over and do a full reverse. But if he did, he would leave Kraken to face those guns alone.

Firewatch shook with a ferocity that jarred his vision and left his head throbbing.

"Direct hit on Turret One, sir," Commander Ban reported. "No survivors."

This was combat. This was what he'd trained for. Not to fight light cruisers though, not a hopeless fight. Their plan was solid; it should have worked. No one could have predicted three ships laying doggo, nor could they have expected his squadron to cripple a battleship.

No one.

Except Grimm. He seemed to see it all.

"Sir! *Interceptor* has altered course, changing bearing toward the enemy formation," Ban said.

"Can we reach them?" Hatwal asked.

"No, sir. Laser-link is down and our radios are jammed."

Ganesh tried to figure out what the man was up to, but other than a suicide run against those ships, he couldn't figure it out.

Commander Novak swore as *Kraken* attempted again to put herself between the enemy and Griffin. Every time she did, though, the light cruisers would alter course and at least one of them would have a clear shot.

DesRon Nine's flag ship wouldn't last much longer. Not to mention, they were drawing ever closer to guaranteed kill range of the Caliphate's main guns. Nothing was going the way they planned. She was feeling like a trapped Gil-rat and hated it.

"Ma'am, *Interceptor* is accelerating toward the enemy ships. Right at them. What is she doing?" Lieutenant Kantor, her XO, asked.

Was he going to suicide? No... he was buying them time.

"Weapons, load the forward tubes with MKIV's. We need to cover that ship."

So far, the Caliphate cruisers hadn't noticed *Interceptor*, or didn't care about her. The range was coming down and once they hit four hundred thousand, he could fire the Long 9 or wait to see if he could close the distance a little more. The cruisers were focused on *Firewatch* and hadn't altered course to avoid *Interceptor*.

"Four hundred thousand, Skipper," PO Oliv whispered.

He glanced at the plot on his MFD. Plasma bolts rained down on Griffin from three different ships.

Kraken popped up suddenly, firing four torpedoes toward the empty space between the enemy and *Interceptor*. Electronic decoys flared to life, speeding ahead of the formation and flooding space with electronic noise.

Two of the torpedoes angled to cross Interceptor's prow, shielding her from the enemy.

"Devi, lock on to Tango-Lima Two."

"Aye, aye, Skipper. Tango-Lima Two," Suresh confirmed.

"PO Ignatius, load the gun."

Ignatius sent the order down to the gun crew. Jacob imagined them lifting the heavy ship-killer round up and into the coil before the loading mechanism jammed it in.

"Long 9 is ready, Skipper," Ignatius said.

The two decoy torpedoes sped across space, blasting away with their heat and electromagnetic noise, temporarily blinding the enemy.

———

Captain Ali frowned. EW torpedoes flared across the screen, confusing the image.

"Don't worry, sir. Their decoys are good, but the range is too close. They'll only work for a minute," his XO said.

The ships vanished as the torpedoes blinded his sensors, but his own turrets continued to fire, guessing where the target would be. As the noise expanded, he caught sight of the smallest of the destroyers making a mad dash toward them before it disappeared behind a wall of interference.

"Starboard twenty degrees. Now dammit, now," he yelled.

———

Tango-Lima One, the ship Captain Ali commanded, turned frantically, her turrets next shots firing wide due to the unexpected maneuver.

However, it wasn't Lima One, *Interceptor* targeted.

Commander Novak's decoys bought Jacob a full extra

minute. In that time, *Interceptor* closed the range to three-hundred and fifty thousand klicks.

"Fire," Jacob ordered. His ship shuddered as the nine-kilogram shot accelerated to thirty percent of the speed of light. The steel casing used to propel the round through the magnetic coils flew apart, revealing the ship-killing, nano-hardened, carbon-tungsten arrow.

Interceptor was "above" the enemy ships as they focused firing at *Griffin*. The arrow crossed the distance, expertly aimed by Chief Suresh, heading for where the targeted cruiser would be.

Nine kilos of armor piercing arrow struck amid ship, impacting with turret three. The six men inside never knew what hit them, vaporized before their brains registered their death. From there it crossed into the ammo locker below, igniting the plasma bolts, before bursting through the other eighteen decks and out through the gravcoil.

Secondary explosions rocked the ship as she lost power and tumbled through space.

Jacob shouted for joy at the direct hit.

"Chief, Sierra Bravo, let's not play around with these guys. Weapons, resume turret firing, target that ship that changed course right before we fired. I think that might be the squadron commander."

Both non-comms confirmed the order.

Interceptor shook as the turrets opened fire and her gravity wavered at the same time.

"Yeah, they're firing on us now, sir," PO Oliv said.

Alarms rang and his plot flashed as the two remaining light cruisers targeted his ship.

"Come on, *Griffin*, disengage," Jacob muttered. "Chief, bring us zero-five degrees starboard. I want to avoid the arc of their forward batteries when we pass by."

Ganesh slumped back in his chair, sighing with relief. He couldn't understand why Grimm had done that. It made no sense. Killing one ship wasn't worth the cost of his own.

"Helm, fifteen degrees down bubble. Maintain acceleration and let's see if we can get out of this mess," Ganesh ordered.

The plot showed Tizón almost out of active sensor range.

Grimm's plan clicked.

"I got it," Ganesh said excitedly. "He sent *Tizón* off opposite of us." It was clever. By forcing the light cruisers to focus on *Interceptor,* it freed up the rest of the squadron to escape.

Ganesh's brief excitement dimmed as he realized Commander Jacob T. Grimm had just traded the lives of those aboard *Interceptor* for the mission and the rest of the lives in the squadron.

By the time the enemy destroyed Grimm's ship, and they would, since he had obliterated one of their own, it would be too late to stop the rest of DesRon Nine.

In that moment, Captain (JG) Ganesh Hatwal knew what it was to command a ship in combat and make the ultimate sacrifice. Not so that he might win, but so that others could.

"Godspeed, Captain Grimm," he whispered.

Interceptor shook as a plasma bolt tore down her portside, slagging armor and the superstructure underneath. Alarms screamed and Jacob struggled to keep his focus through the pounding his beloved ship endured.

"Deck two, frames seven through eleven, are open to space. Rerouting power runs," Boudreaux said from her comms. The XO maintained a running dialogue for the captain, making him at least peripherally aware of the ship's damage. "No casualties."

Jacob gripped his command chair, willing his ship to survive as a hail of plasma bolts leaped out at them.

"Contacts are going to max accel, Skipper. It looks like they're trying to close with us," PO Oliv said.

"Understood," he said. "Where's *Griffin*?" he asked.

"She's pulling away slowly. For some reason the contacts are focusing their fire on us," Oliv said.

"Must have pissed them off somehow. Would it help if I apologized?"

PO Collins wished she could wipe her palms on something, but the suit wouldn't allow that. Her turret rotated, fired, and rotated again as the enemy ships changed position. *Interceptor's* distributed nodes handled the firing calculations and the actual firing; she was the manual back up, ready to pull the trigger or even aim if needed. The two spacers below her loaded the weapon and the other two brought fresh magazines from the stores.

"PO," Spacer First-Class Nessie shouted from below. "We can't get to forward ammo storage. There's too much debris."

"Roger that. One second." She checked the ammo count. Four thirty-round magazines were stored locally, and the one in the gun was about to run dry. Each box of ammo lasted a minute and change. She made a quick call to turret two and found they were in a worse spot, with only two minutes left.

"Bridge, Turret One, we lost access to forward ammo storage. We're going to run out of ammo on Two in one-mike, thirty seconds. Ammo dry on One in four mikes."

"Roger that, Turret One," Ensign Brown's voice came back. "Will advise. Please standby."

She tapped her trigger as the seconds passed. "Nessie, if you had a couple of torches could you burn through?" she asked.

"Yeah, but PO, if we don't hustle to the aft storage now, we're going to run dry. We can't do both," Spacer Nessie said.

The ship shook violently, banging Collins' helmeted head against the cushioned headrest. Alarms in her suit blared to life, showing a hull breach. They'd drained the can long before coming into battle, but breaches still posed a threat to the crew.

"Ops, we're going to try to burn through," she said.

"Roger that, Turret One. Keep us apprised."

"Nessie, get down to main engineering, grab a plasma torch, and get cutting," she ordered.

"Aye ma'am, on it."

Ensign Kai had never experienced battle, and he wasn't sure he had yet. Wrapped in his suit and secured in a chair next to the fusion reactor, he felt oddly disconnected from the events outside. *Interceptor* occasionally shook, the gravity shifted around like a drunken aircar driver, and red lights flared to life on his panel, but otherwise, nothing.

He should be afraid or worried, but instead he focused on his panel and did his job.

Power requirements ebbed and flowed as different systems charged. Virtually all the ship's systems were directly powered by a series of batteries and supercapacitors. From the Long 9 to the coilgun turrets and the torpedo tubes, each system required power regulation and flow. If one system lost power, or if the reactor wasn't producing enough, it was Ensign Kai's job to fix the problem. That was it. That was his whole job. He loved science and engineering, but he felt like there was nothing for him to contribute.

Lights on his panel flashed a warning as the reactor temperature fluctuated rapidly.

"Chief, what's going on?"

Redfern's station was situated across the chamber and the two could see each other.

"On it. It's the borrowed Anvil, sir. We don't have the fine tune control over it that we had on our own. One second and I'll have it."

Ensign Kai reached for his harness release to assist the Chief. *Interceptor* banked, forcing the gravity to shift just as a plasma bolt struck portside aft, obliterating the armor above the gravcoil. White hot shrapnel penetrated the superstructure, annihilating the Armory, causing secondary explosions to ripple forward into the fabricator room, killing two spacers instantly and maiming the PO manning the station.

Shrapnel pinged off the closed hatches leading to engineering. It prevented any further damage, but it knocked the ships stern enough that it forced the secondary gravcoil to compensate with increased gravity just as Ensign Kai triggered the release on his harness.

His right arm was still through the harness when the world lifted and Kai was thrown hard to the port. His trapped arm kept him from slamming into the hull, but the crack of his elbow breaking sounded like a gunshot in his ears.

"Ensign," Redfern shouted as he held on for dear life. "Medical to Engineering."

Laying on the deck, Kai shook his head. He looked up to see an arm tangled in the harness, but the elbow pointed up and he couldn't figure out whose it was. A cold sweat broke out across his skin as he realized.

He used his good arm to pull himself up. Someone yelled at

him through his helmet comms, but the sound came from very far away. It took him a moment to untangle his limb and it fell uselessly to his side, almost like it wasn't connected by bone anymore.

"Chief," he said. His voice sounded off to him, the words were slurred. "What's the heat situation?" Too calmly, he seated himself back in the station, slinging his good side through the harness before attaching the whole thing around his bad arm.

"Uh, sir, the Anvil's producing fuel at the wrong rate. At any given moment we have too much or too little, forcing the reactor to work overtime. Hence the heat buildup. Medical is on the way, sir. Just hang in there."

The hatch leading to the passageway opened and Spacer Whips rushed over to Kai.

"How you doing, sir?" Whips asked.

Kai glanced at the enlisted man with the red cross on his chest. "Just fine, spacer. You?"

"Hanging in there, sir. I think you're in shock."

Whips placed the bad arm against Kai's chest, then sealed it to the suit to prevent mobility.

"You're very good at your job, spacer," Ensign Kai said.

"Thank you, sir. You too," Whips replied.

Whips keyed into Kai's suit controls, and Kai felt a cold rush through his body that cleared his mind and allowed the dull ache of his arm to hit him.

"Ow," Kai said.

"Sorry sir. I triggered the pain killers before the norepinephrine. Your injuries aren't life threatening. Can you maintain your post?" Whips asked.

For some reason Kai thought any injury would result in a trip to sickbay. Here he was with one arm absolutely ruined, and the young man with five minutes of training wanted to know if *Kai* was good to stay at his post.

"Full speed ahead," Kai said.

Whips grinned, patted the Ensign on his good shoulder and stood.

"Chief, you need anything?" he asked.

"Could you have the captain stop at the next coffee shop?"

Whips gave him a thumbs up and headed back out the hatch, making sure it sealed behind him.

"This hurts like hell, Chief," Kai said.

"Aye, sir. But you stayed. And that's what matters."

CHAPTER FORTY-EIGHT

Admiral Endo sighed in relief as the *USS Enterprise* appeared on his scope. The kilometer long battleship, while older and less advanced than his own capital ships, was still a battle wagon. Packed with armor and weapons, it really was a one-ship-navy. Not to mention the escorts emerging one by one behind her.

They had suspended normal wormhole operations to move the battlegroup through. Endo was grateful, even if it created a parking lot of freighters that were sitting tree-ducks if anyone attacked. It wouldn't take them long to clear traffic through the anomaly once things moved again.

"Comms, send Admiral Spencer my regards and ask him if he would like to join us for dinner."

"Aye, sir," Lieutenant Matsuda answered.

Endo's flag bridge sat high up on the superstructure of his ship, the regular bridge below. Every station the regular bridge had, he had, along with a large holographic tank that showed the local area and all the ships. His command crew was for waging a war, not for the individual ship-to-ship engagements.

He frowned as the last of the *Enterprise's* escorts appeared and accelerated toward the three heavy cruisers. Once clear of the wormhole, the lights on his scope started lining up to enter. His console showed them coming to a stop a few hundred klicks from his flag cruiser in a little less than ten minutes.

What made him frown was the lack of ships. Even his own nation, which tended to employ fewer, larger, and more advanced ships, would consider the battlegroup on his screen less than half strength. Three heavy cruisers, four light, and no destroyers. Endo recalled Captain Hatwal saying something about belonging to this battle group, but even so, there should be three times as many ships.

He'd hardly call it a battlegroup. More like a reinforced squadron. Did the Alliance not understand the situation he was in? They had a treaty obligation to help, and yet they sent as few ships as seemed possible.

Endo couldn't help but wonder if the rumors he'd heard about political unrest in the Alliance had credence. He knew they were gun-shy after the Great War, and had let their navy lapse somewhat, but to ignore the Caliphate threat, or treat it as not a threat, seemed egregiously ignorant. The Caliphate had literally declared they would not rest until the Consortium and Alliance were subjugated under their rule. When the enemy speaks, common sense demands he listened.

"Sir, I'm getting a message. It's weak, but you should hear this," Matsuda said.

"Put it on."

"Admiral Endo, this is ... Hatwal. We have enco...... significant Caliphate forces heading for the .... At least one reinforced ......group. Details ... embedded. You must evacuate .... We won't likely make it back, ... hop.... and pray... this gets to you in time. DesRon .... out."

"Can you clean that up, Lieutenant?"

"Negative sir. The interference was at the source, not with our equipment."

Endo listened to the message several more times, trying to glean what he could from it. He couldn't be too hard on the Alliance, then. DesRon Nine just saved the lives of every man and woman in his command.

"Get me the *Enterprise* and signal battle alert. All hands."

CHAPTER FORTY-NINE

Interceptor flopped like a lame duck as she bucked from another hit.

"Torpedo room three is gone sir, as well as two frames into cold storage," his XO said. The loss of the weapon wasn't critical, and thankfully, the forward torpedo rooms were only manned when they were in use.

Jacob's mind registered the information, but his thoughts were glued to the plot. The two remaining light cruisers altered course to stay with him, even as he drew them away from *Griffin* and *Kraken*.

"Devi, maintain flank and change to Sierra-Charlie," he ordered.

"Aye, aye, sir, maintain flank and go to Sierra-Charlie."

Ships had many options for evasive maneuvers, but at the end of the day, the idea was to run away and not get hit. However, once again, *Interceptor* found herself in the position of needing to draw an enemy away from other forces.

"Oliv, let me know the moment *Griffin* and *Kraken* are clear of the engagement."

"Aye, sir," she said.

Several bolts flashed within a few hundred klicks. They'd taken a number of glancing blows, but between *Interceptor's* maneuverability, ECM, and small size, the enemy was having trouble tracking her.

Jacob glanced at Midship Rugger, who worked his EW panel like a musician, alternating frequency and power to keep the enemy guessing.

"Any hits, Rob?" he asked PO Ignatius.

"A few, but no significant damage based on debris. Sorry sir."

"Hits are hits, Rob. Keep it up."

The range continued to climb. If *Interceptor* maintained her acceleration, she would lose the enemy soon. Now it was a numbers game. How fast could *Interceptor* clear the enemy weapons?

"Devi, alter overall course six degrees starboard and five degrees down bubble," he ordered. She repeated his orders back to him as she changed the course of the ship.

Far out on the plot were the eight heavy cruisers heading for the wormhole. If he could parallel their course, then maybe they could also warn the ships at the wormhole if the other destroyers failed... though the farther the light cruisers chased him, the less that seemed likely.

Interceptor's sensors didn't register *Tizón* anymore, only the last place they knew for certain she was. However, detection wasn't absolute. Even radar returned bad readings, and lidar only worked at close range. Beyond a million klicks, all they had were the gravity sensors, and those weren't exact either. If they couldn't see the destroyer, then he knew the enemy couldn't. That was one ship that would make it to fight another day.

Interceptor heaved like a mad bull, slamming everyone down into their seats as the secondary coil fought to keep them alive.

Yousef growled as the little ship continued to run, despite the sheer volume of fire *Glimmer of Dawn* and *Autumn's Favor* had rained down on it. If he had his full command, then the ship would be no more. Somehow, though, that inferior ship had destroyed *two* light cruisers.

Two light cruisers!

Lost under his command. No matter how the battle ended, his career, and his life, were likely over. He would finish it with honor and a measure of his own pride and batter the destroyer to bits.

"Weapons, load and fire the torpedoes, continuous barrage," he ordered. His XO glanced his way, a questioning look that Yousef dismissed. "If nothing else, I will have that ship destroyed."

Sensors showed it was the same one they had chased before. If he had destroyed it then, none of this would be happening. Their captain was a clever man. Dead, but clever.

"Yes sir, torpedoes away. Helm, come five degrees to port, go rapid fire on the turrets to cover us."

Rapid fire would deplete their ammo, but they had that to burn. It would also increase the heat of the ship, but since they hadn't drained their atmosphere, they could simply pump the hot air out of the compartments and pump cool air in.

"Torpedoes in space," PO Tefiti said.

The last hit had taken out several centimeters of armor along their starboard side, shaking the ship badly, but nothing more than cosmetic damage and a few bumps and bruises.

"Torpedoes?" Jacob said glancing down at Boudreaux.

"They must be getting desperate, Skipper. Hoping for a lucky hit?" Lieutenant Boudreaux said.

Jacob agreed. "Switch turrets three and four to point defense. Keep one and two on target," he ordered.

Ignatius acknowledged the order and immediately changed the target package of the stern turrets.

The plot flashed, updating to show each light cruiser launching torpedoes. They appeared in front of the ships, then sped to their target. *Interceptor*.

A total of eight torpedoes lashed out through space at him. Ignatius immediately went to work and the crews of the rear turrets didn't disappoint. The turret crews switched to rapid fire and took out the torpedoes one by one, the last detonating ten-thousand klicks astern.

Jacob wanted to return fire with his own torpedoes, but with two ships focus firing, the risk of a lucky hit outweighed the benefit.

"They've gone to rapid fire, Skipper," Oliv said. "They're also spreading out. It's costing them some velocity, but it's going to get much more difficult to evade. They'll have us in an Anvil in ten minutes."

An Anvil meant *Interceptor* would take fire from two different angles, making it twice as hard to avoid. Jacob fervently wished he could find some way to increase the velocity of his ship, but they were already at flank, pulling away from the enemy slowly but surely.

The mission clock read an hour and a half. It was hard for him to believe they had arrived in system that long ago, but battle was like that. Over so quick the brain didn't have time to register, or dragging on so long a spacer could drop from exhaustion.

"Radiation surge, Tango-Lima Three," Oliv announced.

"Roll the ship!" he shouted.

Chief Petty Officer Devi Suresh reacted with the speed of a lifetime of training and experience. Reaction thrusters on the side of the ship flared to life as she pushed the HOTAS to the port while at the same time using the aft thrusters to move the ship as one, rather than just changing vector.

Jacob had never seen a pulse-plasma laser used before. Since virtually no one serving in the Alliance Navy had seen battle in the last war, there weren't a lot of opportunities to view the deadly weapon. Heavy cruisers like the one *Interceptor* ran from in Medial weren't maneuverable enough to have used it against *Interceptor*.

Terawatts of power surged through space, blasting by his ship with such ferocity that alarms wailed from incidental radiation assaulting their shielding.

"Back over, back over!" Jacob yelled as he realized his mistake. He watched in horror, helpless to make a difference as Devi jerked the controls hard back the other way.

Energy readings from the first shot hid the second shot. The first one was designed to push *Interceptor* to the port so the second cruiser could get the kill shot.

A beam of racing electrons powered by a terawatt laser and turned into plasma that surfed the EM field of the laser beam, rushed out at near the speed of light. Two meters wide at its focal point, it struck *Interceptor* portside aft. Five centimeters of nano-reinforced steel that protected her hull vaporized under the weapon before it slashed through Marine country, running along the keel like a scalpel, right through the forward computer node, killing Spacers Peck and PO Watson instantly.

Ensign Kai hardly had time to scream when part of engineering turned into a blazing sun as the beam incinerated the deck two meters from his station, leaving a hole that opened out into space.

Immense sheering forces were imparted on the destroyer as

vast quantities of kinetic energy hit. The secondary gravcoil clamped down hard just as the harness retracted, restraining the crew as best it could. Nothing could deflect the forces entirely, though.

Seven crew members weren't harnessed and were killed when they slammed across compartments and crashed into the walls. Another five were injured by flying debris.

That wasn't the worst of it, though. Despite her years of experience and training, it took Chief Suresh five full seconds to recover from the hit. Five seconds in which *Interceptor* flew true, unable to evade.

Two plasma bolts ripped through the boat bay, turning the Corsair her into a cloud of shrapnel that shredded the Mudcat and ripped through PO Stawarski's suit, pinning him to the bulkhead. The suit pumped him full of pain killers and sealed the breaches while medical nanites kept him alive, hopefully until help arrived.

Torpedo Room Five, PO Richards, and four spacers were hit by a second bolt, their compartment turned to hell as five thousand degrees of burning plasma burned through the armor and hull and incinerated the men and women inside.

Another hit the gravcoil, glancing off the armored exoskeleton of the rings, but not before disrupting the flow of gravity and killing *Interceptor*'s acceleration.

Lights on the bridge flickered and died. Consoles flashed as emergency power kicked in. Jacob tried to focus on his MFD, but the hit they took had shaken him like a dog with a bone.

"Status," he managed to spit out.

"Acceleration is down. I can maybe get back half," Suresh said.

"I've lost power to the turrets," PO Ignatius reported.

The only saving grace, Jacob thought, was they couldn't pull that trick again. However, they wouldn't have to. With *Inter-*

ceptor's acceleration down, they would close and kill with their turrets.

She was done for. His people were done for... unless... he could surrender. If there was a formal declaration of war, his people would be protected somewhat by that status. Without it, though, the Caliphate could claim whatever they wanted. However, where there was life, there was hope.

"Do we have comms?" he asked.

"Aye sir," Midship Rugger said.

Jacob prepared to make the single hardest call of his life. With no weapons and no ability to run, he had no choice.

CHAPTER FIFTY

Admiral Endo watched his scope with glee. For two hours, his ships, along with the Alliance battlegroup, had accelerated as hard as they could. With the limited information DesRon Nine had sent them, they knew exactly where the heavy cruisers were going to be.

After they set the right course, they decreased their drive power and ran silent. Sure enough, just as they were told, eight Caliphate heavy cruisers appeared on screen, driving hard for the wormhole.

Those eight ships would have filled him with fear before. They would have caused an evacuation and possibly the loss of the war before it began in earnest. Without the Alliance's reinforcements, he honestly didn't know if the Consortium could defeat the larger navy.

However, with the forces arrayed around him, and the fact that it would be a surprise attack, there was no hope the enemy ships would prevail.

The only question would be what kind of enemy commander were they facing? A Caliphate officer who would fight to the death, refusing to surrender even as his ships were blown apart around him? Or a more reasonable officer who would save his people by surrendering when given the chance.

"Admiral, this is your space," Admiral Spencer said from the comms. "We can legitimately open fire with no warning if you wish."

Endo seriously considered it. The horrors these people had inflicted on his, though, was no excuse to act dishonorable. His forces far outmatched the enemy. It would be a tactical and strategic victory if he offered them the chance to surrender. "We must make the offer. Perhaps it will have a better chance of being accepted if it comes from you, Admiral."

Spencer nodded.

Captain Irfan sipped his dark coffee while his ship hummed efficiently around him. He wasn't fond of leaving the admiral behind, but it wasn't like he could say no. Orders were orders. By all accounts, the enemy forces were outmatched. The most the Consortium could hope for was to escape through the wormhole.

He had no appetite for killing civilians, and didn't want to bomb anything he wasn't ordered to. If they arrived and the system was clear, all the better.

"Sir, I'm picking up a signal from up ahead. Close. Maybe three hundred thousand klicks?"

"Play it." He glanced at his passive sensors; nothing showed on the scope.

"Caliphate forces, this is Admiral Spencer of the USS *Enterprise* battlegroup. We have your forces zeroed in and are prepared to destroy you. Please kill your drives and power down your weapons. You have twenty seconds to comply."

Battlegroup? What? There were no battlegroups in Praetor. Their intel was solid and only a week old.

"Sir, active radar!"

Alarms wailed as eleven different radars lit up their ships. The computer immediately flagged one of them as a battleship. Maybe, Irfan thought, *maybe* if it wasn't an ambush, he could fight through them... but like this? His entire command would be destroyed for nothing. He triggered the fleet comms. "All ships, shut your drives down and power off all turrets."

In a matter of seconds, he had gone from glorious victory to ignominious defeat. With any luck, he would spend the next ten years in a POW camp. If he had to return to the Caliphate, an executioner's sword would be his only reward.

CHAPTER FIFTY-ONE

Jacob stood with his officers and senior enlisted in the mess. The clunk of metal on metal reverberated through the hull from the Caliphate shuttle docking. It had taken almost four hours for the three ships to equalize their velocity.

"Detail, attention," he said. With atmosphere returned to the ship, their suits were still on but they had their helmets off. He didn't want the Caliphate captain thinking he was trying something with the atmosphere.

He prayed he hadn't condemned his crew to a lifetime of slavery. There was simply no choice, though. With no weapons and half his drive in ruins, his ship couldn't fight or run. Watching her get pounded to utter destruction with no gain wasn't an option. As it was, they had already made the sacrifice needed to win the engagement, if not the battle.

Jacob couldn't know for sure, but he was ninety percent positive one of the messages had gotten through. The Caliphate fleet would arrive at the wormhole and find it abandoned.

The hatch opened and an aquiline-nosed man with a long thick beard stepped through. He wore the Caliph version of an

ELS suit, helmet, and sidearm, though to Jacob's great relief, the weapon wasn't drawn. None of his people were armed, not even Jennings, who protested mightily when he informed her they had surrendered.

"Captain Ali?" Jacob asked.

The man nodded. "I am."

Jacob snapped to attention, "Commander Jacob T. Grimm, USS *Interceptor*. I formally surrender my ship and crew, sir. I ask that my people to be treated as POWs by the Treaty of Okinawa-Deruta." It was a formal way to say he hoped they wouldn't summarily execute his people on the spot. Surrendering was against everything he held dear, except for the lives of his crew.

"Commander Grimm, on behalf of my Caliph, I accept your surrender. While I can't speak for what happens after you leave my ship, sir, you have fought with honor and skill. I will respect you and your crew… even the women." The slight dip in his voice worried Jacob, but clearly the man intended to abide by the treaty. At least for as long as he could.

Ali signaled the men behind him, and armed soldiers flooded in, separating the officers from the enlisted, and mag-cuffing all. Jennings bristled as they turned her and her Marines around to cuff them. She looked to Grimm, and he tried to reassure her it would be okay.

"Sir, these are my senior officers and enlisted, except for the wounded who are under treatment in sickbay," Jacob said.

"Very good, Commander. I will post men there, but of course I won't interrupt treatment of the wounded. I would offer our own medical facilities, but they are also quite busy now."

Jacob wasn't sure if the man had complimented him, or was angry about it.

"I assure you, sir, I do my best to avoid violence that isn't necessary. I'm sorry for the crew you've lost, truly," Jacob said, and he was. Loss of life was always regrettable. Unavoidable, and sometimes necessary, but regrettable all the same.

Captain Ali looked hard at him for a moment, their eyes meeting, and Jacob thought they came to an understanding. It surprised him. Up until this point, he'd seen the Caliphate as more of an ideological enemy, a life destroying force with no soul. Maybe, though, he'd been wrong. Or maybe just about some of them.

"As a warrior, I appreciate your concern, Captain. I also wish to inform you we have survivors from your destroyer *Glorious Crusade*. About fifty of them, if I recall correctly."

Jacob heaved a sigh of relief. He had worried from the moment *Sabre* had collided with the enemy ship that all hands were lost.

"Thank you for telling me. I appreciate it."

Captain Ali seemed to look more closely at Jacob, breaking through the lies and propaganda.

"Commander Grimm, would you be so kind as to show me your bridge?"

Jacob motioned to the hatch. "Right this way, sir. The lifts have no power, so we'll have to use the ladders."

"I would have it no other way."

Despite the situation, which to Jacob was just shy of the worst possible outcome, he found himself liking Captain Ali. Under different circumstances, he thought they might even be friends. As it was, Jacob's people and himself were about to be prisoners of war to an empire that didn't treat their own people with respect, let alone prisoners.

One of the armed soldiers came up to Captain Ali and handed him a small device, something Jacob assumed was a communications apparatus. The soldier said something in their native tongue that Jacob didn't understand. He realized Captain

Ali had no need to translate Alliance common. Jacob chided himself for not understanding their tongue. If he survived this, he would dedicate himself to learning their language. It reminded him of a quote his mom was fond of saying whenever Jacob had trouble with the kids at school: "If you know the enemy and know yourself, you need not fear the result of a hundred battles. If you know yourself but not the enemy, for every victory gained, you will also suffer a defeat. If you know neither the enemy nor yourself, you will succumb in every battle."

He'd been thrilled to discover the book she'd quoted from years after her death. He'd read it along with dozens of others while at the Academy. Hopefully, he would live long enough to learn from his mistake.

The color drained from Captain Ali's face. He looked to his men, then to Jacob. He handed the device back to his soldier.

"Captain Grimm, it seems Allah has decided a different fate for us this day."

"I'm afraid I don't understand, sir."

"My XO just detected a battlegroup heading our way. They will be here within the hour. It seems it is my turn to surrender to you."

Instant and utter elation shot through Jacob, and though he tried, he knew he couldn't hide his grin. A battlegroup? The promised reinforcements must have arrived in time to thwart the heavy cruiser attack and come to the rescue.

While Jacob's face showed undeniable delight, Captain Ali frowned, looking at his men.

"Sir, I want you to know I had no idea. I'm delighted, but I did not know. I've had some experience with a captain from the Caliphate before and he told me you were all taught we are barbarians. We may be, but we treat our POWs with respect.

You will be given meals, a place to exercise, and most importantly, your religious freedom will be permitted."

Captain Ali appeared to relax. "Now it is I that am in your debt."

"Acting with honor is its own reward, Captain." Jacob held his hand out and the man took it with a firm shake.

CHAPTER FIFTY-TWO

Nadia limped down the hospital stairs, pulling her coat tight around her, hiding her hurt arm. She hadn't checked out and had no intention of telling anyone she'd departed. It wouldn't take long for NCIS and DNI to figure out who leaked the information to the press, information that was damming to congress, the civilian intelligence community, and the government as a whole, and she hoped to be where she was hard to find.

Once the minor new agencies started showing the evidence, ANN had to report on it or risk losing the scoop. Before leaving her room, she hacked into the spaceport's security network and copied the video of Representative Simmons murdering DNI agents and admitting to being a Caliphate spy.

She dumped all of it onto the net, along with everything else she had obtained, including Speaker Bradford's interrogation.

She was a wanted person now. Even the admiral, with all his connections, couldn't save her. It was a small sacrifice to make sure the people who perpetrated the deception against the Alliance paid in blood.

A holovid in the background blared the alarming discovery of spies in the government. She grinned as she pushed her way out, knowing the crap storm she had ignited.

The vid switched to a picture of Bradford, obviously taken from his presidential campaign. A distorted voice, one she knew was hers, played.

"Promise me that once you are president, you will concede the wormhole to us as reparations for your arrogance in the last war."

"If you honor the ISB's agreement to help me get elected, then yes, I'll do it."

Despite her situation, hearing his traitorous words spoken to billions of people lifted her heart. Things were about to change. She just wasn't going to be around to see it.

Like any good spook, she'd planned for the day she would need to disappear. After her first retirement, she had almost raided her exit strategy but decided that she might one day need the money and cover IDs. After she started seeing Jacob regularly, she found the perfect place to hide it. Someplace no one would ever find.

Once on the street, she called an air taxi, painfully climbed in and rested in the backseat. "Bridge City," she said. With her good hand, she activated her NavPad to pay the aircar and block any tracking tech that might be on her or aimed at her person. The automated car took off, flying south for its long trip. Bridge was the only city in the southern hemisphere with a spaceport, which was exactly where her trail would lead.

Not that she had any intention of going off planet. She just needed everyone to think she had.

———

Admiral DeBeck ignored the incoming call light on his NavPad. In his cabin, cradling a hot cup of joe, sitting in his favorite chair, he contemplated the last few weeks.

Two things were apparent. Other than the Navy, the government was severely compromised. Dozens of sleeper cells, from small town mayors, to low-level government employees in three letter agencies, to elected officials in both the house and senate, were rooted out. When ONI analysts looked at Congressmen Simmons' past, then compared it with Daisy's, they found one thing in common; both were adopted through the same agency. Not every kid who went through the agency was a sleeper, but all the sleepers passed through those doors. Once they raided the company, they were able to find the names and start bringing people in.

Some turned themselves in, not wanting to die in an Alliance raid... or a Caliphate sweeper team. Others, they didn't get to in time, arriving at their homes to find them already dead, either by their own hand or by a hidden ISB cell. However, most they were able to take alive. That still left far too many for any Alliance citizen to sleep well.

His NavPad beeped again.

Of all the law enforcement, intelligence, and analyst agencies, only ONI was free of spies. Because of their connection to Bradford, the SECNAV and CNO resigned before the sun rose over Anchorage Bay. At first, the speaker tried to deny it, but once Nadia's footage of him leaked, he resigned seconds before police arrived to arrest him.

His NavPad kept ringing.

When the House met, minus eighteen members who were either spies or compromised by them, they immediately and unanimously declared war on the Caliphate. The Senate, minus four members, and now led by St. John, endorsed the declaration and it went to President Axwell, who signed it into law.

The Alliance was at war.

Which was why he refused to answer his NavPad.

"Wit, you in there?" Admiral Villanueva asked from outside.

Stifling his surprise at her appearance, he knocked back the rest of his coffee, feeling the burn from the heat and the added alcohol.

"Come in," he said.

The door, with its many holes from coilgun fire, swung on its creaking hinges.

Immaculate in her stark white SDWs and cradling her stiff combination cover under her arm, she walked in. "Is housekeeping taking the year off?"

"It's all part of the last month of activity," he said. "I suppose you're here to arrest me?"

Her eyebrow shot up. "Is there something I should know?"

Wit really looked at her. He was tired. Exhausted really. The mess of the last few days—what Nadia Dagher had dumped on the world—changed everything. His anger at her impulsive action and admiration at her moral stand warred with each other. On the one hand, she violated every oath and dozens of laws to do what she did. On the other, it was unequivocally the right thing to do. And he shouldn't have doubted her. She hid her tracks well. She even made sure everything pointed to her, not him. Since no one even knew she worked for him, he was free and clear.

"Nothing you would want to know," he replied.

She walked around to the coffee pot, poured herself a cup, before moving to the living room to sit sideways on a low table. The only other piece of furniture that still stood.

"I had a feeling you were behind the intel dump, but rest assured, nothing points to you. Believe me, DNI is looking hard too. So far, they're saying it was a 'rogue agent' who hacked into the database and leaked it to the media. Was she rogue?" Noele asked.

"She is now," he said, before he realized she shouldn't know who Nadia was. He cocked his head to the side and she gave him a knowing nod.

"Regardless, that's not why I'm here or why the president's assistant has called you a dozen times."

"Why are you here?" He leaned forward, elbows on knees.

"We need a new SECNAV, and you're it 'till you quit or you're dead."

Wit felt something stir in his chest. Mirth played on his face and he let out a roar of laughter that echoed through his open door and down the mountainside.

After he finally calmed down, he shook his head. "You can't be serious. I'm no politician. Get someone else."

"No. The president himself asked me who would win this war for him, and I told him you. We need you, Wit. We need your cunning, your tactical awareness, and your ability to see things beyond just what is there. Yes, it's true, the SECNAV is a political position, and you would be retiring your uniform. But think of all the good you could do. I'm needed where I am. Fleet tactics is what I do best. We need you fighting the big picture. You know as well as I do, if we don't win this war, there won't be another. The president has very few people he can trust. You're one of them. The President of the Systems Alliance has just asked you to serve your people. Are you really going to say no?"

He wanted to be mad, to let his rage build, but all he felt was a sense of resignation. Wit DeBeck was a spy. It was the entirety of his identity. He had always thought he would either die in office or retire a spy.

"You're asking me to give everything up that I've worked for my whole life..."

She put a hand on his knee.

"It's already gone, Wit. Even though ONI was untouched by the scandal, you'll have to go. But, because we know you're clean, President Axwell wants you where you can do the most good. Say yes, Wit. Say yes for me. Say yes and then let's go kick some Caliphate ass."

Admiral Wit DeBeck looked Fleet Admiral Noele Villanueva in the eyes and grinned. "When you put it that way, Noele... Yes."

While *Enterprise* was the smallest of the Alliance's four battleships, she wasn't any less impressive. Maybe a bit more well used on the inside than *Alexander*—her passageways were painted a dull brown, with lots of scrapes and scuffs where heavy equipment was moved—but she was still in fighting shape. The boat bay doors were adorned with a plaque listing every award the ship had won in its twenty years in service, not to mention the large E for excellence. Her crew even referred to her as the "Big E."

Once Jacob's crew were aboard, they had placed the *Interceptor* against the topside hull using magnetic clamps. His ship, for all intents and purposes, was dead. With the gravcoil busted, she couldn't accelerate. Her hull had multiple breaches and entire frames were vaporized. She'd taken a pounding and held together, but it cost her everything.

And it could cost him everything. The Navy didn't look kindly on officers who surrendered their command. It triggered an automatic court-martial.

In the meantime, he had a small office where he could conduct his business. Much of which involved writing reports for command. His crew came by to check on him. Somehow, PO

Mendez managed to find time to bring him food and orange drink.

"Skipper," Lieutenant Boudreaux asked while knocking on his open hatch.

"Come in, Viv. And just Commander, or Jacob. I'm nominally assigned to Interceptor, but she's not under her own power at the moment."

"Aye sir. I just wanted to give you the final numbers." From her NavPad, she sent him the crew casualty numbers.

It wasn't nearly as bad as he feared. The families of the dead wouldn't see it that way, of course. Twenty-one dead, six wounded bad enough they were placed on *Kraken* for medivac to Zuckabar. Dozens more wounded but recovering aboard *Enterprise*.

Boudreaux stood silently as she watched her captain absorb the information. Watched as the weight of the dead fell on his shoulders and pulled him down. Watched as his eyes sank and his heart broke. She knew he would never forgive himself for the price they paid. He would, forever and always, think he could have found another way, made some clever tactical move that turned the battle around.

He would be wrong, but he would never admit that. This was the burden of command. The sacrifice a good officer made to lead their crew. It was what made him the best officer she knew, and a man she would follow to hell if he commanded.

"Thank you, XO. That will be all."

"Aye sir. And sir?"

He looked up at her with watery eyes but a strong visage.

"You did everything you could, sir. No one could have done more and everyone aboard knows," she said.

"Thank you, Viv, I appreciate it. Dismissed."

When she was gone, Jacob turned his chair to face the empty bulkhead. On his NavPad he reviewed the names of the dead, committing their faces to memory, along with any anecdotes or awards he could find about them. Each letter he wrote was personal. No form letters, no "we regret to inform you." His people deserved better than that. They gave everything for him. He could give this to their families.

Dear Mister and Misses Lopez, it is with a heavy heart I inform you that your son, Ensign Mateo Lopez was killed in the line of duty. Mateo died saving the lives of his fellow spacers. He was brave, bold, and decisive. While I didn't serve as his CO for very long, I can tell you this: there is no greater act than to give one's life to save another. During his time on the Interceptor...

He continued on, letter after letter, message after message. Some to parents, others to husbands and wives, some to children. It got no easier and hurt just as badly each time.

Dear Mrs. Richards. There is no easy way to tell you of your husband's sacrifice in the line of duty. I hope this letter fills you with pride for the enormous amount of good John Richards did in his long naval career. He personally saved lives and—

Not all of it saddened him. Some of the letters were of the positive variety.

To: NAVPER
  From: CDR J.T. Grimm
  It is with my full recommendation that Midship Rugger be promoted to LT (JG) upon successful completion of the academy. He conducted himself in an exemplary manner and performed his duty above and beyond...

When he was finally finished, he reviewed the receipts and

sent them off in the next packet. They deserved to know soonest, not a month, or six months later, but as soon as he could manage to inform them.

Rear Admiral Spencer's unused desk sat underneath a large viewscreen displaying the wormhole in the void. He preferred working from the small bar that ran the starboard side of his flag office—that way he could drink, eat, and not worry about having to clean his desk.

Currently, he was working through the after-action reports from the many battles that had happened in the last two weeks. From the *Interceptor*'s action against the Caliphate, to the light cruiser disabling of a *battleship*. (How in God's name did four destroyers manage that one?) Along with capturing a nearly intact Caliph battle fleet. In a lot of ways, Commander Grimm was the luckiest man serving in the Navy.

His actions against the light cruiser, the ambush and the subsequent boarding, were of dubious legality. He technically didn't fire first, but it was by the slimmest of margins. A court-martial would have a hard time distinguishing the difference.

Luckily, they weren't going to have a trial. He thought back to the meeting he just concluded, where Captain Ganesh Hatwal had stood his ground.

"Admiral, I'm telling you, sir, if it weren't for the actions of Jacob Grimm, we wouldn't be having this conversation. My entire squadron would be obliterated. Worse, the wormhole would be in the hands of the Caliphate and that would be the end of the Consortium."

Spencer hadn't believed Ganesh at first.

"Captain, your own initial reports show Commander Grimm doing this exact thing in a training exercise. He's clearly put thought into this kind of engagement. With his record of reckless behavior, surely these are slam dunk courts-martial."

Ganesh stood in parade rest and spoke with a formality that was not required, but he clearly felt appropriate. "Sir, what you see as reckless, I see as a brilliant tactic. Commander Grimm broke no ROE. As his squadron CO, I will testify to such in front of any court. He deserves a medal, sir, not punishment."

Admiral Spencer truly didn't have an opinion the matter. He'd read Grimm's files, even the blacked-out ones he'd managed to pry from a friend at ONI. To some officers, Grimm *was* reckless, but Spencer preferred the term "bold." Decisive even.

After Ganesh departed, he took one more look at the file and came to his final determination. "Commander Rupert, could you show the commander in?"

"Aye aye, sir," Rupert replied.

A second later, the hatch opened and Commander Jacob T. Grimm marched in wearing his SDWs. He paused, his stride hiccupping when the admiral wasn't at his desk. Missing only the one step, he executed a left face and stopped in front of the admiral at attention.

"Commander Jacob T. Grimm reporting as ordered, sir."

Jacob held attention for almost a minute while the admiral perused his files.

"At ease, Commander. May I call you Jake or Jacob?"

No one ever called him Jake.

"Jacob is fine, sir."

Spencer nodded. He held his NavPad in front of him, scrolling over files.

"Surrendering one's ship is a court-martial offense, Jacob, you're aware of that?"

Jacob had feared this moment since he had uttered the words, *"We surrender."*

"Yes, sir. I'm aware."

Spencer took a swig of the brown liquid in his square glass on the bar.

"Then tell me why you did it?"

"Sir, our goal wasn't victory in battle. Our victory came in signaling Admiral Endo of the attack. Once I was sure that was achieved, and after we took the hit to the gravcoil, there was no further point in fighting. The longer we spent running, the more of my crewmembers died. It was clear there was no escape, sir. At that point, surrender was the only chance for my remaining crew to survive, even if it meant ending up as POWs. As long as they were alive, there would be a way. My people have beaten worse odds."

"Yes, they have. I figured that would be your answer, Commander. You'll be pleased to know that I'm closing the case on the surrendering of the *Interceptor*. There's no point in punishing you for the right decision, and I don't need JAG to tell me they don't have a case."

Jacob stood in stunned silence. He'd thought courts-martial were automatic after the loss of a ship... Rank had its privileges, he guessed.

"Thank you, sir. I mean that."

"I know you do. I've commanded my fair share of ships, but I don't think anyone has seen as much combat or had to make the hard decisions you have, Commander. I'm hardly going to sit here from my high horse and second-guess you. Now, with that clear, I have some regrettable news."

Jacob braced himself for the worst. No courts-martial, but were they going to kick him out anyway?

"My engineer tells me that *Interceptor*'s gravcoil is more than seventy percent severed from the frame. I'm afraid she's done for, son. I'm very sorry to be the one to tell you."

The admiral didn't know—*couldn't* know—that Jacob's career was tied to that little ship. If she was out, so was he. Shock and regret passed over him, and his heart banged away in his ears. He missed what the admiral said next but he was sure it wasn't important.

The *Interceptor* was gone...

"Your crew all gave statements, as did Captain Hatwal, and they all seem to think very highly of you, Jacob. I like officers who command the respect of the people they in turn command. It's all too rare these days. You know, I was Admiral Villanueva's XO on *Victory* a million years ago."

What did that have to do with anything? Fleet Admiral Villanueva had assured Jacob she would keep him in the Navy as long as she could, but that once *Interceptor* was gone, she couldn't do anything more. Not with the enemies they had both made over the last few years.

"I have some other news that might interest you. It will be general knowledge here pretty soon, anyway. There was some kind of kerfuffle back on Alexandria. FleetCom has shuffled. There's a new SECNAV and CNO, among other things. Not to mention Congress voted to go to war against the Caliphate, and the president signed it. We're at war, son. I know that's not news anyone wants to ever hear, but I think you're more aware than most of the inevitability of this action."

Jacob was still reeling over the loss of his beloved ship, and now the admiral was telling him about spies and wars? A surge of relief went through him that the politicians had *finally* decided to do the right thing, to seek justice for those the Caliphate had slain on Alexander.

"That's good to hear, sir, in a weird sort of way. I guess I'll learn all about it on the trip back to Alexander."

"Why? Are you planning on going AWOL?"

Jacob blinked in confusion. "Sir, I assumed, with my ship out of action, I would be heading for home. There were… conditions to my service in the Navy that you might not be aware of."

"If I'm not aware of them, then they don't exist. Task Force 16 needs an XO, son. They sent us out here with too few people and not nearly enough ships, which I'm sure you can sympathize with. I've got no one watching my back. I need someone I can trust."

A grin spreading uncontrollably on Jacob's face. "Sir? You want me to be your XO?"

"Don't make me repeat myself, Grimm. I don't like it. The job sucks. You won't sleep, and you can forget going home for a while. But the reward is you get to be in on the high-level strategy meetings and you'll only answer to your God, the President"—he leaned forward and poked his thumb into his own chest—"and me. Got it?"

"I get you, sir. I would be honored."

"We'll see if that sentiment holds when I'm done with you. Like I said, I'm light, so I'm absorbing your crew into mine to make up the difference. I noticed you frocked a warrant? Should she stay an officer?"

"Sir, Lieutenant Boudreaux is the finest naval aviator in the business, but she made an even better XO."

Admiral Spencer made a note on his NavPad. "Good enough for me. With the war on, I can dispense with some of the regulations. Her promotion is permanent. She can be *your* XO until such time as we can get her back for OCS. Dismissed, Commander Grimm."

"Aye aye, sir." Though the Navy didn't often salute aboard

ship, the weight of the moment made it feel right and Jacob snapped to attention and saluted his new CO.

Admiral James Spencer stood and returned it with parade-ground perfection.

JACOB T. GRIMM WILL RETURN IN *KNOW THY ENEMY*, GRIMM'S WAR BOOK 5.

LAST STAND ON KREMLIN STATION

A GRIMM'S WAR STORY

JAMES S. AARON

© 2022 James S. Aaron

CHAPTER ONE

As the wind howled outside the thin walls of the Alliance Naval barracks in Zuckabar Central, Chief Warrant Officer Vivienne Boudreaux studied her cards and smiled. Across from her sat Chief Petty Officer Echo Redfern and two of his newer spacers, Chancey and Karls, on leave from the *Interceptor*.

Redfern was a big man with broad shoulders and a placid face that hid the currents moving underneath. One of the first pieces of information she'd learned when coming aboard the *Interceptor* was that Redfern could fix anything; more importantly, Redfern could *get* anything. In her opinion, both skills were sorely lacking in the modern Navy.

A newcomer to Zuckabar might have thought a wild storm tore at the building, but this was normal weather for an icy planet only decades into its terraforming process. Boudreaux noted with interest that, every time the wind scraped and banged against the metal walls, Redfern hunched slightly, as if the sounds reminded him of something he didn't want to remember. Then he would catch himself slipping back into his usual calm study of his cards. From the outside, he reminded her of the best mechanics she'd known, people who wanted to tear the galaxy apart and figure out how it worked.

Redfern met her eyes, flashing that dry humor, and then gave his cards a hard look.

Beside him, Spacer First Class Karls studied the pot. His round face, quick to smile, reminded Boudreaux of an otter. He shook his head and tossed his cards on the table. "I don't get paid enough for this. I'm out."

"None of us do," Redfern said, raising an eyebrow. "If you're here for the money, you chose the wrong career."

The jolly spacer sucked his cheeks. "I didn't choose the Navy. The Navy chose me."

Chancey chuckled and pushed cash toward the pile. She was a slight woman with a mechanic's hands, bony and oil-stained, her red hair bobbed to keep it out of her face. She looked up at Boudreaux. "I'll stay in if you put up a ride in the Corsair, Chief. That's what I want."

Boudreaux shrugged. "That's too cheap. I play bus driver all day."

Chancey shook her head. "I want a real ride. I want a simulated attack run."

The excitement on the kid's face was too pure for Boudreaux to hit her with the truth of her job, which was mostly ferrying people and supplies from the planet's stormy surface to their stranded ship the USS *Interceptor*, which had been without its main gravcoil for three months now. Hope was starting to turn sour in the crew, and more were looking to get planetside to find whatever entertainment they could on the icy colony.

"I'll tell you what," Boudreaux said. "I'll put up a ride— a real ride, if one of you mechanical geniuses puts up a replacement gyro for the reticle on my ten-millimeter canon. I've had that request in since the day after I reported for duty on the *Interceptor*."

She purposefully didn't look at Redfern as she made the offer. Boudreaux didn't blame him for not being able to source the parts—except she *did* because parts were his responsibility and he was resourceful. So maybe it was a matter of *priority*, or her task to build a little *rapport* with Redfern. Everything was hard to source on this God-forsaken rock. They didn't even have the raw material to fab anything. She was the primary maintainer for her bird, and damnit, she *needed* that reticle.

Oblivious to Boudreaux's secondary game, the two spacers watched their chief as he leaned back on his crate and considered his cards, rubbing his clean-shaven jaw. Even on leave, Redfern kept himself cleaned up.

Boudreaux waited, wondering if she'd overestimated the strength of her hand. She'd learned to count cards from an uncle who made a shifty career of gambling in taverns and casinos across Verdant, and she had a good idea of the chances each of them had at beating her. They were low.

"Let me ask you this, Chief," Redfern said. "You still reading those paperback romances?"

"Paperback?" Karls scoffed. "Why would you bother with that?"

Boudreaux slapped her cargo pocket and pulled out a dog-eared book. She traded them with a network of enthusiasts that included everyone from naval top brass to lower enlisted.

"This is the best communication tech ever invented," she said. "Doesn't lose connectivity. Easily transportable. Practically indestructible." She glanced at Redfern. "Doesn't leave me trying to win at cards to get parts. And I don't just read romances. I read everything. Anything I can trade for, really. I just finished a history of early Alliance economics."

The young spacer rolled his eyes. "If you say so, Chief."

"Have you finished that one yet?" Redfern accepted the book from her and briefly inspected it, opening it to her bookmark. She wasn't a corner-folder.

Boudreaux shrugged. "I've already read it. Waiting on another shipment that may never arrive."

Redfern closed the book. "I'll tell you what. You give me and Chancey a ride, let me have this book and maybe a few more, and I'll get your reticle gyro for you."

She pounced. "You've got the part? Why have you been holding out on me this whole time? That could have cost someone's life if I was in a firefight."

"Well, you haven't been."

"Readiness is a matter of life and death," Boudreaux said. "I think I've heard you say that once or twice. Without that gyro I'm maneuvering the whole Corsair to make fire adjustments. Accounting for a hundred other factors as I'm trying to get covering fire laid down. That reticle is necessary combat equipment."

Redfern nodded. "You don't have to convince me, Chief. Here's the thing. I don't have your part. But I've got a good idea where we might get one, as long as you're willing to work with me. I know for a fact that Chancey ordered your part, but like a lot of things coming into Kremlin and Zuckabar, it probably took the roundabout slow boat."

Boudreaux stopped herself, realizing how angry she'd gotten. She didn't mean to take it out on the engineers. They were doing the best they could with a terrible situation. She'd never heard of a Navy vessel going so long without a gravcoil. And now they were all stuck on this ice cube in the middle of nowhere, with no good indication that the Navy gave a damn about any of them. Hell of a way to treat people who *mostly* cared. But that was the Alliance Navy.

"Sorry, got a little angry there." She held up her hands. "I've been stressed out by this assignment. I'm happy to ferry people around all day long. That's my job. But I hate that there's no end in sight."

"I know what you mean." Redfern returned the paperback. "Be glad you don't have two ankle biters following you around, asking questions about everything, thinking they know how the Navy works. Almost as bad as an ensign. At least I can teach a spacer."

"Hey," Karls complained.

Redfern chuckled. "You're staying here with the gear. Read those manuals I gave you. When we get back, we might just be helping the chief out repairing her gun. That's not a repair job you get to do often."

Boudreaux rubbed her hands to ward off the cold creeping through the metal walls. "So we're headed to Kremlin? I'll need to request a clearance. Shouldn't be a problem, but they get snippy if I don't file a flight plan."

Standing to his full height, Redfern looked like he should have been a Marine rather than a mechanic. "Not Kremlin. We're heading out to Terraforming Point Thirty-six."

"On Zuckabar?"

Karls hooted a laugh and pointed at Chancey. "And you thought you were going for a joy ride. Better find a coat."

"There are no parts on a Terraforming landfall," Boudreaux said.

Redfern gave her an enigmatic smile. "Be patient, Chief."

CHAPTER TWO

The Corsair cruised at four thousand meters above the surface of Zuckabar. A thick cloud layer hid the wild storms beneath them, and the planet seemed almost peaceful rather than deadly. On the edge of the horizon at regular intervals shimmered the silver lines of the terraforming points, transferring raw materials between orbital substations and the volatile surface.

As she expected, the air got weird as they approached the transfer station. What had looked like gleaming silver became something akin to a tight tornado glimmering with ice crystals. The Corsair's engines fought the heavier winds and Boudreaux gave Redfern a grin.

"Tell Chancey she's about to get her real flying experience."

"I should have put her in the copilot's seat."

"If she loses her cookies, I want her in back."

A hard updraft hit the bird and Boudreaux turned her focus on the Corsair, balancing every bit of information in the cockpit display with the gut-level data from the complaining airframe around her as they dove into the storm. The engines wound up like mini tornadoes themselves, and she kept a careful eye on her gyros and pressure levels. All they needed was to blow a line in the middle of these brutal crosswinds. It was like Zuckabar didn't want anybody getting close to a wound, and the wind fought her every second of the descent.

They were under ten klicks from the ground station when Boudreaux lost control of a rear stabilizers. The Corsair's nose turned down, forcing the dropship into a near dive.

Redfern gave her a sideways glance, voice neutral. "Is this normal?"

Boudreaux gripped her controls and kept her focus on her display, ignoring the windscreen. Ice crystals nearly covered the glass, turning the outside world into a white sheet. She stared at her controls, trying to determine the problem. The icy windscreens suggested it was ice on the hull affecting her lift and overall performance.

"We good?" Redfern sounded exceedingly calm, despite the hand gripping his harness.

"Slight change in flight conditions, that's all." Boudreaux took stock of her bird again, checking the rest of the flight stabilization system and hull temperature sensors as she compensated with increased thrust from the engines. The whining jets were almost louder than the outside wind.

Again the nose dropped, the wind growing stronger as they neared the tornado. Boudreaux muttered every curse she'd heard from her mother, her uncles, even the crusty old warrant officer who had taught her every failure mode she knew. The Corsair continued to fight her until she finally brought the engines into equilibrium.

"Keep breathing," she told Redfern. "We're about to get weightless."

Holding the vessel horizontal as it bucked and twisted in the wind, she killed the thrust.

Boudreaux took a deep breath to steady her stomach as the

nose finally rose slightly, and then the back of the bird slid groundward. The altimeter squawked at the abrupt change and the windscreen turned white with clouds as they dropped. Boudreaux took long, slow breaths to keep her lunch from climbing her throat, counting the seconds as they fell.

The instant the light changed in the ice-covered windscreen, indicating they'd dropped below the freezing clouds, she shifted the engines to drop mode and forced them to full power. The Corsair rocked side to side as the gyros fought the wind, and then finally evened out.

"I don't know what you did, but that sure looked like some good flying." Redfern wiped sweat off his brow.

"We haven't landed yet, Chief."

Boudreaux glanced back to find Chancey still hard asleep in her seat, drool trailing down the side of her cheek.

With less than a thousand meters to the icy ground, Boudreaux shifted the bird into combat hover. The engines noise dropped and she breathed a sigh of relief as the servos did their jobs, kicking thrust against the gray-and-white plain beneath them. She patted the one clear space in her console where the paint had been rubbed smooth by other pilots before her, thanking the bird for getting her through another rough bit of air.

"You were worried?" Redfern asked.

She shot him a grin. "What doesn't kill you makes you stronger, right?"

Through the blowing snow, the squat form of the transfer station's control building came into view, a gray line beneath the maelstrom that churned into the clouds above. Even with the noise dampeners in the Corsair, Boudreaux could hear the screaming winds.

"Chancey!" Redfern shouted, throwing off his harness. "Look alive, we're here."

The spacer jerked awake and looked around, wiping her face. "What? Already? I remember take off."

Climbing past the two of them, Boudreaux dug in one of the lockers for the old parkas Redfern had scavenged from the barracks. Certainly not Navy issue, they bore the patches of the Terraforming Guild, proof that he'd been out here before.

"You've got those books?" Redfern asked.

Boudreaux slapped her cargo pocket. "Three, like you asked."

"Why do you like those things anyway? I figured you too serious for romance."

"Everybody needs an escape, Chief. What do you do for fun?"

Redfern paused in the doorway. "I solve problems."

"Lying and cheating?"

He laughed and jumped out of the bird, pulling his parka tight around him as the wind immediately tried to tear it away. She didn't catch his response.

With the Corsair secured behind them, they fought the gale to cross an icy landing pad toward the low building. Boudreaux gazed up at the vortex above them, amazed at the constant swirl of glittering ice and the shifting colors of what had to be other terraforming elements. She didn't know much about terraforming but understood that this was nearly the same tech as a space elevator, driving raw materials into the atmosphere to speed the gradual process of warming the planet. Someday after she was long gone, Zuckabar would be covered in oceans and teeming with life. At least that was what the colony believed, and she wasn't going to rob anyone of their faith, especially in a place like this.

A trench in the ice sliced from the landing pad, sheltering them from the wind as Redfern led the way to the transfer station. At the scarred metal door into the building, he ignored the security scanner and pounded instead. After the first three bangs, he paused, gave two more strikes, then stepped back.

In a minute, the door was opened by a thin man in a gray work suit with the Terraforming patch on his chest. His look of suspicion turned to a smile as he recognized Redfern.

"Well, if it isn't Redfern. And you bring friends. Who are you hiding from today? Did you get a new gravcoil finally? How did that abornite work out for you?"

When the door was slammed close against the wind, Redfern paused in the concrete corridor to nod at the Terraformer. "Andrew, this is Chief Boudreaux and Spacer First Class Chancey. Andrew Carwell here is a Terraformer Fourth Tier. Sole administrator for the station."

The bit of respect Redfern showed the man brought some color to his pale cheeks. He waved for them to follow him deeper into the facility, where the walls vibrated from activity deep below and the air grew steadily warmer.

The station's control room was a brightly lit space filled with various consoles tracking the vortex outside, meters rising and following with element counts, temperatures, and geothermal charting. It all looked impressive until Boudreaux got close enough to one of the geo charts to read its scale, which was tracking in tenths of degrees—a reminder that this was a *very* slow process.

The entire back wall of the chamber was made of a translucent material that allowed a direct view into the vortex. The material must have been polarized because it lacked the harsh white brilliance of their flight in. Darkened and adjusted, crystalline chemicals flashed rainbow daggers as they spiraled from the surface for dispersion in the atmosphere.

Chancey was mesmerized by everything in the spare control room, staring up into the vortex. Boudreaux was too distracted by the stabilization system failure to give the operation more than a passing glance. She wanted to get back out to the Corsair to run checks. She was dealing with flight failures now. That was a problem. The *Interceptor* might be dead in space, but she'd be damned if her bird was grounded.

She'd be damned if she had to beg Redfern for more parts.

Boudreaux figured she would have to barter for more than just the reticle, now.

Redfern was chatting amiably with the Terraformer near a table in in the middle of the room. The big chief petty officer was a good listener. He asked questions showing he was interested, and was able to draw out information that the technician probably shouldn't have shared. Redfern seemed to have a knack for getting the taciturn man to go on about his work, their progress, even the Guild shipping schedule from outside Zuckabar system, until finally Redfern made small mention of it being good to visit, which seemed to remind Carwell why they had come. It was masterful, like a beautiful bit of sustained flying in a glider, navigating uplifts.

Carwell clapped his hands together in anticipation and gave Boudreaux an almost hungry look. She was used to lusty stares; Carwell wanted something else.

"You brought them like you promised?" he asked. "I don't blame you if you fibbed. I get it, Chief. We can still trade. But when you made *this* offer? If you've got them, I'll be honest, you can have pretty much anything I've got. It's not like anybody's tracking supply levels."

The technician closed his mouth abruptly, maybe realizing he'd just given up any leverage he might have had.

"You've got the fertilizer?" Redfern asked.

Carwell squinted. "That's really all you want? Wait, show me the trade first."

Redfern looked at Boudreaux. "Chief, your books?"

Digging in her cargo pockets, Boudreaux produced a

romance novel, a history of Alliance First Era Economics, and a thick novel told from the perspective of a group of rabbits.

Carwell stared at the books for a second before grabbing up the rabbit book. He flipped pages, then looked at Redfern.

"How many tons do you need?" he asked.

CHAPTER THREE

The flight back to Zuckabar Central was a cakewalk compared to the ride into the vortex. Boudreaux kept her eye on the stabilizers the whole time, but the winds never reached the temps that had forced the earlier failure.

Chancey fell asleep again as soon as the engines roared, probably beat after loading in the pallets of solid fertilizer chemicals. Boudreaux didn't dwell on how much wealth those blocks probably represented. Like Caswell, she was putting her trust in Redfern the same way he trusted her skills as a pilot. And why wouldn't he? She was the best drop pilot this side of the Alliance Central and she had been looking forward to serving on a patrol boat. It had been a huge disappointment to find the *Interceptor* dead in space with little hope of change. She wasn't foolish enough to long for action—she'd seen enough combat to shake that desire—but she wanted something meaningful to do. She wanted a *mission*, to do her duty. That was all any of them wanted, as far as she had seen. The *Interceptor* had a good crew and the Navy was wasting them, for reasons she didn't understand.

"You're good at that," she observed as Chancey snored behind them, drool trailing from her open mouth.

"What's that?" the big man asked placidly.

"Bartering, trading, whatever you call it."

He grinned. "Solving problems. I like people. You talk to people; they generally share their problems, what they want, things like that. You talk to enough people, and you see how we can help each other."

"Too bad you can't trade for a new gravcoil."

That was a misstep. His face darkened like she'd mentioned his greatest failure.

"That's a whole other problem in itself." He muttered under his breath. "You don't think I'm going to get your reticle, do you?"

She recalled his face when the wind had been attacking the barracks, like ghouls trying to claw inside. He dreaded some failure. Most of the time he hid it behind a calm face, but it was there. He wanted people to believe in him; they were alike that way.

"You'll find it," she said.

"It's not a matter of finding it. Command isn't helping. A gravcoil should be important to the Navy. Without it the *Interceptor* is dead. How do you let a ship die?"

Maybe that was the heart of the inner conflict she kept glimpsing. He was losing trust in the Navy, in his fellow spacers.

Redfern fell into a funk, staring out the window at the icy plain flowing beneath them. He needed a win.

Boudreaux pursed her lips. *They all needed a win.*

CHAPTER FOUR

"Echo Redfern!" a woman's deep voice called across the underground greenhouse. "You have been too long away from me. I told you to come back soon. I have sweets for you."

"Hello, Brevka." Redfern stood at the end of a long hydroponic bed that ran nearly twenty meters into the cavern as the woman he had identified as Brevka Rozhenko walked toward him.

She was solid, with the muscular curves of the first colonists and jet-black hair with a sharp nose and blue eyes. Her voice carried across the long caverns of the underground greenhouse where Redfern had explained she grew corn for liquor production.

"Who are these dolls you've brought with you, Echo? I've told you a man of your stature needs a woman to match. When will you listen?"

Redfern winked at her and introduced Spacer Chancey and then Chief Boudreaux. When Brevka learned she was a pilot, her demeanor changed.

"You looking for work? I keep you well-funded for one or

two runs to the station, maybe even your Navy ship, I take care of you. We are businesswomen, you and me."

"I'll think about it," Boudreaux said with a smile, following Redfern's easy noncommittal attitude.

The greenhouse was underground in the northern section of Zuckabar Central, under what had looked like an unassuming warehouse where most of the activity was drone transport vehicles roaring to and from the spaceport. According to Brevka, these were the oldest parts of the colony, where the first landing had lived underground while Central and then Kremlin Station were built.

"This is our heart." She brought a fist to her chest, nodding. "Our history."

The air was humid, probably from the stills at the far end of the cavern, as well as the open water tanks that ran the length of the raised grow beds. Boudreaux spotted catfish rolling in the tanks and was surprised to see chickens scratching among corn husks that covered the stone floors. A hen flapped up to a grow bed and pecked at the base of a corn stalk, then eyed them suspiciously as they walked by, Brevka's voice echoing as she explained her operation.

"All is closed system. Engineers have drones that do their bidding, I have worms, chickens, and yeast. Some yeast makes bread rise. Mine make alcohol. Oldest drone in human history."

Fermentation tanks lined each side of the geothermal-powered stills at the end of the chamber, an enclosed operation that made Brevka beam with pride as she showed it off. Workers filled bottles with clear vodka that were then loaded into crates and stacked. There had to be thousands of crates in this section of the greenhouse alone.

"We make the finest vodka in all of Zuckabar," Brevka said with a sweep of her arm.

Redfern chuckled. "Aren't you the only distiller in the colony?"

Rather than bristle at the jibe, Brevka practically cooed under the joke. "Such a strong and naïve man. Upstarts everywhere. Bathtub gin, sugar vodka." She wrinkled her nose. "I service all finest restaurants on Kremlin Station. And maintain largest underground garden. We are reliable source of calories when times get bad. Some snobs say you can't make vodka from corn, only wheat and potato. Wheat is the aristocrats, potato is the people. Corn is Zuckabar ingenuity. I will make vodka from anything but pure sugar. That has no soul, and makes yeast go crazy. Also is a waste of sugar."

"You might be the most resourceful person I know," Redfern told her. "The engineering in your greenhouse is impressive."

"While I can listen to sweet words all day, I am busy. What can I do for you, Chief Redfern?"

Redfern didn't answer immediately. He asked about her latest distillation runs and how the crops were doing. Brevka maintained her business facade for a few more minutes, then gave in to his easy manner.

Boudreaux and Chancey followed at a few meters distance, giving the chief time to work his magic. The smells of sweet corn, soil, and alcohol from the steaming distillation equipment mixed to give the greenhouse a sleepy feel, and Boudreaux thought she might be willing to run liquor if she could spend a few afternoons in the place reading.

Maybe it was the plants, but the workers all seemed relaxed as well, which was a change from the hard attitudes of most colonists she'd dealt with at ground level and above.

Brevka's voice rose abruptly. "No. That is special batch for governor only. You know how long it takes to grow enough potatoes, to run mash, readjust distillation equipment? True vodka is too special for Navy. I am sorry, sweetness. Even for you, this I cannot do."

Boudreaux knew little about liquor aside from color, but she understood how rare true potato-based vodka was to the colonists. It was probably worth more than the *Interceptor*'s gravcoil replacement. The corn liquor that Brevka's operation could produce almost daily, when distilled properly, had little to no flavor and could still be called vodka and sold at a higher price than the purely industrial stuff that was just alcohol cut with water. Potatoes were a rarity in themselves on the battered planet, where growing medium was at a premium. Most food was transported in from Kremlin Station.

Redfern raised a hand to calm the tall woman and called for Chancey. "Bring over that block."

Chancey had been charged with carrying one of the heavy blocks of fertilizer from the Corsair. She nodded and jogged back to the entry. When she returned, grunting with the effort, Redfern directed her to hand the block to Brevka.

The distiller lifted the block with ease and turned it in her hands. Giving Redfern a suspicious glance, she lifted the fertilizer and sniffed it, then touched it lightly with the tip of her tongue.

"This is pure. Very pure. Still, not enough."

"I've got two pallets for you," Redfern said. "Enough to feed a hundred crops of potatoes and the rest of your corn for months. And if we play our cards right, it could be a reliable supply. Think of what you could do with a steady pipeline."

Brevka widened her eyes, watching the chief. "You make me want to keep you forever, Echo. You will never be getting that gravcoil at this point."

"I think you make beautiful things. I like to support you while I can."

The colonist stared at him, then abruptly tossed the fertilizer cube back at Chancey and crossed her arms over her chest. The spacer lunged for the cube and barely caught it before it shattered on the stone floor.

Boudreaux looked between the woman and Chief Redfern. Had he crossed the line with his flattery? Maybe he wasn't as good as he thought.

Then she realized the woman's eyes weren't angry, they were wet with what might have been tears.

Spreading her arms, Brevka surprised Chief Redfern with a hug that lifted him off the floor. He held his hands out for a second, then slowly closed his arms on her in return and patted her back.

Brevka pushed him away, kissing both is cheeks. "You are beautiful man. But there will be no deal."

"No deal?" Redfern asked.

"No deal unless I take you to dinner, beautiful man." Brevka looked at Boudreaux. "Of course, yes?"

Boudreaux found herself grinning. "Of course."

Redfern cleared his throat as he realized he'd been caught.

CHAPTER FIVE

The air in the cockpit smelled of oil and the remnants of Brevka's perfume stuck to Redfern's uniform. Finished the checking the stabilizer tolerance one more time, Boudreaux wrinkled her nose as she glanced into the troop area.

"You better stay awake this time, Chancey. You'll want to be ready at least when we cross the Richman Field in Kremlin. It's going to feel like a tickle party."

The spacer looked at Redfern. "Really?"

"No," the chief said. "Well, maybe a tickle party where they throw you around a room first. Besides, you need to keep an eye on those bottles when we hit zero g. Any of those break and we'll have wasted our time."

Strapped into the seat next to Chancey was a wooden crate carrying twelve precious bottles of Brevka Rozhenko's special recipe vodka. They'd had a toast before leaving and Boudreaux had been forced to wave off another shot before the first had finished burning her throat. She was no connoisseur, but Brevka assured them it tasted of history and love.

Rather than take shots, Redfern had filled a small flask and shoved in a cargo pocket. He seemed satisfied with the transaction, though he offered no details on how many more stops he planned for the evening.

"I've got a duty call in four hours," Boudreaux warned him. "We going to get this done before then?"

Redfern checked his watch and did some mental math. "As long as the bird doesn't try to drop again. We've got two more stops, both on Kremlin."

Boudreaux weighed the time. She could turn around now and make her duty call, push off fixing the reticle until later. Her earlier speech about readiness hung on her mind; she meant what she'd said.

"Can we put this off until later?" she asked.

"As far as my plan goes, everything is lining up perfectly. I don't expect anything to slow us down, but the last two stops are probably the most—complicated."

Boudreaux frowned. "What does that mean? Where are we going next?"

"A bar that hates the Navy." Redfern checked his watch again. "At last call. And after that the governor's mansion. He also hates the Navy."

The proximity alert for the Kremlin approach went off and a curse died in Boudreaux's throat. She was forced to ready for their transition through Kremlin's Richman field, the barrier that maintained the orbital station's atmosphere and allowed entry from space. The Corsair would need to maintain present velocity while transitioning its engines from vacuum to atmosphere. Normally the maneuver didn't cause her any stress. The stabilization failure had her worried, though, and she didn't know what else on her bird was going to decide to hiccup when she needed it most.

"I'm getting my parts, right?"

Redfern gave a mechanic's shrug that she knew all too well.

"There are no guarantees in life, Chief. Signs are looking good. I didn't expect to get this far, honestly. But you never know how these things are going to work out."

Keeping her focus on the controls, Boudreaux couldn't roll her eyes at him. "You strike me as the kind of person who has a pretty good idea of how things are going to work out. And you've probably got your own deal going in the midst of these other trades."

At that, Chief Redfern just grinned like a little kid.

They hit the field and Chancey groaned from behind them. Boudreaux experienced the familiar twist in her stomach. She was too focused on her engines to worry about it. The Corsair shivered, velocity shearing across its frame, then the engines transitioned and maintained speed relative to the station. They were in atmosphere.

"You all right, Chancey? There's a bucket under your seat if you're going to lose it."

The spacer shook her head with her lips sealed, looking green. Redfern gave her a thumbs up.

Once she had verified transition with Kremlin control, Boudreaux relaxed in her seat. "All right, Redfern. What's the name of this bar?"

CHAPTER SIX

A dull sign that read "Carly's Place" flickered above a battered metal door, the only light in the dim alley off a side street in the Kremlin shipping sector. If the area was any indicator, Boudreaux expected to find their destination empty, or sparsely populated by beat-down dock workers.

Redfern paused at the door as Chancey caught up with them, then knocked in an obvious pattern.

"Can I set these down, Chief?" Chancey complained, adjusting the crate against her stomach.

"Drive on, spacer." He knocked one more time, and the door opened immediately this time.

A blunt-faced man peered at Redfern, then expanded his scrutiny to Boudreaux and Chancey. He stared at the crate in the spacer's weakening grip.

"What do you want, Redfern. You know Carly's isn't too happy with you."

"Goff, I appreciate the tip. I'm here with a gift to smooth things over."

"Carly doesn't want uniforms in the bar."

"Does she want a case of Brevka's best?"

The bouncer scowled at Chancey. "We've got plenty of corn liquor."

"This is the special reserve." Redfern reached into a chest pocket and pulled out the flask he'd filled at Brevka's. "I saved a taste for you."

Goff gave him a distrustful glance and unscrewed the flask, sniffed it, and then took a tentative sip. His eyes widened and he looked at the case in Chancey's arms with renewed interest.

"That's a full case," Redfern said. "Carly's going to notice if any go missing. But I think we may have something worked out with Brevka if Carly likes this sample."

"Is that all you want?"

"I'd like to talk to Carly."

The bouncer grunted and pulled the door open, stepping back to take a longer pull on the flask.

Redfern walked confidently in. Boudreaux let Chancey follow him and she took up the rear. The door opened into a short hallway that reminded her too much of a kill box, with another metal door that currently stood open. The dull roar of a crowd came from the other side of that door, which hadn't made it to the street outside.

Boudreaux was surprised to find the bar packed. A long rectangular space, the room's center was taken up by another fenced square. Patrons jammed against the railing, grumbling and murmuring with bottled intensity as something happened in the center space. From this distance, Boudreaux couldn't see what they were watching.

Chief Redfern paid no attention to the middle of the room. He skirted the crowd with Chancey at his back, heading straight for the long bar on the side of the room. A lean woman with red hair stood behind the bar, a white towel thrown over one shoulder. From her calculating expression, Boudreaux figured that was Carly, the owner.

Following Redfern at a distance, Boudreaux's curiosity got the better of her and she pushed between two docks workers to get a look at the central space.

Inside the fence, two men sat at a small square table with a chess board between them. Both wore dockworker's coveralls, their hands and other exposed skin stained from oil and bitter cold. One was bearded and the other so clean-shaven his skin looked blue. A barely touched bottle of vodka sat beside the table, with two shot glasses. From the number of dead pieces, it looked like the game had been either very short, or very long.

The bearded man raised a hand and hovered it over the board. The tension in the room went up a notch, and a wave of murmurs went through the crowd. When Beard took one of Blue Jaw's pawns with a knight, the room burst into the conversation and noise that Boudreaux had heard outside. It quickly subsided as Blue Jaw raised his own hand to respond to the move.

"Boudreaux," Redfern called from the bar. "Come meet Carly."

One of the workers near Boudreaux looked at her and grimaced at her uniform. His attention was quickly drawn back to the game.

"You like chess?" Carly asked her when she reached the bar. The case of vodka sat on a bar stool, one of its unlabeled bottles in front of Redfern.

"I can't play worth a damn," Boudreaux said. "But I can appreciate what looks like a good match."

"These two don't go for theatrics. They could die tomorrow. Chess right now is all they have."

Boudreaux nodded and sat in the offered stool.

"Drink?" Carly asked.

Brevka's shots had been too much. "Water? I'm flying."

"You're a pilot? I can't read the uniforms. They all look the same to me." She gave Redfern a teasing glance. "You should have told me, Redfern. Pilots don't grace our dirty bar very often."

"I thought you didn't like the Navy," Chancey said, glancing back at the middle of the room like she expected to get shot.

Another teasing smile. "We don't. You came anyway. I make no guarantees of protection for anybody, especially Alliance Navy. But I can usually promise an interesting time."

Some move from the middle of the room brought a round of cheers, much louder this time. Someone must have been put in check.

Redfern motioned toward the vodka bottle. "So what do you think? We have a deal?"

"For the pistol? No."

He frowned. "This is worth ten times that pistol."

"Your desire is priceless."

The chief leaned back in his seat, and the Boudreaux was amused to see him finally look flummoxed. Chancey didn't seem to like it either.

"I distinctly remember you saying you would do anything for a case of Brevka's reserve. We got a whole class in vodka, particularly Zuckabar vodka. This is the top. This usually goes to the governor."

Carly nodded toward the crowd. "My people drink vodka like this and it only reminds them how bad life is. They don't want good vodka. They want fire they can bite down and hold in their bellies. You would understand if you weren't so soft, Echo."

Boudreaux sipped her water and reminded herself that the

colonists weren't a monolith, as much as the Navy liked to think they were. Even this frozen rock on the edge of civilized space had factions, and maybe the governing family didn't rule as tightly as they believed.

"Well, what will you trade for it, then?" Redfern asked.

"For the vodka?" Carly leaned in slightly.

"For the pistol. You know what I want."

"It goes up in value every time you mention it."

There was another cheer from the crowd watching the game. It dropped quickly as all attention drew tight on the chess game. Blue Jaw appeared ready to make the killing stroke.

Carly shook her head. "That one. Antony Bayuk. He's going to win his game and then think he owns the place. If he wins, he owns the crowd, at least for tonight. That makes things difficult for me."

She flashed a secret smile. "Throw him out, Echo Redfern, and I will give you the pistol."

Boudreaux dropped her hand to the service pistol at her belt. "You want him out, I'll get him out."

The owner shook her head. "No guns. No one is killed."

Redfern surveyed the crowd again, looking to Boudreaux for backup. "This is going to be a hell of a fight."

"Mate!" someone in the crowd shouted. Bayuk gave his bearded opponent a vicious smile, and then ignored the offered handshake. Instead, he grabbed the untouched liquor bottle from the table and drank deeply, his Adam's apple throbbing as he gulped. When he finally dropped the bottle, he cheered with the watching crowd and accepted the rush of patrons coming into the central square.

Standing, Redfern removed the more fragile insignia from his uniform and shoved them in a pocket. He cracked his knuckles and shook out his neck.

"You ready, Chief?"

"Ready, Chief." Boudreaux finished her water. Wiping her mouth, she pointed at the case of vodka in the seat beside her.

"Chancey, you guard the booze."

The wide-eyed spacer nodded.

Boudreaux and Redfern waded into the crowd.

CHAPTER SEVEN

Working her bruised jaw, Boudreaux brought the Corsair around the central section of Kremlin Station and aligned on the landing pad on the roof of the governor's mansion. While everyone on station called it a mansion, it was a compound in the heart of Kremlin where the Rasputin family ran their operations.

The zone had separate air clearance. Redfern said, "Tell them we've got a message for the governor's office."

Boudreaux had been here enough times with Commander Cole and Lieutenant Yuki to know the approach and even where they liked to park visiting vessels, and she was relatively confident the landing area guards weren't going to ask too many questions. Many off-the-books visits took place at the Rasputin compound, and they weren't some random bird requesting clearance.

When they were on the ground, Redfern grabbed two bottles from the vodka case and handed them to Chancey.

"Carry these for me." He took a third bottle and jumped out as soon as the troop hatch slid open.

"Hold on," Boudreaux said before Redfern disappeared.

"What's the plan here exactly? You've got an antique pistol and three bottles of vodka. What are you expecting to get out of this place? We're not safe here, and it's definitely getting back to command that we were here. The Alliance Navy doesn't just drop in on Governor Rasputin."

A hard wind was blowing across the landing area. Two space-worthy shuttle craft and another Corsair sat on the flight line, cockpits dark.

Redfern stood fast against the wind, not flashing his conniving smile anymore.

"This is our last stop. I've got an in with one of Rasputin's captains, the guy who handles his supply payments and all the warehouses on the station. They're all criminal enterprises, and they all make payments to my friend Gorky. He wants this pistol, and he's going to get me your reticle."

"That sounds like another stop after this."

"I'll have the part for you, Chief. Trust me."

She shook her head. "I do trust you, that's why I'm getting tired of this. I need to report to Commander Cole in two hours. We going to make it?"

Chancey yawned, swaying on her feet. For a second it looked like she was going to drop one of the bottles. She caught herself, blinking.

They crossed the tarmac to a guard shack, where Redfern chatted up the single guard and got him to make a call inside the compound. After a few minutes, a response came back from Redfern's contact.

"He says you can come, Chief Redfern. Your pilot can come as well. Your guard must stay here."

Redfern considered the news, then asked Boudreaux to carry his bottle and took the two from Chancey.

"She can wait in the bird," Boudreaux said.

"Excuse me," the guard said. "She must stay here with me."

Boudreaux gave Redfern a hard look. Chancey wasn't armed, while the young Rasputin guard was carrying a service rifle. It was older than a Navy MP-17 but looked like he maintained it, at least. She unfastened her holster from her duty belt and handed her personal weapon to Chancey.

"Put that on your belt. There's an extra magazine on the backside of the holster."

Chancey nodded and slid the holster into place. The Rasputin guard watched impassively.

When Chancey had the pistol, Redfern handed back one bottle of vodka. "Before you start shooting, see if you can talk or trade your way out of the situation."

"Don't let anybody near my bird," Boudreaux said.

Chancey gave another anxious nod. In a few minutes, Boudreaux and Redfern climbed into a utility car that arrived for them, and they left Chancey sitting on a metal chair in the back of the guard shack, the two lower enlisted looking equally awkward with each other.

CHAPTER EIGHT

There was no knowing if Jose Gorky had already been up and working at the late hour, or his day had never ended. His blue business suit was sharply creased, and his hair looked freshly cut, as if a barber followed him around to freshen him up every ten minutes. He stood from a big wooden desk as Boudreaux and Redfern were shown into his office, flashing a genuine smile that didn't ease the pit growing in Boudreaux's stomach.

While Gorky wore an expensive suit with all the trappings of wealth, his face had lines from worry and planning, dominated by a nose that had been smashed so many times it resembled a cauliflower. His handshake was rough and solid. This was a man who had worked his way to the top of his organization.

They had passed through multiple layers of security and surveillance. No one had asked their names, but they were wearing Alliance naval uniforms and arrived in a naval vessel that would be noted by interested parties. She was going to need a story for Commander Cole, if they got out of here at all.

Redfern might work below command's notice most of the time; she had to maintain flight logs.

"Chief Redfern, it's so wonderful to see you again. And what a surprise to have you drop in like this. I hope everything is all right?"

Boudreaux heard the plain questions and probably veiled threat in the greeting. If Redfern heard it, he didn't bother with being worried.

"Gorky, I had something come into my possession that I recalled you expressed an interest in during our last conversation. Chief Boudreaux here had a little free flight time, so she offered to bring me over."

"Is that vodka?" Gorky pointed at the bottles. "I love vodka but it's not worth a special trip."

Redfern presented the bottles. "These are for you. Brevka's reserve. From potatoes, she says. I'm not an expert on distilling."

"The reserve! Well, very beautiful. You must have impressed her greatly, Chief Redfern. I have only tasted the reserve with the governor. Here, we must have a toast."

Gorky couldn't be convinced otherwise. For him, it was neither too late nor too early. And this was business, after all. They should seal it with Brevka's reserve.

Looking around the office as she held her shot glass, Boudreaux looked at prominently displayed pictures of Gorky's wife, children, and then a display with a map of Kremlin's port area, with markers for locations that had to be warehouses.

They raised their glasses and tossed back the burning shots. Boudreaux's eyes watered from the shot, and this time she thought she tasted earthy potatoes, or maybe just dirt.

"It is a fortuitous night, my friend." Gorky studied his glass contemplatively. "I had thought you might be coming with something for me. Something I expected. But I did not expect you."

Boudreaux frowned at the phrasing. Gorky and Redfern were talking past each other.

Redfern set down his glass and reached into the back of his belt where he'd hidden the antique pistol.

Gorky noted the motion and immediately threw his shot glass to the side and went for his own pistol in a shoulder holster under his jacket.

He thought they were here to kill him.

Shouting for both of them to stop, Boudreaux threw up her hands. "Stop, Mr. Gorky. We're not here for that. Redfern has a pistol for you. He said you wanted it."

The Zuckabar crime lord stood with a snub-nosed pistol in his fist, finger poised on the trigger. The thing looked like a large enough caliber to blow a hole through Redfern and probably keep going.

"This is true?" Gorky asked.

"Yes." Redfern's breathing was cool and even as he stood frozen, one hand in the small of his back.

"Take it out, then. Slowly."

Redfern drew out the pistol, a long thing made of ornate steel with wooden grips. It had an octagonal barrel, and was an even larger caliber than Gorky's hand cannon. He reversed it quickly and extended it toward the other man.

Still holding his pistol, Gorky blinked at the offered weapon. Several emotions crossed his face, and he looked like he was going to cry.

"This is a great gift, Echo. Please, set it on the desk."

"Will you put down your pistol?" Boudreaux kept her voice even.

He stared at her, then lowered his pistol. "Yes, I apologize.

I'm tense tonight. You see, Rasputin has sent a kill order for me. Tonight I die."

Gorky shoved his pistol into its holster. Instead of picking up the antique, he took a shot glass from the tray on his desk and poured another drink from the reserve. He emptied the glass.

"That tastes like family," he said gratefully. "Now, let's see this. How did you get Carly to give it up finally? She told me I would never get my hands on it."

He turned the pistol over his in hands, running his thumb along the worn grips. While the metal was adorned with scrollwork, it wasn't ostentatious, and the smooth grips were uncarved, indicating the pistol had always been meant to be carried. Maybe a law enforcement weapon.

"This belonged to my great-great-grandfather," he said finally. "He was a foreman at the first inbound dock on Zuckabar, back when they were living in caves. Brevka's garden is one of those former caves. Once Kremlin was finished, he did everything he could to bring his family here. To work his way in with the older Governor Rasputin. That family will be the death of us. You know I pay him sixty percent of everything I make from my warehouses. If I don't like it, I pay the price personally. Well, I suppose I am about to pay. I can't allow my children to continue to pay this price."

"Where is your family?" Redfern asked quietly.

Gorky chuckled softly. "Thank you for asking, Echo. You are a good man, even if you are Alliance Navy. We all make our own deals. They are safe. I saw the writing on the wall and moved them out. Sergei Rasputin was notified of my actions and that may have hurried his hand against me."

Somewhere in the distance, the sound of weapons fire thudded through the walls. Gorky raised his gaze to the door behind Redfern, his eyes wet. Another mix of emotions crossed his face, like he was deciding what to do. For a second, Boudreaux hoped the pistol in his hands wasn't loaded. She didn't want to be part of handing him a suicide weapon.

Gorky's expression settled on cold anger. He narrowed his eyes, the solid peasant's face taking on a shade of the determination she had seen in Brevka and Carly. They were all Zuckabar colonists stock, fatalist yet determined. Life might be terrible, but they would not give up without fighting.

Was she reading him correctly? Her next question was what they were going to do if he chose to fight.

Ignoring his guests, Gorky set his father's pistol on his desk and picked up a small communication device. He issued a set of precise orders to his people in the building, received an update that the attack was in an outer admin area.

"They are five minutes from my office." Gorky slipped the communicator into his suit pocket. "Between here and their breach point is a small warehouse we use for high value items. They probably mean to kill me and take ownership of those things. I will fight them there. It is the best place."

"Can you win this?" Redfern asked. "We've got transportation. Come back to the landing pad with us. We can get you out of here. We can probably move a good portion of your security detail as well."

Gorky gave a fatalistic smile. "And do what then? We live in a fishbowl, my friend. I might live like a rat hiding on an outbound freighter. Nothing hides from Sergei Rasputin. You face him and die. Or face him and prove your strength, so you might live to face him again. This is our way."

A distant explosion shook the building.

Boudreaux grimaced. *Anti-personnel grenades.*

This was getting serious fast. They had passed through the warehouse where Gorky wanted to make his last stand on the way to his office. If they had to take the same path back to the landing pad, they needed to get moving.

"We need to go," she told Redfern. "We can't get caught up in this. It would be an international incident."

Gorky motioned toward the door. "Absolutely. I understand. You have given me more than I expected. I only wish I could repay you. I know you came looking for a favor. We will have to see if that is possible when all that is finished."

"I'd stay to help," Redfern said, shaking his head. "But Chief Boudreaux is right. We can't get caught up in a fight here. It was enough of a risk landing without naval clearance."

"I understand. Come with me and we'll get you clear of this."

Gorky picked up his father's pistol again and checked its magazine, as well as several additional magazines slotted in his shoulder holster. Fixing his suit jacket like he was walking into a board room, he walked around the desk and led the way out the door.

CHAPTER NINE

Heading back down two levels, Gorky led the way across the ground floor of the building. As on the way up, Boudreaux found herself amused by how normal the office space was, like most of the work of running a criminal shipping business was in the accounting.

The sounds of fighting grew louder as they reached a set of double doors. Three guards in the same gray uniform as the landing pad soldier were propped against the wall, clutching at wounds. One of the guards perked up at the sight of Gorky, staring at him with eyes bright from shock.

"Captain, we're fighting them off. You should run while you can. Greshev said she would send you the message."

Gorky knelt and squeezed the man's arm. "I got her message. I'm not leaving."

The guard nodded forcefully, wincing. With effort, he lifted his combat rifle to hand it to Gorky. Like the guard at the landing pad, it was old but well-maintained.

"Kill those bastards for me, Captain."

Boudreaux didn't pretend to understand what honor worked among mercenaries in the same organization. The extra fire power would be useful, though. She grabbed a rifle from one of the unconscious soldiers, checked its action and the magazine.

"You sure about that?" Redfern asked.

"I'm getting out of here in one piece, even if I have to drag you behind me, Chief."

He nodded and picked up the other rifle, familiarizing himself with the foreign action. Another grenade exploded on the other side of the door, followed by heavier gunfire. One side had brought in a heavy machine gun, and Boudreaux figured it probably wasn't Gorky's people. Rasputin really wanted to take Gorky down, and they must not have cared much about whatever valuables were stored in the warehouse.

"I'm going in," Gorky said with a hand on one of the doors. "If you keep to the right as I draw their fire, there is another exit on the south wall. There's a stack of shipping crates over there now, hiding it. That stairwell will take you back to the roof and the landing pad.

He raised his father's pistol and kissed the barrel, then shoved the door open and ran into the warehouse firing. The door slammed closed behind him.

"I'm not doing that." Boudreaux put her hand on the door and eased it open, raising the volume of the fight on the other side. "Come on."

Keeping low, Boudreaux took cover behind a nearby forklift and tried to get a sense of what was going on. The problem was that everyone was wearing the same uniforms except for Gorky. The space was well lit, a regular warehouse with stacks of crates, packing stations, and a loft against one wall where a desk looked over the whole operation. There was no knowing if any of these crates were going to stop projectiles, and several were already blown apart and smoking from the grenades she had heard earlier. Guards in gray uniforms lay dead on both sides of the warehouse.

She couldn't see the door where Gorky had directed them to run, only a wall of crates beneath the loft that might have been what he was talking about. There were at least two guards in front of that wall with rifles, tracking the movement of Gorky's people on the other side. They didn't seem to be moving, only watching for the others so they could kill them. The fight might have reached a short standoff before Gorky ran into the room. The bursts of weapons fire had died down again.

Gorky's voice boomed against the concrete walls as he cursed the attackers.

"Got any ideas?" she asked Redfern.

"I fire, you move. Repeat until we get over there?"

She looked around again, then at the steering wheel of the forklift above them. It looked like the driver had jumped from the seat without killing the drive. The simple console was still green.

"Let's see what kind of distraction we can get going first."

Quickly grasping her plan, Redfern produced some wire from a cargo pocket and went to work on setting the steering wheel and accelerator as Boudreaux covered him.

If Gorky's guards had been content with a standoff, he was not. The blue-suited captain appeared behind different crates and fired on their attackers, slinging every curse at his disposal. There appeared to be many. His father's pistol tore holes in crates and attacking guards, filling air with debris and blood. His ferocity pushed the other group back for a little while, until one of their leaders started shouting with equal anger. Rasputin had apparently promised quite the reward for Gorky's oversized nose.

None of them seemed to be paying attention to Boudreaux and Redfern, until the forklift wound up faster than expected and shot across the warehouse toward the wall hiding their door.

"Run!" Boudreaux shouted, firing on the two guards in front of them while trying to keep pace with the wild vehicle.

At least Gorky had the presence of mind to use the distraction; he directed his people forward, the pistol booming. More crates exploded. These must have been full of pottery because they filled the air with ceramic shrapnel. Boudreaux took a wave of debris in her side and arm. She ignored the pain, focused on the wall of crates.

A gray uniformed guard appeared in front of her and she shot him center mass, just as another explosion shook the middle of the room. The attackers had found more grenades.

Ears ringing, Boudreaux reached the wall of crates and immediately dropped into a cover position as Redfern sprinted in behind her.

"There's the door," Redfern said. Boudreaux prayed it was unlocked.

She looked back at the center of the warehouse in time to see Gorky appear through the smoke from the grenade, arm raised with the pistol spitting fire as he chose targets.

"With me! Follow me." He shouted and cursed, rallying his guards. "We'll beat down Rasputin's door and bring justice!"

Just as three of his guards emerged behind him, four rounds hit Gorky in a line across his chest. The impacts stopped him. A look of surprise flashed across his face and the pistol dropped slightly. Then he raised it again, face contorted with anger and determination. He took a pained step forward. More projectiles hit him, knocking him back, and then his guards ran for cover and left him alone as he fell.

"Come on." Redfern waved from the open exit. Boudreaux took one last look at the fallen captain and hoped his family was going to be all right, then ran after Redfern for the stairs.

CHAPTER TEN

The guard sitting with Chancey stood when they arrived, showing no knowledge of the fight below. He checked them out on the antiquated terminal at his desk, then gave Chancey an awkward smile and half-hearted wave as she left the guard shack. Chancey didn't appear interested in continuing whatever interaction they'd had while she waited.

Boudreaux had accepted that she wasn't going to get her aiming gyro. She would double down on the other sources she had been working, outside the system. The Corsair was a fairly common bird and there were still supply depots in the inner Alliance where parts could be found for the right price. She would pay it, even if the Navy wouldn't.

Redfern had apologized as they climbed the stairs to the landing pad, assuring her he had other resources to get into the warehouses. They were all run by criminals with a price.

Boudreaux could only shake her head. "I'd rather you didn't risk your neck again dealing with these people. They're dangerous."

"Isn't that why we joined the Navy?"

"I prefer to do my fighting with a ten-millimeter canon."

As the Rasputin compound shrank behind them, still no signs of any internal conflict showing in its windows or outside streets, Redfern glanced back at his spacer and then started.

"Chancey, where's that bottle of vodka I left you with?"

Keeping her focus on the controls, Boudreaux couldn't see the spacer's expression, but she could hear something mischievous in her voice. "I found a use for it."

"Did you get drunk? I told you not to drink that stuff. It was to save your ass if you needed it to get out of there."

"I traded it, Chief. For this."

Redfern accepted something from the spacer and leaned back in his seat, holding the object in front of him so he could inspect it in the low console light.

Boudreaux glanced over and started. "That's an aiming gyro." She turned in her seat to find Chancey grinning at her. "How did you get that?"

"I asked the guard back there, Nevi, about the Corsair sitting on their line. Turns out it was a junker Rasputin bought at salvage and they didn't have anybody qualified to work on it. I traded him the bottle if I could take a look. I'm lucky these things are so modular. Two panels and a locking pin and I had it out."

"I'll be damned, Chancey. How did you get so crafty?"

The spacer smiled sheepishly. "I learned by watching you, Chief."

Redfern's outer calm cracked. He stared at Chancey, mouth open.

Boudreaux couldn't help thinking of his earlier despair at the state of things, and here was a spacer first class proving there was hope. Maybe

The chief caught himself and gave an affirmative nod.

"Well, there's hope for this Navy after all."

They were still five minutes out from the Richman field. Boudreaux checked the nearby airspace as she formulated a plan; it was still clear above the compound. Chancey's resourcefulness deserved a reward, even if she was no good at poker.

"Buckle in, Chancey." Boudreaux shot the spacer a grin. "You're about to get that ride you asked for."

The shift of confusion to disbelief to *joy* on Chancey's face was all Boudreaux could have asked for. Chancey barely had time to tighten down her harness and grab the case of vodka before Boudreaux opened up the engines, and then flipped into a barrel roll.

Chancey's hoots of joy were music to her ears.

As she climbed for another long dive, Boudreaux glanced over at Redfern. "You're off the hook this time, Chief, but you still owe me for that bet. And no cheating this time."

He grinned, clearly in a better mood now. "Cheating? I never cheat at cards. But with everything else? If you ain't cheating, you ain't trying."

CHAPTER ELEVEN

They arrived at the *Interceptor*'s flight deck with half an hour to spare. Boudreaux engaged the Corsair's landing configuration and breathed a sigh of relief when the stabilizers held. As the ship settled onto the deck, she leaned over to pat the reticle gyro sitting in the copilot's seat. Throwing off her harness, she grabbed the part and strode aft to lock it in a storage cabinet. She would have time after the commander's trip to get her hands dirty installing it. Or maybe she would get some sleep and do it later.

Strangely, she didn't feel tired. The long night with Redfern and Chancey had left her feeling more alive than she had in months.

Her boots hit the deck and she scanned the flight line for the commander. Instead, she spotted Lieutenant Yuki standing near the control desk, talking to one of the chiefs. Boudreaux waved and jogged toward her, then came up short when she realized the XO's eyes were bloodshot and she wasn't standing with her usual stiffness. Yuki looked like someone had punched her in the gut and kept on hitting.

Boudreaux saluted. "Ma'am, I'm ready whenever Commander Cole wants to leave."

Yuki gave a distracted nod. "You were almost late. That's not like you, Chief."

Acknowledging the slight reprimand, Boudreaux figured she should give some reasoning. "I was chasing down parts all night, ma'am. The job ran a little longer than I expected."

"I appreciate all the work you put in, Chief. Everyone. We don't get enough thanks for what we do." Her voice trailed off.

"Is everything all right, ma'am?"

Yuki caught herself and straightened. "There's been a change of plans. We won't be going down to Zuckabar. I've got a meeting with Governor Rasputin on Kremlin."

A sizzle went down Boudreaux's spine. Had word already gotten back that she and Redfern had been at the compound?

"Just you, ma'am? Not Commander Cole?"

The XO seemed to steady herself again. "I'm notifying the civilian authorities in person. We haven't announced this to the crew yet."

Boudreaux frowned. "Announced what, ma'am?"

Had the gravcoil finally arrived? Were they leaving Zuckabar?

"Commander Cole is dead."

The information took a second to sink in. Abruptly Boudreaux felt tired. It wasn't just the long night; it was a general ache that had built over the months they had all been trapped in this system. And now the one man who could get them out was dead.

What would happen to the Interceptor *now? Was the Navy going to abandon the ship in space?*

"How?"

"I can't go into that now. Right now, I have orders to inform Governor Rasputin in person."

Boudreaux set her jaw. Those were questions for another day. Her job was to escort the XO and do her duty. She gave the XO a resolute expression, and the other woman seemed to take strength from her resolve.

She came to attention and snapped another sharp salute, recognizing the XO as the acting commander, whether Yuki had been promoted or not. That was the weight on Yuki's shoulders, and she would need all the help she could get.

"Are you ready to leave then, ma'am?"

"Yes, Chief. Thank you."

Boudreaux made an about-face, discipline propelling her now. Together, they crossed the flight line for the Corsair.

James S. Aaron is an army veteran and half-acre farmer. He's the author of *Aeon 14: Sentience Wars, Galactic Law*, and *Vagabond Space*, coming soon from Aethon Books. You can learn more about his work at https://tertiaryeffects.com/list/

ALSO IN SERIES

AGAINST ALL ODDS
WITH GRIMM RESOLVE
ONE DECISIVE VICTORY
A GRIMM SACRIFICE

THANK YOU FOR READING A GRIMM SACRIFICE

We hope you enjoyed it as much as we enjoyed bringing it to you. We just wanted to take a moment to encourage you to review the book. Follow this link: A Grimm Sacrifice to be directed to the book's Amazon product page to leave your review.

Every review helps further the author's reach and, ultimately, helps them continue writing fantastic books for us all to enjoy.

ALSO IN SERIES
AGAINST ALL ODDS
WITH GRIMM RESOLVE
ONE DECISIVE VICTORY
A GRIMM SACRIFICE
KNOW THY ENEMY

You can also join our non-spam mailing list by visiting www.subscribepage.com/AethonReadersGroup and never miss out on future releases. You'll also receive three full books completely Free as our thanks to you.

Facebook | Instagram | Twitter | Website

Want to discuss our books with other readers and even the authors? Join our Discord server today and be a part of the Aethon community.

LOOKING FOR MORE GREAT SCIENCE FICTION AND FANTASY?

For the last Supersoldier left in the Galaxy, it's kill or be killed... Despite the genetic enhancements inherited from her father, Victoria Anetti never wanted to be a supersoldier. She'd rather spend her life fixing starships, free from family expectations. Then her father and his comrades vanish on a mission to find a lost warship, leaving her the last supersoldier left alive. Now she must flee from planet to planet in order to evade government agents—like her estranged mother—who want to use her as a pawn in a simmering interstellar conflict. To escape yet another capture attempt, Victoria reluctantly joins her uncle's salvage crew who are attempting to complete her father's mission. But when clues surface that her father might be alive, Victoria must choose whether to disappear again to avoid sparking another war, or embrace her supersoldier legacy to save the only family she has left.

Get Robber Barrons Now!

For all our Sci-Fi books, visit our website.

ABOUT THE AUTHOR

Join Jeffery on his mailing list to receive the latest information about his writing. Find his other books on Amazon.com under Jeffery H. Haskell.

https://goo.gl/LJdYDn

Or via his website @ Jefferyhhaskell.com

A quick note on technology.

I expect that in one thousand years things will be very different than how I imagine. In fact, I would bet they will be unrecognizable. If you go back a thousand years from today, to 1022, it would be almost impossible for those people to understand the technology of today. Swords and lances were the hi-tech weapons of war.

I don't pretend I'm doing anything new with my writing. I love military sci-fi for the stories of survival and brotherhood they tell. Seeing a crew pull together to overcome adversity and succeed against overwhelming odds. For those stories to work, for the technology and the ships to play an important part in those stories, the author and the reader must understand them fully.

Thus I chose to limit the advance of technology even though it's a thousand years in the future. I didn't want to spend all my time reading about quantum physics and nano-carbon tubes in order to write. I spend enough time doing that for fun as it is!

Instead I kept things at a level that I could understand well enough to describe in a way that average readers will understand. When they launch torpedoes, you can see it. When the ship shakes from the turrets firing, you can feel it.

There are spots for high-technology, but I try to keep it grounded in what we know today. You may be surprised to learn (or not, you all are pretty intelligent) that the gravity coil FTL is based on a theory about gravity manifolds that actually exist as a natural phenomenon.

Pretty cool if you ask me.

I strive to improve with each book. I'm not satisfied to stand still and just do what I did before. If you do see a cool piece of tech out there you think would be a good fit for the Grimmverse, let me know at Jeffery.haskell@gmail.com I'd love to hear from you.